CW00692872

THE BAD BARGAIN

CRYSTAL KASWELL

Copyright

This is a work of fiction. Similarities to real people, places, or events are entirely coincidental.

Also by Crystal Kaswell

Inked Love

The Best Friend Bargain - Forest — coming in 2019

Standalones

<u>*Broken*</u> - Trent & Delilah

<u>*Come Undone*</u> - A Love Triangle

Dirty Rich

<u>*Dirty Deal*</u> - Blake

<u>*Dirty Boss*</u> - Nick

<u>Sign up for the Crystal Kaswell mailing list</u>

Chapter One

ARIEL

"**I**'m sorry, Ariel." Phillip's voice fills with apology. He holds my gaze for a second—less even—then his eyes shift to the clean white tablecloth.

This is a nice place. The kind of place that covers its square tables in actual cloth. That sets a candle between lovestruck diners. That adorns its brick walls in images of Italian actors.

It's not a place where you say *I'm sorry, Ariel*.

This isn't a conversation that starts with *I'm sorry, Ariel*.

My boyfriend is awkward, but he's not that awkward. He's not stupid enough to start a proposal with *I'm sorry, Ariel*.

I press my palms into my dress. It's red and tight and expensive. Forest helped me pick it out. Even though he doesn't think Phillip is good enough for me. Even though he doesn't think I'm ready to get married. Even though he doesn't think an Italian restaurant in Marina Del Rey is a nice enough spot for a proposal.

I try to find my boyfriend's gaze, but his eyes refuse to

budge. He watches the candle cast shadows over the white tablecloth.

It casts highlights over his face. His angular chin, wide nose, dark eyes, black hair.

He's so handsome. And more than that, his face is familiar. I know every shade of brown in his eyes. Every grey in his coarse hair. Every curve of his soft lips.

I know this expression.

It's not *I'm sorry, Ariel, but I couldn't find the ring you liked. It wasn't available in your size—did Holden tell you I asked? Or was it Forest? Your brothers are gossips.*

It's not *I'm sorry, Ariel, I should have picked a nicer restaurant.*

It's not even *I'm sorry, Ariel, but I need more time.*

I know the words before they're out of his mouth.

"I can't do this." Finally, he pries his eyes from the table. Stares at me with those soulful browns. "It's not you."

It's not me? That's ridiculous. I'm the one with the ticking clock. With the ultimatum. With the expiration date that changes everything. "Then what?" I want to believe him. I want it to be something else. His parents. School. Friends.

Anything but my sudden need for a baby.

"I love you." He reaches across the table. Places his palm on mine.

His tan skin covers my pale fingers.

Much like my namesake, I'm as pale as the moon. I can't sing, or hold my breath, or move with grace, but I have the pale as the moon thing down.

Phillip is Vietnamese. He's darker. I always loved that. The way our skin tones contrasted. It was just sexy.

God, I'm already thinking in past tense. We used to look perfect together. The pale math geek and the tan doctor. Same black hair. Same five-foot-seven frame. Same love of nature documentaries.

Now this.

I stare at his hand. I can't move my eyes. I can't move my lips, my shoulders, my feet.

This doesn't make sense. It's been three years. We've talked about it. Sure, I'm changing the timeline, but what's that matter?

We both want this.

Or we did.

He did.

"Ariel…" Apology drips into his voice. "I hate doing this."

"Your parents?" They emigrated here when he was a baby. They're traditional. At first, they hated that he was dating a white girl. But they softened when I asked them to teach me to cook. Which took a million years. I'm so hopeless in the kitchen.

"They love you." He squeezes my hand. "They want this."

"You told them?"

"I wouldn't—"

"You're the only one—" I suck a breath through my teeth, but it's too shallow to calm me.

"I know."

"You can't—"

"I won't."

"Seriously, Phil, if Forest or Holden finds out." I am going to tell my brothers. And my dad. And my friends. Eventually.

"They'll support you. Like always."

Something catches in my eye. Something salty and hot. Fuck, it stings. Why does it sting like this?

"Sweetie—" Phillip reaches for my cheek—with his other hand. His fingers brush my skin. He catches a tear on his thumb.

I'm crying.

That isn't okay. Not here. Not now.

I haven't cried over it yet.

I don't cry over anything but Mom.

Another tear catches on my lashes. Then another.

I blink and my eyes are full of them. The room gets blurry. Like when I take off my glasses.

The same fucking glasses as Phillip. We always joke about how we dress the same—thick black frames, black jeans, black tops. Why waste time deciding what to wear? There are puzzles to solve, PhDs to complete, undergrads to teach.

"Ariel." He says my name the way he always does. Like he loves me. Like he wants the best for me. Like he's promising he'll be by my side forever.

"Are you scared?"

"Not like that." He stresses the last word, so I know he's not scared about the disease that killed my mother. He's not scared of losing me. He's scared of keeping me.

"Like what?" I pull my hands free. Finally. But they do a terrible job wiping my eyes.

I can't cry here. That's why he picked this place. Not because I love Italian food. Not because it's soft and romantic. Because it's *nice*.

It's not the kind of place where you throw a fit over a breakup.

Which is ridiculous. I've never thrown a fit. In three years, I've always—

We're calm, even people. We don't throw fits. Why would I start now?

"I hate this as much you do." He sets his hands in my lap. "I love you, Ariel. I don't want to leave."

I press my lips together. It helps stem the tears. Not enough, but some. "Then why?"

"You only have a year."

"But I—"

"I thought I was ready, but I'm not… I'm not sure I want that anymore."

"What?" I pinch myself. Still here. Not dreaming. He doesn't want this anymore? He's always wanted this. "Since when?"

"I don't know."

"But—" There isn't enough time for someone else. A year and change. Which really means four or five months, max. After that, the odds are too bad.

I want this, yes, but I'm a woman of science. I know a sure thing when I see it. I know a death sentence when I see it.

"If there's anything I can do…" He presses his lips into a smile. "Anything, really."

"What if you didn't have to be involved?" The words tumble out of my mouth. They don't stop in my brain. Or my heart.

His brow furrows. That look he gets when he complains about coworkers who fail to grasp simple concepts.

The words keep coming. "What if it was just a… donation?"

"Ariel—"

"Breakup sex." My voice is fast. Desperate. Some tone I haven't heard since Mom… "Please."

"I'm sorry, but I don't know if I want to be a father anymore."

"I understand." Kind of. I mean, before I saw the test results, I wasn't sure either. The *positive* changed something. Made it obvious what I had to do.

"I wish things were different."

"I know." It's sweet, really. It's not what I want, but it's honest. It's all I can ask for.

Phillip isn't ready to be a father.

Which means I have four months to find a guy to knock me up.

No, four months to actually get pregnant.

I'm completely and totally fucked.

Chapter Two

CHASE

"You're not keeping that up." Forest points to the banner hanging over the foyer. The one that reads *Congratulations, Mrs. Nguyen*.

"Why not?" Holden makes a show of scratching his head. So we know it's the stupidest question in the world.

"She's not taking his name." Forest turns to me, requesting backup. Anything to prove he's right. Same as me.

No, I stop at teamwork. That's one of the many ways my best friend is a better person than I am.

"It's the thought that counts." I decline to take a side. I've been good friends with the Ballard family for a long time. Since high school. Forest and I were on the basketball team together.

I hung out here all the time. Got to know his little brother Holden and his little sister Ariel.

She's different. Passionate about things that go way over my head. Math, science, the gender politics of taking your boyfriend's last name.

My stomach twists. This is too familiar. I swear, I can

CRYSTAL KASWELL

see the ring on Grace's finger. Feel the weight of it. Her palm pressing into mine. *I'm sorry, Chase. I can't.*

Tears catching on her long lashes. Smudging her dark eyeliner. Rolling down her apple cheeks.

Her red nails digging into her hoodie—red, of course. It was her favorite color. It's still her favorite color.

"Fuck, Chase hates it too?" Holden shakes his head, sending his waves in every direction. He's named after the titular character of *Catcher in the Rye* and he lives to be even more annoying than Holden Caulfield.

"Chase is too nice to say it," Forest says.

Holden looks from his older brother to me. "Chase isn't nice."

"She's your sister." Yeah, I'm an unforgiving asshole. But when I care about someone, I do my best.

It's just that's never been good enough.

My best didn't help Mom keep her shit together. It didn't convince my little brother to get sober. It sure as fuck didn't make Grace happy.

Maybe these guys should do the opposite of my best. That has a better chance of working.

And I—

I need to go somewhere I can breathe. "I should get out of here." I shrug my hoodie off my shoulders. It's too much, too hot. Even with the AC turned up high, I'm melting.

Forest and I play basketball once a week. It's perfect. We don't talk about life or love or work—he's a tattoo artist, same as I am.

We play until we collapse.

No feelings involved.

No chance to hurt another person I care about.

"She shouldn't take his name." Holden hops onto the

8

counter—actually hops—and reaches for the banner. "I shouldn't encourage her."

"Why'd you buy that?" Forest shoots me a look *what's wrong with him?*

"I need to shower." It's the only excuse that comes to mind.

"Hot date tonight?" Holden raises a brow. "You holding out on me, Keating? You know I like dirt."

Forest rolls his eyes *grow up*.

"Something like that." The only hot date I have lately is with my hand. It's not lack of options. Women are interested. Most of my female clients drop hints or leave their number. Sometimes, they flat out proposition me. *I don't usually do this, but I feel like I can trust you. Do you want to come to my place tonight?*

I never say yes.

My friends consider that a sign of dysfunction. What healthy man declines casual sex?

But it's not like that.

Those women don't want me. They want the idea of some bad boy who put ink to their skin. They think that if they can trust me with their body in the chair, they can trust me with their body anywhere.

They're wrong.

With my tattoo gun in my hands, I know what I'm doing. I'm a master of the fucking universe.

When I set it down—

The record speaks for itself.

"Good. You need to get laid. Bad." Holden shakes his head *so fucking bad*, turns to the banner, reaches for it, stops.

Forest nods *it is pretty bad*.

Maybe they're right. Maybe my standards are too high. What is it they say—that perfect is the enemy of the good?

Yeah, I can't have Grace. But I can have any number of women.

I can take them home, roll their panties to their knees, lick them until they're groaning my name.

My body is on board with the idea. Even my head is willing to consider it. But my heart?

It's already too fucking heavy. I like Holden and Forest's little sister, Ariel. I do. She's sweet. She deserves happiness.

I want that for her.

So long as I don't have to watch.

"Someone you met at Inked Hearts?" Holden jumps off the counter. He motions to the sash *it's staying there.* "You have a pic? Taking some tonight?" He raises a brow *don't hold out on me.*

Forest shoots him a look. Some brotherly thing I don't understand.

I used to have that kind of language with my brothers. But…

I suck a breath through my teeth. Shrug my shoulders. It doesn't break up the tension, but it conveys a certain *I don't give a fuck* attitude.

"Fuck, dude doesn't realize how good he has it." Holden shakes his head. "I wish Oddball had the clientele you have at Inked Hearts. The girls there…" He presses his hand to his heart. Then to his crotch. "It's not fair. And we—"

"Don't." Forest cuts him off. Shoots him another one of those brotherly looks.

I don't try to understand it. "Thanks for the game." I motion to the backyard. It's huge. A perk of hanging at your rich parents' place. Not that I can talk. My parents have plenty.

Forest nods, sure. "Do you have a minute, Chase—"

The front door creaks open.

Forest turns to his brother. Drops his voice to a whisper. "It's too early."

"Maybe he blew his load early." Holden shrugs like he doesn't care, but concern is written all over his face. Their mom died when they were teenagers. It wrecked their dad for a while, so they stepped up to take care of their little sister. They're more protective than anyone I know.

"Chase?" Ariel's footsteps move into the kitchen. She brings her hand to her cheek. Wipes a tear.

Her eyes are puffy, but they're not lined in smudged makeup. She isn't wearing any makeup, save for something making her lips red and shiny.

It's a faint red, not like the fire engine shade Grace used to wear.

But that dress—

Fuck, she looks good in that tight crimson thing. It shows off her tits. Hugs her narrow waist. Her curvy hips.

Has Ariel always looked like this?

Or is Holden right? Do I need to get laid so badly I'm desperate?

Ariel is like a little sister. She's crying. She's vulnerable. It's not the time to think about her tits.

"What are you—" She looks around the room. The clean oak table. The cake on the counter. The banner reading *Congratulations, Mrs. Nguyen.*

Her composure breaks.

She presses her lips together. Turns her gaze to the ground. "I… uh… excuse me." She moves up the stairs. Slams the door. Turns her music on.

It's something from the 80s, a synth-pop jam that is somehow peppy and depressing at once.

I want to follow her up there. To knock on the door. Wrap my arms around her. Whisper *it's going to be okay.*

But I can't promise that.

I have no idea how to get over my broken heart. How am I supposed to help with hers?

———

Forest talks me into playing another round. Then a third. A fourth.

The sun sets. The automatic lights turn on. My thoughts betray me.

This place is too familiar. Too constant.

When I close my eyes, I can see her here. Sitting on the taupe patio furniture. Sketching as Forest and I played. Humming along to her iPod.

Pressing her bright lips into a smile.

Fuck, I need a break.

"Water." I motion to the kitchen.

Forest nods *sure*. He takes the ball from me. Turns to the hoop. Lines it up just right—

Swoosh.

Nothing but net.

I'm almost jealous. It's hard to get competitive about sports now. I'm almost thirty and I'm—

Let's just say my life is nothing like I thought it would be two years ago.

No marriage. No kids. No white picket fence around my two-million-dollar house in Santa Monica.

Because it's a good school district. Because the kids are worth it.

My throat tightens. There she is. Trying to invade my thoughts.

Fuck that.

I suck a breath through my nose. Push an exhale through my teeth.

That needs to be my universe. My breath. Stillness. All

that new age shit.

After a few deep breaths, the image of Grace fades. My throat relaxes. My feet obey my commands.

I move through the sliding glass doors.

Ariel is sitting at the kitchen table, fingers wrapped around a glass of liquor. Vodka or gin. Something clear.

Her dark eyes flit to mine. "You want one?"

I shake my head *no thanks*, but the look on her face makes me reconsider.

Fuck, I know that look.

I *own* that look. "You know what—" I pull the sliding door closed. Which is wrong. We shouldn't be alone. Not with both of us single. "I'll have one."

No, I'm overthinking this.

The girl is heartbroken.

Yeah, I'll probably fuck it up if I try to help, but I can share a drink with her.

"It's a Moscow Mule," she says. "With ginger liqueur. It's great, but sweet."

"Make it the way you like."

"You sure?" She stands. Moves to the fridge. Pulls out vodka, liqueur, club soda, ice. "If you know what you want, why—"

"Maybe I don't know what I want."

She tries to laugh, but it comes out more like a cry. "Sorry, I—"

"Why are you sorry?"

"Is it obvious?"

Huh?

Her eyes fix on mine for a moment. "The *Loser* printed on my forehead?"

"'Cause you got dumped?"

She hesitates. "Yeah."

"Happens to everyone."

"Not Holden." Her gaze shifts to her brother's bedroom upstairs. Not that he lives there. It's just Ariel and her dad. Who's away on business.

After Forest leaves, it's just her.

My stomach twists. I don't like the thought of her drinking by herself.

I don't like the hurt spread over her face.

Because she's like a sister.

Not because her red lips make me think of—

They don't actually. Ariel is nothing like my ex. She's the polar opposite of my ex.

Ariel is steady, quiet, calm to a fault. Whereas Grace was… is. She's an artist. Wears her feelings on her sleeves. Rides her ups and downs like they're a roller coaster.

"You have to be with someone to get dumped," I say.

She nods *true*. Turns to the counter, fixes my drink, brings it to the table.

I sit across from her.

She looks different up close. Same black hair pinned to her head. Same thick glasses. Same freckles covering her nose.

But the red lips—

My heart twists. My stomach flutters. My balls tighten.

"Thanks." The drink is crisp. Sweet, yeah, but spicy too.

"Is it too much?"

This conversation is, but that's not what she's asking. "Just right."

"It doesn't matter now."

"Huh?"

"If I drink. I might as well today. Because it's not happening soon."

"What's not?"

Her eyes meet mine. "Nothing." She pushes her glasses up her nose.

God, those glasses are perfect on her. Between the fancy updo and the classy dress, she looks like a sexy professor. Like she's going to invite me to her office for some extracurricular—

It has been too long.

There's no way in hell I'm thinking about fucking Ariel Ballard.

Sure, she's gorgeous. Dark eyes. Long legs. Soft lips. And—

Not helping.

"Did you ever get over it?" she asks.

"Over what?"

"Grace?"

My heart twists.

Her eyes turn down. "I didn't mean—"

"I know."

"I just… tell me it gets easier."

"It does." Mostly.

"Do you… Do you think it's weird if I burn this dress?"

I can't help but laugh. "No."

"Holden thought it was."

"He doesn't know."

She nods *he doesn't*. "I hate red, anyway. I only bought it for Phil, and I guess it worked. He said I looked beautiful."

My eyes fail to obey my command. They trace a line from her dainty chin to her strong shoulders to her lush tits. Fuck, she's wearing that dress. "You do."

"Thank you." Her cheeks flush. "I… I want to ask you something…"

My body cuts in. *Yeah, I'd love to fuck you. Take off the dress. Show me what you're wearing under it.*

Tell me it's that same shade of red.

It's fucking perfect on you.

Her eyes bore into mine. "A favor. But you have to promise not to tell anyone."

I try to find a no. Or better yet *I really like you, Ariel, but I don't think this is appropriate for our relationship.*

Instead, I stare back into her eyes. "Shoot."

Chapter Three

ARIEL

W*ill you help me get pregnant?*
No. That's too obvious. And it's not what I'm asking either.

Chase is a good guy. He's tall—like ridiculously tall. Like our hypothetical kids would be basketball players.

He *is* a basketball player.

God, the day he and Forest celebrated over making the varsity team, and Chase had too much cheap vodka, and he hugged me like he wanted me, like he loved me—

That's exactly why Chase isn't an option.

Sure, I'm a grown woman. I'm over my schoolgirl crush. But he's so handsome. And sweet.

Maybe sweet isn't the right word. Chase is like... he's like the ice princess in *Frozen*. He has a supernatural ability to push people away or cut them down with his stare.

"Ariel?" Chase's blue eyes fix on me. They're deep and clear. They're beautiful.

Mom had blue eyes.

Maybe I carry the recessive gene.

Maybe our daughter would have blue eyes. And I'd be as evil as Mom and name her after ice princess Elsa.

The ocean princess and the ice princess.

It's kind of adorable.

Ahem.

I like Chase. A lot. So much that I want him to continue breathing. If Forest found out Chase and I slept together, that Chase got me pregnant—

My baby daddy would be dead before he hit the ground.

I'm already thinking *baby daddy*. How ridiculous.

"Remember when you were a kid?" His voice lifts to some tone I can't place. (Which is normal. I'm terrible at placing tones).

"What specifically?" I suck another sip of Moscow Mule from my straw. Spicy ginger, crisp vodka, tart lime, sweet liquor.

"The birthday where Holden bought you a *Little Mermaid* costume?"

I stick my tongue out. Before Mom got sick, my family enjoyed how much I hated my name. They teased. Constantly.

Chase chuckles. "He convinced you to put it on."

"Mom's smile convinced me to put it on." It did a bunch of times. She loved when I dressed as *that* Ariel. The Halloween before she died—

"I called you princess all day."

My knees press together. My stomach flutters. Chase calling me princess. God, that's… I had such a crush on him.

"You are a princess."

"I'm not—"

"Maybe you don't have the swimming down—"

"I do okay."

His lips curl into a half-smile. "There's something about you."

"Thank you." I think.

"What do you need, princess?" His eyes light up. With desire. Then surprise.

It sounds so good on his tongue. *Princess.*

For a second, I forget Phil dumped me. I forget I have four months to get pregnant. I forget everything except that day Chase first called me princess.

I need to keep this in the back of my mind. Can you do that? Can you make me forget my boyfriend of three years decided he doesn't want to have kids with me? Can you make me forget I had to issue that terrible ultimatum because I'm carrying the gene for the cancer that killed my mother and I need to have a baby now or give up on it forever?

Please, Chase, make me forget.

God, I'm losing track of my point. Maybe it's the Moscow Mules. Maybe I've had too many. Or too few.

"Do you want another round?" I ask.

He nods *sure.*

I take his cup, fix two more.

Chase eyes me curiously. It's different than his normal gaze. Filled with concern and something else. Something I've never seen in his eyes.

At least, not directed at me.

He holds up his drink.

I do the same. "What to?"

"Heartbreak."

I'm not sure I want to toast to the thing making my body ache, but I do it anyway.

Clink.

"It'll hurt for a while." A sigh rolls off his lips. It's low. Deep. Pure pleasure. "Then less every day."

"Right." I don't want to call Chase a liar, but he's not a

shining example of his point. His fiancée left two years ago and he's still completely miserable.

I mean, Chase has never been happy go lucky. But he did love her.

For a while, I hated how happy in love they were. Then I got over my schoolgirl crush and—

Why is my stomach fluttering the way it did then?

His eyes are so blue. And intense. And he's staring at me like he's staring through me.

That must be it.

The guy has a penetrating gaze.

Like he's a cop and I'm a murder suspect he's interrogating.

Like he doesn't believe a word I say.

Anyone would feel nervous under that kind of scrutiny.

"Ariel, I get what you're feeling." He leans in closer. "We're good friends."

"Yeah…"

"But we can't—" His eyes flit to my chest. His cheeks flush. Just barely. "We can't cross that line."

"What line?"

His gaze shifts to my bedroom upstairs.

Oh.

No.

I shake my head. "Of course."

He stares at me like I'm crazy. "I'm flattered. But—"

"I don't want to have sex with you."

Surprise streaks his expression.

Okay, that isn't exactly true. I do want to have sex with Chase. In the way I want to have sex with Idris Elba. Because he's attractive, intense, commanding. Because I touched myself to thoughts of him in high school.

Not because it makes sense today.

I don't have time for casual sex.

I have four months.

"I…" God, how do I explain this to him? I can't tell him about my situation. I can't trust him to keep it to himself. "I want to find someone else."

"You need my help?"

"Yeah." I need someone's help. And I can't ask a coworker. I certainly can't ask Skye. "You know a lot of guys."

"I guess."

"And you're very attractive."

A chuckle falls from his lips. "You sure you're not buttering me up?"

"Not for that."

His shoulders relax. "For what then?"

"Can I trust you?" I swallow a sip. Let the liquor warm my throat. According to my fertility app, today is the last viable day of this cycle. Which gives me approximately three weeks to find someone. That doesn't leave a lot of time for caution.

He raises a brow *can't you?*

Maybe. He picked me up at prom after my date made a move. He never told Forest or Holden.

If he kept that secret—

I nod *okay*. "I need to find someone."

"You're a beautiful woman. You don't need my help."

My heartbeat picks up. He thinks I'm beautiful. He thinks I'm a woman. Not a girl. Not a kid. Not his friend's little sister. A woman.

"That's what guys care about." He shakes his head. "Fuck, ignore that."

"Oh."

"You deserve better than some guy who wants a warm place to stick his dick."

My tongue slides over my lip. He's so… concerned. It shouldn't do things to me. But it does.

Maybe he is what I need. Maybe casual sex is what I need. One night to get over Phillip. To put me on the path to finding a… um, suitor.

"No, I… I want more than that," I say.

He tilts his head to one side *huh*.

"I don't want to find some guy to ease the loneliness." Well, that's not criteria number one.

He stares back at me.

"I need someone who will get me pregnant."

Chapter Four

CHASE

I *need someone who will get me pregnant.*

My fingers dig into the glass. Find too little friction. Slip.

Ariel Ballard wants someone to get her pregnant.

What the actual fuck?

She's twenty-four. A kid. A good kid on a clear path.

She's getting a PhD in statistics.

She's living with her dad to save money.

She's crying over her doctor boyfriend dumping her.

But then—

The banner is a crumbled mess on the counter. *Congratulations, Mrs. Nguyen.*

Forest and Holden didn't have anything to say about why Ariel was expecting a proposal.

They had a lot to say about her boyfriend—*I don't care if he's a doctor, he's not good enough for her. He spends all his time working*—but they were convinced the proposal was imminent.

That Ariel was going to be Mrs. Phillip Nguyen in no time, flat.

"What?" I press my palms into the table. Blink twice.

She's still sitting across from me. Her brown eyes are still boring into mine. Pleading *please help me*.

"Don't you—" She has friends. Female friends. Coworkers. Other people more qualified to help. "Why?"

"I need to get pregnant in the next four months."

That doesn't clarify anything. "Why?"

"That doesn't matter."

I shake my head. That sure as hell matters.

"Can you help? Or do I need to ask someone else?"

"Ariel—"

Her eyes turn down. She stares into her drink like it might offer answers.

I try to formulate a response. Something more coherent than *Ariel*. Something both firm and kind. Between *hell no, I'm going to stand outside your bedroom door so this doesn't happen* and *I wish I could Ariel. But are you sure this is a good idea?*

"Princess—" My balls tighten. Calling her princess is supposed to send me back to when we first met. It's not supposed to fill my head with ideas of bending her over and growling *take off your panties, princess*.

The sliding door opens, cutting me off. Forest steps inside. He surveys the scene and raises a brow.

His eyes meet mine. They ask *is she okay?*

They don't ask *what the fuck are you doing?* Or *are you taking advantage of my sister* or *are you gonna fuck the drunk, lonely girl because you're that desperate?*

He trusts me with his sister. He trusts me to act like an honorary brother. To end stupid ideas like getting knocked up at twenty-four.

Ariel presses her lips together. She shoots me a different look. *Please don't tell him.*

"I gotta go." I can't say no. Not until I convince her this

is a bad idea. "Let's talk tomorrow." I look to Forest. "You coming by Inked Hearts?"

He nods *yeah*. "We'll get dinner after." He looks to Ariel. "Why don't you come?"

Her eyes light up. "Yeah. That's a good idea." She finishes her drink. Stands. "I, uh, I'll see you later, Chase. Think about what I said, okay?"

As if I'll think about anything else.

Chapter Five

CHASE

"How much will it hurt?" My client presses her lips together. She taps her toes against the tile floor. Pushes out a sharp exhale.

"This is your first?" It's obvious from her nervous eyes and her bare wrists. I know this kind of girl. She wants something tiny on a delicate spot. Wrists, ankles, hips, ribs.

For some reason, it's always the small, feminine women who pick the most painful spots for tattoos.

And Sara here—

She's torturing herself.

"It will hurt." I never lie to clients. Ever. But sometimes it's better to skip the gory details. "But you can handle it."

"Uh…"

"Sara, look at me."

Her blue eyes fix on mine. They're the same shade as Grace's. For once, that's not where my brain goes.

It goes to the nerves in Ariel's dark eyes. The same as this girl's nerves. Like she's about to jump off a cliff.

Tattoos are scary and painful, but compared to love? Starting a family?

It's nothing.

"Tell me about the design." I know everything there is to know about this design. *Omnia vincit amor.* Surrounded by lilies.

It doesn't take a genius to put those pieces together.

Love conquers all. Funeral flowers.

Either Sara lost someone or she's a big fan of the movie *Titanic*.

"I um… Well, it's kind of personal." She tugs at her jeans.

"You're wearing tape as a top."

She nods *true*. Motions to the gauze covering her breasts. "It's different."

"What is?"

I swab a cotton ball with rubbing alcohol. Run it over her ribs. Blow to help it dry.

Her eyelids flutter closed. A groan falls from her lips. The one that usually means *God, I want the hot tattoo artist.* "What's it matter if you see my body?"

"What does it matter?"

"It's personal, yeah. Sometimes it's sexy. But it's not like when you reveal your heart to someone."

I nod.

"Sure, it hurts if someone rejects your body—"

"Who rejects your body?" I tape the stencil to her ribs.

"Well…"

"You can't lie when someone is this close." Sara is a knockout. Big tits, narrow ribs, perky ass.

If things were different, if I was the kind of guy who cared more about the look of a woman's body than—

Fuck, I don't even know what people look for in casual sex.

Her laugh is nervous. "They're fake." She motions to her chest.

This is Southern California. That isn't rare. "A lot are."

"Yeah, I, uh, well, I was really small as a teenager. And I thought I needed that to feel beautiful. It helped, but it attracted a different sort of guy too."

"Besides the one—" I motion to the trace paper.

"Yeah." She sucks in a sharp inhale. "Can we start?"

I'm pushing too far. It's not like me. I don't usually ask clients personal questions. If they offer, I listen. But I don't pry.

My head is in a weird place today.

It keeps going back to Ariel.

The hurt streaking her eyes.

The desperate plea.

The heaving chest.

Some asshole taking advantage of her. Failing to appreciate her math puns and her begrudging love of Disney films and the way her black glasses frame her brown eyes.

The way she blushes when I call her *princess*.

Fuck, not going there.

She's not asking *me* to get her pregnant.

She's—

I swear, I'm out of my mind. It's the lack of sleep. The lack of coffee. The mental image that shouldn't be in my head.

"On the count of three." I pick up the gun. Dip it in ink.

Sara nods.

"On, two." I turn the gun on. Bring the needle to her skin. "Three."

She yelps. "Fuck." For a split second, her eyes press together, her teeth sink into her lip, her fingers dig into the teal vinyl.

Then she sighs and releases.

"It hurts," she says.

I nod *yeah*.

"But knowing how it does... that makes it less scary. Why?"

"The unknown is always scary."

"True." She wraps her fingers around the chair. Still bracing, but not so tightly. "You, um... you do a lot of these?"

"Latin quotes?"

"I guess."

"Some." I do a lot. A lot of this quote specifically. But never with lilies. "Not many like this."

"For someone... you think that will make it hurt more or less?"

"What will?" I finish tracing the first word. Move onto the second.

She yelps as the needle hits her skin. "Have you ever lost someone?"

"Not the way you mean."

"But you have?"

"I was engaged for a while."

Her eyes flit to my left hand. "Your glove is in the way."

"You can ask."

"Is there a ring?"

I shake my head.

"Did she... is she gone?"

"She's around." Just not around me. I never once thought that would be better. I love Grace. I want her in the world. I want to stop loving her, but not because she's gone. Because I don't care anymore.

"What happened?"

I trace the *a*. Study her expression through the mirror. She wants a distraction. A connection. A reason to spill her guts.

Usually, I run away from that.

Right now—

There's too much in my head. I need to talk to someone. I need someone to understand.

To whisper *it's not your fault, Chase. You're not the reason everyone around you is fucked. You're capable of making someone happy.*

I want to hear that.

I want it to be true.

But this isn't about what I need. It's about Sara. "I tried to make her happy. But I didn't."

Through the mirror, her eyes meet mine. "You miss her?"

"Sometimes," I lie. Return to the letters. "Do you miss your—"

"Yeah, but it's different than a breakup."

"Forever?"

She nods *yeah*. "He knew he was... it was, I swear it was like a Nicholas Sparks movie. I knew he had a terminal illness when we fell in love. He told me to stay away. He even left at one point."

"He didn't want you to hurt?"

"Maybe. I think it was more... he was scared, you know? To have someone there to watch. To have something to lose."

Fuck, I can't imagine.

"I... I used to tell him this. That love conquers all. Even death. He thought it was stupid." She nods to the tattoo. "He'd hate it."

"You really think so?"

"Yeah, but he'd love it too. Because..." She blinks and a tear catches on her lashes. "Sorry."

"It happens."

She presses her lips together. "It isn't easier."

I move to the next letter.

"Adding the memory. But nothing will ever hurt that much. Or like that."

"You ever think he was right?"

Her eyes turn down.

"Sorry. None of my—"

"No. People usually dance around it." She pushes out an exhale. "At first, I thought it wasn't. I missed him so badly. I couldn't get out of bed. But eventually the cloud lifted. And now… I'm glad we had that time."

"Yeah?"

"Better to have some than nothing."

I used to think that too. But now—

"Fuck, it really does hurt."

"It does."

She grimaces. "And the shading—"

"Even worse."

She nods *that's what I thought*. "I, uh…"

"Tell me about him."

She does. It gets her through the words, the outline of the flowers, the fill, the shading.

She doesn't cry, really cry, until she's cleaned up and staring at her new ink in the mirror.

Sara throws her arms around me. "Thank you."

Usually, this kind of touch sucks away my oxygen. Female clients like to hug goodbye. It's too much intimacy. Too much closeness. Too much pain.

The love in her eyes tugs at the hole in my gut.

This girl lost her boyfriend young. She barely had any time with him. But she still looks at their relationship as the best thing that ever happened to her.

If I made Grace half as happy as she is—

Maybe I'd believe that too.

My younger brother Wes watches as I check her out. He whispers to his best friend Griffin. Something about me, no doubt. The two of them have been working together for half a decade. They've been friends since day two. They're always hanging on the sidelines, trading gossip.

I try to ignore them as I walk Sara to the door.

She hugs me goodbye, presses her business card into my palm, mumbles something about a date. *I'm still not over him, but if you ever want something casual with someone incapable of loving you... I know, it's a great offer, isn't it?*

They do me the courtesy of waiting until she leaves to launch.

Wes makes an *o* with his thumb and first two fingers. He takes his other hand, presses his index and middle finger together and goes for it.

His blue eyes light up as he mimes penetration. This is where he lives. Making stupid jokes. Pretending like he doesn't give a shit about anything.

Griffin shakes his head, sending dark waves in every direction. Unlike Wes, he actually enjoys hanging on the sidelines, staying out of things.

He's blunt as hell and he doesn't see anything wrong with his lack of tact. "You gotta warm her up first."

Wes drops the mimed penetration. Brings his first two fingers to his mouth to make a *v*.

Like in high school.

Griffin nods *yeah*.

Wes shakes his head. "We have any evidence Chase is a—"

"Cunning linguist?" Griffin chuckles. "That really what you were going to say?"

"Yeah." Wes shrugs. "You got a problem with that? Jeez." He runs his hand through his sandy hair. "You're as moody as Chase."

"I'm moody?" Griffin raises a brow.

Wes nods yeah.

"'Cause I'd rather call things what they are?" Griffin asks.

Wes groans. "Jesus, Griff, I'm trying to have a little class."

"Let's use real words. Does Chase eat pussy?" Griffin asks.

Wes cringes. "Pussy? And I'm in high school?"

"You think I haven't seen your sexts?" Griffin asks.

"You two have a point?" If I don't stop them, they'll go all day.

"Yeah, Griff wants to know if you're eating pussy." Wes chuckles.

Griffin nods *it's a fair question*.

"She was cute. Into you," Wes says.

"Crying. That's your type," Griffin says.

Wes shakes his head. "Jesus, Griff, tact!"

"Chase is miserable. She's miserable. Seems like they'd get along." Griffin shrugs *it's the truth. Do you want me to lie?*

He doesn't realize most people don't appreciate his level of honesty.

I don't mind. I'd rather hear the truth, even if it hurts.

I know what people think of me. They don't have to dance around it.

"Maybe. If Chase finds one of those *I want my ex to die in a car crash* chicks it might encourage his worst impulses." Wes's sandy hair falls over his head as he tilts his head to one side. "Maybe he needs someone like Quinn." He sighs with bliss as he refers to his girlfriend.

"A virgin?" Griffin chuckles. "You're the only one obsessed with conquering. Unless—" He looks to me and raises a brow. "Is that why you've been holding back?"

"You got me," I deadpan. "I can't fuck a woman unless I'm her first."

Wes and Griffin share a look. One at my expense.

The details elude me. I used to know all of Wes's looks —he is my baby brother. But shit changed when I kicked our brother Hunter out of our old shop.

It was necessary. Hunter lied about getting sober. Promised to quit then didn't. Letting him stay would have been enabling him. It would have pushed him toward a path that ended in—

Well, in a tattoo with lilies.

Sometimes you have to hurt someone to help them.

It's true.

Only no one tells you that hurting someone burns that bridge forever.

It's not that I hold a grudge. I want to forgive him. To trust him again.

I just can't.

Bing-bong. The bell's ring interrupts Rosencrantz and Guildenstern.

Ariel steps inside. Her eyes meet mine. Her red lips curl into a smile.

It's not like last night. They don't make me think of Grace. They send my head straight to the gutter.

Her lips on my neck. My chest. My cock.

Fuck, there's something about her request. It's not even for me, but it's doing shit to me.

I always wanted that. A family. But I wanted it with my ex. When she left, I swept it aside. Put it in the same box as the ring.

Now—

She's not even asking you. She doesn't want you filling her. Doesn't matter that she'd melt if you ordered her to get on her knees.

"Shit," Wes whispers to Griff. "There's a girl."

Griffin nods *yeah*.

"Too cute for him."

"Chase is handsome. It's his personality—"

"You two have work to do?" I ask.

They share a look. *He's irritated. He must like her.*

I do. That's the problem. I don't want to hurt Ariel. But I have to.

Somehow, I have to talk her out of this.

Chapter Six

CHASE

"What are we drinking to?" Wes holds up his glass of white wine. "Tell me it's Chase—"

I don't want to know where that sentence is going. "Do we need an occasion?" I shoot him a death glare. It's bad enough he invited himself to dinner. Whatever this is—

I want nothing to do with it.

"Was gonna say to Chase drinking." Wes returns my look. *Bro, please. I'm the one with social skills. Give me that.* "It's rare."

Griffin isn't here to add *Chase quit drinking regularly when he realized Mom was an alcoholic. Now that she's half-assing recovery, again—*

Not going there.

"It is." Forest holds up his glass—a Moscow Mule, the same as his sister. He taps his glass against Ariel's. Then mine. Wes's. "You're drinking wine."

"I'm a classy bastard." Wes takes a long sip of his white wine. Sighs like he can't get enough.

"His girlfriend is into wine," I say.

Ariel's gaze flits from me to Wes then back to me. "What's she like?"

"Smart," Wes says. "Cute. Nervous. Thick glasses." He winks at Ariel. "Always dig a smart girl with glasses."

She looks me in the eyes, asking if he's serious.

He is. In his way. I nod.

"Too bad you and I were never single at the same time." Wes raises his glass. Winks at Ariel. "Or we really could have had some fun."

"I'm not sure Forest would allow that." Her smile softens. Her shoulders fall from her ears. "He's a little—"

"Over-protective older brother. I get it." Wes reaches to me and musses my hair. "They're difficult."

She laughs. "They are." She turns to Forest, whispers something in his ear.

He whispers back.

She nods. "Excuse me. I, um, I need to make a call."

"Me too." It's a bad lie, but I don't care. I need to talk to her alone.

Her lips purse. This isn't the outcome she wants. But I don't care about that either.

"I'll walk with you," I say.

"Actually…" She looks to Forest for help.

He nods *it's okay*.

She turns to me. "We…"

I motion to the door *let's go*. Cut through the cozy tables. This is a cute place. A Mexican restaurant in the trendy Abbot Kinney area. It brims with homey charm. Streamers in white, green, and red. Flower print vinyl table-clothes. Cactus string lights.

Ariel follows me to the street.

The sun sinks into the horizon, streaking the sky orange. It's something out of a postcard. Quiet street, smell of salt, low roar of the ocean.

Or maybe that's my imagination. We're half a dozen blocks from the beach. And since when do postcards include smell or sound?

"Chase, I, uh… I'm not really good with subtlety. So I'm just going to say this." Ariel turns her body toward mine. She takes a step toward me. So there are only six inches between us.

Fuck, there's something about the heat of her body. She smells good. Like tangerines. "Yeah?"

"I have other people I can ask. For help. But I trust you. We've been friends a long time. You've always looked out for me." Her voice gets serious. "I understand you're friends with Forest."

"He's been there a long time."

"He's not here to help me. He wants to ask a work favor."

"Oh?"

"I'm not supposed to tell you. He… he's like you. Proud."

I chuckle.

"He hates the idea of charity." Her dark eyes fix on me. "You're the same."

"Mostly."

"That's why I… Honestly, if I can only pick one favor, I'm going to be selfish."

I try to figure out what she's getting at, but I can't. "What are you asking?"

She pushes a breath through her teeth. Sucks an inhale through her nose. Her gaze shifts to the ground—to her black shoes. To my black shoes.

She traces a line up my body.

Slowly.

Like she's savoring every inch.

Or maybe like she's analyzing me, looking for cracks,

deciding what will convince me.

"There's a flood at Oddball. Forest and Holden need a place to work for a while. They're hoping they can borrow suites at Inked Hearts." Her eyes meet mine. Her voice stays even. "He's going to pretend like it's not a big deal, but it is."

"Of course." We always need more artists. We'd be lucky to have them. Even for a few months.

And, well, I could use the brownie points.

Everyone at Inked Hearts thinks I'm an asshole who doesn't participate.

They're right.

But I can't get behind the whole *the shop is my family* thing. I tried that at my old shop, Blacklist. I worked with my actual family. Adopted everyone else as de facto family.

It made everything with Hunter complicated.

It's one thing firing an artist for drinking on the job. It's another when he's your brother and your other brother is going to glare at you forever, both at work and at home, for it.

I learned my lesson. Business is business. Family is family. Period.

"Okay." She leans back on her heels. "Are you sure?"

"I have to ask the owners. But they'll say yes."

"Good." Her lips curl into a smile. Her brow relaxes. She wants the best for her brothers. "I… uh… Thank you."

"Don't thank me."

Her gaze shifts to the street as a Honda pulls up to the curb. The driver rolls the window down. Calls out a name.

A couple—a short guy and a tall woman—skips to the car. He opens the door for her. She giggles as he slaps her ass.

They're happy.

In love.

My lips curl into a frown instinctively.

Ariel's do the same. "How long does that last?"

"You tell me."

Her voice softens. "Is that why you don't want to help?"

"Who says I—"

"I'm not that oblivious." She slides her hands into her pocket. She's back in her usual attire. Black jeans. Tight black t-shirt. Black sneakers.

Fuck, the way the cotton hugs her curves.

My body begs me to touch her. To trace the curve of her waist. To rest my palm on my shoulder. To run my fingers over her cheek.

I want to comfort her.

Fuck her.

Hold her.

None of that is happening.

My brain is demented. It activated some sort of *Daddy* protocol. The same as it did that month Grace was late. She was freaking out—she wasn't ready to be a mother. I tried to be supportive. To stand by whatever she wanted.

I would have stood by her choice, whatever it was.

But, fuck, I wanted to see two pink lines on that test.

I wanted to tape an ultrasound to the fridge.

I wanted to buy tiny red Converse.

"You think I'm crazy?" Ariel asks.

Grace wasn't pregnant. She was just stressed. We never had to make that choice. We never made plans to cross that bridge.

"Chase?" she asks. "Please don't say something stupid, like, 'it's not a good idea.'"

"It's not."

"It is." Her brown eyes fill with determination. She's sure this is right. That this is exactly what she needs.

"You're a kid."

"I'm twenty-four." She fingers the edge of her black t-shirt. "Are you sure you can keep a secret?"

My eyes go straight to her pale stomach.

Fuck, I never had a thing for pale girls, but there's something about the way her light skin contrasts with the dark top.

I want to see her in black lingerie.

On my black sheets.

Naked.

Blood flees my brain. "Of course." I inhale slowly. Exhale deeply. I'm not fucking her. That's out of the question.

"My mom… the kind of cancer she had. It's genetic. I waited to do the testing. I was scared, I guess."

I get that.

"I didn't think it would matter. Phil and I talked about marriage and kids, but it was never urgent. It was always maybe. He knew there was a possibility—"

My stomach clenches. My voice drops. "Are you—"

"Sick? No. But I will be. I have the same gene mutation. That's what the test said."

"Ariel—"

"It's not… well, it is a big deal. But it's preventable. It's just the prevention…" Her lips press together. "My doctor wanted me to do it right away. But we compromised on twenty-five."

"Do what?" It's a stupid question. Her mom died of ovarian cancer. Prevention of that must mean—

"A hysterectomy. And a double mastectomy. Otherwise, I have a ninety-five percent chance… It's an aggressive treatment, some people wait longer, until thirty or thirty-five. But since my mom was so young—"

"I'm sorry."

"It was, um, the same thing happened to Angelina Jolie. But hers was a different gene. Just her—" She nods to her chest. "I should be able to keep my nipples. That's the good news. They can do a mastectomy that keeps the skin. There are so many breakthroughs in medicine, but there are so many things they can't figure out too."

"Fuck, Ariel." I want to offer something better, something comforting, but nothing comes.

"I only found out last week."

"Jesus."

"Yeah, I, uh… I never thought I needed to have kids. It was something I might want one day. But when I saw the *positive* on those test results—" Her eyes meet mine. "Something clicked, you know?"

I do.

"I just knew. That I needed to have kids. Well… a kid, I guess. There isn't time for two."

"But you…" Fuck, I have so many questions. "Your boyfriend didn't want that?"

She nods. "Something clicked for him when I asked. Only the other way."

"He thought he did?"

"Yeah. I… I don't blame him though. He answered as quickly as he could. He just—"

"It sucks, feeling like you're not enough for someone."

"Yeah." She reaches out. Takes my hand. Squeezes tightly.

She's comforting me.

She's telling me that she's going to develop a deadly, aggressive cancer if she doesn't remove her organs, and she's comforting me.

"That's why I have to do this now," she says.

I squeeze her hand back. "But why—"

"Do I want your help?" she asks.

I nod.

She's so calm. And certain.

This is not how I expected this conversation to go.

"I need someone's help. And I trust you. Please, Chase. I don't know who else to ask." She stares up at me. "Please help me."

Chapter Seven

ARIEL

C hase's blue eyes fill with concern.

It's familiar—he's been worried about me so many times—but it's different too.

This isn't an *older brother* task. It's not an *older brother's friend* task. It's not a small errand.

Sure, I'm not asking *him* to get me pregnant—

Though…

"Can I think about it?" His eyes stay trained on me.

I try to read him. To figure out if this is a probably or a probably not. But I can't. I'm not good at reading people and Chase is a brick wall.

I guess I only have one choice.

I can tell him what I need. He can accept it or not. "Twenty-four hours."

"We're negotiating?"

"I only have four months. And I… I'll be fertile in twenty-one days."

A chuckle falls off his lips.

"What?"

"Nothing." His laugh gets louder. Bigger. Big enough to light up his eyes.

"Something."

"You're matter-of-fact."

"There's a short window. Six days. I need to find someone by the first of those. He needs to be available every day."

His smile spreads over his cheeks.

"What?"

"You're just… you're Ariel."

"Who else would I be?"

"It's perfect."

"So you'll—"

"Sleep on it." He offers me his hand.

I shake. "Twenty-four hours."

He nods. "Twenty-four hours."

―――――

FOREST AND CHASE HAVE THEIR PRIVATE CONVERSATION. Return with their typical *I'm an impenetrable badass* stares.

Wes teases me about my glasses. And my all black outfit. And my non-fiction book.

He even hints I'm too good for Chase, that I can do better than someone so brooding and miserable. (Ridiculous. Chase is crazy, stupid hot).

Our conversations join. Shift to work. To tattoo techniques and irritating clients and even more irritating coworkers. A lot of hinting that the people at the table are the most irritating coworkers of all.

I don't have anything to add to the discussion, but I don't mind. It's nice, hanging on the sidelines, observing everyone.

My social skills are… lacking. Something in me

stopped growing when Mom died. I never learned the nuances of flirting or negotiation or secrets.

Maybe it's a good thing. Sure, I'm a little awkward and overly blunt, but that helps me cut to the point.

After dinner, Forest drops me off at home. He hugs me goodbye, asks if I'm okay, begrudgingly accepts a yes.

The house is quiet. It always is. Whether Dad is here or out of town.

At the moment, he's in New York. Or Chicago. Or maybe Boston. All those big cities run together. Cold, rain, snow, skyscrapers, attitude.

Los Angeles has its faults, but, God, the weather—

I love the sun. And the beach. And the warm air.

I love our house. Even though I'm usually alone. Especially because I'm usually alone.

Dad works in sales. His job requires travel. Before Mom got sick… she kept the house so warm and sweet and full of love.

I missed Dad, but I never felt like he was far away.

When Mom got sick, Dad put family first. He took a leave of absence. Stayed home to nurse her. To watch her die. To take care of us.

It stalled his career for a while.

Once I was in college, we convinced Dad to finally put his career first.

I live here to save money. And to stay close to Dad. He took Mom's death the hardest. For a long time, he was a shell of himself. Not that I can talk.

It's been more than a decade, but I can still feel her presence. She's in the purple couch (still my favorite color), the framed art on the wall (Lichtenstein, of course), the shelves of graphic novels and Disney DVDs, the giant TV.

It's a new TV (Forest found a Black Friday deal and

surprised us), but it's still her. She loved movies. All movies. Especially animation.

It's where I got my name.

The Little Mermaid was her favorite.

For a long time, she showered me in symbols of it. Walls in cerulean and aquamarine sponge-paint. Framed posters of aquatic animals. Mermaid t-shirts. Flounder plushie.

It's still there.

My walls are still painted like the ocean. Still adorned in Mom's favorites. Still childlike and innocent.

How could I cover the sponge-painting she did?

That's just…

Maybe I need to channel Ice Princess Elsa and let it go. But that feels more like forgetting.

I'm not giving up the gifts Mom left.

And, well… I kinda like Disney now. Even *The Little Mermaid*. Sure, it's the bane of my existence. Every person I meet asks if I can swim or sing or turn into a mermaid.

The movie is still one hundred percent Charlotte Ballard.

It's our connection.

When I watch an animated movie or pick up a graphic novel, it's like she's here. Smiling at me. Wrapping me in a blanket. Dropping hot cocoa on my desk.

She missed so many things.

Everything.

And now, she's going to miss this.

My hand goes to my lower abdomen reflexively.

It's silly. There's no chance I'm pregnant. I had my IUD removed a few days after I saw the test. A few days ago.

I haven't had sex since.

That's the great thing about a copper IUD. I can get pregnant immediately. In theory.

But…

Ahem.

I open my laptop. Pull up my thesis. Play Soft Cell.

Mom's favorite. Okay, second favorite. She loved loved loved Madonna, but I just can't with the Queen of Pop.

The familiar song fills the room. Between the moody vocals and the puzzle in my thesis, I slip into work.

It's hard to describe my feelings about statistics. There isn't a romantic language, the way there is with art. But it's the same love.

This is where I live.

This is what makes sense.

This is what makes my heart sing.

A bunch of data with no clear question or answer?

There's nothing better.

I work until my stomach growls, then I make a hot chocolate, and I work some more.

When I finally stop, shower, change into pajamas, I spot the notification on my phone.

Text message from Chase Keating.

I press my eyelids together. Suck a breath through my nose. I need a yes. I need his help. I need someone I trust —someone who isn't saddled with the baggage of Mom's death.

I press my thumb to the pad to unlock my cell.

One, two—

There.

Chase: Why not use a sperm donor?

It's none of his business, but that response isn't going to get me anywhere.

Ariel: There's a lot of paperwork. It's a time-consuming process.

Chase: That's it?

No. But why does he need every part of my motivation?

A sperm donor is too impersonal. I need someone I know. I need a night of—

Not love. But something equally beautiful.

Something other than a cup of semen and a turkey baster. Not that professionals use actual turkey basters. Or that I'd attempt such a method. Just, um…

Ariel: I want to do this now.

Chase: You'll need to have unprotected sex.

Ariel: You think?

Chase: I'm just saying.

Ariel: I'm not eight. I know how pregnancy works.

Chase: Unprotected sex leaves you at risk.

Ariel: I'm aware.

Chase: A sperm bank tests all its material. You can't trust a guy's results.

Ariel: He can get a test.

Chase: He could still have an STI. Some take months to show up.

Ariel: I know.

It's sweet he's worried, but I'm not going to take his condescending attitude.

I double majored in math and statistics.

Phil and I watched science documentaries every weekend forever.

I have the actual baby-hosting equipment.

I know how this works.

Ariel: I'm aware of the risks.

Chase: I'm not helping you contract a disease.

Ariel: I'll find someone who's been abstinent for six months.

Chase: Who's willing to get you pregnant the old-fashioned way?

Ariel: Yes.

Chase: You really think that's happening?

Ariel: A guy who hasn't had any in a while will probably be more eager.

Chase: Or he has his reasons.

Ariel: You haven't been with anyone.

Chase: And?

Ariel: Have you?

Chase: Have I?

Ariel: Slept with anyone since Grace?

Chase: No.

Ariel: Why not?

Chase: Because I was waiting for a stranger to ask me to knock her up.

I can't help my chuckle. It does sound absurd like that.

Ariel: I knew it.

Chase: Yeah, it's too bad I already know you.

Ariel: I could end your blue balls.

Chase: I'll live.

Ariel: What's the real reason?

Chase: Why do you want someone you know?

Ariel: I want it to be special.

I stare at the cell, waiting for a response. It's his turn now. He needs to offer his reason.

Why hasn't Chase been with anyone since his ex?

He must have opportunities. A lot. Holden acts like any guy who doesn't mow through women is an idiot. But Chase is smart. And he's certain he's making the right choice.

There must be a reason. Something he's waiting for.

Chase: Like your first time?

I press my lips together. I can ask. Demand an answer. Or I can let him change the subject.

I want to know.

I want to know more about him.

But I'm the one asking him a favor. It's not the time to pry.

Ariel: No. Not like that. Ow.

Chase: I haven't heard this story.

Ariel: Of course not. You're friends with the enemy.

Chase: The enemy?

Ariel: Forest.

Chase: Your brother is your enemy?

Ariel: My brother would like to imagine I'm a virgin. Or at least that I only sleep with geeky doctors.

Chase: Most guys would be happy their little sister bagged a doctor.

Ariel: Most guys.

Chase: You know?

Ariel: Know?

I flick the light off. Slide into bed. Hug the cell to my chest.

There's something about talking to Chase like this, in my giant The Cure t-shirt and my black panties (it's the most practical color), surrounded by my royal purple bedspread and my lilac sheets.

It's intimate.

Illicit even.

My stomach flutters. My nipples pang. My sex clenches.

Chase hasn't been with anyone since his ex. That's almost two years. More even.

He must know if he's disease free.

And he's so tall and blue eyed and intense.

We'd have cute babies.

It's totally, completely out of the question—

But we really would have cute babies.

Chase: Your brothers didn't think Phil was good enough for you.

Ariel: But they got a banner.

Chase: They're trying to support you.

Ariel: Is it because he's short?

Chase: That came up.

Ariel: He's the same height as me.

Chase: Did I say anything?

Ariel: You don't have to say it. You live it.

Chase: I live it?

Ariel: What are you? Six three?

Chase: About that.

Ariel: That's ridiculous.

Chase: How?

Ariel: You're in the top three percentile.

Chase: That sounds good.

Ariel: In the abstract, sure, but it means only three percent of guys are your height or taller.

Chase: And?

Ariel: Why do Forest and Holden think I need that?

Chase: It's not about height.

It's about something. They've never thought Phil was good enough. They try to hide it, sure, but it's clear.

Chase: They'll never think anyone is good enough.

Ariel: Are you like that?

Chase: With my brothers? No. They were never really looking to settle down.

Ariel: They were sluts?

Chase: You say 'sluts'?

Ariel: You would have thought it was weird if I said 'they were promiscuous.'

Chase: No. I would have thought you were Ariel.

Ariel: Not everyone finds that charming.

Chase: I do.

My stomach flutters.

My body buzzes.

He's so…

He's flirting. I think. I'm not good at this. Maybe he's stating facts.

He's tall. I'm charming in a quirky way.

This is business. Well, it's personal, but it's a mission.

I can't let his beautiful blue eyes distract me.

Ariel: Maybe this will help you too.

Chase: Finding you a baby daddy will help me?

Ariel: Help you get over Grace.

Chase: Uh-huh.

Ariel: Trying new things is the number one way to get over a break up.

Chase: I thought it was getting under someone else.

Ariel: What do you mean?

Oh.

I…

I never considered that.

Ariel: Is that your preferred position?

Chase: You're so Ariel.

Ariel: Can I not ask?

Chase: It's the way you asked.

Ariel: Okay, how about this: what's your favorite way to fuck?

Chase: With purpose.

Ariel: What kind of purpose?

Chase: Connection.

He doesn't want a connection with a stranger. Or he wants more than that.

He wants to fall in love again.

He wants to trust someone.

Or maybe I'm reading into things. This isn't about Chase's sex life. It's about mine.

Kind of.

Ariel: What position?

Okay, I ask anyway. I just… I already have such a beautiful mental picture. I need that detail.

His lips on my neck. His hands on my thighs. His cock—

Fuck. Since when do I think about guys like this?

Sure, I enjoyed sex with Phil, but it wasn't the kind of thing I see in the movies. It was… nice.

We both came, we felt closer, we cuddled after. It didn't set the world on fire, but I didn't need that. I needed his love.

With Chase…

Ahem.

Ariel: There's no scientific proof it's best for a woman to be on her back for conception, but most people try anyway. Why not get gravity on your side?

Chase: Makes sense.

Ariel: So, um, I guess we should find a guy who doesn't mind being on top.

Chase: That's not going to be a problem.

Ariel: No?

Chase: How many guys have you been with?

Ariel: Why does that matter?

Chase: That isn't how they think.

Oh. I kinda see what he's saying. Almost.

Chase: If I wanted to fuck a woman, I'd fuck her in any position she liked.

Ariel: But you must have a preference?

Chase: I like being in control.

Ariel: Bondage?

Chase: Not usually.

Ariel: Sometimes?

Chase: We shouldn't have this conversation.

But we should.

He's so sexy. Why is he so sexy?

Chase: You want to fix my broken heart?

Ariel: Yeah.

I really do.

Chase: What about yours?

Better not to think about it.

Ariel: I can worry about that when I'm pregnant.

Chase: You're sure you want this?

Ariel: Is that a yes?

Chase: I'm going to regret this.

Ariel: You won't. I promise.

Chase: Yes.

Chapter Eight

CHASE

"I appreciate it." Forest holds out his hand.

I shake.

He pulls me into a hug. "It's a big favor."

"It's nothing." I step backward. Nod to the guy sitting in his chair. Well, to the guy's bare back. This is the second session of his back piece. A hammerhead shark surrounded by black waves. It's still in the outline stage, but it's already badass. "Good business."

He runs a hand through his dark hair. Drops it by his side. "Yeah." He presses his lips together, struggling to find the words.

It's painful to watch. Really, it is. Like looking in a mirror.

We've been friends forever—more than half my life—but we're incapable of admitting vulnerability or expressing gratitude.

It's not that we aren't close. We are. We're just not feelings people.

"Honestly, you're doing us a favor." I motion to the empty suite in the back. "Half the shop's on vacation."

His dark eyes light up *you're so full of shit* but he still nods *sure*. "Then I'll keep an extra ten percent."

"Over my boss's dead body," I say.

"You'd rat me out?" I ask.

"He does the books."

"What's a little fraud between friends?" His shoulders relax with his smile.

Mine do too. It's easier teasing. A different way of communicating, I guess. "Maybe if you cut me in on the deal."

"You can take twenty percent of the extra," he says.

"When I'm taking all the risk?" I shake my head *hell no*. "Fifty-fifty."

The door to the office creaks open. My brother Wes and his best friend Griffin enter the main room. Survey the scene.

"Or—" Wes skips to the middle of the room. He leans down. Lowers his voice to a stage whisper, "You give me fifty percent so I don't rat you out." He winks at me. Then Forest. "You must have really fucked up some shit to end up here."

"You kidding?" He motions to the counter. Hunter's girlfriend Emma is sitting at the computer, working on the schedule. She's ten years younger than Forest, but he still smiles *check out the babe*. "Best place around."

"Puh-lease." Wes shakes his head. "You're as miserable and alone as Chase."

"It's sad, really." Griffin joins us. "Like you had to bring him here so you'd seem less pathetic."

"You got me." I shrug. I don't mind the teasing. Hell, it's kind of nice, being a part of it.

"Only you're even more bitter than Forest." Griffin shakes his head *it's sad really*.

Wes chuckles and pats his friend's shoulder. "You gotta

admire the guy's willingness to say whatever pops through his mind."

"You think this is what goes through my mind?" Griffin asks.

Wes nods *yeah*.

"You don't know your best friend as well as you think you do," I say.

Forest nods. "Even I know Griff better than that."

Griffin nods *hell yeah*. "Right now, I'm thinking about the taste of my wife's cunt."

Wes rolls his eyes. "We can see the ring. We don't need the reminder you're married every ten seconds."

"Jealous your lady doesn't want to make it official?" Griffin asks.

Forest laughs. "She's holding out on you?"

"No. I'm respecting her desire to focus on her career." Wes shrugs *jeez*. "She's crazy about me."

Forest copies Wes's *that's so sad head shake*. "Take it from me, kid, if she doesn't want to make it official—"

"She does too." Wes throws his arms in the air. "I could call her right now. She'd say yes. Excuse me for wanting it to be special. And not the result of half a bottle of tequila." He refers to Griffin's Vegas wedding.

Which doesn't bother Griffin. At all. "Don't hate me 'cause you ain't me."

"Are you fourteen?" Wes asks. "That's so—"

"You're practically green," I say.

Wes's eyes flit to mine. For a second, he studies me. Tries to figure out what I'm after. "I'm jealous?"

"Yeah. It's sad. As you say." My smile spreads a little wider. For once, this is easy. I'm not thinking about our mom or our middle brother or all the tension that came with them.

I'm teasing my baby brother about how much he loves his girlfriend.

"I do say." Wes folds his arms. "It's sad you can't see that my and Quinn's love is more powerful than anything."

"Aww." Griffin reaches out and musses his hair. "Isn't he cute?"

Wes slaps his hands away. "Stop it—"

I copy Griffin's gesture.

Wes folds his arms over his chest. He huffs an exhale so exaggerated it could be a panel in a comic book.

Forest chuckles. "You're just like Holden."

Wes drops the faux irritation. "In his dreams."

"What a nightmare." I shudder.

Forest nods.

"You realize he's coming in later?" Griffin looks from me to Forest. "Both of 'em are gonna be here."

"Horrible," I say.

Forest nods. "True pain."

Griffin chuckles. "You have competition."

"In his dreams." Wes rolls his eyes *he wishes*. "You're lucky to have me. I know that's what you're thinking." He nods a *later* and moves to his suite.

Griffin heads to the empty suite in back. Pulls out his sketchbook. Drifts into concentration.

Forest shifts his weight between his feet. It's still there, that sense that he owes me. But he doesn't.

I'm not doing this as a favor to a friend.

I asked the owners if they could find spots for Forest and Holden because it's good business.

That's it.

Favors are great. When they stay professional. When you start to make exceptions for friends and family—

Not making that mistake again.

"I think I've given him a long enough break." Forest

motions to his client, who's still lying in the chair, tapping messages on his cell.

The guy looks grateful for the reprieve, but I'm not about to argue.

I nod *sure*. Open my mouth to say something about how I'm glad to have him here.

The ringing door interrupts me.

Ariel steps inside.

Light surrounds her like a halo. Casts highlights off her dark hair, her pale skin, her snug black dress.

God damn, that thing hugs her waist like it was made for it.

And it's short. Shows off her strong legs.

I want to push her on the counter and whisper *you wearing black under that too?*

That's so fucking out of the question.

And it's ridiculous. I haven't wanted to fuck a woman since Grace. Not like this. Not with my entire fucking body.

"Thanks." Forest motions to his sister.

My stomach drops. He knows something. Something he shouldn't. What the fuck am I going to say? *Listen, I know I'm helping your sister get pregnant, but it's not like I'm the one doing it. Though, for some reason, I can't stop thinking about that. Which is probably worse. That I woke up to sticky sheets and an incredibly vivid dream about her sprawled under me.*

"For helping with her project."

"Right."

He looks at me like he knows I'm lying, but he doesn't press the subject. "She can be a lot."

"She's a sweet kid."

"If she says anything about Phil…"

I nod. "Of course."

"She thought he was the one." His eyes drift to the window.

For a moment, he stares at the sky, lost in a memory of the girl who broke his heart. Then he waves hello to his sister.

"I'll let you know."

Of course, I'm not going to tell him about our plan, so I can't really say I'm fulfilling my duties as a friend.

———

"THIS ISN'T NECESSARY." ARIEL HOLDS HER HAND OVER her eyes. Looks up at the sky like it's a thing of beauty and wonder. "The office—"

"With your brother ten feet away?"

"In the zone." Her gaze shifts to the bright white sidewalk.

"Still."

"I never saw you as…" A laugh spill from her lips. "Never mind."

"Never mind?" I keep pace with her. She walks with purpose. Like she doesn't have a second to waste. I guess she doesn't. But, fuck, there's something about this—

The two of us walking to a coffee shop on a bright, clear day.

The sun bouncing off her dark hair.

The smile forming on her red lips. The same soft red. From some kind of gloss. Her lips are shiny. Kissable as fuck.

Not that it matters.

I don't care that Ariel has perfect tits, a cute ass, soft lips.

Only that she needs my help.

Which means I need my head in gear. "You think I'm a coward?"

"I was going to say cautious."

"You never saw me as cautious?"

"Never."

"Really?"

Her dark eyes meet mine. They light up with something. Joy or humor or curiosity. I'm not sure.

But I like it.

I really fucking like it.

"Really." Ariel's gaze shifts to the palm trees lining the sidewalk. The quiet street. The row of shops ahead. "You go for what you want."

"I do."

She laughs. "Where's the disagreement?"

"I value my life."

"Forest wouldn't—"

"Wouldn't he?"

"Well… I… I value your life too." She motions to the coffee shop across the street. *That work?*

I nod *sure.* "Sweet of you."

"That's why I didn't ask you."

"Why you—"

"To be my, ahem, donor." Her cheeks flush. "You… uh… It would be more convenient than finding someone else. But I figured. God." Her blush deepens.

My balls stir. She thought about asking me. She wants to ask me. She wants to fuck me.

It shouldn't be surprising—a lot of women want to fuck me—but it is.

Ariel Ballard wants me.

God dammit, it's too hot today. I'm not sure why I'm surprised. We're not far enough into fall for the weather to cool.

The afternoons here never cool.

Even in the dead of winter, it hits seventy and sunny.

"I shouldn't have said that." She stops at the crosswalk. Presses the button.

"Is it true?"

"I'm not sure I've ever lied."

"Never?"

Her brow furrows with concentration. She presses her glasses up her nose. "I've declined to spill the whole truth, but—"

"Isn't that the same?"

"I guess so." The light turns green. She looks both ways, steps into the street, moves quickly.

I follow her. "I'm not a fan either."

"If it's too much, keeping this from Forest, we can…" She steps onto the sidewalk. Stops in front of the coffee shop. "I like you, Chase. You're the only guy I trust for this. But I need to know you're all in. I don't have time for you to get cold feet."

"I'm in." I'm out of my fucking mind, but I am in.

"Are you sure?" Her eyes bore into mine. "If you have any doubts—"

"You begged me to do this."

"I know."

"Which is it?"

"I want you. If you're ready to commit, a hundred percent."

"We should decide what that entails."

"Isn't that why we're here?" Her voice is matter-of-fact. Like this is incredibly obvious.

Maybe it is. Maybe I'm missing something or dense. I can't say I've ever been in this position before. "When are you gonna tell your bothers?"

"When I'm sure." Her hand goes to her stomach. "After that—"

"The first trimester?"

"The likelihood of a miscarriage—"

"I know." I did my own research. A lot of it. My browser history is all baby, all the time. I'm going to get ads for diapers until the day I die.

"Oh. Good." Her gaze shifts to the shop. "It's only a few months of keeping the full story to ourselves."

There's something about her expression. Like I'm holding her heart in my hand. Like I have the power to crush her.

I can't.

I don't want to.

I really fucking like her.

In a way that means I want to help her. Not in a way that means I want her. Not like that.

I pull the door open for her. "Come on. Let's make a plan."

"Yeah?"

I nod. "I'll buy the coffee."

"Chai. But sure." She steps into the door. "Let's make a plan."

Chapter Nine

ARIEL

"What do you want from the guy?" Chase's voice is dead serious.

It's fair. This conversation is a big deal.

But I'm so tired of serious.

Since the day Dad sat us down to explain Mom's diagnosis, my life has been serious. My family has looked at me like I might have that same ticking time bomb inside me.

It's been there, in the back of my head, since I understood what cancer was.

This is serious, yes.

But it's not ugly, the way that is. It shouldn't feel heavy. It should be… not fun or easy.

Joyful maybe.

I guess asking for Chase's help and expecting joyful is foolish.

But he is capable of that. I saw him with Grace. He was happy. He—

He really does have a beautiful smile.

"Do you want a guy who will come inside you then never call again?" he asks.

I choke on my tea. Oh my God. Cinnamon and ginger burn. They're delicious on my tongue. But stuck in my throat—

I just barely swallow.

Ow. I take another sip. It helps. This chai is sweet, spicy perfection. It's a lot of caffeine, given my goals, but I'm not ready to give that up too. "Do you have to say it like that?"

"Yeah."

"But—"

"Call things what they are."

Okay. I guess it's strange to use words like ejaculate and semen and conception. Clinical isn't sexy. "Okay."

"Is it okay, princess?" His blue eyes light up. With delight. He loves the way the nickname sounds on his tongue.

I love it too. It's the opposite of clinical.

He's as direct as I am, but he makes his demands seem sexy. Whereas I use words like ejaculate and promiscuous.

I'm a stuffy nerd.

Chase is…

Skye would say he's yummy. Skye does say he's yummy. And she's right. He is yummy.

He's really, really yummy.

See, I can express things in a normal, non-clinical, totally sexy way.

Chase is yummy.

Chase is freaking delicious.

Chase is more delicious than the best chai latte in the world.

And that's really, incredibly delicious.

"Ariel?" He takes a long sip of his cold brew. Sighs a sigh of deep, pure pleasure.

Which is so freaking yummy.

Not that it matters.

"I don't want him involved." I can't take another person abandoning me. I'm not about to put my daughter or son through that. It's hard enough losing a parent to cancer. Losing them to disinterest?

No way.

"So he fucks you and leaves?" Chase asks.

"Yeah."

"How do you know it works?"

"I guess he sticks around until I'm pregnant."

"And if you—"

"Miscarry?" My lips purse.

He studies my expression. "You don't like talking about it?"

"It's a possibility."

"That scares you." It's a statement, not a question.

This entire thing scares me. I'm trying to find a stranger to knock me up. "Of course."

"I have to be honest."

"Yeah."

"It's stupid, looking for someone."

Okay…

"A sperm bank will give you exactly what you need."

My chest flares. Who the hell does he think he is telling me what to do? I just… UGH. Are all men bossy know-it-alls or just the ones in my immediate vicinity? "Your opinion is noted."

He stares back at me *is that really your response?*

I suck a breath through my nose. Push an exhale through my teeth.

I'm asking for his help.

I have to be cordial. No matter how irritating he's being.

"You gonna pull some 'my way or the highway' shit?" He arches a brow.

"It's my—"

"That's kind of my thing."

"I know."

"Gotta be honest." His voice softens. "It's not really working out for me."

He's giving me space. I think.

He's so hard to read.

I stare into his deep blue eyes. "Isn't it?"

His expression gets contemplative. "Depends on the definition."

I press my lips together. I don't know all the details of Chase's life. Only the broad strokes.

About two years ago, his high school sweetheart left him.

Half a year later, he kicked Hunter out of Blacklist Tattoo—Holden and Forest talked about it for months.

Forest thought it was the right move. Hunter lied about his drinking. Chase needed to use a, uh, firm hand.

Holden thought it was a dick move. That Chase's brother needed unconditional love and support.

I don't know what I would have done. If it was Holden or Forest who was lying about drinking, if I could tell they had a problem, if I had no idea how best to help them.

Would I be willing to risk our relationship for their well-being?

I'm not sure I'm brave enough for that.

"You work with Hunter now," I say.

His brow knits. "Technically."

"He never forgave you?"

"He did." His gaze shifts to his coffee. He takes a long sip. Swallows hard.

"So you…"

"It's only a suggestion." He completely ignores my question. "If you insist on finding a guy the old-fashioned way."

"It's not old-fashioned."

He raises a brow.

"We're using the Internet. It's modern."

His gaze shifts to my shiny silver laptop. "It's your decision, Ariel. But are you sure you don't want a donor?"

Maybe it's not a logical decision. Maybe it's not the result of hours of crunching numbers. Maybe the numbers aren't even on my side.

But I know it in my gut.

I'm not giving that up.

"Have you used the Internet to date before?" he asks.

I shoot him a *really* look.

He returns it.

"I wasn't born yesterday."

"You're swiping right on any hot guy?"

"Who interests me, sure."

"And DMing any guy over six feet tall?" He smiles. He's teasing me.

Mmm. I like the feeling of him teasing me. "Oh my God." My lips curl into a smile. "That isn't what matters."

"You sure?"

"Why are you so obsessed?"

"Look at me." He motions to his long legs. Covered in snug jeans. A dark blue denim that begs for my hands. "One of the few things I have going for me."

"Besides the blue eyes." Which are even more inviting than his strong legs. I want to stare into them for hours. As I climb into his lap. As I wrap my hand around—

Jesus. Since when do I think about sex like *that*?

I shouldn't be thinking about the feel of Chase's cock. That's just... so wrong. Beyond wrong. Beyond ridiculous.

"And the tattoos." He sets his hand on the table like his arms need no explanation.

Black and grey sleeve on the right. Colorful sleeve on the left. The two sides of his personality.

The serious guy he shows the world.

And this other guy, the one who can't help but smile, who teases me, who finds my awkwardness charming.

Who's willing to risk anything to do the right thing.

He's…

He's an amazing person.

He'd make such a good father.

Which is exactly why I can't ask him for a *donation*. Chase deserves a family. His family. It would kill him to stay away.

I think.

He is in love with his ex.

Maybe. I'm really not the person to ask. I'm doing everything I can to avoid thinking about *my* ex.

"You didn't have any when you started seeing Grace?" I press my lips together. It doesn't take the words back. There's lack of tact then there's asking the most not-over-his-ex guy in the universe a question about his ex.

He doesn't want to talk about it. I shouldn't push. It's really none of my business.

"Not that you could see." His eyes flare with something I can't place. Then his expression softens. Settles into nostalgia. He stands. Pulls his t-shirt up his stomach.

My gaze goes straight to his bare skin. Yummy doesn't begin to cover it. Tan skin stretches over hard muscles. Contrasts with curvy black lines of ink.

He turns to show off said ink.

I try to focus on the design, but my eyes disobey my command. He's so strong and hard and beautiful.

I've never thought of men as beautiful before. Chase is

certainly not a guy most would call beautiful. He's incredibly masculine.

But this is fucking beautiful.

My fingers reach for his skin.

Thankfully, he's too far away. I manage to press them into the table. To look with my eyes.

Semper ad meliora

Always toward better things.

"Hunter did it." His eyes turn down. "We used to be—"

"I'm sorry."

"Don't be—"

"Not for asking. I'm sorry things are strained. I can't imagine."

His voice is steady. Sure. "It's not his fault things are strained."

"He was the one who lied."

"Yeah, but he couldn't help it. That's what addiction does to people. It turns them into monsters who will destroy anything in the way of their next fix."

That's perceptive. "You sympathize?"

"Not exactly."

"But you haven't forgiven him?"

"It's not a logical thing."

For once, I understand. "It's hard."

"Yeah." His gaze darts around the room. Stops on a woman gawking at his stomach. "Shit." He chuckles as he drops his shirt. "I must look like Wes."

"A little." His little brother does like showing off. But Chase does it in a different way. He's making a point. Saying *this is me, take it or leave it.*

Sure, he's inviting stares, but—

It's hard to explain.

It's just…

Yummy.

God, I should ask Skye for help with adjectives.

Right now, my brain is a neon sign flashing *yummy, yummy, yummy*.

He's sitting, staring at me, ready to discuss important things.

And I'm picturing him shirtless.

But God he really is yummy.

"You okay?" he asks.

I force my eyes to the table. It's expensive. Well made. Solid wood.

My cheeks flame.

Then my chest.

God, this is so…

I need a response. Now. "It's a lot to consider." I open my laptop. So we can get started. I need to stay on task or I'm going to ask him to take off his clothes.

"You have a site in mind?"

"I already started."

He chuckles. "Of course."

"It's all rough. I figured… you're better with people than I am."

"That's the first time anyone has ever said that."

"It's true though."

His chuckle deepens. "Maybe." He stands, moves around the table, sits next to me.

"Definitely."

"That's sad for you."

"It's my cross to bear." I offer him a smile.

He smiles back.

I melt.

Chapter Ten

ARIEL

Chase's blue eyes fix on my laptop screen. He reads my profile like his life depends on it.

His toes tap the tile floor.

His fingers curl around his drink.

He wraps his lips around the straw. Finds only melted ice.

I should buy him another round. Offer that immediately. Do something besides stare at his soft lips, wondering what they'd feel like on my neck.

My chest.

My *ahem*.

I don't…

I may not be the most experienced woman in the world, but I'm not a blushing virgin either. My high school boyfriend and I did a lot. We helped each other learn the basics, so to speak.

Then there was a fling my first year of college. Not that I realized it. At the time, I thought the (way out of my league senior quarterback) guy wanted the same thing I did.

I missed all the signals. Let myself believe what I wanted to believe.

He made it clear he wanted something short and fun.

I didn't hear him.

It was short and fun. Then he moved onto a new play-mate and I felt like the stupidest person in the world. Like there was something deeply, truly wrong with me. I guess there was. There is. I suck at picking up signals.

With Phillip, I was crystal clear. I wanted something serious. Something with forever potential. Something that would end in marriage and kids and a house in the suburbs.

I wanted a partner.

And he was a partner. He made me dinner, rubbed my back when it ached, held my hand when I went to visit Mom.

He even brought the flowers. From his mom's garden.

He was a good boyfriend.

But not in the way Chase…

There was never a burning passion. I didn't want to tear his clothes off. I didn't lose myself in daydreams of his soft lips. I didn't demand he go down on me.

Don't get me wrong. The sex was good. He was generous. And we… we had fun. But it wasn't *oh my God I need it now.*

It wasn't the same as it is with Chase.

I mean, the way it is in my mind. Which is still thinking up delicious dirty images.

Him rolling my jeans—and my panties—to my knees. Sliding his fingers inside me. Groaning into my ear.

But…

Uh…

I'm still staring at his lips.

They're just so soft and pink and lush. I never understood the word lush. Isn't it for blooming green jungles, not flesh?

Right now, it makes perfect sense.

It's his lips.

Such beautiful—

Ahem.

"You want another round?" I force my eyes to my watch. I only have an hour. Less even. My next class is at three and it takes forever to get to the university. "On me."

"I got it." He reaches for his wallet.

I stop him. "It's the least I can do."

His eyes meet mine. Study mine. He must decide I'm in the right, because he nods *sure*.

"Same thing?"

"Yeah."

I take his glass and mine. "You, uh, you can start changing—"

"I will."

"Great." I force my lips into a smile. Which does nothing to settle the flutter in my stomach. Or the lightness in my chest. It's something between *oh my God I want you* and *oh my God, you're going to judge my complete inability to masquerade as a normal human.*

I drop our cups at the bus tray, move into line, order a second round. Another cold brew, splash of milk, dash of simple syrup for him. Another chai for me.

I will cut down on caffeine. By the time I'm ready for the next, uh, round.

Chase stays laser focused on the computer. Even as I grab our drinks and return to the table.

I take a long sip. The mix of sweet and spicy isn't comforting. It's cloying. Too much sugar. Not enough cinnamon or ginger. Not even a hint of cardamom. How can the second be so much less good?

It's the same drink.

It must be something else.

The look in his eyes screaming *Ariel is so out of her depths*.

Sip. Swallow. Sigh. "What's the verdict?"

He reaches for his drink, eyes still on the computer, takes a long sip, lets out that deep, beautiful sigh of pleasure. "When's the last time you dated?"

"Don't sugar coat."

"It's a little clinical."

"I should be to the point."

"Yeah." Finally, he looks at me. "But think about it from the guy's perspective."

"He gets to have unprotected sex."

A laugh spills from his lips. A full-blown belly laugh. He doubles over, clutching his stomach.

His cheeks turn red.

His eyes light up.

It's so beautiful. I don't even care that he's laughing at me. Only that he's laughing.

I need to make this happen again. To bring that joy to his eyes.

It's so…

Yummy.

Delicious.

Amazing.

Wonderful.

Fascinating.

Fulfilling.

Thrilling.

None of the adjectives that come to mind properly convey the magnitude of Chase's laugh.

"What?" My cheeks blush. I want him to keep laughing. I do. But I want to be in on the joke too. "Is that not accurate?"

"No, it is." He presses his palms into the table. Struggles through a breath. "It's perfect."

"So what's the problem—"

"This." He turns the laptop screen to me. Points to the text in the profile. Reads it aloud. "I'm not going to waste your time and I hope you won't waste mine either. I'm looking for a man who's willing to get me pregnant. You'll need to work around my schedule. To provide *donations* every day I'm ovulating—" He looks at me. "Should I keep going?"

"It's not—"

"You're right. There are three reasons a guy would say yes to this." He counts *one* with this finger. "He's a good Samaritan who wants to help a woman in need—"

"Is that too much to ask?"

Chase nods *yeah*. Holds up a second finger. "He's excited about the idea of unprotected sex with you."

"What's wrong with—"

He holds up a third finger. "Or he's so into the idea of his DNA living on he's willing to overlook the weirdness of the situation."

"And… what, those guys go to sperm banks?"

"Yeah. But I won't push that."

"Thank you."

He nods *sure*. Looks at me funny. With this mix of respect and understanding. "You really know what you want."

"Is there something wrong with that?"

"It's different."

"Different how?"

"My ex… she was all over the place."

"Oh." I press my palms into my thighs. I am not asking about his ex. I am not seething with jealousy over his ex. I am not struggling to breathe because I hate that his ex owns his heart. It. So. Doesn't. Matter.

"At work… nobody stands up to me."

"No?"

"They mostly ignore me. Let me do my own thing."

"Isn't that how tattoo shops work?"

"Sometimes." He pulls up a word document. "We need something more like this." He reads the new profile. "I'm looking for someone to knock me up. No strings attached. A few weeks of fun, unprotected sex. Then we part ways."

"Is it that different?"

"Guys are dumb. You have to spell it out."

I can't help but laugh. "Isn't that… I'll probably get lots of people who aren't willing to commit."

He nods *true*. "So we add something to weed out guys who can't commit."

"What?"

"Ask for a pic of their latest test results. In a message with a specific code."

"A code?"

"So you know they're listening."

Okay… "I love going bareback?"

He chuckles. "More subtle, maybe."

"I thought we had to spell it out."

"How about this: 'the baby bargain.'"

"Like a discount?" That's… unflattering. And not at all what I want. Sure, I don't need Prince Charming. But I want something special.

"Like an agreement."

I guess that works. I nod *okay*.

He puts in the new profile. Adds a few details about scheduling. And a minimum height. Of course.

It's ridiculous.

But maybe it's practical. Lots of studies show tall

people have more advantages. A tall, handsome, emotionally stable father—

That's a good thing. DNA wise.

Chase hits the *submit* button. Turns to me. "There's one more thing."

"Oh?"

"Your photo."

"What about it?" My chest tenses. I'm not as naturally beautiful as Chase, but I try. At least, there are times where I try.

"You're a pretty girl—"

"Thank you—"

"This photo doesn't show that."

"So…"

"It doesn't say *don't you want to get me pregnant*."

"What would?"

He motions to my purse. "Give me your phone."

"That's—"

"Just the pictures."

Okay, I guess that's fair. I pull my cell from my purse. Open the photos app. Place it in his palm.

His fingers brush mine as he takes it. He swipes through the pictures, his gaze fixed on the screen.

His lips press together.

His eyes light up.

There.

"Perfect." He brandishes a photo from one of the days Phillip and I went to the beach. I'm sitting on the sand, sheer dress over my black bikini, hair blowing in the breeze, lips curled into a smile.

"Isn't it a little—"

"Promiscuous?" he offers.

I can't help but laugh. "Yeah."

"Usually, I'd say yes, but in this case, I think we need to

appeal to baser instincts."

"You mean—"

"Find a guy who sees this and thinks 'I need to come on those tits.'"

My cheeks flush. "But, uh, he would have to *ahem* inside me—"

"Trust me. There's no guy in his right mind who's gonna see this picture and think anything but *I need to fuck her*."

"So—" Any guy who looks at that picture will want to fuck me. He's a guy. He's looking at it now. That must mean he wants to.

Oh my God.

Deep breath.

Slow exhale.

Ultimate confidence.

I am not thinking about Chase naked. I'm not. "What now?"

"We wait."

Chapter Eleven

CHASE

Most of the time, my life is rote. Work. Gym. Dinner. TV. Sleep. Repeat.

Sometimes, I go out with Griffin or Wes.

Occasionally, I see my entire family.

I visit Mom once a week. But we're so far past the point of catching up. We're both transparent.

It's like I'm screaming *are you really staying sober this time?*

Like she's a kid, throwing a tantrum *are you ever going to trust me?*

It's a fair question. It's the question at the center of my entire universe.

People act like figuring out your shit fixes things, but it doesn't.

I know why I don't trust my mom. I know why things are strained with Hunter. I know why my heart refuses to let go of Grace.

The knowledge doesn't make it easier to forgive or trust or move on.

Hell, I don't know where the line is anymore. I don't know what normal is anymore.

I understand why Hunter lied to me. I understand why he slipped. Why he failed.

I blame him a lot less than I blame Mom. With that kind of role model—

It's amazing Wes and I aren't dodging rehab right now.

I'm not mad at Hunter. I'm not holding out for an apology.

It's clear he's sorry. It's clear he wants to make up. It's clear he loves me.

I love him too.

He's my brother. I'll always love him.

But I can't forgive him.

Everyone thinks I'm a bitter asshole. I guess my taste in music—I'm currently playing my favorite album, a pop-punk classic filled with equal parts *I hate you and hope you die in a car crash* and *I don't even think about you, you mean nothing to me, why do you think this song is about you anyway*—does nothing to help my reputation.

But that's not why I enjoy this genre.

I just like the same shit I liked in high school.

What fifteen-year-old isn't pissed at the world?

Maybe there are normal, well-adjusted people out there somewhere. But I don't know any of them.

With Mom already MIA—

I loved this song when I was a kid, because it felt like it was speaking to me. And, yeah, I dug the style. I got more into it. That stuck too.

It doesn't mean I still want the people who wrong me to drive off a bridge.

I don't see anyone accusing Griffin of wanting to score benzos because he listens to musicians who sound like they're about to overdose.

I don't see anyone accusing Dean or Chloe of doing

heroin and looking for apartments in Seattle because they love grunge.

This is what I play—

Well, all the time.

It's one of the few constants in my life. One of the only things I've had since I was a kid.

I'm not giving that up, no matter how little the adolescent attitude suits a twenty-nine-year-old man.

The album hums as I fix beef and broccoli. It's a simple stir fry. It's easy to make for myself. With leftovers to spare.

Anyone who cooks will tell you the same thing—

It's not the same making dishes for one.

It's hard to find the motivation.

I take care of myself. Wes would say obsessively. But it's not about vanity.

It's about discipline.

Strong body, strong mind. I work out ten hours a week because it keeps me centered. Because I need it. If I don't force myself to follow a routine—

Who knows where my head will go? What I'll do with that free time?

It doesn't escape me—the genetic predisposition to addiction.

Yeah, fixing dinner for one is a little sad, but it's better than the alternative.

I finish cooking. Set the burner to warm. Check the rice.

A knock on the door cuts through the music.

Then a soft voice. "Chase. Hey?" Ariel doesn't wait for a response. She launches right into her explanation. "I know we're supposed to meet on Friday, but I don't want to waste a prime date night."

She's driven. Incredibly driven. I've never seen anyone approach a goal with this velocity.

But I guess she doesn't have much time.

I thought a mom who abandoned me for a bottle was bad. But losing my mom completely? Knowing I was doomed to follow in her footsteps if I didn't take action?

All right, maybe it's not that far removed from my life.

But it's a hell of a lot more drastic.

I lift weights, avoid sugar, skip alcohol.

She's—

I really can't imagine.

"Sure." I move to the door. Pull it open. "Come in."

"Thanks." Her eyes move around the room. Take in the simple decorations. Black couch. Black walls. Bookshelf overflowing with comics.

Then they fix on me.

Her cheeks flush.

Her tongue slides over her lips—

It hits both of us at the same time. I'm only wearing a towel.

And, fuck, the way she's staring like she wants to tear it off and drop to her knees.

Blood rushes to my cock.

Not okay. There's no way to hide the situation in this.

I turn. So she won't notice the way the cotton is straining over my cock. "Why don't you set up?" I motion to the table. "I'll get dressed."

"Sure." She keeps staring.

I can't see her, but I can feel her gaze. I swear to God, I can feel her heartbeat picking up.

Or maybe that's mine.

It's been a long time since I've had a woman here. No, I've never had a woman here.

I moved out of the place I shared with Grace after she ended things.

This apartment is small, but it's mine. No memories of her. No floral shampoo scenting the crimson drapes. No Van Gogh prints adorning the wall.

No women.

Until now.

Now, Ariel is sitting at my table. The smell of oranges is wafting into my nostrils.

Her shampoo.

Fuck, I want to wrap my arms around her and inhale it.

Which is beyond out of the question.

My friends are right. I need to get laid. As soon as she leaves, I'm calling Griffin and Wes. Demanding they join me at a club and play wingman.

Not that I need their help. Or their commentary. I'm perfectly capable of calling—

God, I don't even remember her name. Any of them. Five clients left cards this week and I can't envision a single one. My head is too full of Ariel.

Fuck, this is not productive.

I move into the bedroom. Recite the Dodgers line up. Change into boxers, jeans, a t-shirt. I don't even check the colors. My head isn't here.

In the main room, Ariel is sitting at the kitchen table, eyes pressed together, deep in thought.

I move to the kitchen counter. "You eat dinner?"

Her gaze follows me. It moves over me slowly. Studying me. Like I'm an animal in the zoo. Or maybe like she's deciding if she wants to do me like we're a video on the Discovery Channel. "I came straight from work."

"Teaching?"

"If you can call it that." She opens her laptop. "It's more like... babysitting."

"Really?"

She nods *yeah*. "I'm always stuck with 101 classes. Most of the students are there as a requirement. They don't care about math."

"Some must."

She nods *maybe*. "I usually have one."

"Who's the one?"

"Mandy. She's smart, but shy. She doesn't like to ask questions. It's almost like she's embarrassed she's smart."

"Maybe she is."

Her brow furrows with confusion. "Why would you hide that?"

"It intimidates guys."

"Why would you want a guy who's scared of your brain?"

"You're asking me?"

She nods *hell yeah*. "Your ex was..." She clears her throat. "She wasn't book smart, exactly."

"She was an artist." My stomach twists. The thought of Grace still makes me sick. But it's necessary. The verbal equivalent of a cold shower.

"Were you threatened by that?"

"Never." I shake my head. "We were competitive, sure, but the same way Forest and I are about basketball."

"He's better than you."

I can't help but laugh. "Most people wouldn't say that."

"Sorry." Her nose scrunches. "Do you not want the truth?"

My laugh gets bigger. Louder.

She stares at me with confusion.

"It's perfect."

"You sure?"

"Yeah." Fuck, there's something about her lack of decorum. Something I really like.

After years tiptoeing around Grace's feelings—

It's a relief to hear *you're not that good at basketball.*

Or *you're kind of obsessed with your ex.*

Or *yeah, you're hot, Chase, but your head is a mess. Why would anyone date you?*

The furrow in her brow deepens. "Why would any guy be threatened by a woman's intellect?"

"Insecurity."

"That's stupid." Her dark eyes fill with frustration. "You're not like that, though."

"I try not to be."

"Good." Her gaze shifts to the food. "That looks good."

"Beef and broccoli."

"Oh. Am I interrupting? I texted, but you didn't reply and—"

"You're not." It's strange, having her here. But in a good way. In a really good way. "You want a plate?"

Her tongue slides over her lips. "Yeah." She pauses, like she's catching herself. Reminding herself of the rules of politeness. "If you have enough. I don't want to impose."

"Glad to share."

"You sure?"

I nod *yeah.* "Gets depressing cooking for one." I fix her a plate.

"You can come over. Cook for two." Her toes tap the carpet. "I… uh… Phil's parents taught me. But that's… I tried making spring rolls yesterday and I started crying."

"It's hard, walking away from someone."

"Yeah. I… uh… It's really all I know how to cook, Vietnamese food. They were so sweet. And I… uh… this looks good."

"It's not too close?"

"No. Vietnamese food is all fish sauce. This is soy sauce."

"You have a good nose."

"You can't really miss fish sauce." Her smile is sad. "This, um, this really does look good."

"Thanks." I bring the plates to the table.

She waits until I drop off silverware and waters. "You're a really paternal guy."

"You could say that?"

Her eyes fix on me. "Sorry… I just… uh…" She picks up her chopsticks. Uses them to grab a piece of broccoli. "Thank you."

"My pleasure."

She brings the broccoli to her mouth. Chews. Swallows. "Can I be honest?"

"Can I stop you?"

Her lips curl into a half-smile. "Remember when you told me to listen to this album?"

"After the guy in high school dumped you."

"Yeah. You thought it would help. And I guess it did. But only because this guy—" She motions to the speaker— "Annoyed me so much, I started thinking 'maybe all men are terrible. I'm better off single.'"

I can't help but laugh. "What about him?"

"He's so obsessed with his ex, but he can't even admit it. It's like… get over it, dude. You know?"

"You realize who you're talking to?"

Her eyes meet mine. "At least you know."

"Still can't get over it."

"Maybe." She presses her lips together. "Or maybe that's just the story you tell yourself."

Fuck, I have no idea how to respond to that.

"You still listen to what you loved in high school," she says.

"You don't?"

Her laugh is light. "I guess that's fair." Her gaze shifts to the speakers. "It's weird. I hated this band at first. But I'd hear you and Forest playing it and, after a while, it made me think of you. I like you. So I like it."

"You like me?"

Her cheeks flush. "You've always been a good friend." She trips over her last word. Like it's not accurate enough for the situation.

It's not. But then what do you call our current relationship? There's no word for *the woman you're helping find another man to get her pregnant.*

Which is why she's here.

Not to talk about my taste in music, or gush over my cooking, or cuddle up on the couch.

She's not mine.

We're not together.

It's that familiarity in my brain. I don't invite people into my space. I don't invite women into my space. Not since Grace.

It's normal that I want to hold Ariel. That I want to take her to bed. Take care of her.

That's what I do.

Just—

I need to do it a different way here.

"So, I, uh… you were right." Her blush spreads to her chest. "A lot of guys replied. About a third followed directions."

"Good." My stomach sinks. It's not good. I hate it. I hate that some other guy is going to—

Fuck, I can't even think it.

I force my lips into a smile. "How many prospects do we have?"

"I narrowed it down to ten."

"Perfect." I'm happy to help. I want to help. I don't want to be the one knocking her up.

I certainly don't want to stick around to raise her kid.

That would be ridiculous.

Chapter Twelve

CHASE

After we eat, we go through Ariel's prospects.

Every guy who saw her profile offered to impregnate her.

No surprise.

She's fucking gorgeous.

And, men, well, we're not exactly mysterious. Most guys are motivated by their dicks. The ones who use their brains are still driven by biology.

Must stick it everywhere.

Must pass on genes.

Must fuck eager babe.

This is what she wants. Men who are willing to do the job then walk away.

It doesn't bother me.

At all.

I go through her finalists. Ten guys who follow directions well. Who have clean bills of health. Who, well—

They're all attractive, at least as far as their pictures are concerned.

It's not what I expect from Ariel. Not that her ex is a

troll. Yeah, he's on the shorter side, but he's a good-looking guy. Symmetrical features, dark hair, broad shoulders.

These guys are a mélange of different jobs, looks, races, but they're all super fucking hot.

I'm not afraid to admit when a man is attractive. Some things are just facts.

I know the effect I have on women.

And I know these guys—

I'm not surprised hot guys are lining up to help Ariel.

But the nausea in my gut—

That's less obvious.

"What's your number one priority?" I study the first profile. A college student. He's younger than her. A soccer player who's studying chemistry. Who loves nerdy girls with thick glasses.

"I want to have a connection." She wraps her lips around her cup. "Is that stupid?"

"Does it matter to you?"

She nods.

"Then it's not stupid."

She takes a long sip. Swallows hard. "It… um… do you have anything sweet?"

"Sweet?"

"Dessert?"

"Oh." I can't help but chuckle. "I'm not big on sweets."

"Can I look?"

"Go for it." I motion to the kitchen.

She moves there. Pores over the fridge, freezer, counters. Settles on a basket of strawberries.

I try to judge bachelor number two—another athlete.

He's tall. Blond. Fun loving. His message is practically an essay about his interest in hiking, surfing, traveling.

Number three has a similar look. But with more tattoos and black clothes. He's some kind of musician. One who either makes a good living or pulls from a big trust fund. Expensive haircut. Designer jeans. Black nail polish.

The kind of guy Grace is dating.

Last I heard.

It's not that I'm jealous. More that I'm acutely aware of how we compare.

Most guys do the same thing. Most people do the same thing. We judge our ex's new partners to see how we stack up.

Yeah, I'm taller. I'm better looking. My tattoos are a hell of a lot nicer.

He makes more money. Knows more about the world. Has a better education.

Those aren't the things that matter though.

Does he make her come so hard she wakes the neighbors?

Does she dissolve between his arms?

Does she love him in a way she's never loved anyone?

Does he—

"You're just like Forest." Ariel's laugh is soft. "Eighty-five percent or bust."

"Less than that and it's barely chocolate."

She sets a bowl of strawberries on the table. Sits. Unwraps the chocolate, breaks it in half, hands a chunk to me.

Her fingers brush my palm.

Mine close around the chocolate.

"It's going to melt if you hold it like that." She breaks a square. Places it on her tongue.

Her eyelids flutter closed.

Her brow softens.

Her lips part with a sigh.

Her cheeks flush. Then her neck. Her chest.

Her tits heave with her inhale.

She's wearing the same thing as always—a tight black outfit. It looks perfect on her.

But I need it on the ground.

I need her in my bed.

I need her sighing like that for me.

Shit. The chocolate is melting. I place it on the table. Lick it off my palm.

Which only fills my head with ideas.

But I can keep those to myself. "You don't really have a type."

"I don't know." She swallows her treat. Picks up a strawberry. "I like guys who are—"

"Hot?"

Her blush deepens. "Who bring something new to my life."

"Like a kid?"

"A passion." She motions to the framed prints on the walls. "It doesn't matter what it's for—art or medicine or soccer. As long as I can see it all over their face."

How about you sit on my face?

Fuck. New subject.

I bring my pointer finger to my chest. "My face?"

"It's a nice face."

Princess, you have no idea. "Full of passion?"

"Of course." Her gaze shifts to the strawberry in her palm. "You love what you do."

"You feel like that too?"

Her eyes light up. "There's nothing better than solving a hard problem."

Isn't that life? "So you want a guy who's passionate? That's the biggest thing?"

"And hot." She teases. "Of course."

"Of course." I go through the profiles again. These

guys are passionate, as a group. But some more so than others.

I knock out the bottom five. Turn the screen to her. One guy in each tab. "Let's pick three. Set up meetings."

She nods *okay*. Studies the screen. Knocks out two guys. The baseball player. And the doctor. "Now what?"

"We write back."

"And say, what, 'please impregnate me'?"

"I was thinking you'd start with coffee," I say. "But if you'd rather jump to that—"

"No." She shakes her head. "Coffee is good." She sinks her teeth into the fruit.

Juice spills over her lips. Dribbles off her chin.

She laughs as she wipes her face.

Fuck, this is not where my head should be going. Not at all. "You want me to reply?"

"Uh, sure. Do you need help or could I—" She motions to the TV.

"Go for it."

"Thanks, Chase. Really." She takes her bowl. Moves to the TV.

I put the music on pause. Try to channel a guy who desperately wants to knock up a stranger, no strings attached. What does that guy want to hear? Besides "Baby, I can't wait to take your cock?"

Not that I'm imagining those words falling off Ariel's lips.

I'm not ruled by my dick.

She settles into the couch as I figure out replies. It takes me a while, but I manage to strike the right tone. Sixty percent *baby, I can't wait to take your cock* and forty percent *I have strict rules about this and you're gonna have to meet all of them, on my timeline.*

When I finish, she's glued to the TV, watching *Jurassic Park* on some streaming service.

Her cheeks flush. "I can finish at home." She looks to the clock. "It's getting late."

"No, stay."

Her teeth sink into her lip. "I can't take your couch."

"Who said you are?" I take a seat next to her.

Her knee brushes mine. Our jeans are in the way, but I can still feel the heat of her skin.

Her eyes meet mine then they go back to the screen.

"Okay, but then I have to restart. You need to see the whole thing," she says.

"I've seen it before."

"Not with me." She taps the remote.

"Let me guess: take it or leave it?"

Her lips curl into a smile. "Exactly."

"I'll take it."

Her smile widens. "Perfect." She turns back to the TV, but I can still feel her attention.

The whole fucking movie, her attention stays on me.

She watches me watch.

Then we put on the sequel.

She falls asleep in my lap.

And, fuck, it feels more right than anything has in a long, long time.

Chapter Thirteen

ARIEL

I wake on Chase's couch, pillow beneath my head, blanket over my body.

It's warm and safe and comfortable and completely inappropriate.

We need boundaries.

No, I need boundaries. I need to draw that line between *person helping me get the thing I want more than anything* and—

Okay, I'm not really sure where the boundaries are. But I will figure it out.

We, uh… we're friends. That's a good enough word.

I find the sketchpad on his counter. Leave a note.

Thanks for everything. I have to get to work. I'll call you when I have some responses. I want to set up a date for Friday.

I want it to be with him.

I want to watch *The Lost World* and *Jurassic Park Three* and even the unfortunate reboots. (Which are nonsense, but also full of dinosaurs).

Then, I want to study his selection of comic books, to see where our tastes overlap. Does he obsess over heroes who are energetic and clever like *Spider-Man*? Is he more into brooding martyrs like *Daredevil*?

Does he like dark, gritty storylines or fun, bright ones?

Does he prefer people who work alone or dysfunctional teams?

I want to know more about him. I want to know everything about him.

My fingers move over the paper. It's filled with tattoo mock-ups.

His style.

Big and bold like something out of an old comic.

Thick lines. Bright colors. Strong shading.

Mom would love it.

Mom would love him.

She'd tell me I'm crazy for doing this with anyone else.

I think. She rushed through the talk—she wanted to be the one to give it to me—but she underlined a few things: Sex should be fun, beautiful, and totally consensual.

I need to trust my gut.

And I should always follow my heart.

It's what I'm doing. Mostly. There is something in my gut begging me to stay here. Demanding I write *Chase, I have another thought. How about I delete my dating profile, you head to the clinic for a test, and we rendezvous at your place for some baby making?*

Though I won't actually be fertile until next week.

We can start now anyway. Practice.

Practice makes perfect, you know.

The logical part of my brain pushes it aside. There are so many reasons why I can't ask him that. More every day.

The more I see Chase, see how much he needs to take care of other people—

I can't deprive him of that.

I really can't.

I sign the note *Ariel Ballard*, leave it on the counter, collect my stuff.

Okay, so I do check out his bookshelf for way too long.

No surprise, Chase favors the brooding martyrs. (He has so many issues of *Daredevil*).

But there are quite a few dysfunctional teams too.

He makes a huge point of severing ties with people who hurt him. If he wants this kind of connection—

There must be this well of emptiness in his gut.

Which is another reason why I can't ask him.

He'll think this will fill him, but it won't. And you can't fix other people. You certainly can't fix damaged boys.

Even if Chase is twenty-nine and a man in every sense of the word.

And, uh—

I'm leaving. I am.

I hug my bag to my chest, slip into my shoes, lock the door on my way out.

Then I drive home, shower, fix breakfast, head to work.

I barely think of Chase.

I mean, I think of him when Spotify plays one of those songs he loves (I just happen to be in the mood for pop-punk music). And as I drink my chai. And the second chai.

And when I catch sight of students' tattoos.

And when I close my eyes.

But that's only every free moment in my day.

I barely think of him at all.

———

MY THOUGHTS FORK IN TWO DIRECTIONS.

In one, I'm a doting mother, raising a baby girl (Charlotte, after my mom) in my old room. My brothers are constantly hovering. They're practically co-parents. They shower her with so much love and attention she's spoiled rotten.

We play with blocks. I dress her in tiny black Converse *and* little pink dresses. I rock her while I'm studying. And bring her to defend my thesis.

She doesn't come into the room with me. She stays outside, with Forest. And Dad. And Holden.

When I'm finally awarded my PhD, we celebrate at a big, chain restaurant instead of some fancy local place. Because they have high seats and kids menus and crayons.

She's the center of my life. And that life is so big and full. It bursts with love from family and friends. I kick ass at my job, but I still go home at five every night, and take her to the park on the weekends, and watch her run around the waves in the summer.

There isn't a man involved. There are three—Dad, Forest, Holden. But they know I'm the one in charge. They help when I need it. Help more than I need it. But it's still me and my little girl against the world.

Then there's the typical, domestic path. The one I used to imagine with Phillip.

I'm a million months pregnant in a lacy white wedding dress. We kiss at a ceremony on the beach. He holds my hand in the delivery room. Holds Charlotte when I'm sleeping.

He's there, turning her mobile, rocking her to sleep, cooing over her smile.

He's at the park, holding my hand, as we try so, so hard to let her play with other kids. It's scary. She might hurt herself. Someone might pick on her. But we have to let her go.

He's there, holding her hand as she runs through the water, teaching her to swim, then surf, then run.

Handing her a basketball and challenging her to get past him.

Teaching her to draw. Teasing *you must take after your mom* when she scribbles a crooked stick figure.

Smiling at me.

And I'm smiling back. And my heart is so full I'm sure it's going to burst.

Because, God, Chase really would be a great father.

I try to sub in other guys, but it's always Chase.

I haven't even kissed the guy and I'm already imagining our baby.

This is exactly the kind of behavior that gets women labeled "crazy." Which is rude and reductive. Crazy isn't even a scientific term.

But, God, this is crazy.

And so out of the question.

But the more I stare at my inbox, waiting for responses from potential baby daddies, reading responses from potential baby daddies, imagining doing the deed with potential baby daddies, going through an entire pregnancy on my own—

I keep wanting it to be Chase.

But that's still so out of the question.

So I imagine what I can with my, ahem, suitors. Soft lips on my neck. Rough hands on my hips. A hard body over mine.

Sure, Chase makes his way into those fantasies. But so does Phillip. And Idris Elba.

It's just a fantasy.

It doesn't mean anything.

I'm still doing this.

I'm still meeting these guys.

Chapter Fourteen

ARIEL

I can't do this.

How the hell can I do this?

I sit at my computer for an hour straight, reading over replies from Bachelors One, Two, and Three, trying to formulate a response.

Everything I type is wrong. Too desperate or too disinterested. Too explicit or too vague. Too base or too clinical.

It's too much, deciding where to have coffee with the future father of my child.

Potential future father of my child.

It's just…

It's way too much.

I bring my laptop downstairs. Heat up the leftovers I made with Dad. Pasta with marinara, broccoli, peppers, and Italian sausage. It's good. Rich, savory, comforting.

A dessert of seventy percent chocolate comforts, but it fails to illuminate.

This. Is. Way. Too. Much.

Deep breath.

Slow exhale.

One step at a time. Read. Reply. Meet.

Save the overwhelming thoughts for later. All that *uh, my boyfriend of three years just left me* and *I'm really trying to have a baby* and *maybe I waited too long* and *maybe I'll get sick anyway, and she'll lose her mother. I can't do that to her. Especially if she doesn't have a father.*

I'm not diving into that.

I can deal with it once I'm pregnant. Really pregnant. Second trimester, ready to tell people, sure of my decision pregnant.

This is step one.

Read the first message.

Hey Ariel,

I know what you mean. I was raised by a single mom. She was a badass. She worked hard, but she was always there to make dinner and tuck me in.

You seem like you'll be a great mom. I want to help.

And, well, I hope you don't think this is out of line: I find you incredibly attractive. It's not just that I want to sleep with you. I do. But I also want to make it something we both remember.

His name is right there, but I still call him Bachelor Number One. I can't get attached to him. Not until I'm sure he's in.

It's a sweet message. Exactly what I want. Completely perfect.

It should be easy to reply.

Hey Bachelor Number One,

I have to admit—I also find you incredibly attractive. I think we'll have a lot of fun making babies. Do people still call sex "baby making?" I'm not with the times. But I know I like you.

Let's meet Friday at this little shop in Venice. They have great herbal tea and it's close to my place.

Sincerely,

Ariel

106

That's normal. Reasonable. Personable.

But is it right?

I have no idea.

I need another opinion.

I grab my cell. Call Chase.

He picks up on the second ring. "Most people text these days."

"I have long messages to read to you."

His chuckle is soft. "Of course."

"Oh." This isn't what normal people do. "Am I interrupting? If you're busy, I can call back."

"You're good. I just got out of the shower."

My cheeks flush at the mental image of him in a towel. "Yeah?"

"I'll put you on speaker while I cook."

"Of course." My heart thuds against my chest. I want to invite him here. Offer him the food I made. Wrap my arms around him. Ask him if I'm making the right decision.

But I don't want his input.

Yes, I need his help convincing normal guys to agree to my request. But that's where it ends. That's where it has to end.

"Three guys replied. I'll read them one at a time." I pull up Bachelor Two and Three's messages. "Ready?"

"Shoot."

I relay the first message.

The second is a little dirtier. A little more focused on the actual baby making and how much the guy wants to do me doggie style.

"Did he just say *I want to see that round ass bounce as I fuck you*?"

"Uh…" Okay, it's incredibly explicit. But this isn't romance. It's sex. "Yeah."

"No way."

"He's cute."

"They're all cute." Chase's voice drops to a familiar paternal tone. "A guy who will say that in his second message will say a lot worse shit—"

"What's wrong with that?"

"It's not wrong, exactly."

"Maybe I like dirty talk." My cheeks flare. I hate that he's casting me as this good girl. But I love that he's over-protective. I hate that I love that he's over-protective. "Maybe I want to reply *hell yeah, baby, for our second session, I want to feel your cock in my ass.*"

Oh my God.

I didn't say that.

Did I just say that?

A low groan flows through the speakers. It's stilted. Like he's trying to swallow it.

It still makes my sex clench.

And my heart race.

And my breath catch.

Am I breathing? I'm not sure anymore.

Chase is so sexy.

So much sexier than Bachelor Number Two.

But also so unavailable. That beautiful mental image that's been playing in my head for the last few days—

It's a fantasy.

Even if I could ask Chase—and I can't—he's in love with his ex-girlfriend.

There's no room in his heart for me.

Which is good. It means he won't get jealous or confused or possessive.

That's logical.

It makes perfect sense.

So why is my stomach fluttering?

Why is my body buzzing?

I…

Uh…

"You're right." His voice is sure. "If you want a guy who will look at you like a piece of meat, go with him."

I swallow hard. That's not fair. It's an over-simplification. "It's better if he just wants sex. No risk of getting attached."

"What did I say?"

"You said it in a—"

"It's what you want, princess. Not what I think is best for you."

"So you—"

"A guy like that doesn't respect you."

"But you…" My heart thuds against my chest. "Are you telling me you don't dirty talk?"

"That's different."

"How?"

"It just is." He's quiet for a moment, like he's trying to think of an explanation. But he doesn't offer one. "Read the third message."

It's halfway between the first two. A little dirty. A little sweet. A lot of talk of practicalities.

Which is good.

Sensible.

Even if it's dry. Like he's only doing this because it works for his schedule.

That shouldn't matter—I need his sperm, not his everlasting love—but it does.

Chase waits until I'm finished. "What do you think?"

None of them are perfect. But this isn't a fairy tale. I can't wait for perfect. "I should meet all three of them. That's the best way to see if there's chemistry."

"Okay." Apprehension drips into his voice.

I ignore it. "What do you think of my reply? To the first one?" I read it word for word.

"It's good."

"Just good."

"It's you. It's perfect."

"Okay." I hit send. Close my eyes. Suck a breath through my teeth. "Help me with the other two?"

"Sure."

"This second guy... I think..." That I can't read dirty talk to Chase on the phone or I'm going to start touching myself right here.

Dad is upstairs in his room, asleep. He has an early meeting and the thought of waking him up with my—

So out of the question.

"Give me a second. I... uh... I'm putting you on speaker." I set the phone on the table. Try typing a response.

Bachelor Number Two,

I like the sound of that. I really like the thought of you pinning me to the bed and fucking me from behind. Not because I'd imagine some other guy who slipped and mentioned he likes it rough. Not because I want to feel his hands on my shoulders and his lips on my neck. Because you—

UGH.

Okay.

Maybe more to the point.

Bachelor Number Two,

That sounds fun. I'd say we should meet for a drink, but I'm skipping alcohol for obvious reasons. Let's get coffee at this shop by my place. Say Saturday night?

Looking forward to it!

Ariel

That's normal. Ish. Or is it not sexy enough?

"All you need for that guy is a time and place. He'll show up," Chase says.

I clear my throat.

"He wants to fuck you. That's it."

"I need someone who will commit to fucking me a lot." My cheeks flare. Chase is so difficult. He's acting like he doesn't have an attitude, but he does.

"You wanted my help—"

"Your help, not your judgment."

"I'm not—"

"You are." My face flames. "You think there's something wrong with me wanting panty-melting sex."

"I don't."

"You obviously do." My fingers dig into the table. "Or you wouldn't have this attitude."

He's quiet for a moment.

Which is so…

UGH.

Who does he think he is, judging me in silence?

God, he thinks he knows everything.

He doesn't.

I…

He…

Ugh.

Deep breath.

Slow exhale.

Chase is helping me.

I asked him to help me.

I asked him for a favor.

I can't snap now. Even if he's so—

"It's not that." His voice softens.

"Yes it is." My voice gets snippy. I don't recognize it. I never get snippy. "I'm the one doing this. I'm having sex with this guy. Unprotected sex. And if I want a guy who will make that hot and dirty and nothing else, then I'll fuck that guy." Blood rushes through my veins. I stand. Press my palms together.

Pace.

My body is buzzing in the strangest way. It's not quite desire, but it's an equally potent rush.

I feel good. Awake. Alive. Like I can handle telling any bossy man in my life to shove it.

"You're not the one fucking him. You don't get to tell me what I want" The electric current rushes to my fingers and toes. I don't talk like this. Not with this tone or this profanity or this focus on what I want in bed.

"You're right." His voice stays even. "But I don't trust that guy. I'm going with you."

"On my date?"

"I'll be at the shop. Just in case."

I should say no. Just to prove a point. To make sure he knows I'm in charge. But I want him there. I want him protecting me. I hate how much I want him protecting me. "Okay."

Ding. New Message. "Oh." I skim it quickly. "Bachelor One wants to meet Friday. At seven." *Please come. Watch over me. Don't tell me what to do but stay nearby. So I feel safe.*

"You want me to come?"

"Isn't that what you want?" My fingers curl into my jeans. I hate that I want his comfort. But I do.

"I'll be there."

"Thanks, Chase. I… I appreciate your help. But, uh—"

"Watch the sass?"

"Yeah."

"Not sure I can agree to that," he says.

"Oh. Well…"

"Kidding."

"Oh." I knew that. Totally. "I just… I'll see you Friday. Meet me here at six thirty. Help me pick out my outfit."

"Until then."

I hang up the phone.

Then I go straight to my room.

I try to push thoughts of Chase from my head. I try to stop imagining him rolling my jeans off my hips, dragging his hand over my thighs, growling dirty demands—

I fail.

Chapter Fifteen

ARIEL

For the tenth time, I smooth my dress.

It still hugs my curves.

It still screams *look at me, I'm sexy*.

It still makes me sick.

This is my break-up dress. The sexiest garment I own and the thing that reminds me I'm a loveless loser.

Not that I—

It's easy to not think of Phillip when I stay focused on my task. When I leave gaps—

Well, I guess, lately, my head's been going to Chase. But it's still there, that dull sense of loss.

I don't want Phillip, exactly.

But I miss him. I miss his laugh and his arms and his shampoo.

I miss being half of a whole.

I miss coming home to sweet texts. Cooking dinner together. Sharing stories about our days.

Sure, that stuff was rarer the last year. He was busy with residency. I always thought... I don't know. That it would change once he settled in.

Maybe I was missing all the signs.

Maybe he checked out way before I asked him to go all in.

"Damn, where are you going?" Forest stops in my doorframe.

"A date." I keep my eyes on the mirror. The dress is good. It will keep my head in the right place. In a *there's no way I'm handing over my heart* place. That's important. Even if it means a dull sense of nausea. "Why are you here?"

"Meeting Skye."

The girl next door. Literally. Skye and Forest have been best friends since the day he accidentally hit her with a basketball.

They're joined at the hip.

But he's so, so sure he's not into her.

And she always insists she's not into him.

He did spend years with a girl who was all wrong for him. I get why she's hesitant.

But come on, Forest. Get your shit together.

"So you come here to terrorize your sister?" I ask.

He nods *yeah*. "Is this a Tinder date?"

"Gross."

"I thought I was too prudish about your sex life?"

"Just don't comment." I have enough over-protective bullshit with Chase. Not that I can complain without giving my plan away. "How is Skye?"

"Stressed."

"Well, yeah, she can't find—"

He shoots me a familiar look. *You're not helping.*

Ahem. "I'm sure you can find a way to comfort her." I try to drop my voice to that teasing tone Holden uses, the one that says *and by comfort her, I mean with your body*, but I don't come close.

Forest rolls his eyes. "I get enough of this from Holden."

"We only speak the truth."

He shoots me some serious side-eye. "Why are you dressed like that?"

"Like a woman going on a date with a man?" I roll my eyes. Twice. Then I grab my lipstick. Focus on applying just enough Raspberry Rhapsody.

"Like you're in a porno from the 1950s?"

"This is the look." My red sheath dress is both classy and modern. "You helped me pick it out!"

"Skye picked it out."

Mostly true. Further proof their lives are intertwined. Not the right thing to say at the moment. "Does she dress like she's in a 1950s porno?"

He chuckles *no, more like a goth princess porno*, but he doesn't say anything. "Who's the guy?"

"Internet date." That's true enough. I set my lipstick down. Pick up my mascara. Forest and Holden tried to step up and teach me the ways of the feminine arts, but they were terrible. Skye filled in what she could, but her style is a lot bolder than mine.

"Then why's Chase coming over?" Apprehension drips into his voice.

"The statistics project." I rattle off some details about the data I need.

Forest nods along, only barely following.

Thank God most people don't understand statistics. "He's coming straight from work. Said this was the best time."

"He worked this morning."

Shit. "I guess he had another appointment."

Forest makes eye contact through the mirror. "He's still in love with Grace."

"And?"

"He's a good guy. He is. But he'll break your heart. He'll have no idea he's doing it. But he will."

"He's helping with school."

"Your boobs are out."

"For my date." I suck in a deep breath. My chest heaves, adding credence to the *my boobs are out* theory. "With a man who isn't Chase."

"I hate saying it, Ari. He's a good friend. He'd take good care of you. But he'd never be there." He places his hand over his heart. "He doesn't know how to let her go."

My stomach flip-flops. It's true. Chase can't get over his ex. I don't understand why. They had an ugly breakup, sure, but it was a long time ago.

But maybe I don't understand love. The kind of real, true love that leaves a mark on your soul.

That leaves you crushed when you lose someone.

Like Dad was after Mom died. It took him years to find his smile.

This is different, but—

"You're thinking about it," Forest says.

"Thinking about how you're projecting your feelings for Skye."

He scoffs *yeah right*.

I reach for a better comeback, but the opening door interrupts me.

"Hey." Chase's voice echoes through the room. "You here, princess?"

"He calls you princess?" Forest whispers.

"He always did," I whisper back.

Forest shakes his head *no way*.

I nod *yes way*.

"Seriously, Ariel. Be careful. I know how you feel about him."

"I don't—"

"You always have. I get it. He's a cute, older guy. He's brooding and miserable—"

"You're brooding and miserable."

"That's how I know."

That's ridiculous. I toss my mascara on my desk. Shove my lipstick in my purse. March toward the door.

Stumble.

March a little slower.

"Hey, Chase." I move down the stairs. "Forest was just —" Ugh, what the hell can I say he's doing? "Leaving."

"Nope," Forest says.

Whatever.

I hold the banister to steady myself.

Chase's eyes fix on me.

His pupils dilate.

His jaw drops.

"Fuck, princess." The words fall off his lips. "You're gonna knock 'em dead."

"On my date. With another man. Which is none of your business." I flip Forest off.

He shakes his head *you're going to get hurt. Don't be stupid. Listen to me. I'm never stupid like this.* Yeah, he's behind me, but I can tell.

I move faster.

Trip on the last stair.

Chase rushes to help me. Wraps his arm around me. Pulls my body into his.

God, he's so warm and hard and strong.

My fingers dig into his t-shirt. "I, uh, let's um… talk on the walk. I think Forest and Skye want their privacy."

Chase chuckles. "They would."

Forest continues shaking his head. "Be careful."

"I will." I turn and follow Chase out the door.

It hits me as I step onto the sidewalk. I'm actually doing this. I'm actually meeting this guy. I'm actually holding Chase's hand.

The last one is the strongest.

But that doesn't mean anything.

———

CHASE SQUEEZES MY HAND.

I squeeze back. It's not enough to keep me steady. Not in these shoes. Three inch wedges. The shoes I wore to graduation. The only nice pair of shoes I own.

Okay, that isn't exactly true. I own a lot of nice business attire. When I interviewed for internships, I went all out. Mom imparted that wisdom before she left.

Looks shouldn't matter, but they do.

Sure, scientists get cut a lot of slack. But less when they're women. If I head into an interview in my usual outfit—black jeans, black tank top, black hoodie, black shoes—I get a look.

She's some goth weirdo.

She doesn't understand how to fit in.

She doesn't care enough to dress to impress.

It's ridiculous. Black goes with black. It hides stains. It holds color.

It's a very practical choice.

And, well, it brings out my coffee eyes. Complements my dark hair. That's what Mom always said when Dad would try to get me in color.

Not that it stopped her from buying every *Little Mermaid* themed dress in the world.

Sure, I look good in crimson-red and regal-purple.

But they make me think of Mom.

So…

I guess that's a fun, new association for this dress. Break-up dress. *Mad Men* porn parody. Late mother.

Wonderful.

"You okay?" Chase turns to me. Studies my expression.

I try a smile, but it's stiff. "Nervous."

"This guy might father your child." Something slips into his tone, something I can't place. The he blinks and it's gone. "It's normal."

"Right. Yeah." I suck a breath through my teeth. Push out an exhale. "Forest thinks I have a crush on you." My cheeks flush. Why did I say that? It's so not the thing to say.

"Do you?"

"Oh." I don't know how to respond to that. I'm not a good liar. "I did. When I was younger."

"I know." He chuckles. "You were cute."

"I was not cute."

He nods *you were*. "You'd come into Forest's room when he stepped out, all sly, like you got away with something."

My blush deepens. "I did not."

"You did." His lips curl into a smile. "You'd crouch next to me. Try to make eye contact. Stare at the ground." His eyes meet mine. "Your cheeks would turn bright red." His fingers brush the strap of my dress. "This red."

I shake my head *no way*.

"You'd rest your hand on my sketchbook. Ask if you could see what I was drawing."

"Maybe I was interested in art."

"Maybe." He laughs.

"It's possible."

"Don't tell me if it's true. It would bruise my ego too much," he teases.

"And you'd rather I stroke it?" The words fall off my lips without passing through my brain. "Oh, I mean—"

"I know." His smile widens. "Yeah. I'm a bitter asshole who can't get over his ex or forgive his brother—"

"You're not—"

"You gotta give me something."

"I'm sure a lot of women want to… stroke it."

"Yeah."

My cheeks flare, but not with desire. With something else. That same uneasy feeling I got when Phillip talked about his boss. About how smart and competent and stylish she was. "So…" I'm not jealous. That would be stupid. "Why don't you?"

"Act on it?" he offers.

"Yeah."

"You ever have casual sex?"

"Well… there was this guy in college. I thought it was serious, but he didn't. I, uh, when I look back, it was obvious. He was dropping a lot of hints. But I missed them." Deep breath. Slow exhale. Steady steps. "I guess that's a no."

"I used to. Before Grace. It was exciting while it happened. But, after, I'd feel worse. Empty."

"Empty like you… ahem." I motion to his crotch, which really doesn't get the point across in a graceful way.

But he must get it, because he laughs. It's that same *Ariel, you're so ridiculous* laugh.

My stomach flutters.

My heart thuds.

My veins buzz.

Not because I like him.

Because… uh…

"No." His laugh gets deeper. "In my head. And my heart. I thought maybe that was sex. Until Grace. We waited a while. It was her first time. She was scared. By the time we finally—"

"Had sex?"

"Yeah. I was already in love with her. It was so different. Like I could feel her soul connecting with mine." He breaks our touch to run his hand through his hair. "Fuck, it sounds so cheesy like that."

"I know what you mean. With Phillip… maybe I couldn't feel our souls. But it was always about connecting, more than… getting off."

"Did he not—"

"No, he did. I… uh… so you never get…" I try to find a tactful word. Fail. "Horny?"

His laugh gets louder. "I have a hand, don't I?"

"Oh." Must not imagine Chase fucking himself. Must not imagine Chase fucking himself. Must come up with a coherent response. "Two, actually."

"True." His laugh gets louder. "But I stick with one."

"Which one?" Oh my God. Why can't I stop words from falling off my lips? I… He… UGH.

"You gonna stop shaking that one? I wash thoroughly." His voice is teasing, playful, like he wants me to know which hand he uses to fuck himself.

Like he wants me picturing him wrapping his hand around his cock.

Or pressing his palm to my thighs.

Or tugging my panties to my ankles.

Not that I…

Ahem.

"No, it's um, healthy to masturbate. Lowers blood pressure, helps you sleep, relieves stress. It's um… It's good. I do it a lot too." OH MY GOD, WHY CAN'T I STOP TALKING?!?!?!

Chase just laughs.

"I just mean… it's normal."

"I'm not laughing at you."

It's that *Ariel is adorable* laugh again. I should hate it, but I don't. I really don't. "I… um, well, uh—" I am changing the subject away from masturbation. I am no longer asking him about his masturbation habits. I am done picturing Chase's lips parting with a groan. "We're almost here, huh." I pick up my pace.

He nods *yeah*. Follows me to the coffee shop.

Shit.

He's here.

Bachelor Number One.

He's here and the only thing I can think about is Chase's groan.

This date is going to go so well.

Chapter Sixteen

CHASE

Ariel's chest heaves with her inhale. Falls with her exhale.

I shouldn't look at her tits. I should look at her dark eyes. Or at least her red lips.

But my eyes refuse my command.

They trace a line down her curvy body.

That dress is perfect on her.

Though I'm currently picturing it on my floor. Her in my bed. Me growling *show me how you touch yourself, princess. I want to watch you come.*

It's way too vivid.

Incredibly fucking inappropriate.

Impossible to ignore.

But that isn't why we're here.

"He's there." She takes a step backward, so she's out of view of Bachelor Number One. "He's wearing jeans. You think I overdressed?"

"He won't mind."

"You sure?"

One hundred percent. "You made an effort." I can't

exactly say *your tits look fucking amazing. I need them in my hands. Need you groaning as I play with your nipples.*

How do you like it, princess?

Soft and teasing? Hard and aggressive? Slow and steady?

"But it's so much." She shifts her weight between her heels. Teeters on her black shoes. "It's—"

"You look perfect."

"Really?"

"Yeah." I squeeze her hand. Try to ignore the question flitting through my head—*do you touch yourself with this hand, princess?* Step backward. "I'll go in first."

"Sure, yeah."

"If you need anything, I'm there." I hold up my cell, so she knows she can text. Not that I'm going to be far. I want to hear this.

Not enough to pry.

Enough to help.

"Okay." Her gaze flits from me to Bachelor Number One then back to me. "Thank you, Chase. Really." She moves forward. Wraps her arms around me.

Fuck, that feels good. Way too good.

I soak her in for a moment, then I release her, nod *good luck*.

She shoots me an *okay*. It's awkward and adorable and perfect.

Fuck, she really is cute.

Not that it matters to me. More that I'm trying to help her with this date.

That's it.

I move into the coffee shop. Pass Bachelor Number One on the way to the line.

He's not as tall as his profile suggests. But he's just as handsome. Like an Abercrombie model. A star quarterback. A guy who could play *Captain America*.

It's too late for caffeine. I order a cold brew anyway. I need to stay alert. In case this guy crosses a line. Or pushes too hard. Or scares Ariel.

She deserves the best.

Not an asshole who misrepresents his height.

Okay, the difference is an inch or two at most. And maybe I'm not the person to judge. Most guys under six feet tall look the same to me.

Height isn't important.

As long as he's healthy and he treats her well—

Fuck, how do you judge what matters in a sperm donor who's doing things the old-fashioned way?

I fix my drink, take a seat, pull my sketchbook and pencils from my pocket. So it's not obvious I'm eavesdropping.

Tomorrow morning's design stares back at me. A couple's tattoo. A locked heart and a key. Classic. Simple. Perfect.

Loving someone enough to mark your skin—

I used to be there. I was there. I thought it meant we were forever.

But the ink stays longer than the relationship.

I should text this duo. Tell them they're making a mistake. That they'll grow to regret this decision.

I want to. Everything inside me screams *run the fuck away*.

But I can't. They're happy. They're in love. Nothing I say will get through.

I remember that feeling—like someone else completes you, like you can't live without them, like you want nothing more than their happiness.

My heartbeat picks up as Ariel steps inside. She waves to Bachelor Number One.

It's a big, friendly wave. A lot. But he just smiles, endeared.

She crosses the room to meet him.

They shake. Exchange hellos and names.

He motions to the line. She nods *thanks*, follows him to the counter, lets him pay for her drink.

She's good at this. Better than she thinks she is. Better than she has any right to be.

That shouldn't be surprising.

Yeah, Ariel is a little blunt and unaware of social mores, but she's passionate, charming, smart.

What guy wouldn't fall in love with her?

I hate to admit it, but Bachelor Number One is a gentleman. He waits for her drink to arrive, leads her back to the table, leans in for personal conversation.

I only catch a few things. Normal date stuff. Where they're from. His classes at UCLA. His love of smart women.

Her love of athletes. (Her ex was a swimmer).

His soccer scholarship.

How me must have strong legs.

How much she wants to feel those legs against her palms. Around her hips—

Okay, that's my fucking brain. They're having a perfectly chaste conversation. He *is* a gentleman. And even if he wasn't—

The goal of this is getting him in her bed by next Friday. (I know her cycle better than I know my work schedule at this point).

She should talk about his thighs. And how much she wants his body over hers. And how much she wants to take his cock.

It doesn't bother me.

I'm not jealous.

I'm happy for her.

Happy they're hitting it off.

It's fucking fantastic.

It's everything I want for her.

It is.

I suck coffee through my straw. It's the same rich, chocolate it was yesterday, but it doesn't satisfy.

I don't want coffee.

I want Ariel in my bed. Away from this asshole who's not remotely an asshole. Away from this whole stupid idea.

She deserves better than a stranger.

She deserves more than a one-time thing.

She deserves everything.

It's not my fucking decision. She wants someone who isn't involved. That's her choice. Not mine.

If she wanted me, she'd ask.

It's not like she needs her kid to inherit my genetic predisposition to alcoholism.

Even if everything else about this made sense, that doesn't.

The more I repeat the mantra—*It's her decision*-the less I feel it.

I *know* it's her choice, her body, her life.

But the sound of her date's laugh still makes me sick.

For an hour, I sketch. They talk. She giggles. He laughs.

Finally, they hug goodbye. She watches him leave. Waits.

Moves to me. "What do you think?" Her smile spreads wider. "He was really nice. And on board. I think he gets it."

"Perfect." I try to smile, but it's impossibly forced.

"You think so? He's not too…"

"You like him?"

She presses her lips together. "He's a good guy."

"Then I like him."

———

I HATE HIM.

Bachelor Number Two flirts more openly. It's just dirty enough to keep her engaged. Comments about how nicely her dress hugs her figure. How much he loves her dark hair. How beautiful her eyes look when she laughs.

Yeah, her dress—this tight black thing that stops just below her ass—makes her look like a goddess.

Yeah, any sane guy would want to see her dark hair in his hands.

Yeah, her eyes are beautiful when she laughs.

Yeah, I can't stop imagining what they look like when she comes.

But this isn't about me.

It's about this guy who makes her laugh, and touches her arm, and glances at her tits in a way that says *I want you, but I care enough to look you in the eyes when we talk.*

They flirt through two rounds of drinks. Decaf coffee for him. Herbal tea for her.

He kisses her goodbye.

She steps backward, blushing and nervous. Whispers a promise to call him. Watches him leave.

Then she goes to me, looking for my stamp of approval.

What the fuck can I say? *I hate that it isn't me?*

I force a smile. "Do you like him?"

She chews on her bottom lip. "He seems like he understands what I want."

"If you like him, I like him."

She nods *good*, but the look she returns is off. Like she doesn't believe me.

———

THE WEEK IS TORTURE. I WORK. I HIT THE GYM. I COOK. I text Ariel all night. About my comic book collection. And hers. And why Batman is overdone. But I must love him, because he's so dark and brooding and he carries the world around on his shoulders.

And, yeah, maybe I invite her over to watch sci-fi.

Maybe she suggests the *Daredevil* TV show. Because isn't Matt Murdock even more of a mopey motherfucker than I am?

Maybe I watch her more than I watch the action. Maybe she falls asleep in my lap, again.

Maybe I can't handle how much the TV show makes me think of my brother Hunter—it's his favorite.

So I think about her instead. About her red lips on my neck. Her soft thighs around my hips. Her short nails on my back.

It doesn't mean anything.

We still end every conversation with *you ready for Bachelor Number Three?*

On Thursday, they meet at that same coffee shop. She's back in her red dress and done with her shyness. She struts into the place like she owns it. Stares at this guy—a handsome Asian dude with swimmer's shoulders—like she knows he wants her.

And he does.

They flirt for two hours straight. Hug goodbye. Part.

She waits until he leaves. Comes to me. Studies my sketch.

It's nonsense at the moment. Doodles. A ripped heart stitched together in different styles.

Water color.

Classic line art.

Modern comic book.

Classic comic book—the stuff with the shaded dots.

Greyscale.

Her fingers brush the pages. "Those are perfect."

"You want one?"

"No." She wraps her arms around her chest, suddenly shy. "I, um, I'm scared of needles."

"It's not as bad as it looks."

She shakes her head *it is too*. "Yours are nice though. I always... I always thought they were sexy." Her cheeks flush. "I mean, they are. Right now." Her fingers brush my forearm. They trace the lines of a black and grey rose. "I like the pop art look. But this is more you."

"Should I get it right here?" I press my palm to my chest.

Her eyes go to the exposed skin between my t-shirt and my neck. "Definitely."

"Advertise my broken status to the world?"

"Show you believe you'll heal yourself."

I'm not sure about that, but it's a nice idea.

She offers her hand. "Walk me home?"

"Of course."

I pack my bag, take her hand, follow her out of the coffee shop.

We make small talk for a while. Dance around the only question that matters.

Finally, we approach her place.

Maybe I should wait, give her space, but I have to ask. "What do you think?"

"Hmm?" She turns her attention to the sidewalk. Moves with shaky steps.

"About the guys?"

"Oh."

"Is one of them Mr. Right?"

"I, uh… I have thought about that."

"Yeah?" I ask.

"I think I know who I want."

My stomach clenches.

"I just… I guess I have to ask him."

Right. Of course. She has to make it official. With one of these guys.

I hate it.

Most of me hates it.

There's a part that's happy for her. "Who is he? Which guy do you want to knock you up?"

Chapter Seventeen

ARIEL

I can't say this.

   I can't ask this.

   I can't.

Chase is already offering so much. He's already helping so much. And there's nothing wrong with any of my eligible bachelors.

They're good guys. Attractive. Intelligent. Respectful.

On board.

Not in love with their exes.

I mean, maybe they are in love with their exes. I don't know and I don't want to know. That's why they're good options. Because we have clearly drawn boundaries.

That isn't the case with Chase.

Yes, he's not over his ex.

Yes, that makes him a safe choice in certain ways. It dampens my fear he'll get attached. It keeps me from getting the wrong idea. It's basically this dress.

Chase is into his ex.

Chase is never going to love me.

Chase is never going to want a partnership with me.

I know that. I understand it. I accept it. Hell, I embrace it.

Chase's locked heart is perfect for this mission.

But now he's doodling mended hearts.

And he's looking at me with all this concern.

And my stomach is fluttering.

The lines are fading already. If we start taking off our clothes?

I can't do it.

Sex is one thing.

Friendship is another.

Respect is, um, a third.

Sex with a friend I respect and desperately want to fuck? All for the purposes of making a baby?

That's something else.

"Princess?" His voice is soft. Concerned.

"Yeah."

His fingers brush my wrist. He takes my hands. Turns his body toward mine. Stares into my eyes. "You okay?"

No. "Yeah."

"If you're not sure—"

"No, I'm sure."

He looks at me funny, like he's not following. "You don't want to tell me?"

"No, I do."

His blue eyes bore into mine.

I suck a breath through my teeth. It's easy. One sentence. Three words.

I can do that.

No problem.

Really.

"It won't hurt my feelings if it's Bachelor Number Two." His fingers brush my wrist. "If you want dirty—"

"I want you."

His eyes go wide.

God, there's no backing out now. I just have to say it. "I don't want bachelor one, two, or three. I don't want some other anonymous guy. I want you, Chase." Deep breath. Slow exhale. "I want you to get me pregnant."

He stares back at me dumbstruck.

It's not a yes or a hell yes or a let's go right now.

But it's not a no either.

It's something.

God, I really hope it's something.

Chapter Eighteen

CHASE

I *want you to get me pregnant.*

All my breath leaves my body.

All my blood leaves my brain.

My heart—

It's a mess.

I want to help Ariel.

I want to fuck Ariel.

Hell, I want to give in to my primal urge to pass on my DNA.

But I need to be sure.

"Oh… I…" She reaches for the door. "I'm sorry. That was out of line. I won't—"

"What do you mean?"

"Do I need to explain the biology?"

My laugh is impossibly awkward. "No. What do you want?"

"I want us to—" She nods to her bedroom window. "I mean, not now. Well, it could be now. I… uh… I can make you one of those Moscow Mules. I can't have one. But you could."

"No." I suck a breath through my teeth. "What do you want from me?"

"You're saying yes?"

Fuck yes. Take off your dress, princess. I want to see that pretty cunt. "Will it be like with Bachelor Number Two?"

Her eyes go wide. "Dirty?"

My balls tighten. It's going to be dirty. That isn't a question. And it's not what I need to clarify. "Wham, bam, thank you ma'am?"

"Oh… well… you're my friend."

"Yeah."

"I wouldn't want us to stop being friends."

I nod.

"And, um, I wouldn't want things to get weird with Forest. I could… I don't have to tell him it's you. I can. But I don't have to."

"So you want to do this and part ways?"

"Well…" She chews on her bottom lip. "I know how you feel."

What?

"About Grace. You're still in love with her."

Usually, I'd agree. Today, the words feel wrong. My heart is empty, sure, but not because Grace fills it. Because she took it with her and I don't know how to get it back.

"That's good." Her voice wavers. "I mean, not for you. It kinda sucks for you."

I can't help but laugh. "It does."

"But for us. I know your heart is locked. I know you won't fall for me. And I won't fall for you either."

"Okay."

"I know you want a family. But, um, I don't think it should be like this. I mean, it's your life, do what you want. But I'm only asking for a donation."

"What if I want more?"

Her dark eyes meet mine. "More how?"

"We're gonna stay friends."

"I hope so."

"Am I supposed to pretend this kid is a stranger?"

"Oh. Right." She presses her palms to her dress. "I haven't really... I mean, if it was someone else, you'd be Uncle Chase, right?"

"Yeah."

"I want that. You're Uncle Chase. If you want drop off a teddy bear or see him on his birthday, great. But I don't want to confuse him. I don't want him to think you're—"

"More than Uncle Chase?"

She bites her lip. "Yeah. If that's not okay—"

"My mom's an alcoholic."

"I know." Her eyes bore into mine. "You're not."

"But I'm genetically predisposed."

Her lips press together. "No one has perfect DNA."

Maybe. But this is far from imperfect. "What if your kid inherits that?"

"Are there any other illnesses in your family?"

Nothing off the top of my head. "No."

Her gaze shifts to the concrete. "If you're not interested... You don't need to break it to me gently or make an excuse. Just tell me you're not—"

"Can I sleep on it?"

"Yeah. Okay. But I, uh..."

"Want to start tomorrow?"

Her cheeks flush. "You remember?"

"You text me updates every day."

"Oh. Right." Slowly, she meets my gaze. Holds out her hand to shake. "Sleep on it. And if it's a no, I understand. I just..."

"Need a firm answer."

"Yeah."

I take her hand.

"I need a commitment. A hundred percent commitment. Which is a lot to ask."

"Yeah."

She shakes. Releases me. "I, um, I like you a lot Chase. You're a good friend. I'd hate to mess that up."

"Me too." I wrap my arms around her.

She rests her head on my shoulder. Digs her fingers into my arms.

She's so soft and pliable and right.

I haven't felt that since Grace, that sense that someone's body belongs near mine.

There have been plenty of hugs, embraces, dates Griffin pushed me into.

But this—

It's something else.

"I'll sleep on it." I release her.

She steps backward. Looks at me like she's not sure how we're supposed to say goodbye.

I'm not either.

So I nod, turn, move to my car.

She watches me drive away.

She stays in my thoughts all fucking night.

Do I want to get Ariel pregnant is an easy question to answer.

Can I do that without getting invested, without falling in love with her kid, without falling in love with her?

That's a lot harder.

Chapter Nineteen

CHASE

Sleep and coffee prove equally useless in the clarity front.

My thoughts circle as I walk to work. My favorite album flows through my headphones. Blocks the sounds of traffic, surf, conversation.

Usually, this song makes me think of Grace. Usually, every fucking song makes me think of Grace.

It's not that I'm still in love with her.

I still don't get it.

The look of relief on her face when she pressed the ring into my hand.

It was the first time I saw her relax in forever.

When we started, we were over the moon. I loved every fucking thing about her. The sharp laugh. The red nails. The birthmark on her collarbone.

The way she scribbled lyrics on my arm in sharpie. Traced my tattoos. Gushed about the art history class we shared. Bragged when she earned a higher test score than I did.

Yeah, we fought a lot. But when we made up—

Fuck, the sex was amazing.

For a while, it was a cycle. I'd pull her closer. She'd pull me closer. Then she'd push me away. Push me until I broke. We'd fight. I'd demand more of her heart. She'd promise it. We'd make up with hot, sweaty, needy sex.

Repeat the process.

I guess, when I put it that way, it makes sense. Logically, it makes sense.

But then I think about her smile. All those times she melted into my arm. That she whispered *I love you* and clung to me like she was terrified I'd leave.

She thought I was scared of her moods. That I'd leave her when I realized she was crazy. That one day I'd wake up and put the pieces together.

Yeah, she had issues, but they never pushed me away. As long as she was dealing with them, taking care of herself—

I guess that was the problem.

It makes so much sense, when I think about it. I can articulate the words as well as any therapist. I couldn't save my mom (jury's out on the final results there, but at the time Mom was drinking heavily and unwilling to listen to ideas about help) so I tried to save my girlfriend.

I thought I could love her enough to convince her to stop hurting herself.

It was stupid. Love doesn't work like that. Self-loathing doesn't work like that.

I *know* that.

But knowing something and really believing it are different.

My head gets it. My heart?

I still want to stitch her heart together.

Even though—

I have no idea how her heart is doing. Maybe she's fine.

Maybe she's happy. Maybe she's taking her meds and eating right and exercising.

Maybe I was the problem all along.

I certainly can't—

Fuck, I don't even know.

The singer's groan ceases as I pause the song. I'm already on the band's second album. In some ways, it's like the first. There's still anger and energy and that youthful need to take over the world.

But there's something else too. The guy drops his defenses. He stops bragging about how little he cares about his ex. Starts admitting how much the world is slipping through his fingers.

I'm not sure who I am in this metaphor—the lyricist or the listener. Both, maybe.

I should clarify—there's something about this string of albums; they always underline my thoughts—but it doesn't.

My head is still a mess.

I want to help Ariel. That's clear.

But when I start thinking about more than that—

Maybe it's better if I cut the line there. I don't fix situations. I make them worse. I'm smart enough to understand that and stay away from people who are…

Whatever I should call it.

Ariel isn't broken or damaged or confused. Yeah, she's hurting over her ex. She's in a tough spot. She's young.

But she knows what she wants.

She tells me when I'm overstepping.

She demands people meet her needs.

For all intents and purposes, Ariel is a well-functioning, well-adjusted member of society.

If I'm not trying to fix her, maybe I won't break her worse.

Maybe I can actually help her.

Maybe it will be good for me.

Even if it hurts worse when we part. Hell, that's progress. I'm thinking about another woman. Wanting more time with another woman.

If it was just sex, it would be an easy question.

But it's more than sex. There's another life at stake. A tiny, helpless life.

There's a big part of me that thinks it's best I stay away. I can't fuck it up if I'm not involved.

Then there's this other part, the one that can't stop imagining a kid in tiny black Converse.

"Fuck, what happened to you?" Wes interrupts my quiet contemplation. He's leaning against the shop window, sucking cold brew through a straw. He takes a long look at me and shakes his head. "You start obsessing over Grace's Facebook or something?"

No, I haven't checked her social media in forever. Since she posted the pic with the musician.

She looked so fucking happy.

I want that for her. I do. It's just—

Why couldn't I accomplish that?

"You got me." I make a show of rolling my eyes, but it doesn't come across as playful. More pained.

Wes's nose scrunches. "It's not about Grace?"

"I have work to do."

"You're an hour early." He follows me into the shop. Offers me his cold brew.

I take a sip. It's good shit. Rich, creamy, a little sweet. "Have to catch up on design."

"Here?" Wes raises a brow. "And not at your apartment? Where it's quiet? And free of irritating family members?"

I can't help but laugh.

"So it's not hopeless." He smiles. "That's a start."

I hand back his cold brew. "A lot on my mind."

"Isn't there always?"

"Not all of us are as enlightened as you."

He nods *true*. "It is freeing, only thinking of babes and wine."

"You're still selling this story about you loving wine?"

"Jealousy doesn't look good on you."

"Uh-huh."

"It's sickening."

"Your concern is heartwarming," I deadpan.

He plays his role. "You know how hard it is being the only one who cares about your happiness?"

I shoot him a *get real* look.

He shrugs *I am real*.

I move into my suite. Drop my sketchbook on the chair.

Wes leans against the half-wall. Drops his pained persona. Taps his toe against the tile floor, the picture of casual. "I always wonder: is Chase secretly like me, only he's picturing tortured chicks with too much eyeliner?"

"Who says it's too much?"

His laugh gets bigger. "I get it. You hit puberty when the emo look was big. Now, you're helpless against a chick with flat-ironed hair and eyeliner."

"You know me so well."

"Same thing happened to me with Quinn. The glasses. She was the first girl I wanted to fuck—"

"And now you fuck her every day?"

"Well, yeah, but—"

"Somehow you always manage to work that in." My voice lifts to something teasing. This can be easy. That's possible.

"Look at her."

"You won't hit me?" I ask.

"If you look with your eyes." He offers his drink again. "I know she's not your type."

"Do you?" I take the drink, sip, offer it back.

He motions *keep it*. "Not enough eyeliner."

"I thought I was into the babe—"

"Ariel? Is that why you're in a mood?"

"I'm not in a mood."

"Don't think this counts against your thing for emo and goth chicks. She was dressed entirely in black," Wes says.

I open my sketchbook to the page I doodled at the coffee shop. The mended heart.

I always thought I was the thread in this metaphor, but maybe I'm not.

Maybe I'm the broken heart.

It's not inaccurate.

Only—

I can't go into this expecting anything but sex.

"Ariel isn't like that," I say.

Wes's eyes go wide. "You're into her."

"Isn't that your point?"

"Yeah, but I didn't think it would stick." He pushes off the wall. Moves closer. "You had a look."

"What look."

"When I said Ariel." His light eyes fill with an equal mix of enthusiasm and victory. "Like that."

"Maybe I watched *The Little Mermaid* when I was going through puberty?"

"Maybe you're making up fantasies of the cute math geek." He jumps—actually jumps—and claps his hands together. "Fuck, you are."

I shrug like I don't care.

His smile gets wider. "Griffin is gonna shit himself."

"You two talk about me?"

"Fuck yeah. Usually shit about how you're hopeless and miserable."

"You sound like him."

"No." Wes's laugh is knowing. "He says a lot worse shit."

I can imagine. "We're just friends."

"That always means you're not just friends."

"If that's what you want to believe."

He nods *hell yeah, it's what I want to believe.* "You want to fuck her."

"Look at her."

He laughs so hard he doubles over. He clutches his stomach, stomps his feet, reaches for something steady. "Oh my God."

"Glad to amuse you."

"Oh my fucking God." He stifles a laugh. "You think —" Wes breaks into another giggle fit. So much that he drops to his ass. Kicks the ground with his feet. "That works—" A giggle breaks up his sentence. "Coming from you?"

"Yeah…"

He shakes his head. Struggles through an inhale. "You don't look at girls."

"I'm twenty-nine."

"You don't look at women." His laugh steadies. He stands. Looks at me like I'm ridiculous. "You rejected three chicks yesterday."

"Maybe I'm picky."

"One of them was wearing enough eyeliner to open a Sephora." He jumps to his feet.

"You know about Sephora?"

He smiles. "I support my girlfriend if she wants to go to the mall."

"'Cause she'll model the dresses she tries on for you?"

"And then I'll sneak into the dressing room with her and make her come." He rolls his eyes *obviously*.

Fuck, I miss that. Wanting to be around someone so much I gladly joined her at the mall.

And, well—

I had my share of dressing room sex.

It was always fucking amazing.

Would Ariel be into that? She doesn't seem like the mall type. More the *buying all my clothes online, on a site that sells reasonable but high quality basics* type.

She has to get those tight black jeans somewhere.

There has to be somewhere I can demand she bend over and roll them to her knees, so they're binding her thighs as I fuck her.

Somewhere besides her bedroom.

"Shit. I got you started." Wes shakes his head. "I know it's been a while since you thought about fucking anyone. Don't forget to keep it in your pants."

"Thanks for the tip."

He laughs. "If you must, the bathroom's over there." He motions to the bathroom in back.

"Thanks. I almost forget." I can't help but laugh. It's absurd. That it's been so long since I've openly wanted someone. That Wes and I are talking about fucking ourselves in the bathroom. That this conversation is so easy.

"You fuck her yet?"

"She's Forest's kid sister."

"And?"

"You think he wants someone like me with his sister?"

"You're not as awful as you think you are," Wes says.

I almost blush. I want to believe that. I really do. "You sure about that?"

Wes nods *yeah*.

The door rings *bing-bong* as someone enters. Footsteps move closer. Steady ones.

Hunter moves into the main room. His blue eyes—a shade lighter than mine—move over me and Wes.

He reads the room. Keeps his distance.

Wes shakes his head *this is stupid*. "Not to get all Griffin, but if you want me to pretend it's normal you two don't speak, well—" He looks from Hunter to me. "Get the fuck over yourself, Chase."

"I'm just sitting here." I turn the page in my sketchbook. Pick up my pen. I need something to steady my thoughts. A way out of this conversation that doesn't make me a bitter asshole.

"Putting out vibes," Wes says.

"I thought I was vibing on Ariel?" My shoulders tense. There's a storm cloud over this conversation. It's not Hunter. It's me. My inability to let go, forgive, trust, move on.

"Ariel Ballard?" Hunter takes a step closer. It's tiny, a test. Like I'm a wounded cat that might run at any moment.

"Yeah," Wes says. "She doesn't even wear eyeliner."

Hunter's laugh is easy. "But she dresses exclusively in black." His eyes meet mine. His lips curl into a smile. "She's smart."

"Too smart for him," Wes says.

"Not that smart if she's into him," Hunter teases.

I try to laugh, but it's stilted. I can tolerate listening to the conversation. But I'm not at participating. Not like this.

"He does have a good body," Wes says.

"And the tattoos." Hunter nods. "Some girls are into it."

"With tattoo artist older brothers?" Wes shakes his head *I don't think so*. "Did that work for you?"

"I'm with Emma, aren't I?" Hunter asks.

"Yeah, but you have a certain charm." Wes looks from Hunter to me. "Nah, actually, you and Chase are both miserable assholes. If there's hope for you, there's hope for him."

Hunter flips him off.

I do the same.

Maybe I can do this. Maybe I can have an honest, easy conversation with my brother. "It did work for you, Hunter." There isn't enough lightness to my voice. But there's some.

For a second Wes's eyes go wide with surprise. Then he blinks and launches into teasing. "Yeah, not like Hunter has anything else going for him."

Hunter nods *yeah*, still dumbstruck.

I run my hand through my hair, trying to project an easy, breezy attitude and failing miserably. "She… Uh…"

The opening door saves me. Footsteps move closer.

Forest and Holden move into the main room.

So much for salvation.

"Hey." Forest nods his usual hello. He takes in the scene —the three of us close enough to talk—and shoots me a look. *Is everything okay?*

I nod *sure*.

He stays apprehensive, but he doesn't push. "Can I borrow Chase?" He nods hellos to my brothers.

Wes shakes his head *fuck, this is gonna blow up*. He and Hunter exchange one of those brotherly looks—one I'm not a part of—then they grab Holden and move into the main room.

I brace myself for *what the fuck do you think you're doing offering to impregnate my sister? You think I'd let someone like you touch her?*

But Forest's voice drops to a completely different tone. An all business tone. "It's about work."

"Sure." I nod to the lobby.

He follows me into the empty space. Drops his voice to a whisper. "Oddball is closing. Owner is selling. We don't know if the new owner will want to keep us."

"I can talk to Brendon."

His eyes light up. "You sure?"

"We'd be lucky to have you permanently."

His shoulders drop with relief. "I hate asking—"

"Seriously, Forest. It's not a problem." If anything, it's a solution. At least, if I've been reading the owners here right. "You're doing me a favor."

"Yeah?" He raises a brow *that's bullshit*.

"You think they keep me around for my sunny disposition?"

He chuckles. "Why else?"

I share his laugh. "Maybe it's the looks."

He makes that *you're okay* motion. Offers me his hand.

I shake.

He pulls me into a hug. Pats me on the back. "You're a good friend."

But all I hear is *then why the fuck are you keeping secrets? You want to push him away too?*

Chapter Twenty

CHASE

My day is back-to-back appointments. Short break for lunch. Another for coffee. Then the steady buzz of the needle and the groans of Emma's favorite music.

My brother's girlfriend slash the part-time manager has the same taste in music as I do.

Maybe that should embarrass me—she's nearly ten years my junior—but it doesn't. I've never been embarrassed by the things I love.

The band she plays isn't my favorite, but they're familiar. I can see Grace singing their lyrics, squealing over tickets to a show, promising I was way hotter than their lead singer.

And I can see Ariel sitting on my couch, laughing about my taste, humming to the melody, looking at me with all the understanding in the world.

Fuck, I want her. I really do.

So much that I need to do the right thing. I need to stay out of her life. So I don't fuck that up too.

I practice explanations on my walk to the gym, during

my bench presses, during my shower, as I cook dinner (for two, just in case she's early), while I set the table.

The second she steps into my apartment, I lose my train of thought.

"Hey." She looks up at me with those big, brown eyes. "Did you..." She crosses the room to me. Takes my hand. Squeezes tightly. "Did you decide?"

This is where I say *no, I'm sorry. I like you too much to risk fucking you up.*

But I don't.

I stare into her dark eyes, and I say, "I'll do it."

Chapter Twenty-One

CHASE

A riel's smile spreads over her face. It lights up her dark eyes until they're brighter than the sun. "Really?"

I nod. "Really." I'm out of my mind. I am. My head is still screaming *what the fuck are you doing?* But my heart?

For the first time, my heart is full. Warm. Easy.

This is right.

As long as I manage to keep from fucking shit up, this is right.

I can do that. I just have to look at the past. See the patterns. Avoid them.

Mom, Hunter, Grace—I tried to fix something.

There's nothing to fix here. And even if there is, if I find something—

I'm not doing that again.

Maybe I'm not capable of loving someone in a way that makes them happy.

Maybe I'm not capable of loving someone in a way that makes me happy.

But I can do this.

Fuck, I really want to do this.

Ariel throws her arms around me. "Thank you." She squeezes tightly. "I... oh my God, Chase. I..." Her fingers dig into my bare arms. "I don't know what to say."

"Thank you is good."

"Right. Um..." She looks up at me. "You're not wearing a shirt."

"Yeah." I can't help but chuckle. "You keep showing up right after my shower."

"I try to be early, but if I'm too early—"

"It's good." I release her. "I like the way you stare."

She takes a small step backward. It's nothing. It only puts six inches between us. Her eyes move over me slowly. Shoulders, chest, stomach, hips.

"That."

"Oh." Her tongue slides over her lips. "This... well... we're doing this."

"Yeah." We're doing this. I'm doing this. I'm helping her without fucking shit up. Giving her exactly what she wants and nothing else.

"So I should look at you like that."

"You always look at me like that, princess." My voice drops to something low and demanding. It's easy shifting to sex with her. Easier than it should be.

But, then again, I've been fucking myself to thoughts of her for two weeks straight.

This is already a replay.

Ariel's teeth sink into her bottom lip. She takes another step backward. Smooths her tight black jeans. "I... Uh... You're eating dinner?"

"Yeah." I motion to the plate on the table. "You eat?"

She shakes her head. "No, but maybe... maybe we could eat after?"

"After?"

She nods. "Unless… I mean, I'd like to start today. Not just because I'm fertile." Her nose scrunches. "Sorry, I know that's kind of clinical."

"I'm used to it."

"Still, it's like we said." Her cheeks flush. "It's not just that I'm—"

"Primed?" I offer.

Her laugh is nervous. "Yeah. I also… I want to have sex with you." Her blush deepens. "Is that too blunt?"

"It's perfect." I motion to the couch. "You want a drink?"

"Just water. I'm—"

"I know."

"I don't mind if you have something." She moves to the couch. Sits next to the armchair on the right, the one closest to me.

I store the food in the fridge, pour two glasses of water, bring them to the couch.

Her fingers brush mine as she takes it. "Thank you." Her throat quivers as she swallows. "We don't have to—"

I nod. "I know."

"It's… uh… this is kind of awkward, huh?"

I sit on the middle cushion. A foot away from her. So she can come to me. Or maybe so I can breathe. It's hard to say.

"Like…" Ariel turns toward me. "All of a sudden everything is loaded." She takes a long sip. "Before we were just—"

"Here to talk about the possibility of me getting you pregnant?"

"Yeah, I guess, that's… A good point. And that brings me to something else." She leans forward. Sets her glass on the table. "Have you been tested?"

I can't help but chuckle.

"What?" She stammers. "How was I supposed to ask that?"

"No, that was perfect." I drop my glass next to hers. "Hold on—"

"Then why?"

"I was just thinking." I stand. Move toward the bedroom. "This is the first time I've been accused of fucking someone post-Grace."

"I trust you, but—"

"You don't have to justify anything." I turn. Go straight to the dresser. Find my last test results. They're buried deep, under several pairs of jeans.

It means something, that I kept these, that I got tested every six months despite abstinence.

I move into the main room. Hand Ariel the stack.

"Oh." She riffles through the tests. "There are a lot of these."

"Every six months, right?"

"Yeah." She sets the papers on the coffee table. "But, um, if you didn't sleep with anyone since Grace, then why…"

"Habit, I guess." Or maybe some part of me was ready for this.

Her brow furrows like she's working something out. "I, uh, you saw mine."

"I did."

She presses her lips together. "Is it weird if I say this is weird again?"

I shake my head. "Most people drink to skip the awkwardness."

"Right." She nods. "I really don't mind if you do. If that's your routine."

Maybe I should. It might settle the nerves in my stomach. But I want to feel this. Every second of it.

"So… um… are you ready to start today?" Vulnerability streaks her expression.

I want to say yes, but I can't lie to her. "I'm not sure."

"You have technical issues?" Her voice is matter-of-fact, even as her gaze goes right to my crotch.

"No." I can't help but laugh. I haven't had sex in two years. I get hard like *that*. Fuck, it's happening now, all from the eager look in her eyes. "It's more—"

"Emotional?"

"Yeah." I turn toward her. "I haven't kissed anyone in two years."

She nods with understanding.

Fuck, Ariel is something else. Empathetic, smart, funny, quirky.

Beautiful.

It's hard believe she wants me for this.

She has her pick of guys—the entire state of California is lining up for the job—and she wants me.

"We don't have to kiss." Her eyes stay on my face. They study my expression.

"We do."

"Oh."

I need those soft red lips against mine. "It's not a physical problem, princess." The pet name falls off my lips. Pushes my mind to dirty places. "I want to throw you on the bed, roll those jeans to your ankles, and split you in half."

Her pupils dilate.

"Just saying it makes me hard."

"Chase—"

"But I'm not sure I can… No, I can. Physically. It's more—" I try to find a good way to explain it. I barely understand it myself. It's tricky. "I haven't tried. I don't know how it's gonna go. I might freeze."

Her fingers curl around my wrist. "You're scared?"

"That's a good way of putting it."

Her laugh is easy. "I am too." She looks up at me. "It's um, well, my mom, before she died, she always talked about consent."

"Yeah?"

"Well, not always. Just the one time, really." Her cheeks flush. She's as nervous as I am. More even. "I was young when she died."

"Fuck, Ariel, I'm sorry."

"Thank you. But I don't want to talk about that right now."

I nod *sure*.

"She gave me the talk before she… She only hit a few points. Listen to my instincts—"

"Does that work?"

"Not usually, but that's why I'm here. There's something about you. My gut likes you."

I can't help but laugh. "Lucky me."

"Yeah." Her laugh is more nervous. "And also to follow my heart, even if it's not practical." She runs her thumb over my skin. Softly. Like she can't help but touch me. "And consent. I should never let a boy do anything I don't want him to do. I should say no if I don't like something, and yes if I do. And I shouldn't leave it all up to him. I should tell him what I want."

"Was that awkward?"

"Yeah." Her blush deepens. "My first homecoming dance, I met my date at school. And, right away, I told him: you can touch me here—" She places her hands on her hips. "And here." Then her waist. "And here." Then her shoulders. "During the slow song, if you want to kiss me, lean closer, and I'll kiss you."

"How'd he take it?"

"He laughed and stared at the ground a lot."

"Did he—"

"Touch me?" She swallows hard. "He was polite."

"Did he lean in?"

"Oh." Her laugh lights up her eyes. "No. But I respected that. He didn't want to kiss me."

"Or he was scared."

"And I wasn't?" Her chest spills into her tight tank top as she leans closer. "Mom underlined that too. I should make sure I get consent from boys. Because sex shouldn't be this thing where boys try to unlock girls' panties—"

"Did she say really say 'unlock girls' panties'?" I need to stop looking at her chest. I need to look her in the eyes. To feel this.

Or maybe that's all wrong. Maybe I need to stare at her round tits and her narrow waist and her lush hips. To make this base and dirty and nothing else.

It's not possible.

I can't fuck Ariel without feeling something.

I'm not sure I can *fuck* Ariel at all.

No matter how dirty or rough or aggressive this gets, it's intimate.

I can take the emptiness that used to come with casual shit.

But the fullness that comes with—

Fuck.

"Your mom was a badass." I try to steer my thoughts to where they need to go. Anywhere but the lightness in my chest.

"She was. She liked you. She'd like you now." She leans back. Releases my arm. "So, I, uh… if you want to stop, that's okay. But I have to be honest. I don't read signals very well."

"You think?" I try to drop into teasing her. Get most of the way there.

She smiles. "Okay, maybe it's obvious. I just… I want you to know that I respect whatever you want. If you're trying to say something and I'm not getting it, it's because I don't get it. Just tell me. Even if it's awkward or it kills the mood. Because nothing would be worse for the mood than finding out you didn't want to—"

Fuck, she's too adorable.

I lean in. Bring my lips to hers.

She wraps her hands around my arms. Holds on tightly as she kisses back.

She's soft, eager, pliable.

She tastes so fucking good, like spearmint and like Ariel.

She pulls back with a sigh. "Oh."

"Too fast?"

"No?" She shakes her head. "Perfect." She leans in. Digs her fingers into my skin. Kisses me.

Her lips part.

I slip my tongue into her mouth. Play with hers.

Softly.

Then harder.

She groans against my lips. Brings her hands to my shoulders. Climbs into my lap. "Does this mean we're—"

"Yeah."

"Thank God." She stares down at me, her brown eyes full of desire. "I really want to fuck you."

Chapter Twenty-Two

CHASE

A riel digs her fingers into my shoulders. "This isn't fair."

"Yeah?"

She traces the tattoo covering my right shoulder. "You have all this—"

"The ink?"

Her nod is heavy. She watches her finger glide over my skin, her pupils wide, her cheeks flushed. "You're a sex god and I'm—" She swallows hard. "I…"

She's nervous.

Fuck, I'm not sure which of us is more nervous.

It's been two years for me, but she's the one with purpose. She's the one changing her life.

When I think about it—

My limbs get light. My whole body gets light. Like I'm about to float off the couch.

I need to be here. Need to feel every inch of her skin against mine. Need her soft lips on my—

I need to keep this physical. To keep my brain tuned to her perfect tits and her red lips.

If I start thinking about—

If I start thinking, period—

"Come here." I bring my hands to her hips. Pull her closer. Closer—

Her eyes go wide as she brushes against me. "You're already—"

"I told you."

"But—"

"I've got a knock-out in my lap and she's staring at me like she's desperate to get her hand around my cock—"

Her blush deepens.

"Of course, I'm hard."

"Chase... I..."

"You want to touch me, princess?" The words are awkward on my tongue. It's been too long. She's too real.

My fantasies of Ariel are hot as fuck, but they're smooth in an otherworldly way. That makes it easy to forget all the scratches on the record.

Actually having her in my lap, smelling her tangerine shampoo—

Fuck.

Her nod is heavy. Needy.

It makes my balls tighten.

She *is* a sex goddess. Sweet. Adorable. Innocent. How is it possible she doesn't see it?

Those dark glasses alone—

I bring my hand to her hair. Undo the tie pinning it to the back of her head.

Dark strands fall over her shoulders. Frame her coffee eyes in the perfect shade of deep brown.

She turns her head to one side, suddenly shy.

My heart thuds against my chest. There's no way to deny it. This is Ariel in my lap. The sweet kid who used to beg for peeks of my sketches. The girl who lectured me about drinking in moderation. The friend who's asking me to bring another life into this world.

It's a lot.

Too much at once.

I press my eyelids together. Suck a breath through my teeth. Push my thoughts to dirty places.

"Take off your tank top." I make my voice low. Demanding. The voice I use when I'm ready to issue orders.

It sends my head in too many different directions.

Then Ariel turns to me and looks me right in the eyes and all my thoughts tune to her.

"I like that." She brings her hands to the bottom of her shirt. "When you get bossy."

"Off now." I drop my voice another octave.

Her chest heaves with her inhale. She nods *yes*, rolls her black tank top up her torso and over her head.

It lands on the floor with a thud.

She shifts her hips, settling into my lap. "Now, we're even." Her fingers brush my bare shoulders, collarbones, chest.

Her touch is soft. Intimate. Eager.

Her hand feels so fucking good on my skin.

I need it everywhere.

I need that pretty hand wrapped around my cock.

But, first, I need to make her come.

I really need to make her come.

"No." I bring my hand to her chest. Trace a line over the bottom of her lacy black bra.

"No…" Her eyelids flutter together. Her head falls to one side. Her fingers dig into my skin.

"Not even close, princess."

She lets out a soft groan.

CRYSTAL KASWELL

It's fucking music. Better than my favorite album. Better than anything.

I trace the top of her bra. Left to right. Then back. Again. Again.

Her nails scrape my skin. "Chase…" My name falls off her lips like it was made for it.

I need more of that.

I need her groaning my name as she comes.

But one thing at a time.

"I…" She rocks her hips against me. "You're really good at this."

I was, once upon a time. Now, I'm not so sure. But I can't let my head go there.

I don't want to think about that shit.

I don't want to think at all.

We're exactly where we're supposed to be. Maybe nothing else makes sense. But Ariel groaning over my touch—

It's perfect.

I bring my lips to her neck. Kiss her softly. Then harder. Harder.

She squeezes me with her thighs.

I scrape my teeth against her neck.

"Fuck." She rakes her nails over my chest. "Do that again."

"You like it rough, princess?"

Her response is a groan.

"How rough?"

"I… I never…" She trips over her tongue.

She doesn't know.

I'm the person who helps her figure it out.

What the fuck did I do to get so lucky?

"Like this." I drag my teeth over her skin softly. Not enough to hurt. Just enough she feels it.

"Mm-hmm."

I do it again, a little harder. Hard enough it hurts.

She groans a little louder.

I go a little harder.

"Fuck." Her nails dig into my skin. "Yes."

"This?" I knot my hand in her hair. Tug at her hair to pull her head back.

I do it slowly, softly. Enough she knows I'm in charge, but not enough to hurt.

"Mm-hmm. Chase…" She hooks her arm around my neck. "That. Exactly that. If it's not enough—"

"It's perfect, princess."

The pet name makes her groan.

Blood rushes to my cock.

I want to torture her for hours, but I don't have hours in me. Not today. I've been thinking about this for too fucking long.

"Stand up, princess. I want to watch you strip."

She nods. Presses her palm into my chest to push herself up. But she doesn't reach for her bra or her jeans. She nods to the bedroom.

Fuck, she's a genius.

I follow her into the small space. Press the door closed.

She flicks the light switch.

Everything rearranges.

We're in my fucking bedroom. Ariel is in my fucking bedroom.

It's too familiar. And too different.

My body whines for her soft skin.

My head tells me to get the fuck over it.

But my heart—

It's pounding like a drum.

Ariel's eyes meet mine. She studies my expression. She

must notice something, because her brow furrows. "Is this too much—"

"No." Maybe. I push off the door. Suck a breath through my teeth. I can do this. I want to do this. I really do.

She traces a line down my body, stopping at my crotch. "You're still—"

"Yeah."

"But you…"

"Here—" I turn the main light off. Turn the string lights on. I told Griffin he was an idiot when he insisted on the decor. But I have to admit, he was right.

The soft white glow makes the room feel like something out of a movie. Sweet. Romantic. Fantastical.

It draws a line between the bed I shared with Grace and the bed that's all mine.

I focus on the things that make the room mine. The soft lights. The black curtains. The black sheets.

Ariel staring with confusion in her eyes.

Fuck, even though she's flushed and wanting, her expression is the picture of patience. Like she's ready to wait forever if that's what it takes.

It's not.

I just—

I roll my shoulders back. Suck a breath through my teeth. Push out a slow exhale.

Her voice is soft. "If you want to stop—"

"Fuck no." I'm here. In this moment. Only this moment. "Take off your bra—"

"Are you sure?"

"Now."

She hesitates for a moment. Then something switches in her eyes. She nods *yes*, reaches around her back, unhooks her bra.

She brings one hand to her chest. Holds the black lace in place as the straps fall off her shoulders.

God damn, is she really this demure or is she playing it up for me?

My eyes go to hers. The desire in those soulful browns. The flush in those round cheeks. The part of her red lips.

God dammit, I need those lips on me.

I need those clothes on the floor.

I need her sprawled out under me.

On *my* black sheets.

In *my* space.

In *my* life.

I motion *come closer*.

She takes a shy step. Another. Another.

I wait for her to come to me.

When she does, I run my fingers over the line of her chin. Down her neck. Over her collarbone. All the way to the outline of her bra.

She shudders. Drops the garment on the floor.

Her cheeks flush with equal parts shyness and desire. "Is it—"

I take her hand, bring it to my cock.

She feels me over my jeans. "Chase… I…" She looks up at me with that same shyness. "Can I?"

I'm not sure what she's asking, but whatever it is, the answer's yes. I nod.

She undoes my jeans. Rolls them off my hips. Rubs me over my boxers.

I cup her breast with one hand. Grab her ass with the other.

There's all this fabric in the way, but I can still feel her. Her palm against my cock. Her flesh against my hand.

She's soft and eager.

Fuck, she's too good at this.

My eyelids flutter together. My fingers dig into her skin.

I drag my thumb over her nipple. Softly. Then harder. Harder. There—

She groans that same *fuck, I need you* groan.

"You have perfect tits, princess." I open my eyes. Bring them to her eyes. Cheeks. Lips. Chest.

"Fuck."

"Responsive."

She groans as I bring my other hand to her chest. Toy with both her nipples.

"You like hands or mouth better?"

She pushes out something that's all vowels.

"This?" I draw circles around her nipples until she's groaning. Then I bring my lips to her lips.

She kisses back. Rubs me with her palm as I scrape my teeth over her flesh.

Her groans vibrate down my throat.

I break our kiss. Bring my lips to her chest. Take her nipple into my mouth.

Suck softly.

Then harder.

Then it's the scrape of my teeth. Enough she feels it.

Enough it hurts.

"Fuck." She rubs me harder. "Chase." She presses her lips to my shoulder. "Fuck."

I toy with her. Suck softly. Then harder. Then hard enough she yelps.

I flick my tongue up and down, left to right, in circles and zigzags.

Soft pressure makes her groan.

But the scrape of my teeth—

She melts into me.

Ariel wraps her fingers around my wrist. She brings my hand to the waistband of her jeans. "Chase—"

I unbutton her pants. Roll them off her hips. Down her thighs.

Fuck, those black panties. Soft lacy things that match her bra. Soft lacy things she wore for me.

My cock pulses.

I need to make her come.

Now.

I brush my hand against her. It's soft, barely a touch, but I can feel her.

Soft. Wet. Eager.

I run my fingers over her panties.

"Fuck." She looks up at me with eager eyes. "Chase—"

I push her panties aside. "You always get this wet, princess?"

Her hair falls over her face as she shakes her head.

"Only for me?"

"Chase—"

I tease her with one finger.

Then two.

Her eyelids press together. Her fingers dig into my hips. Her hand stays wrapped around me.

"You keep touching me like that and I'm gonna come in my boxers," I groan.

She nods with understanding, but she keeps her hand where it is.

I watch bliss spread over her expression as I slip one finger insider her. Then two.

Her nails dig into my skin.

Slowly, I push my fingers deeper. Deeper. There—

Her eyelids flutter closed.

Her teeth sink into her lip.

I drive two fingers into her.

She pushes my boxers over my hips. Wraps her hand around me. Works me with steady pumps.

"Princess—" Fuck, that feels too good. "I'm gonna come—"

She cuts me off with her lips.

I drive my fingers into her a little faster.

She works me with that same perfect rhythm.

I bring my hand to her clit. I need to make her come. I need to make her come now, so I can—

Fuck.

"Chase." Her nails scrape my stomach. "You're… Don't stop."

I keep that same pressure. Same speed.

Her brow knits.

Her teeth sink into her lip.

Her chest heaves.

She claws at my skin as I bring her to the edge.

Groans my name as she goes over it.

She keeps working me with those same steady stokes.

I bring her back to the edge.

With the next brush of her hand, I come. I groan her name as I spill into her palm.

Pleasure spreads through my stomach, thighs, chest. All the way to my fingers and toes.

It's different than when I'm alone.

Warmer. Brighter. Bigger.

Like my entire being is brimming with bliss.

I keep working her.

She keeps groaning my name.

Then she's there, raking her nails over my skin, melting into my arms, coming on my hand.

I rub her through her orgasm.

When I release her, she blinks her eyes open. Looks at me with a sheepish. "Sorry."

"Sorry?" What the fuck is she sorry for?

"I got carried away."

Oh. She's—Oh. "Don't fucking apologize."

"Good." Her cheeks flush. "Do you think you have another one in you?"

I can't help but laugh. She's adorable. She's Ariel. "Yeah." I grab a tissue from the nightstand. Bring it to her. "After we eat."

"Need to keep up your strength?" she teases.

"Exactly."

Chapter Twenty-Three

ARIEL

I 'm not scared.

I'm not terrified.

I'm not even nervous.

It's just Chase is too sexy.

That's the only reason.

Sure, there's this voice in my head screaming *oh my God, have you thought this through? It's one thing having sex. It's one thing setting intentions. Hell, it's one thing getting pregnant.*

Actually being a mother—

That's a whole different ballgame.

Can I really handle that?

It's not that I don't want it. God, I want it so badly. Even now, with my pulse racing and my stomach flip-flopping, there's this warmth in my heart.

A voice screaming *want baby now.*

Seriously. It's like something out of a romantic comedy. I'm the baby crazy lady with the ticking biological clock.

Want. Baby. Now.

Terrified. Of. Motherhood.

It's possible to feel two things at once. Conflicting

things. Like my desire to unlock Chase's heart and my desire to stay a thousand miles away.

"Princess?" Chase's voice is sweet. Teasing. The one he uses when I'm drifting off.

Shit, I am drifting off.

"You okay?"

"Yeah. Just..." I turn to him, willing his clear blue eyes to inspire a response. They do. It's just not a verbal one.

My heartbeat picks up.

My stomach flutters.

My fingers curl into my thighs.

He's so pretty. And handsome. And sexy. And sweet. And caring.

"You want something besides water?" He motions to the fridge. It's packed with fresh food. A rainbow of fruits and veggies and a packed meat drawer.

"You cook a lot?"

"Yeah." His chuckle is knowing. "It's less food than it looks like."

"You're a..." How do I say *you are super freaking hot and I want to pounce on you again, so please take this as a compliment, when I say you're clearly a man with a high bodyweight who needs a lot of calories. It's all muscle. It's a lot of muscle. It's not that you're fat. Do you even have any body fat? I'm concerned about your health with your incredibly low level of body fat, but not concerned enough to stop staring at your abs.* "I, um... I know." Okay, there's no good way to say that. "I cook a lot too."

"You've expanded beyond Southeast Asia?"

"Uh, sorta." My heart twists at the memory of Phillip teaching me to make pho. The way he laughed when I tried to sip the broth right away. *We need to let it simmer, sweetheart. Otherwise, we won't enjoy the full depth of the flavors.* "I do pasta also."

"You miss him?"

"No…" My stomach drops. "Yeah. Sorta. I think I miss *it* more."

"The sex?"

My cheeks flush. "The companionship. The stability. Knowing someone was waiting at home for me."

"You live with your dad."

"Yeah, but he's away half the time. I usually went to Phillip's place after work. God, the last few months, I'd be there alone for hours." I force my gaze to the fridge. Chase's eyes are too intense. It's impossible to transition away from the subject of my ex-boyfriend. The one who dumped me because he didn't want a future with me. "Water is good."

"Sure." He fills two glasses. Drops both on the table.

I take a seat. Press my palms to the wood. No touching him. Or myself. Nothing that will make this complicated. "He's busy. He's a resident now. But that started a while ago. I think…"

"It's easy to take shit for granted." He turns to the stove —he's warming dinner in a pan. "We all do it."

"Maybe that's it." I take a long sip of water. It soothes my throat, but it does nothing to ease the *thump-thump* of my heart. "At first, I thought it was a sudden thing. That the only reason why we ended was my ultimatum—"

"You asked him to—"

"Yeah." I swallow another sip. "I told him I'd had my IUD removed and I needed to get pregnant right away."

He chuckles.

"What?"

"Most people don't act that fast."

"I didn't really have a choice."

"Even so…" His laugh is easy. "Most people don't know what they want that clearly."

I guess that's true. Sorta. "He knew. He knew right away that it wasn't what he wanted."

"You sure about that?"

"He broke up with me. I told him I needed to do it now, then, three days later, he broke up with me."

"Doesn't mean he was sure."

What?

"You told him why?"

I nod. "You and Phillip are the only people who know."

"You trust him?"

"Yeah." My chest gets heavy. "He's a good guy. He really is. A little awkward and oblivious sometimes. But smart. Caring. Practical. He was so practical about it. Even though… Is it wrong I hope it hurt him?"

"You're asking me?" He chuckles.

Of course I'm asking him. Sure, Chase isn't over his ex, but he doesn't harbor any ill-will toward her. At least, not as far as I can tell.

It's not like he wants her to die in a fire just because his favorite song is about a guy who wants his ex to die in a fire (even though said guy supposedly doesn't care about said ex).

Sure, Chase likes songs that are filled with toxic masculinity and an undercurrent of misogyny.

But I like songs filled with allusions to—

God, eighties songs are full of messed up shit.

My love of eighties music doesn't make me a rave going swinger.

His love of pop-punk doesn't make him a bitter asshole.

"Why does everyone think you're a bitter asshole?" I bite my lip. Not the most tactful wording.

But he doesn't grimace. He just laughs.

"Sorry." My cheeks flush. "I, uh… I should have asked that in a more—"

"I'm glad you asked it like that."

"It's kind of rude."

"It's true." He turns the burner off. Scoops stir fry onto two plates. Then rice. "Everyone thinks I'm a bitter asshole. It's not like saying 'everyone thinks Chase has a tendency to hold grudges' changes the facts."

"Is that why?" I stand. Move to the counter. Next to him.

God, he's so warm and he smells so good. Like sweat and soap and Chase.

I want to touch him, kiss him, lick him.

I actually want to put my tongue on parts of his body. And not just the normal ones. Though I really want that.

And not just because I'm terrified of what happens if we actually do this.

Uh…

Let's talk about him. And not my fear. That's easier. And more interesting.

"You do hold grudges." I grab the silverware. Forks and chopsticks. In case he doesn't like chopsticks. Or uses them exclusively.

"I wouldn't put it that way."

"I thought you didn't like euphemisms?"

"Yeah, I'd stick with bitter asshole." His lips curl into a half-smile.

I move toward the table. Away from the magnetic pull of his blue eyes.

God, those eyes. I want to stare into them forever. "But you're not."

He arches a brow.

I place our silverware. Sit. Sip. Swallow. "Do you really believe that? Or do you just want me to believe it?"

He sets my plate in front of me. Sits across from me. "Good question."

"I, uh… thanks again. For dinner."

"Sure."

I pick up my chopsticks. Scoop broccoli and rice. "It's a very caring thing to do—"

"I was cooking anyway."

"You didn't have to offer me any."

He arches a brow. "I'm supposed to send you home hungry?"

"Other guys would."

"They have no game."

I laugh. "Is that it?"

"Yeah. If you get hungry, you'll leave."

"So it's just to keep me here."

He nods *yeah*.

"Do you actually believe that?"

His chuckle is soft. "No. But it's true."

I nod. It is.

"Griffin's like you."

"Sexy as hell?" I try to make my voice teasing, but it's more nervous than anything.

"To the ladies, yeah." His eyes light up. "Blunt. Though the way you do it is a lot cuter."

"Thank you." I bite the head of my broccoli, so I won't blush.

"After Grace left, he made a big thing about taking me out to meet someone else."

"Yeah?"

"But I wouldn't play along. I brought books or comics."

"You read?"

"Doesn't seem like I read?" His voice is light. Teasing.

"No, I meant, more—I don't see any books." I motion to his shelf. "What do you read?"

"Don't laugh."

"I'm getting a PhD in statistics. What do you think I read?"

"Books about economics."

"Sometimes." A lot. "But I read fiction too."

"You first," he says.

"I asked first."

He picks up his chopsticks. Scoops beef and rice to his lips. Chews. Swallows. "Mysteries."

"Mysteries." My head flashes with a mental picture. Chase on the couch in his boxers, flipping through a book, gasping at the reveal. "Why mysteries?"

"Why, what do you read?"

"Urban fantasy. It's kind of like comics, but all words."

"People with super powers in the city."

"Exactly." I take another bite. "I guess I like the fantasy of having magic powers. Of being special and competent and—"

"You are."

My cheeks flush. I don't have a response to that. Only a burning desire to sit in his lap and kiss him.

"Your ex. He probably wasn't sure. If he knew about your timeline, he knew he had to jump or let you go."

"But he—"

"It must have hurt, letting you go."

"How do you know that?"

"How could it not?"

My heart thuds against my chest. Is he saying what I think he's saying? Does he even realize it?

Too many things race through my head.

The sad look in Phillip's eyes. The sympathetic tone to his voice. The concern in Chase's expression.

That's so…

Next topic.

I find the thread of our conversation. Clear my throat. Smooth my tank top. "Why mysteries?"

"Never really thought about it." He picks up a broccoli floret. "There's something about getting the answer to a question that's killing you. I have to know."

"Is it the knowing? Or the wanting to know?"

"Both."

That makes sense. You can't have one without the other.

His eyes meet mine. "I guess everyone reads fiction for the same reason."

"To escape?"

"Because it makes sense. There's a logic to fiction. Everything is there for a reason. Everything resolves. No matter how complicated the characters are, you understand them. What they do. What they want. Why they screw things up."

"It's harder with real people." It's half question, half answer.

He nods *yeah*.

My eyes go to his. "Who are you trying to figure out?"

"Everyone."

"You seem… you seem like you understand."

"Maybe it's just Grace then."

My chest gets heavy. I already hate her name. I hate her. She was nothing but pleasant to me. She even bought me a few birthday presents over the years. But I hate her stupid light hair and her tattoos and her ability to apply makeup and her hold on Chase's heart. "You don't hate her."

"Why would I?"

"She broke your heart."

"It wasn't out of malice." His gaze shifts to his plate. "I

don't want to hate her. I don't even want to forget her. She was a big part of my life."

"What do you want?" *Do you want her back?* I have to know, but I can't ask. I'm too afraid of the answer.

"That's a hard fucking question."

"If it's your entire life, sure. But I'm only asking about Grace."

His chuckle is soft.

"I said something stupid?"

"No. It's just…" His eyes meet mine. "Nobody gives me the benefit of the doubt."

"Because…" I'm not sure what he's saying.

"Everyone thinks I'm a lost cause. This guy who's hopelessly in love with his ex. They imagine me sitting around, pining for her, spending every waking moment poring over memories or planning to get her back."

"It can't be every waking moment. I mean, I hope it wasn't—" I nod to the bedroom.

His smile widens. "It wasn't."

"Good." I take another bite. It's good. Better than my last. Crunchy broccoli, chewy beef, firm rice, that perfect mix of savory and salty. "You're a good cook."

"You're…" He laughs. "Whatever you're thinking, it's all over your face."

"Oh?"

"Yeah." He takes a long sip. "You don't think I'm hopeless, but you don't buy that I'm—"

"I know you're not over her." I swallow hard. "But I believe you're capable."

"Do you?" He raises a brow *'cause your face says no fucking way*.

I do. Maybe. "It's not for me to say, is it?"

He nods *fair*. "I'm not sure."

"Not sure?"

"There are too many things I want. That changes every day. But there are a few that stick."

"Yeah?"

"More than anything, I want her to be okay."

"Even if it's with someone else?"

"I don't know." His voice strains. "I try not to think about that."

"But you do want her to be happy?"

"You want Phillip to be happy?"

"Yeah, but not for a little while." I dig my hands into my jeans. I'm back in my jeans and tank top. He's now wearing a t-shirt. But this is more revealing than anything we've done tonight. "I guess it shouldn't matter if we're over. But I don't want it to be easy for him to move on. Even though this was my choice. I want him to have loved me enough that it's hard." I press my lips together. "That's selfish."

"Yeah, but it's normal."

"You're the same?"

"I was."

"But now?"

He chuckles. "Anyone else, they'd be sure I want her pining for me forever."

"Maybe your friends don't know you as well as they think they do."

"Maybe."

"Or maybe that's what you want them to think."

"Maybe it is."

It is. But why? Why does Chase want everyone thinking he's a miserable jerk?

He's even convinced himself.

I should believe him. Keep my heart locked. Keep my focus on the curves of his lips and the lines of his body.

I really should.

But I can't.

I need to help him. I don't know why. It's not logical or reasonable or smart.

But my heart is sure.

He's offering me so much. I need to do something for him too.

I need to help him get over his ex.

No matter what.

———

I CHANGE THE TOPIC TO CHASE'S COMIC BOOK collection, but it stays in my head.

I need to help him.

I need to pry open his heart.

I need to sew it back together.

Okay, maybe not those last two. But I can help him without falling in love with him. Even if we're planning to spend the next few months having sex. And he's giving me everything I want.

And, oh yeah, he's the future father of my baby.

God, he knows so much about art. The passion in his steady voice when he talks about dot shading—

I want to listen to him forever.

I want him to talk me to sleep.

To talk me through dreams.

But he has other plans. When we finish dinner, he stands, offers his hand and nods to the bedroom.

It's time to do this.

For real.

Him inside me. Him coming inside me. Possibly getting me pregnant.

I can handle that.

Totally.

Chapter Twenty-Four

ARIEL

The string lights are tiny stars against the black walls. Like the sky over the ocean in Malibu.

Like the candle flickering between me and Phillip as he said *no, I can't do this with you.*

Would that be easier? If Phillip was the one getting me pregnant? If I was going into this with a partner instead of a…

Friend who's helping me get pregnant.

A friend I'm helping get over his ex.

A friend who is going to make me come until—

Ahem.

I can have sex that's just sex. Sure, I've never done that before. And my feelings for Chase aren't strictly physical. And we're not just having sex. We're trying to make a baby.

But the point stands.

This isn't about an emotional… uh… romantic connection between me and Chase.

"Take off your clothes, princess." His voice is low and demanding.

My body begs me to obey.

My heart sings.

My head—

Ugh.

This is why people drink before sex. To dull the distracting thoughts and turn up the dirty ones.

That isn't an option.

I need to get my head in the game, somehow.

Focus on Chase's impossibly sexy lips, shoulders, chest, stomach, legs, cock—

Focus on how much I want him inside me.

Forget about the implications of that.

I'm capable. Totally. Absolutely.

He takes a step toward me. "I can't let you get carried away this time, princess." He moves closer.

Two feet. One foot. Six inches.

His fingers brush my stomach.

The waistband of my jeans.

The button.

He undoes it with a flick. Then he unzips my jeans. "I need to feel that sweet cunt wrapped around me."

Holy shit. Where did he learn to talk like that? No, I can't ask myself stuff like that. It leads to questions about his ex. And whether or not he's in love with his ex. And all the empty casual sex he had before that. And was it really empty?

And what does that mean about us?

Is this full?

Uh.

So.

Yeah.

Not thinking about that.

Chase's fingers skim my stomach. He brings his hand to my chin. Tilts my head so my eyes meet his.

God, his eyes are so pretty.

"You nervous, princess?" He presses his palm flat against my stomach.

"Yes." There's no sense in hiding that. It's obvious.

"You want me to take it slow—"

"No." I shake my head. "I want you now."

He traces a line down my body. "Clothes off."

I stare into his eyes, trying to find his intentions. They're such pretty eyes. What else matters?

"Now, princess."

God, the demanding tone to his voice. I want to listen to that. To bend to that. To lose myself in that.

Maybe it's possible.

It's worth a shot.

"Keep doing that." I toss my tank top over my head.

His eyes go to my chest. He watches with rapt attention as I do away with my bra. "Keep doing what, princess?"

"The demands."

"They're not demands if you ask for them."

"They are."

He nods *maybe*.

"Will it help if I say please?"

"I'd say it will help if you get on your knees and beg, but I don't trust myself not to come in your pretty mouth."

My sex clenches. He's so… Oh my God.

His eyes find mine. "Take off your pants." His voice shifts to something lower. The same tone he used to tell me to do my homework or stay away from cigarettes.

He's taking care of me.

God, he really is.

He's just so…

Yummy. It really is the best word. And my main focus.

I push my jeans off my hips. Shimmy out of them. Kick them off my feet. It's more awkward than smooth, but I don't care.

I need to be naked with him.

I need to follow his orders.

I need to fuck him.

He looks me up and down slowly, like he's savoring every inch. His eyes move over my lips, shoulders, chest, stomach, hips. They stop at my black panties. "Off."

My heart thuds against my chest as I push my panties off my hips.

His pupils dilate, but his posture stays demanding. In-control. He watches as I kick my panties aside. "Sit on the bed."

I sit at the edge.

"Spread your legs, princess. I want to look at you."

My sex clenches. My stomach flutters. That's so much. It's hot as hell, but it's so much.

I bring my eyes to his. Okay, as long as I don't think about what it means, I can do this.

I spread my legs.

"Wider."

The pet name makes me throb. The way he says it, like I'm the only thing he needs, like the very thought of me makes him hard—

I spread my legs until the sides of my knees hit the bed.

"Fuck." He moves closer. Drops to his knees. Presses his palms into my inner thighs.

I swallow hard.

I've been with guys. Done *this* with guys. But no one has ever stopped to savor the sight of me.

No one has ever looked at me the way Chase is looking at me.

"Fuck, princess." His fingers dig into my skin. "You're beautiful."

"You say that to all the—"

"No. Not here." He leans in. Brings his lips to the inside of my knee. "Lie back."

"I want to look at you," I say.

"Trust me." He scrapes his teeth against my skin.

My legs give out. That's so… he's so… Yes. On my back. So I don't collapse.

I lie on the bed. The black sheets are soft and smooth, and there's something about seeing my pale skin against them—

Seeing his strong hands against them—

Fuck. This is already intense.

I press my eyelids together. Suck a deep breath through my teeth.

It feels like this is the first time. The only time.

"You're still nervous." He nips at my inner thigh.

I nod. "I just—"

"Breathe."

"Okay."

"That's all you need to do."

"Just breathe?"

"Yeah." He bites me a little harder. Hard enough it hurts in the best possible way. "I'll do the rest."

"I want you to enjoy this too—"

"Trust me, princess. I am." He pins my legs to the bed. "You'll know I am."

"Chase—"

"Yeah?"

"I… uh… okay."

He plants a kiss on the inside of my knee. "You have no fucking idea how badly I want to taste your cunt."

My body buzzes.

"I've been thinking about it for weeks." He drags his lips up my thigh. Higher. Higher. Higher. "I've been dreaming about it."

"What do you do?"

"When I think about this?" He stops to nip at my skin.

Fuck. It hurts so good. "Yeah?"

"I fuck myself." His voice is matter-of-fact, like it's both obvious and incredibly hot.

"I do too."

"You fuck yourself to me?" It's more a statement than a question.

I answer anyway. "All the time."

"You imagine coming on my face?"

"Oh my God." My entire body buzzes. He's too hot. It's wrong. It's really, incredibly wrong.

"You like dirty talk, don't you, princess?"

My response is a groan.

"You act sweet and innocent—"

"I am sweet and innocent."

"But you want me to demand you come on my face."

"Chase—"

His fingers curl into my inner thighs. Then it's the soft scrape of his nails. "You want to come on my cock too, princess?"

"Yes."

"You want those pretty lips around my cock?"

"Chase—"

"You want me to turn you over and split you in half?"

Oh my God.

"Or maybe you want your feet at my shoulders?"

"Chase—"

"I like you dirty and demanding, princess." He digs his nails into my thighs a little harder.

Fuck, that feels good.

He scrapes his nails a little harder.

I groan. It hurts. But that only makes it better.

"I'll fuck you until you can't walk straight." He pushes

the heels of his hands into my thighs, pinning my legs to the bed.

Softly.

Then harder.

Mmm. There's something about surrendering to him.

I really like it.

"I'll fuck you any way you like, princess." He places a kiss on my inner thigh. "But I'm the one who makes demands."

"Chase—"

"Is that a yes?"

I nod. "Please."

"You can beg." He drags his lips a little higher. "But it's not gonna help your case."

Holy shit.

He's so…

This is so…

I…

He…

Uh…

I press my eyelids together. "Please." It's all I can say. He's barely touching me and I'm already achy.

I'm empty.

I've never been so acutely aware of how empty I am.

Or how badly I need to be filled.

He drags his lips higher, higher, higher—

There.

His lips brush my sex. Then they're on my other thigh. He works his way down my leg with soft, slow kisses.

Then it's the scrape of his teeth.

The tiniest hint of pain.

Again.

Again.

Again.

Higher and higher and—

There.

His lips brush me.

Softly.

Then harder.

He explores me with his tongue. Flat strokes. Thin strokes. Short. Fast. Hard. Slow. Long. Deep.

He takes his sweet, sweet time. Like he's savoring every moment. Like he can't get enough of me.

He sucks on my outer lips.

Teases me with his tongue.

Brushes his lips against my clit.

He stays so, so close to where I need him. But he keeps me on edge. Keeps me aching and empty.

I reach for Chase. Get his shoulders. His head.

I knot my hands in his hair.

Arch my hips to meet him.

He pins me harder. A reminder I'm his. A reminder he's in control.

A reminder I'm helpless.

Why is that so hot?

Why do I want to give him my body?

That's not…

I'm not…

I don't fucking care what I am or what he is or what this means.

I only care about his soft, wet mouth.

He tortures me with a slow pace. He stays so, so close to exactly what I need.

My nipples pang. My sex aches. My thighs quiver.

It feels like he goes on for hours.

The tension in my sex winds tighter, tighter, tighter—

So, so close.

But so, so far.

Forever and ever.

Finally, he brings his tongue to my clit.

Works me with soft, slow strokes. Hard, fast ones.

He tries every pressure, place, speed.

There—

I groan as he licks me exactly where I need him.

"Please." My hips rock of their own accord. I don't care that begging doesn't speed him. I need to push the words out. I need to do something with the anticipation welling inside me.

This is so—

He's so—

We're so—

Oh my God.

My nails dig into his skin.

He pins me harder.

Licks me harder.

Faster.

There—

"Chase," I breathe. "Fuck."

He keeps that same steady pace.

With every flick of his tongue, my sex winds tighter and tighter.

So tight it hurts.

Tighter.

Tighter.

"Chase—" I tug at his hair. Claw at his shoulders. It's too much. And not enough. "Make me come, baby." The words fall off my lips. I have no idea where they came from and I don't care.

There's only one thing in my head.

Him.

"Please." I rock my hips.

He pins me.

He works me with that same perfect pressure.

Brings me closer and closer and—

Fuck.

With the next flick of his tongue, the tension in my sex unwinds.

"Chase. Fuck."

My world goes white. Soft. Like the string lights glowing against the wall.

Nothing but the beautiful, pure glow of bliss.

I tug at his hair.

But he doesn't stop. He pins me to the bed.

It's so much. Too much. It hurts.

Then it's not enough.

He winds me up again.

Pushes me over the edge again.

He licks me through my orgasm, then he pulls back, tosses his t-shirt over his head, pushes his jeans and boxers off his hips.

He's so hard and ready and I really fucking want that.

His pants collect at his ankles.

He scoops my legs into his hands. Brings my calves to his chest, my feet to his shoulders.

His fingers curl around my ankles. "Look at me, princess."

The desire in his blue eyes dissolves my other thoughts.

I need that.

I really fucking need that.

His nails scrape my skin. Softly. Then harder. Then hard enough to hurt.

Fuck.

My teeth sink into my lips. My fingers dig into the sheets.

He's too far away. I want his body on mine. I want to feel every inch of his skin.

But that's too—something.

This is good. Better. Less personal. More dirty. More—

The scrape of his nails calls all my attention.

He shifts his hips, bringing our bodies closer. Closer. There—

His cock strains against me.

Then it's one inch at a time.

My body stretches over him.

Fuck, that feels good. He feels good. Warm and hard and mine.

He holds us steady for a moment. So it's just him filling me. His body and mine locked together. One.

His eyes bore into mine.

They ask for so many things.

Offer so many things.

Then his eyelids press together.

His nails dig into my skin.

"Hold on to the edge of the bed, princess." His voice is a low growl. "I don't want to hurt you."

I nod and grab the edge.

It helps.

Mostly.

He looks down at me as he pulls back then fills me again. His expression shifts. The softness fades into something dirty and demanding.

I let my eyes close.

Let my head fall.

Sink into the feeling of our bodies joining.

He fills me with slow, steady thrusts.

Then hard, fast ones.

Again. Again. Again.

It's so good, so right, so satisfying. There's no other way to say it.

I'm not empty anymore.

I'm full.

I'm brimming.

I'm—

Fuck.

He holds my legs against his chest as he drives deeper and deeper.

It's so much, so intense it hurts, but in the best possible way.

I look up at Chase.

He looks down at me.

Fills me with steady strokes.

Bring me right to the edge.

My body takes over. I release the bed. Bring my hand to my clit.

He watches, eyes wide, as I rub myself through an orgasm.

Then he pulls me closer, pins my legs tighter, fucks me harder.

His breaths run together.

His eyes close.

His stomach quivers.

I watch bliss spread over his expression as he comes.

It's so fucking beautiful.

His groans bounce around the room.

His cock pulses.

He spills inside me.

He thrusts through his orgasm, then he releases me.

I push myself up reflexively, but he stops me. He reaches down. Pins my shoulders to the bed.

Oh.

Of course.

This is—

I almost forget.

No, I did forget.

And now it's there and it's real and it's the only thing in my head.

This might be it.

The night it happens.

Not that the possibility is going to stop me from fucking Chase every day for the next week.

Nothing is going to stop that.

Chapter Twenty-Five

ARIEL

Skye steps out of the front door—our front door—in her pajamas. A black tank-top and pastel pink bat print shorts that hug her curvy frame.

She pushes her short black hair behind her ear. Presses her berry lips into a smile. "Where have you been?"

I hug my overnight bag to my chest. Tap the electric lock on my car. *Beep-beep.* Like it's screaming *I'm already locked.* "Nowhere."

"Nowhere." Her gaze shifts to my purple bag. "Lot of stuff to bring from nowhere."

"It's—"

"I won't tell Mr. Grumpypants." She raises a perfectly outlined brow. Seriously, she's in a full face of makeup in her pajamas. And not normal pretty, subdued makeup.

Thick eyeliner, long lashes (I'm pretty sure they're extensions), dark lips.

She's devoted to her style. I like to call it goth sex goddess. Not that Skye sees herself as a sex goddess. I'm pretty sure she's less experienced than I am. Which is sad. Or it would be sad if the reason wasn't obvious—

She's totally in love with Forest.

Which is sad in its own way. Since neither of them sees it. At all.

I don't know why they're so oblivious. Even their names are perfect together. Forest and Skye. How much more could they belong together?

Though, it's not like I wanted to go out with the guy in my AP Chem class who said "I'm Eric. You're Ariel. We must belong together."

Uh, no, our parents both happened to love the same incredibly popular movie. Or maybe he was named after his dad or an author or a senator. Eric is a very common name. It's not like I'm giving any guy named Eric a chance.

"Was it okay?" Her voice drops from its playful tone. To one that's serious. Motherly. "Did he do something you didn't—"

"No. It was all very consensual." I clear my throat.

Her eyes light up. She stifles a squeal. (She's very excitable, despite her love of black). "Tell me everything —" She turns toward the slightly open door. Presses her lips together. Motions *shhh*.

Skye moves off the first step. Moves into whispering distance.

She motions to the door *Forest is coming*. "I won't tell him. Really."

It's a nice promise. Maybe she means it. Skye was like a big sister to me, especially after Mom died. I'm sure she believes she won't tell Forest.

But come on. They tell each other everything.

I might as well scream it right here, right now.

That's not happening.

I want Chase alive. I need him for another few months. And I like him. The world is a better place with Chase in it. Even if it's a moodier, more unable to move on place.

If only Skye or Forest were aware of their obvious crush. They could give me some advice about not moving on. Or maybe they're the worst people to ask.

Since they are so obviously stuck.

What could they say, besides *it's not so bad. Let him stay in love with her. Look at me. Sure, it's obvious my heart is devoted to Forest. And, yes, he looks at me like a little sister. But so what? I'm happy.*

It's a whole different story, really.

They're attached at the hip.

Chase's ex is… Where is she? That information is easy enough to find—I'm sure she's all over social media—but I shouldn't pry. It's only going to feed the voice screaming *Chase is doomed to misery*.

I'm going to help him.

In a normal, healthy way.

That's it.

That's totally it.

She leans in to whisper, "Was it good?"

I bite my lip. I want to tell someone. I should tell Skye. It's not like I can hide the reality of the situation from Forest. It's obvious I slept over. "Really good." My chest warms at the memory of Chase's groan. He's just so… mmm.

She stifles a squeal. "On a scale of you almost fell asleep to you're not sure if you can walk straight—"

"That one."

Her eyes go wide. She jumps backward. Claps her hands together. Swallows her smile.

Forest pulls the door open. Looks from me to Skye then back to me. "Where were you?"

She motions *my lips are sealed*.

Not that it matters. Not on this particular detail. "Spending the night with a man."

"What man?" He turns to Skye. Shoots her that *if you know something you better confess* look.

She shrugs like she has no idea. Sells it. A little.

"A man who had sex with me," I say.

Forest rolls his eyes. "This man has a name?"

"Yeah, his name, hmm… it's None of Your Business," I say.

Skye laughs.

Forest does too.

Shit, they're laughing at me. They exchange this look. *Isn't Ariel precious?*

Okay, it's mostly my brother. But still. Talk about a lack of female solidarity.

"That would be cute if you were fourteen," he says.

"As would the over-protective brother routine," I say.

He looks at me funny. "A question is over-protective?"

I slide my bag onto my shoulder. Move past them. Reach for the open door. "It's, um—"

"Are you being safe?" he asks.

"Of course." Not in the way he means. But I am being safe.

He turns to Skye. They exchange one of those best friend looks that I can't begin to comprehend.

He turns to me. "He treats you well?"

"Very," I say.

"And this has been going on for…" He raises a brow.

Skye clears her throat. "Maybe your sister doesn't want to share the details of her sex life."

"Maybe she's hiding something," he says.

Skye shakes her head *I don't think so*.

He nods *yeah, I think so*. "Someone I know?"

"Hmm… How about… Still None of Your Business," I say.

He just laughs. "Be careful, Ariel."

"I'm careful," I say.

"Don't make it more than it is," he says.

I clear my throat. "Goodbye, Forest."

He ignores my clear request to end the conversation. "You're spending the night."

"I was tired after our vigorous sex," I say.

He chuckles *okay, sure.*

Ahem. "I'm a very skilled and athletic lover." Why am I arguing about this with my brother? And why am I trying to sell that story? I take walks, sure, but I don't exactly work out. And I certainly wasn't the one doing the work last night.

"It's true. Remember when we took that pole dancing class together." Skye laughs. "Ariel was a natural."

"I don't want to picture you humping a pole." He turns to his best friend.

"There's no humping. Well…" She chews on her bottom lip. "Sometimes there's humping. But you couldn't do half the moves."

"That a bet?" he asks.

She nods *it is.*

He offers his hand. "What are we wagering?"

"Loser skips sex for a month."

"You won't go on a second date. Who are you going to have sex with?" he asks.

"I don't hear a counter," she says.

"I'll see you guys later." I move toward the door.

"Seriously, Ariel. If you like this guy, great. But make sure you're on the same page," Forest's voice fills with concern. "I don't want to see another—"

"I'm not eighteen anymore." I bite my lip. It's good advice. He's right. How am I supposed to tell him he's a nosy dick when he's completely right? "But I appreciate the concern."

Forest nods *good*.

I wave goodbye. So it's clear I am beyond done with this conversation. "Now, go do whatever you're doing to do—"

"Work," he says.

"Why are you here?" I ask.

"This is my house," he says.

Nerves flash in Skye's eyes. He's here for her. For some reason she doesn't want me to know.

Okay, fine.

I know how to mind my own business. "Have fun at work."

He chuckles *yeah right*. "One more question."

"What?" I just stop myself from rolling my eyes.

"Is it Chase?" he asks.

Time stops.

The sounds of traffic, sprinklers, conversation, wind cease.

The only thing in the world is Forest's concerned voice.

And the super obvious question *is it Chase*?

"That's all I want to know, Ariel," he says. "Because if it is—"

"What? You're going to punch him in the face?" I keep my back to him. Step into the doorframe. Like this is no big deal.

"He doesn't know what he's capable of," Forest says.

I guess we agree on that point.

Forest's voice is the picture of calm reason. "I know you like him, but—"

"We've had this conversation," I say.

"And you haven't answered with a 'no,'" he says.

"Goodbye, Forest." I reach for the door.

Skye whispers something about how it's really not their business.

He replies with a scoff and something about how anyone who hurts his sister becomes his business.

And, sure, maybe I should appreciate that my older brother is looking out for me.

But there's only one thing in my head:

A neon sign flashing "Fuck."

Chapter Twenty-Six

CHASE

I t's a good day.

The sky is bright. The air is sweet. The coffee is strong.

And this mock-up, the one I've been struggling to figure out—

I finally have it.

An anatomical heart complete with four chambers and a home in the biggest.

I outline in black. Snap a picture. Send it to my client.

He sends back a *fuck, that's perfect.*

I lean back in my chair. Bask in the glory of the moment. There's nothing like working out a tough design. The satisfaction is incomparable.

Well, maybe not incomparable.

Last night was—

"Hey." Forest steps into my suite. He leans against the half-wall, easy breezy.

It's not like him. He's not a ball of manic energy the way my little brother Wes is, but he's not exactly the picture of cool either. He cares too much for that.

"Hey." I nod back. Turn my sketchbook to him.

He takes it. Studies the design. "You've been working on this awhile?"

"Yeah." I check my cell. Read the message again. But that's not the only news on here. There's something from Ariel.

Shit, I can't check that with him hovering.

I should change her name to—

Fuck, I don't know. I've never done the whole sneaking around thing. Grace's brother knew what was going on day two. There was no hiding it.

"Talking to someone?" he asks.

"Client."

He nods *of course.* Hands the sketchbook back.

"Don't tell me you don't like it," I say.

His chuckle is easy. "I hate it."

I raise a brow.

"Better than the shit I'm working on today. So fuck you."

"Since when are you the jealous type?"

"Since you walked in here with that smile."

I close my sketchbook. Set it on the shelf. "You didn't see me walk in here."

He nods *yeah.* Studies my expression like he's looking for something. "You're still wearing it."

Is my smile that rare? Maybe it is. Fuck, it's not like I've had a lot of good things in my life lately.

Even after Mom agreed to give rehab another shot—

She's been sober a few months now, but how can I trust that she'll stay that way?

Hunter has a year under his belt. The odds are good. Relatively speaking.

But relatively good odds are still shit.

"And now I'm ruining it." He slides his hands into his

pockets. He's dressed the same as always—dark jeans, dark t-shirt, black motorcycle boots.

"Aren't you hot in those?" I motion to his leather boots.

"You gonna ask me to take it off, Keating? 'Cause you should know I need a little romance first."

"You think I get off on your sweaty feet?"

He nods *yeah*. "Sounds like the perfect fetish for you."

"Maybe if you were a woman with a great ass."

"And thick eyeliner?" he teases.

"Don't tell me Wes and Griffin got to you." I stand. Motion to the Keurig in the lobby. *You want coffee?*

He nods *sure*. Follows me out of the suite, through the lobby, past Hunter's girlfriend Emma.

She looks up from her spot at the counter. Eyes us curiously. Says nothing.

She's the only reason I'm here. After I refused to join Inked Hearts, she showed up at Blacklist, and told me to get the fuck over myself and a) forgive Hunter and b) take the job Hunter got me at Inked Hearts.

At the time, I had no interest in my brother's attempts at reconciliation.

Especially not that attempt. I don't care what his intentions were. Nobody buys my forgiveness.

It would have been a pain finding another shop, sure, but I'm an in demand artist. I can take my clients anywhere.

Hell, I'm still not sure I made the right call. This forced proximity does nothing to warm my heart.

Every time I see Hunter—

I'm not getting closer to forgiving him.

It's all Emma's fault, really. The badass college student ranted at me then fell asleep on our bench. Turned out, she'd been up all night crying after Hunter dumped her.

He dumped her and she still went to bat for him.

It was some bullshit about her brother catching them together. At the time, I thought he was an idiot.

With Forest following me to the coffee maker, walking like he's trying so hard to stay casual—

Maybe I have more in common with Hunter than I want to believe.

No, I do. I have that same genetic disposition to fill the emptiness in my gut with whatever numbs it. One I'm not giving into. Ever.

"You want one?" I try to keep my voice casual, but it doesn't land. Last night was a big deal. There's no getting around that.

I don't need to give away that it was Forest's sister, but I can't act like nothing happened.

"Sure." He takes a seat on the bench. Folds one leg over the other. "Whatever, as long as it's not too dark."

"Doesn't sound like you."

His chuckle is easy.

I think.

Maybe I'm imagining this tension. Maybe I'm projecting.

"I'd go for the darkest thing they have, but it's nothing compared to you," he says.

"Thought I was smiling."

"Yeah." He nods. "Maybe I should switch it up today. Go for the Italian Roast."

"I think they're all the same." I grab a medium roast pod, pop it in the machine, fill it with water from the cooler.

"Equally mediocre."

I nod *exactly*. "There's great coffee four blocks away."

His nose scrunches in distaste. The way Ariel's does. "Add milk and sugar and it all tastes the same." He rests his back against the wall. Even with the blinds down, the sunlight surrounds him in an angelic glow.

I try to focus on picking out a coffee. He's right. They're equally mediocre—this is probably the worst way to make coffee, save for instant. I'm not a snob. Only got into coffee because Hunter did.

Now—

Fuck, I don't even need the caffeine. It's not going to help with my racing heart.

There's no way Forest knows something.

That's impossible.

Sure, Ariel isn't the most skilled liar, but—

She's the worst liar in the world. She wears everything all over her face. It's hot as hell when she's staring at me like she needs me inside her.

But when it's—

"You have a glow, Keating." He leans back, easy breezy. "You finally trade up to a flesh light?"

"You sound like my brother."

He chuckles. "Like mine too." His voice drops to something more serious. "Is there a girl?"

"Since when do you think I'm capable of moving on?"

He chuckles. "I live for surprises."

I match his laugh. I should have a better sense of humor about my misery. I try. It just doesn't happen.

"So…" He arches a brow. Leans in to whisper distance. "Who was she?"

"Don't remember saying there was someone."

"Why else would there be a spring in your step?"

I shrug like I don't know. Wait for the *drip-drip-drip* of the machine to finish. Hand Forest his coffee and the box of fixings.

He nods *thanks*. "Don't tell me it's about the design. I know that look."

"I have that look."

He chuckles *yeah right*. "What was she like?"

"Sweet." I can't deny this. I'm not supplying all the details, but it's not like he's asking.

"Ah." He smiles. "There is someone."

"Yeah." I'm imagining the third degree. This is normal. My friend giving me a hard time the way he always does. That's all it is.

"You finally got laid?"

I can't help but laugh.

"Took you long enough, Keating." He stands and pats me on the back.

Which attracts the attention of my little brother.

What the hell is he doing here? He's not scheduled to work until later.

Wes skips to us. He looks from me to Forest then back to me. "Why's Chase in a good mood?"

"He got laid," Forest says.

My cheeks flush. God, I don't talk about my life like this. It's too much attention.

"Holy shit. Look at that." Wes reaches for my cheek.

I slap his hand away. "Watch it."

"Ohh, he's all pissy about it." Wes presses his hand to his heart. "How cute."

Forest nods *yeah*.

"You like this girl?" Wes asks. "Oh, was it—" His gaze shifts to Forest. Realization spreads over his face. "Oh."

Fuck.

"Oh?" Forest asks.

"Yeah, I just, uh… it was the chick you were talking about the other day." Wes nods *go with me*. "The one who confessed her need for a strong hand."

He's making this worse.

I shrug. "This was more recent."

"Look at you." Wes pats my shoulder. "All casual about finally getting laid. Like it hasn't been two years."

"It's not a big deal." Okay, it is. But that's not something we need to discuss.

"Oh shit." Wes's smile drops.

My stomach clenches. He's smarter than this. He's smarter than he looks.

"You had to pay for it." He tries to hold a poker face, but it cracks immediately.

Forest laughs so hard his cup shakes. Coffee spills over the sides.

He reaches out *stop*, but he keeps laughing.

"Fuck." Forest barely makes it through his words. "That's… fuck… can you imagine?"

My shoulders relax. Wes is a genius. He's distracting Forest from the actual situation.

Fuck, I need to buy my brother dinner or something.

Maybe a trophy that says *you're an asshole, but you're a helpful one*.

"Imagine, what? Why else would a woman touch Chase? Sure, he has those Keating good looks. And, well…" Wes raises a brow.

"Well…?" Forest laughs. "Is that supposed to be something about how everyone knows Keating men are good fucks?"

"I was gonna say well-endowed, but I don't like to brag." Wes winks.

"You forget who you like flirting with?" I ask.

"That was for Emma." He turns and blows the store manager/Hunter's girlfriend a kiss. "You know what's up."

She flips him the bird. "Why are you here?"

"To see your beautiful face," he says.

"What's your girlfriend think about that?" she asks.

"We're secure in our relationship." His smile gets dreamy. That Quinn smile of his.

It's disgusting. Usually.

Right now, it's not so bad. Cute. Sweet even.

I want him to be happy.

I want Hunter and Emma to be happy.

I want the whole world to be happy.

What the fuck?

"You know, it's almost commendable." Wes pats me on the shoulder again. "You know you're a piece of work, that you'll fuck up any woman you touch. So you hire a professional."

I flip him off.

He just laughs.

Forest too. "Do you really think Chase—"

"It makes sense," Wes says.

Forest nods *kind of*. "What do you say, Keating? You hire help for this? Or you find someone willing to fuck your pain away?"

"She knows my pain isn't fuckable," I say.

Forest and Wes exchange a look. Then Forest turns to me. Studies me. "She knows you well?"

Fuck, he is trying to figure something out.

I need to check these texts. But I need to step away first.

No, I need to convince Ariel this secrecy is stupid. I should tell him now. But I won't betray her confidence.

"She knows I'm not gonna fall for her. And she's not gonna fall for me either," I say.

Forest freezes. "Oh? She recently heartbroken too?"

I can't say that. "She doesn't want something serious."

Wes scoffs. "Chase, dude, you're not capable of casual. Remember the girls in high school? The one sophomore year? She threatened to kill herself—"

"Don't start." That's one subject I can't handle.

Wes nods *okay, that's fair*. "I'm just saying. You're not a guy who does casual."

Forest hangs on every word. Then he stops. Looks at his crotch.

Oh, his cell.

He pulls it out. Checks a message. Frowns.

Shit, did she tell him? Did she try to lie and give it away?

I try to relax. If he punches me, it's better I'm relaxed. Less long-term damage.

I'm not gonna stop him.

I'd do the same.

But he doesn't deck me. He turns to us and shakes his head. "Oddball is closing."

"What?" Wes asks.

"Yeah. The owner is selling. At a discount. His divorce is going through. He doesn't want his wife to get it." Forest rolls his eyes *of course*. "He wants to sell as quickly as possible."

"I have an idea." It's either the worst idea I've ever had or the best.

"You don't mean?" Forest asks.

I nod *yeah, I do*.

Chapter Twenty-Seven

CHASE

etween my next appointment and a pow-wow with Forest, my morning flies by.

On my lunch break, I get the fuck out of the shop. Grab a sandwich at a nearby coffee shop. Find space to think.

The smooth, chocolate cold brew hits the spot. It's a million times better than the instant shit. But it's not why I'm here.

Yeah, I usually eat leftovers for lunch. And last night, I gave the other half of dinner to Ariel.

But that—

Well, I guess that is why I'm here.

I stare at her texts, trying to figure out what they mean for us.

Ariel: I got home when Forest was leaving. He gave me the third degree about being safe and not getting my heart broken and blah, blah, blah. But then he asked something weird. He asked if it was you.

Ariel: I didn't say anything, but I think he's suspicious. He knows I had a crush on you. I guess everyone knows.

Ariel: Not that I do now. I like you a lot, but I know what this is. You're helping me. I'm helping you.

Ariel: Just play it cool. You're cool. It should be easy.

She is helping me, but it's not like her to realize that.

Fuck, Ariel is something else. It's easy to talk to her. And the way she looks at me—

For once, it's not *damn, that guy is a lost cause*.

She treats me like an equal. Like a person capable of understanding the complex concepts she studies. Like a person capable of moving on.

And even when she gets that *shit, Chase really is hung up on his ex* expression, it's not in a condescending way.

She gets it.

She must.

She left her boyfriend less than a month ago. She thinks he left her, but that's not how it went.

She made an ultimatum. He said no. She left.

God, it's hard to believe she can't see how much that must hurt him.

All right, I'm not exactly a mind reader. I'm getting a lot of this from his social media. Which I should probably ignore.

But it's more fun checking on her ex than mine.

Grace's feeds—

Fuck, I can't go there. I haven't. Not recently.

The last time I saw her with that new guy, the musician, the smile on her face, the fresh semi-colon tattoo on her wrist—

I'm sparing Ariel this pain.

Okay, that's bullshit. I want to know how I stack up to her ex.

Yeah, I'm taller, broader, more tattooed.

But the dude is a doctor. He's an educated guy who can

keep up with her and buy her the kind of home she deserves.

I do all right, but I'm not destined for a three-hundred-thousand-dollar salary.

Thank fuck he's dull. At least as far as Instagram is concerned.

Phillip Nguyen's profile might as well say *medicine is my life*.

He mostly posts pictures of dinner. Or selfies with his fellow interns.

That's where it's obvious—he's lacking the spark he had a few months ago.

She's that spark. Anyone could see it. Everyone sees it.

I wish I could grab that spark, that I was capable of loving someone without ruining them. But look at where Grace is now compared to where she was when I left.

Look how well Hunter is doing now that I'm out of his life (more or less).

Facts are obvious.

God, I should probably warn Holden and Forest. Tell them Inked Hearts buying Oddball is bad for them. They're better off finding anywhere else to work.

Or maybe I should quit. I'm the problem. If I remove myself from the situation, the problem goes away.

Buzz.

Ariel: Did you really offer to buy Oddball?

Chase: Not exactly.

Ariel: Do you have that kind of money?

Chase: The shop is looking to expand.

Ariel: Don't do this for me.

Chase: I'm not.

I'm doing it for me. Because it makes me feel good. Because I want a percentage of the new shop. Because I want to see Inked Hearts take over the state of California.

Maybe I don't participate, but I still care. I want this place to bloom.

I want Hunter to bloom.

I want my mom to bloom.

Grace—I want that for her too. It's not like I'm hoping the people who hurt me fail.

This might be a big risk, but it's a smart one. Even if it makes my life harder.

The more Forest is around, the quicker he'll discover our lie.

As long as the fallout is—

He's going to find out eventually.

But I—

The guy is my friend. I owe him this much.

Chase: It's a good idea.

Ariel: But won't he be around all the time? He'll get more suspicious.

Chase: We could tell him.

Ariel: Uh…

Chase: What's he gonna do?

Ariel: I don't think he owns a gun, but he might.

Chase: He's a levelheaded guy.

Ariel: So are you.

Chase: And?

Ariel: And I remember what you and Grace were like.

We fought all the time. Loud, screaming fights where we tore each other apart.

At first, I thought it was her.

But it takes two to tango. As Mom used to say. Before she gave up on advice entirely.

Chase: What are you going to tell him?

Ariel: When I'm pregnant?

Chase: Yeah. You can't tell him it was Phillip.

Ariel: That's true.

Chase: Have you thought that far?

Ariel: I will tell him something.

Chase: He should know.

Ariel: Okay, he should know. If it happens.

Chase: It's going to happen.

Ariel: You have no proof of that.

Chase: Should I come over right now? Fuck you senseless?

Ariel: Yeah, but I have back-to-back classes.

Chase: You have an office?

Ariel: I wish.

Chase: Fuck you in an empty classroom then. I always wanted to do a naughty teacher.

Ariel: Wouldn't the teacher be the one doing the punishing?

Chase: You want to be punished?

Ariel: That's not what I meant.

Chase: Do you?

Ariel: Maybe.

Chase: Yes or no, princess.

My balls tighten. This conversation is a bad idea. A terrible idea.

But I can't stop myself.

Ariel does something to me.

Everyone is right. I am different today. The world is different today. It's bigger, better, more beautiful.

Ariel: Yes.

Chase: How?

Ariel: I haven't thought about it.

Chase: Think about it.

Ariel: I'm not sure I'll be able to think about anything else.

Chase: I'm partial to spankings.

Ariel: Oh.

Chase: I could bend you over my lap. Punish you for not giving me the grade I want.

Ariel: Or you could be the professor.

Chase: Yeah?

Ariel: And maybe I wasn't paying attention in class.

Chase: Maybe you disobeyed my order to show up at my place without panties.

Ariel: Is that an order?

Chase: Depends.

Ariel: Oh?

Chase: Are you wet?

Ariel: Yes.

Chase: Then it is.

Ariel: What time?

Chase: I'll be free at six.

Ariel: Seven. I'll bring stuff for dinner.

Chase: You think you'll be able to keep your hands off me that long?

Ariel: I didn't say we'd start with dinner.

Fuck, this girl is going to kill me.

———

IT TAKES MY ENTIRE AFTERNOON BREAK, BUT I MANAGE to compile the paperwork we need to start this process.

After my last appointment, I meet Brendon in the office. I drop the stack of papers on his desk.

He only owns a quarter of Inked Hearts, but he does the majority of the owner duties.

His dark eyes flit to the front page. He reads the words carefully. Like his life depends on it.

I try to keep my posture strong and sure, but it's hard. I'm the same age as the owner. We're about the same height and size. Same general level of *don't fuck with me*.

But he has this confidence I don't. Like he knows he's destined to run this shop. Like his twenty-five percent ownership grants him magic powers.

Maybe it does.

I want that.

I really fucking do.

He looks to me with an impenetrable expression. "You're bringing us this out of goodwill?"

"No. I want a cut."

He nods *fair*. Picks up the stack. Flips to the second page. "You do good work, Chase."

"Thanks." It doesn't sound like a compliment, but I don't know how else to take it.

"You're to the point. I appreciate that." His voice softens. "I used to be the same."

"You're not exactly going into a soliloquy."

His chuckle is low, deep, knowing. "You've been here a year now."

"About that."

"You do good work, you have your own clients, you show up on time."

"And…"

"Do you want to be here?"

Fuck, how am I supposed to answer that?

"It's not a trick question." He sets the papers on the desk. Looks me dead in the eyes. "We'll check this out. See if it's a good deal. If it is, we'll need someone to manage the new shop."

"You want to do it?" My chest gets light. This is good. Great. Fucking fantastic.

He nods *yeah*. "We've been talking about buying another shop for a while. Just have to figure out the name."

"Inked Souls," I tease.

He chuckles. "Inked Love is the frontrunner."

I nod *sure*. It's close but not too close. It has that same vaguely romantic, vaguely fourteen-year-old emo kid vibe. "I like souls better."

"Maybe for the third shop."

I can't help but laugh.

He nods *I know, it's ridiculous*. "Forest and Holden do good work."

"They're good guys."

"Friends of yours."

It's not a question, but I answer anyway. "Yeah."

"Would you rather work with them?" His eyes bore into me.

"Than?"

He raises a brow *really, do I have to spell it out?*

I guess it's obvious how I feel. I make a point of requesting any shift my brother isn't working. "I'm comfortable here."

"There's no chance you're managing here."

It's a big opportunity. "I appreciate the candor."

He nods *of course*. "I hear you have a reputation for issuing orders." He chuckles. "Doesn't help with an actual office."

He would know. The guys here never tire of teasing Brendon about his taste for handcuffs.

His girlfriend is the sweetest thing too. A curvy blonde with blue glasses and innocent green eyes. Ten years his junior. Constantly attached to a book. Madly in love with Disney movies.

I didn't know him that well in high school. He was friends with Hunter, not me. I have to assume he heard Hunter's side of things.

Which is fine. I'm not here to make friends or win people over. I'm here to work. And Brendon is a professional enough guy. Maybe he thinks I'm a bitter asshole, but he doesn't hold it against me.

He's…

Not the same, exactly. But he's also a serious guy who knows family isn't easy.

"Hunter's a good friend. But you are too," Brendon says.

"What?"

He chuckles. "Yeah, we haven't done karaoke together—"

"Is that an invitation?"

"If we buy the shop, yeah. We're gonna celebrate. You ever meet Wes and Dean?"

"It's terrifying when they're together."

He shakes his head *nah*. "They get so caught up in one-upping each other, they forget to terrorize the rest of us."

That might be true.

"There are a lot of ways this can go, Chase. But, no matter what, Inked Hearts isn't going to be far."

Okay…

"I'm not gonna step in and mediate whatever's going on with you and your brother."

"It won't be a problem."

He makes that *I'm not sure I believe you* sound. "You'd be a good manager. It's a good idea."

"When do you need an answer?" I ask.

"Paperwork should take a few weeks. Months maybe." His eyes meet mine. "Can you get the money to buy?"

"Yeah." I have healthy savings.

"I'll get you numbers as soon as I can."

"Yeah."

Compassion drips into his voice. "No one is going to think less of you if you decide you need distance."

That's not true. Everyone is going to think I'm a bitter asshole.

But it's not like that's a change from their current opinions.

I'm the guy who can't make nice with his brother.

I'm the guy who can't move on.

Am I ready to make a permanent status?

Am I ready to give up on a real relationship with Hunter?

That's a hard fucking question.

I offer Brendon my hand. "I will, thanks."

He nods *sure* like he knows which way I'll go.

Maybe he's right.

Maybe I am hopeless.

Chapter Twenty-Eight

ARIEL

I press the *power* button. The hum of my Prius ceases. The music disappears. The air goes still.

Chase's apartment is right there. Right across the street. He lives in the suburban part of Venice with plenty of parking.

It's close to our place. I could walk.

But not with these, uh, conditions.

Seven o'clock. My place. No panties.

My sex clenches at the thought of his dirty demand. There's something about the low tone of his voice, something I've never felt before.

It wakes up some place that's sleeping.

It turns on something that's been off for far too long.

My skin flushes. I'm not sure if it's him or the car. It's late enough the sky is deep blue.

The air is crisp, not cold. Fall always creeps up on me.

The leaves don't change, but the nights get cold. The days get short. The tourists slow from a tsunami to a trickle.

Work gets heavier. Undergrads need more attention at

midterms and finals. Work on my thesis ebbs and flows, but it's always there, in the back of my mind.

The perfect distraction from other thoughts. To fill the gaps. So I don't start asking myself why every one of my boyfriend's left me. Why Chase so obviously doesn't see me as a romantic possibility. Why I'm even wondering about Chase's ideas of romantic possibilities.

This is casual. There's no reason why Chase should see me as a romantic possibility.

Those aren't even the scary questions.

There's that big one: Can I do this? Am I ready? Will I get it right?

I want to. There's no doubt about that. But it's all happening so quickly. I can't slow down and let that voice in. I don't have time.

Fuck, it's hot in here.

Even without the panties.

My fingers dig into my thighs.

Yes, this is it. This is where I need my head. On Chase's deep voice and his blue eyes and his hard—

No more thinking.

It's time to enjoy the ride.

I step out of the car, grab my purse and groceries, shut the door, hit the lock.

Beep-beep.

The familiar sound is comforting. Like I'm leaving one world for another. Like I'm leaving the shy, inexperienced Ariel behind.

When I'm with Chase—

It's like I really am the sex goddess I am in my fantasies. And the daydreams that have been running through my head—

Those are my focus. Period. End of story.

I shift the groceries to my hip. To get away from the

smell of mint and lime. It makes my mouth water, but it does things to my heart.

His door is open.

I knock then step inside.

He's standing there in jeans—just jeans—water dripping off his hair, shoulders, chest.

God, I want to be that drop of water. I want to glide over every inch of his skin. Especially the low v.

It's an arrow pointing to a prize.

A prize I need desperately.

"Princess, you're gonna make me think you're only in this for my body." He motions for me to come closer.

I do. "Who says I'm not?"

His lips curl into a half-smile. It's small, but it lights up his deep blue eyes.

His eyes are so beautiful filled with joy. It's a rare look on Chase, historically. Lately—

That's another road I can't travel. But, God, it's good to see him smile. To feel his joy. It bounces around the room. Pours into my heart. Makes my entire body warm.

He takes the groceries, sets the bag on the counter, moves everything into the fridge.

"What if I'm hungry now?" I press my lips together. It's a pathetic protest. Yeah, my stomach is growling. But that's nothing compared to the ache between my legs.

"Still need to fridge the meat." He finishes unpacking. Closes the fridge. Turns to me.

I nod *of course*. It's all I can think to say. It's all I can think, period.

The way he stares at me, like he wants to consume me, like he's sure I'll obey every single order.

It's hot in here.

It's so fucking hot in here.

He takes a step toward me. Brings his hands to my

hips. "You follow orders, princess?" He pulls my body into his.

I look up at him. Get lost in his intense blue eyes. "What if I didn't?"

"I'll have to punish you."

My sex clenches. God, that's so hot.

"Is that what you want, princess?" He brings his hand to my lower back. Slips it under my tank top. Runs it over the waistband of my jeans. "You want me to bend you over my lap and spank you?"

My nod is heavy.

"You want me to tease you until you can't take it anymore?"

"Chase—"

"That a yes?" He presses his palm into my lower back to hold my body against his.

He's hard.

He's already hard.

That feels so good. Why does that feel so fucking good?

"It's not a dare." He brings his other hand to my inner thigh. Runs his fingertips over my jeans, pressing the fabric into my skin. "If you don't like it, I want to know."

I nod.

"But the look in your eyes—" He drags his fingertips higher, higher, higher. Over the seam of my jeans. Over my sex.

Fuck, the friction of the denim.

It's rough and soft at the same time.

I reach for something to grab onto. Get his chest. He's so strong and warm, and the sight of my light hands against his tan, tattooed skin—

My heartbeat picks up.

My breath catches in my throat.

My knees knock together.

He holds me steady as he rubs me over my jeans. He does it softly. So softly I barely feel it.

But that only makes it more intense.

Every brush of his hand is a shockwave. Electricity shoots to my fingers. My toes curl. My sex clenches. My nipples pang.

I need more of his hand.

And more of this delicious, perfect pressure.

"You like following orders." He brings his lips to my neck. "Don't you, princess?"

"Yes," I breathe.

He rubs me with that same perfect pressure. "Good girl."

Fuck, that shouldn't be so hot. But it is. It really is.

"You know what that does to me?"

I shake my head.

He shifts his hips so his cock presses against my stomach.

Fuck, I want that. I want it so badly.

He nips at my neck as he rubs me with that same pressure. It winds me tighter, tighter, tighter—

"Chase." I claw at his skin.

"Louder."

"Chase." I hook my other hand around his waist. Hold onto him for dear life. Fuck, he feels so good against my skin. Hard and warm and safe.

There's no other way to explain it.

He feels safe. Like he'll protect me. Like he'll give me everything I want.

Here.

He scrapes his teeth over my neck as he rubs me.

I hold onto him. Melt into his skin.

He winds me tighter, tighter, tighter—

There.

My fingers dig into his skin.

I groan his name as I come. My eyes close. My world goes white. That same soft, sweet light of bliss. Like everything in the universe is shiny and new and beautiful.

He brings his hand to my inner thigh. Brings his lips to mine.

His kiss is hard, aggressive.

He scrapes his teeth against my bottom lip. Then the top. Then he's sucking on my bottom lip.

He toys with my tender flesh, then he slips his tongue into my mouth.

He claims me with his tongue. There's no other way to describe it. It's so fucking clear I'm his.

Not anywhere else. But here? When it's just our bodies?

I want every part of him. Every demand. Every desire. Every inch.

I shift my hips so his cock presses into my stomach.

"You want that, princess?" He keeps his hold on my lower back. Keeps me steady.

I nod.

"Where?"

Where? Is he really asking?

Oh my God.

He's so—

My sex clenches.

He presses his palm against me, pressing my jeans into my tender flesh. "In that pretty cunt?"

I nod.

He drags his fingers over the seam of my jeans, forward, over my clit, then backward, all the way to my—

"In that gorgeous ass?" He brings his hand to my mouth. Catches my lower lip with his thumb. "Or here?"

My nod is heavy.

"You want to wrap those pretty lips around me?"

"Yes." I look up to him, asking for permission. It's absurd. What guy hesitates when offered *that*?

But the way he stares, like he's only going to give me what I want on his terms, on his time—

Fuck, it's so hot.

He cups my ass with his hand. Runs his fingers over my skin, checking for panties. Or double, checking, I guess. "You followed orders."

I nod *yes*.

"Good girls get what they want."

Oh my God.

"On your knees." He offers his hand. Helps me onto my knees.

There's a rug where the coffee table usually goes.

He put this here on purpose.

A padding for our activities.

Fuck, it's so hot and thoughtful and dirty all at once.

I grab onto his hips to steady myself. I'm right where I need to be, and, fuck, I need to do this.

He cups the back of my head with his hand. "Tell me what you want, princess."

I reach for his button.

"Say the words."

"That I want—"

He nods *yeah*.

"I… I can't say that."

He nods *you can*.

My cheeks flush. It's one thing being here. Or following his orders. Or responding to his dirty talk.

Actually saying it?

Is that possible?

I look up at him. Hold his gaze for a second. It's too much, too intense.

My gaze shifts to the floor. It travels up his body. Strong

legs and thighs, narrow hips, massive bulge.

It's so wrong that he's covered in jeans.

I need to undo them.

I need to unleash him.

I really, really need to taste him.

"Say it, princess."

"Chase—"

"You want to suck my cock?" It's only barely a question.

I nod *yes*.

"Then say it."

I look up at him, but that's a no go. Okay, I can do this. It's just a few words. A few super hot, incredibly dirty words unlike anything I've ever said before.

Deep breath.

Slow exhale.

Less thinking. No thinking. Just a direct line from my libido to my mouth.

God, that's—

"I…" I cup him over his jeans. "I want to suck your cock."

He lets out a low, deep groan.

"I want to make you come." I look up at him. Blush. "I want to taste you."

He shakes his head. "I'm coming in that pretty cunt."

My sex clenches. My thoughts try to step in, remind me the whole reason why we're here. I absorb enough to nod.

I know how biology works.

I just… don't care. Not like this. Not when I'm here.

"This time." I'm not sure why I'm trying to negotiate. Only that I have to. "But later—"

"I'll come in your pretty mouth later."

Fuck, the sure, steady tone to his voice—

I'm on fire.

My thoughts slip away.

I undo his button.

He nods, giving me permission. It's so fucking hot, that he's giving me permission, that I have to ask.

He's in control.

And I'm desperate to obey.

I unzip his jeans. Roll them off his hips. Then the boxers.

God, there's something about the sight of him up close. Long, thick, hard.

I wrap my hand around him.

Bring my lips to his tip. A soft brush. Just enough to taste him.

That same soap and underneath that, something all Chase.

Something I need desperately.

I explore him with my lips. Watch him shudder and groan as I taste every part of his tip then every inch of his shaft.

He digs his fingers into my hair. Cups the back of my head. Like he's ready to lead at any moment.

But he doesn't.

He stays patient as I explore him.

I try slow strokes. Then faster ones.

I find the spot that makes him groan.

Flick my tongue against him until he's shaking.

Then I take him into my mouth.

My lips stretch over his flesh. God, there's something about the feel of him in my mouth.

I need it. More of it. All of it.

He looks down at me, his expression equal parts heady and demanding.

He holds me in place with his palm.

I take him deeper.

Deeper.

Fuck.

I swallow to relax my throat.

When I can't take him anymore, I wrap my hand around him. Then I pull back.

I do it again. A little faster.

I run my mouth over him slowly. So I can savor every inch.

Then again.

Again.

Until he's shuddering and tugging at my hair.

Then I do it faster. Faster.

There—

He lets out a low, deep groan. "Ariel."

My sex clenches. I love the way he says my name. I love that I'm the one driving him out of his mind. I love every fucking thing about this.

I work him with that same speed.

He presses his palm into the back of my head, urging me on.

My body buzzes.

I need this.

Need him.

Need his bliss filling me.

I let him lead. Let him drive my mouth over him. Drive himself deeper.

"Fuck." He reaches for my shoulder. Tugs at the strap of my tank top. "Princess—"

I keep going.

"Fuck, I'm gonna…" He tugs at my shoulders, telling me to stand, to stop.

I should follow orders. I should be a good girl. God, even the sound of it makes my sex ache.

But I want to make him come like this.

I want to taste him like this.

I don't stop.

I keep going. Keep driving him deeper and deeper.

His hand knots in my hair.

His groans fill the room.

"Fuck." His voice is low, heavy, like he can barely get the words out.

I take him again.

He tugs at my hair. Hard. Hard enough it hurts.

He pulls me off him. Pulls me to my feet. Pushes me onto the couch.

"Pants off," he growls.

I unzip my jeans.

He pushes them to my thighs.

His hands go to my hips. In one swift motion, he enters me.

Chase holds me in place as he fucks me.

I dig my fingers into the couch for balance.

He drives into me with deep, steady strokes.

It's a lot. Intense enough it hurts.

But that feels good too.

God, he feels so fucking good.

His nails scrape against my skin as he drives deeper and deeper.

Then he's there.

He comes quickly. He tugs at my hair, groaning my name as he fills me.

When he's finished, he helps me onto my back on the couch.

I pull my knees into my chest.

He looks down at me with a smile. "Bad girl."

My cheeks flush.

"You looking to be punished, princess?

"Maybe."

His smile screams *you are and I like it*. "You have a vibrator?"

"What?" I clear my throat. "Why?"

"Pretty sure I'm gonna need one with you."

"Is that a good thing?"

He nods *yeah*. "I want you to come on my cock."

Fuck, the way he says that is so hot.

"If you're not gonna give me time to warm you up—"

"I don't have a vibrator." I try to make my voice confident. Sorta get there. Mostly. "But I—"

"Let's go shopping."

"Tomorrow."

He nods. "Tomorrow." He sits next to me. Pulls my knees over his lap. "Right now, you need to come on my hand."

"I—"

"You…?"

"Okay." My lips curl into a smile.

"Okay? Princess, I need better than okay."

"Yes."

"Yes?"

"Hell yes."

He smiles *good*.

Chapter Twenty-Nine

ARIEL

"You don't have sugar?" I check the cabinet again. There's protein powder and a million vitamins and fifty different spices, but there isn't any sugar.

"Why would I?" He looks at me like the question is ridiculous.

"Because it's sugar?" How can anyone not have sugar? It's an ingredient in most recipes.

His expression stays dumbfounded. "I don't eat it."

"Why?"

His brow furrows. He stares back at me, not at all understanding the inquiry. "Don't consume addictive things."

"What about coffee?"

"Except for coffee."

"You put sugar in your coffee," I say.

"A little simple syrup, yeah."

"So…" I motion to the simple syrup free pantry.

"Drink it black too."

"You don't have honey."

"Or maple syrup, or agave, or coconut sugar." His lips curl into a smile. "They're all sugar."

"But you cook. You must use sugar sometimes."

"Had a jar of honey once." He shrugs like he doesn't know what happened to it or care.

"And now…"

"Do you need sugar?"

"Ideally. But I guess we'll make do." Maybe it's better leaving something out of the recipe. Less familiar.

"I think it's in the fridge—"

"The—"

"Honey." He pulls the fridge open. Scans the top shelf. Nothing. Middle shelf nothing. Bottom shelf, behind the bag of carrots.

Victory.

A honey bear. Mostly unused.

"Griffin puts it in his coffee sometimes," he says.

"You have people over?"

"On occasion."

Immediately, the mental image forms. A friend—I know Griffin—sitting on Chase's couch, watching a movie with him, teasing him about his misery.

Chase nodding and smiling back *yeah, I'm miserable, what's it to you?*

Is he relaxed with other people?

Is he ever relaxed?

Or is he always thinking about her?

Ahem. "And this sugar thing has never been an issue?"

He chuckles. "For you, I'll keep sugar."

"Thanks." I take the honey, run it under warm water. I do like my chai lattes sweet. I'm down to one a day. I know zero would be better, but it's hard giving up spicy perfection. Especially when Chase is willing to keep honey here for me.

Okay, it's sugar, not an engagement ring.

But the logic does nothing to calm the flutter in my stomach. "Will that mess you up?"

"How?"

"You have a reason for avoiding it."

"My mom's an alcoholic, yeah."

"So you rarely drink."

He nods *of course, you know that.*

"I just… uh… I didn't realize you took it so seriously."

He shrugs like it's not a big deal.

But it is. He avoids addicting substances to the point of eschewing dessert, candy, sweetened coffee even.

It's not the most consistent position, sure, but it's still drastic.

He's that scared of following in his mother's footsteps.

He's that unable to trust himself.

That's…

Fuck, that's really a mess.

His voice is even, effortless. "What if I was one of those guys who was on some low-carb diet?"

"Ugh. Really?"

He chuckles. "No."

"I mean, do what works for you, but please don't tell me about your diet." My eyes meet his. "Are you really?"

"No. But I avoid anything that's bad for me."

"Always?"

"I try."

I guess I'm not that different. I've been a good girl my entire life (and not in the dirty way, though that is a very delicious way). I study hard, I put in hours at work, I cook healthy meals.

But when I want chocolate or cake or ice cream, I eat it.

When I'm tired, I watch trashy TV.

When I'm lazy, I skip my walks.

When I'm lonely—

Okay, I haven't checked on Phillip. But I did stalk Chase's ex. And, God, the shit that went through my mind.

Not healthy choices. At all.

"Isn't that exhausting?" I ask.

"I'm used to it."

My chest gets heavy. He carries around so much pain. Does he see it? He must. He calls himself a bitter asshole.

He's not bitter.

He's not an asshole.

He's just hurting.

I was the same after Mom died. Everything was hard and heavy and ugly. For years.

There was no dramatic change. No moment where the light flipped on. It got a little easier some days. Got worse other days. Then one day, it wasn't so heavy it weighed me down.

"I was like that after my mom," I say.

He wraps his arms around me. Brings his lips to my neck. "You've been through a lot."

"You too."

"But you're happy." Disbelief drips into his voice.

A laugh spills from my lips. "Usually."

"I'm—"

"If you say you're a bitter asshole again, I'm going to hit you."

He chuckles. "Now, I have to say it. I want to see how well you punch."

"Forest convinced me to join his karate class."

"It's aikido."

"Okay, I'll aikido your ass."

"Aikido is about not harming your opponent."

"Yeah, but I'm not very good at it."

He chuckles. "Okay. Say I'm not a bitter asshole. What am I?"

"Hurting."

He nods *fair*. Steps back, releasing me.

My body whines from the loss of contact. I want his warmth, his hardness, his softness. How can one person be two opposite things?

Not that I'm getting attached.

Just… we're friends. Friends notice these things.

"Small saucepan," I say.

He nods *sure*, grabs a pan off the rack.

For a while, I focus on our task. We're making bun cha, a simple dish. Cold rice noodles, savory pork, crunchy vegetables.

There are a lot of steps, but I know them like the back of my hand.

We cook and rinse the noodles.

We boil water, dissolve the honey, combine with fish sauce, garlic, and chili peppers.

Chase cuts the veggies into perfect long rectangles. Like something out of a cookbook. Like he actually knows what julienned means and he doesn't just cut them into whatever size is easiest.

For a while, routine takes over. This was one of the first dishes I learned to make. It's simple, light, refreshing.

But there's something about the smell of fish sauce and mint.

It's too familiar.

I can't see anything but Phillip's mom's smile as she showed me how to stir the sauce.

His laugh.

Them teasing each other in Vietnamese. I never knew what they were saying, but I knew it was about me.

I knew it was good.

Conversation is half body language and a third tone. The actual words are the least important part.

Chase sets two plates on the counter. He turns to me, his clear blue eyes filled with concern. "We can order take out."

I shake my head. I'm okay. Mostly. I need to get past this. I'm not giving up the food I know best, that I love most, that feels like home. Like a home that's not there anymore.

Shit.

I blink and a tear catches on my lashes.

What the hell? I don't cry. I don't get upset. I don't get emotional.

All of a sudden, everything is stirring inside me.

Was it Phillip leaving? Or is it something else?

I still don't get it. Why he left. Why I wasn't enough. Why he stopped wanting the storybook ending.

"Ariel." Chase wraps his arms around my waist. He pulls my body into his.

My forehead goes to his chest. Then my cheek. My hands.

God, he feels so safe. There's no other word for it. It's almost scary how safe he feels.

No, it is scary. And overwhelming. Because Phillip felt like that too. And Phillip left.

He's gone.

I'm alone.

I'm doing this on my own.

I—

Fuck.

I press my eyelids together, but tears still well. "Sorry."

"What for?"

"We're not…"

"We're friends."

"Yeah, but…" I motion to the food. "It's getting cold."

"It's supposed to be cold."

"Only the noodles." The meat is supposed to be warm. So you get both sensations.

Not that it matters.

It's only dinner.

What's it matter if everything is lukewarm?

I can do this. I just have to breathe.

"You want to sit down?" he asks.

I shake my head and lean in a little closer.

He pulls me tighter. Wraps one hand around me. Brings the other to the back of my head. Runs his fingers through my hair.

It's soft, gentle, caring.

I want that.

Not with Chase. Not exactly.

I miss that. The love, connection, closeness.

The safety.

But that was an illusion. There is no safety. This isn't safe. This is the most dangerous thing I've ever done.

"You can talk if you want." His fingers brush my back. "You don't have to. But you can."

"I… I think I'm hungry."

His chuckle is low. "You're hungry crying?"

"No, it just… it can't be helping." I force myself to step backward. It's so cold, letting go of him. So empty. But that's a good sign. That's a warning. I'm getting too close. Too comfortable.

"I can make something else."

"No. I want this. It was the first thing Quyen taught me to make. The first time I tasted it, it was like home."

"I get that."

"I'd forgotten about that. When my mom was here… every day, I felt that. She always kissed us goodbye, sat with us at dinner, tucked us in at night. Even when I was ten, when I insisted I was too old for that, she came in to wish me good night." I wipe tears with my thumb. "She filled the world with so much love."

"I wish I'd known her better."

"Me too." Something catches on my lips. Something hot and salty. A tear. "She liked you."

"I'm sorry."

"Why?"

"That she's gone."

I've heard that so many times. It never felt like more than a platitude. But this… I don't know. "I miss her. I miss talking about her. Ever since she died… I blocked out those memories. I hate that."

"Sometimes it hurts too much."

I don't know what to say, so I nod. I take a seat. Let Chase bring dinner to the table.

He pours waters, brings silverware and napkins and sriracha, sits with me. "Thank you."

"For?"

"Making this."

"You did a lot."

"With your help." His fingers brush the back of my hand. "I wish I had more than *I'm sorry*. The first time I thought my mom was gone… fuck, it killed me."

I nod *thanks*. "It has to be harder that way."

"She's still here."

"Is she though?"

His chuckle is low. Knowing. "Maybe. She went through rehab."

"She's still sober?"

"Three months now." His gaze shifts to the rice noodles. "But I don't know if I can let her break my heart again."

I know exactly what he means.

"I had this thought when I got that call—"

"The car crash?"

He nods. "I thought she was dead. And I was relieved for a minute. At least, it was finally over. She'd stop destroying herself. Stop destroying me." He picks up his fork. "It's fucking terrible."

"No, I get it." I pick up my fork. Spin noodles around it. "It was like that when my mom was fading… I didn't want her to go, but at the same time…"

"You couldn't get your hopes up anymore?"

"Yeah." I take a bite. Mint, fish sauce, sriracha. God, it really does taste like home. The chewy noodles, crisp veggies, tender meat. It's perfect.

It hurts more that way.

"I… uh… I don't want to undersell my dad," I say. "When he's home, he's around. We make dinner, talk, watch movies. The ones Mom loved. Though, she kind of loved everything. She loved film…" I suck in a deep breath. "He's a good dad, but it's different."

"You always feel that loss."

"Yeah. I guess… I'm sorry about your mom."

"Thanks."

"I hope you two can be okay."

"Me too."

"Really?"

"Yeah." He takes a bite. Chews slowly. Swallows. "I miss her. The person she was before the alcohol took over."

God, I can't imagine that. It was agony losing Mom. But losing her then seeing a shell of her every day?

I couldn't do it.

I'd run for the hills.

Chase keeps trying. He may do it in a tough love way, but he's still there.

"I, uh, we do Sunday dinners still. You should come." I want that sense Phillip's family had. That I had when I was with him. I want that for my child. For our place to always feel like home.

"Wouldn't Forest—"

"Oh, right." I have to tell my brother something. "We could—"

"Tell him the truth," Chase says.

"Eventually." I take another bite. "I promise."

He nods *okay*.

"I… I don't know if I can do that?"

"Tell your brother?"

No, I can do that. I have to do that. If I don't find a gentle way to break the news, I'll crack and spill and make it a million times worse.

But I can handle that.

I've been my brother's sister for a long time.

This? This is a whole new challenge. "Make a home like that. What if I become like my mom? Or yours?"

"You won't."

"How do you know?"

His eyes meet mine. They fill with certainty. "Ariel, you're the most tenacious person I've ever met."

"That doesn't mean—"

"Yeah, it might not stop a health problem. Or an accident. But nobody can stop that."

That's true. "I just…"

"You're gonna be a great mom."

I press my lips together. I want to believe that. I do.

"You're caring. You're smart. You're creative. You brought a whole grocery store here just to make me dinner."

"It was only a few things." Okay, a dozen. But it was easy to grab them.

He nods to the massive bag on the counter. "The way you treat me—"

"Am I too involved?" God, is it obvious I want to help him?

He shakes his head *no*. "You believe in me. You believe I'm capable of being better. And it makes me want to be better."

"You can—"

"But you don't bullshit me either. You're incapable of bullshit."

"You mean I can't lie?"

"Yeah." His lips curl into a smile. "You might be a little quirky, sure. Maybe you're not the most tactful. But your heart is full of love. This honest, pure, unafraid love. Anyone would be lucky to have that."

"Any kid?"

He blinks. Shifts back in his seat. "Anyone."

I swallow hard. "Phillip didn't want that." I asked him to do this with me, and he said no. He didn't want it.

"You gave him an ultimatum. You left."

What? No. "He didn't want kids with me. He didn't think we could do it."

"Maybe he didn't want kids."

"He did before."

"It's different when it's an abstract discussion."

"How do you know?" I ask.

"Grace had a scare."

Oh.

"She wasn't pregnant. But if she was... I wanted that. So fucking badly. I always knew I did. But when she told me it was an actual possibility, something flipped in my brain. I forget how terrified I was of my kid becoming an alcoholic. I forget how terrified I was of becoming my mom. I just—"

"You just knew?"

"Yeah."

He just knew that he wanted to be a father. "Do you still want that?"

"One day."

But he's doing this for me. He's not getting that. God, I want him to have that.

"Your ex is a doctor."

"A resident. He's still in training."

"And, he's what, twenty-five?"

"Twenty-seven."

"A twenty-seven-year-old who has no free time."

It makes sense when he says it that way. But—"People do it."

"When they want it badly."

"So he didn't want me," I say.

"Or he didn't want kids."

Maybe. It's just… so hard to believe.

"He's miserable."

"How do you know?"

His expression gets sheepish. "I check on his social media."

"Maybe it's a different Phillip Nguyen."

"Who posts pictures with you?"

Okay, that seems unlikely.

I take another bite. Chew. Swallow.

It helps.

I am hungry.

I need nourishment. And space. And a lock for my heart.

Men are just—

They're too difficult and untrustworthy.

"He's not the same without you," Chase says.

"Free?" Finally able to screw his hot boss.

He shakes his head. "Miserable."

I bite my lip. That can't be possible. It can't.

Chase holds my gaze. "I can show you."

Maybe. I want to know, but it's a bad idea. I should move forward, not backward. "Only if I can show you Grace."

His face goes white.

"You want her to be happy, right?"

His voice is uncertain. "I think so." His shoulders tense. His jaw cricks. All of a sudden, he's the picture of discomfort. "You follow her?"

I twirl noodles around my fork. "Her Instagram is public."

He swallows hard.

"If you don't want to know—"

"Do you?"

Maybe. I think so. "I'll jump if you will."

Chapter Thirty

CHASE

My heart is in my throat.

Do I want to know if my ex-girlfriend is happy?

Do I want to see the visual evidence that I added to her pain?

Do I want to know, with certainty, that everyone I've ever loved does better without me?

My fingers curl into my fork. I try to move the noodles to my mouth, but my hand stays in place.

It's ridiculous. I'm starving. And this dish is delicious.

Chewy noodles. Crunchy vegetables. Tender meat.

All that love Ariel poured into it. The love that's still with Phillip. The love she's forming for her future child.

It could be there.

She could be pregnant right now.

Maybe that too fast fuck on the couch was—

Even if she's not, she's going to get there. And when she does.

If I'm a fucking virus, I need to know. I can't spread

that to her kid. Even if I want to be in her life. In their lives.

"It's okay if you don't want to." She slurps noodles into her mouth. Chews. Swallows.

Every molecule of my body is screaming to know.

But the possibility that I'm the cause of all this shit?

Fuck, I don't know if I can take that evidence.

Maybe I need some kind of twelve step program. Hi, I'm Chase Keating and I destroy everyone I love. As soon as I remove myself, they get better.

After I kicked out Hunter—

After I gave Mom an ultimatum—

After Grace left.

She landed a seventy-two-hour hold while she was with me.

And now—

"It's healthy, to move on." She sets her fork down.

It's possible.

"Maybe… maybe this is a step. To moving on. Seeing that we're all better off."

Most of us, at least.

"It's up to you, Chase. I… hate the way you talk about yourself." Her voice softens. "You're such a great guy. But you… you're like Batman or Daredevil."

"I'm like Daredevil?"

"Of course." Her voice is dead serious. "Don't tell me the metaphor escapes you." She motions to my bookshelf. "You have like every issue."

"And…"

"And we watched the show together."

"You wanted to watch it."

"Well, yeah. It's got amazing action."

I can't help but laugh. "You convince me to watch superhero shows for the action. I stay for the themes."

"Oh, 'cause I'm a girl." She rolls her eyes. "Grow up, Chase. I've been reading comic books since—"

"I was reading comic books when you were born."

"Okay, but I bet I've read more."

"I'll take that bet." I try to offer her my hand, but my arm is too stiff. I roll my shoulders back. Suck in a deep breath. Push out a full exhale.

She's defusing this already.

She doesn't realize it.

Ariel is—

She's going to make someone really fucking happy one day. Some very lucky guy. Someone who doesn't destroy everything he touches.

Maybe—

What the fuck am I hoping here? I want Grace happy and healthy. Even if that means I'm doomed to ruin everyone I love.

It's not that I still love her.

I do.

But not in the same way. I'm not in love with her. I haven't been in love with her for a long time.

It's just—

I'm not sure what the fuck I am toward her.

"All his love interests face horrible fates." That can't be what she means. But it's true.

"Well… yeah. But that's not his fault. It's comic book writers. They can't handle the idea of a woman who finds happiness."

I arch a brow.

"Like that album you love. With the car crashes." She half-smiles. "Why is that guy so obsessed with car crashes?"

"You think I know?"

"You listen to it all the time."

"Don't have a direct line to his head." If I could figure anyone out, it would be myself.

She nods *true*. "No. You're like the Daredevil in the show."

"Charismatic and buff?"

"Yeah." A laugh spills from her lips. Lights up her eyes. For a moment, it wipes away the tension in the room. Then she blinks and it's back. "You have this martyr complex."

"A complex?"

She nods. "You think everyone is better off without you. Even when they tell you otherwise. You think you have to save the whole world all by yourself. Even when other people want to help."

"To the point where it's a complex?"

"Yeah." She presses her lips together. "I mean, at least he has super powers that make him more able to solve problems. And, you know, he has that lust for violence he can't admit to." Her eyes fix on mine. "Maybe you're like that. Maybe you love being miserable."

"Damn."

"Oh." Her brow furrows. "I didn't mean it like… I was just thinking out loud."

"I'm not offended." It's not like I can deny the allegations.

"I mean, he's super hot and kinda dreamy. Usually. Until he goes off with that self-pitying martyr complex. It's annoying. And paternalistic." She rolls her eyes again. "Maybe he has abilities, but so do other people. He takes away their agency by stepping in all the time. Other people can help in their own ways. They want to help. But he pushes them away and makes it his fight and his alone. And that's just… it's bullshit."

I can't help but chuckle.

"What?"

"You really hate Matt Murdock."

"No." She bites her lip. "He's just... get over yourself, you know?"

I shake my head. I don't know. Not enough.

"Not that you're that—"

"Horrible?"

She clears her throat. "I, uh... I mean, there are parallels between the two of you, but I'm not saying you're... he's totally a dreamboat. Usually. So even if you're like him, uh..."

"I'm not offended."

"Oh." She presses her lips together. "Good."

"Just thinking."

She folds her hands in her lap. Stares at me with a nervous expression. Like she's sure she's hurt me.

"He's Hunter's favorite. Daredevil."

She nods *right*. Leans forward like she's expecting insight.

"Maybe... I guess I don't stop to think about how he feels."

"Like he also has that guilt for failing at something that's not his fault?"

"Yeah." I stay away because it's for the best. That's what I tell myself. But maybe that's bullshit. Maybe it's something else.

"But you do want him to be happy?"

I nod *of course*.

"So... uh... I think, um... should I go?"

"Why?"

"That was a horrible thing to say."

"Is it what you think?" I ask.

"Yeah, but not in a bad way, exactly."

"You never have to apologize for telling me what you think," I say.

She crosses and uncrosses her legs. "Oh… Uh…"

"Let's look." I need more evidence. I want her to be right. I want this to be in my head. Even if that means my head is more fucked than I like to believe.

That's fixable. I've seen people work through their shit. Yeah, they always did it after I bailed. They always proved they were better off without me.

But at least I know it's possible.

If only I could work through my shit without me.

That would be something.

"But I show you first." I need to prove I can leave someone better than when I found them.

I need to help her. Period.

I really fucking like Ariel. I want the world for her. I want the best for her.

Whatever that means.

"Okay. Should I get my laptop?" She motions to her backpack.

"I'll get mine." I stand and move into the bedroom. It's dark. Quiet. Cool.

The space that's all mine. That was all mine until she whirled into my life.

Fuck, I really like having her in my life. I love making her laugh or smile or groan.

I love when she falls asleep on my shoulder—

Or melts into my chest.

Or gushes over the food I made.

I don't know what the fuck I'm doing here. There are lines. I'm supposed to keep them firm. So neither one of us gets hurt.

So she doesn't get hurt.

But now…

I find my laptop on my desk. Bring it to the table.

Ariel scoots closer. She brings her half-finished dinner. Slurps noodles. "Here goes nothing."

I nod and pull up her ex's Facebook.

It's quiet. A few posts about medicine that go over my head. A few pictures of his family.

Ariel offers the screen every ounce of her attention. She does everything like that. At one hundred percent.

Her eyes light up at the sight of his parents.

They turn down when she gets to an old picture, of the two of them.

It's older, a Fourth of July barbecue, but it's perfect. They're dressed in matching red, white, and blue outfits. Grilling in his parents' backyard. Happy.

Both of them are happy.

Fuck, the smile on her face does something to me. Makes me warm in places that are usually cold.

She nods. "He's not seeing anyone else yet." She bites her lip. "I thought... I thought he liked his boss."

"Maybe it's a crush."

"Maybe."

"You've never had a crush on another guy?"

"Well... I guess. But I never..." Her eyes meet mine. Her expression gets sheepish. "I... let's see the Instagram."

I nod *sure* and pull it up.

She scrolls backward through the posts. Dinners and coffees. Then dinners and coworkers. Dinners and family. (The guy likes his food).

Dinners and Ariel.

Snapshots of the summer. A sweaty hike in the Malibu hills. A day at the beach. The two of them sharing iced drinks at a hipster cafe.

Her licking an ice cream cone.

Which gives me too many fucking ideas.

Not the time. At all.

But, God damn, she has such a pretty mouth.

At least that—I know I'm good at that. I know what she wants there. I know how to help her there.

She swallows hard. "He was happy." Her gaze shifts to the keyboard. "I thought I'd feel better, but I just—"

"It still hurts when he hurts?"

She nods *yeah*.

"You still love him?"

"No." She scrolls way back, through years and years, all the way to Phillip with a different woman. "I don't get that pang anymore. I don't get sick over the thought of him kissing someone else. But—"

"You still want him to be happy."

"Yeah." Her eyes find mine. "I guess that's… healthy?"

"You're asking me?"

"Right." A laugh spills from her lips. "I can't tell with you."

I arch a brow.

"If you have a good sense of humor about your issues. Or if you're deflecting."

"You sure you're not studying psychology?"

She nods. "If I was, I'd be able to tell."

I can't help but laugh. "Maybe."

She rests her head on my shoulder. Lets out a long sigh. "Do you… do you still want to see Grace?"

"Yeah."

"Can you handle it?"

I have no fucking idea.

Chapter Thirty-One

CHASE

"Do it." I push the laptop to Ariel.

She rests her hands on the keyboard. Keeps her eyes on the screen. Keeps her expression apprehensive.

She doesn't have to say it.

We both know it.

This isn't a place where I excel.

I don't know if I can handle this information, but I need it. I need this piece of the puzzle. I need to know what the hell my future holds.

Ariel's eyes flit to me. She studies my expression for a moment, then she nods, and turns to the computer.

She taps Grace's username into the search bar.

Pulls up her feed.

There's her profile picture. A new version of a classic. Her winking at the camera, light hair spilling over her face, red lips in a smile, makeup dark.

The first few pictures are easy. Latte art in cream and caramel. Red chucks. A screenshot of a Buttercup

Halloween costume on Etsy, with *two weeks until true love* scribbled in red.

Grace hugging a tall guy with dark hair and dark eyes.

The musician. He's effortless in his leather jacket and jeans. Like he just rolled out of bed with perfect hair and *fuck me* eyes.

Her arm is around his waist.

His is around her shoulders.

They're at some crowded event. A gallery.

I nod *that one*.

Ariel bites her lip, but she opens the image.

I love how my baby supports my art.

Then there's his screenname and a bunch of hashtags.

Fuck, I want to reach out and click his name. To see every single way he's better than I am. And every way he's worse.

That ugly, competitive impulse races through my body.

I need to be better than him.

But I'm not.

No matter what I do, he makes her happy. I don't.

I nod to Ariel *go on*.

She tabs back to the original page. Scrolls through weeks of history.

The two of them at dinner. A finished painting. The sketch. The mock-up. The inspiration.

A party with friends.

More latte art and dinner and drinks.

The beach. A hike. Dinner with his family.

Summer parties.

Summer projects.

Mirror selfies of her outfits. The same trendy style she always wore. High waist shorts, crop tops, sneakers, dark makeup.

The semi-colon tattoo on her wrist.

Ariel's finger hovers over the square image. "I… uh… I looked it up."

"Yeah?"

"It's really beautiful, actually." She bites her lip. "The semi-colon project."

"Project semi-colon."

"Oh." Her eyes flit to me. It must be bad, because her frown deepens. "You know about it?"

I nod *of course*. There's way too much to say. Things I should tell her. But I have to start somewhere.

"She kind of lays it out. Uh…" She doesn't wait for my permission. She opens the image. Reads the caption. "Forgive yourself. It's the hardest thing you'll ever have to do. But it's worth it."

I don't need to see the date to know.

Two years since she—

Since I—

My stomach drops. I can't go back to that memory. It steals all my oxygen.

It hits me all at once—

The feeling of her limp body in my arms.

The dial tone that lasted too fucking long.

The 911 operator telling me it would be okay.

The look on her mom's face when she got to the ICU.

"She tried to… I looked it up. You're supposed to say attempted suicide. So it's more clinical. There are all these rules about how you're supposed to talk about it. So you don't cause a contagion." Ariel swallows hard. "It's kind of ridiculous. You're not supposed to talk about it, because it might give people ideas. So how are you supposed to move on? Or admit it happened? Or heal? If you have to dance around the details?" She catches herself rambling. Clears her throat. "Sorry… I… I don't know what to say."

"She did."

"How… uh, you're not supposed to ask that. But I… I promise I'm not at risk." She leans back in her chair. Sets her hands in her lap. "If I'm overstepping…"

"She bought drugs from a friend."

"Oh." Ariel bites her lip. "Do you blame them?"

"No. He didn't know why she wanted them. And she'd have figured something out either way. She was…" Where do I start? Grace was—Grace is full of fire and light. But she's just as full of darkness. "She has bipolar too."

"Shit." She presses her lips together. "That must have been a lot."

"Sometimes." It's there, the semi-colon on her wrist. The one she added after we broke up. "When she was serious about treatment, she was… maybe not happy or easy, but okay."

Ariel nods.

"I thought… I don't know. I guess, when I was younger, I thought I could save her."

"Like you wanted to save your mom?"

I can't help but laugh.

Ariel's brow furrows. "Sorry, was that—"

"You say this shit that everyone is thinking. Hell, there's a part of me thinking it, but I can't quite reach it."

She nods with understanding. "You didn't realize you were—"

"Plagued with mommy issues?"

"Subconsciously repeating a past trauma." Her lips curl into a half-smile. "Yeah, plagued with mommy issues."

My laugh deepens. "No. I just thought… it wasn't like I loved her in spite of her illness. Or because of it. There was no separation in my mind. Grace was Grace. She happened to have a condition. Just like I did."

"But you're not—" Ariel bites her lip. "Or maybe you are."

268

"Maybe I am…"

"You should talk to a professional, not me."

"Is there a diagnosis for plagued with mommy issues?" I ask.

"No." She bites her lip. "But, uh, you do have a lot of the symptoms of… no one really knows what comes first— a chemical imbalance or the negative thought patterns."

"You're gonna have to dumb that down."

"You're like Daredevil."

I arch a brow. "What's that have to do—"

"That guilt and self-loathing and habit of seeing the worst in everything—"

"I see the worst in everything?"

"A lot of things." She pushes her chair back. "It… it might not be your personality."

"What?"

She bites her lip. "I'm sorry. I shouldn't… I should go."

"Why?"

"I… I just should."

She's scared of something. Of me.

She must see it too.

That she needs to get the fuck away, ASAP.

"If you want to leave, you can," I say.

"I don't want to. I just…"

She knows she should. That she needs to protect herself. Avoid a guy who turns everything to shit.

"The story doesn't get better," I say. "All the details I have… they only make it worse."

Ariel bites her lip. "I don't know."

"You don't know?"

"How about…" She moves to the sink. Refills her water. "Tell me. And I'll decide." She turns. Rests her ass against the counter.

Her posture screams *don't come closer*.

I want to. I want to hold her, kiss her, promise her it's going to be okay.

But it's not.

I can't lie to her.

"We met in art class, in high school. She thought I was annoying, that I tried too hard, and always let me know. She was bright, like a star, like the sun. She was big and loud and I fell in love with her right away." Those are good memories. They are. But I always wonder—when did it start? What signs did I miss? "We'd hang out at my place—"

"Or our place," she says.

I nod *yeah*. "When we were good, we were amazing. But our disagreements were explosive. I look back, and I can see where we were expecting too much of each other. We were asking for things that were impossible. I'd be jealous she was talking to another guy. She'd worry I was going to leave her. Beg me to stay. Then avoid me for weeks."

Ariel nods with understanding.

There's something in her eyes, something she isn't saying, but I press on anyway.

"She stayed here for school. I started apprenticing at Blacklist. When I made enough for my own place, I asked her to move in. We did. It was… I loved having her there. I loved that it was our place. That we could argue about which artists to hang and whether or not comic books belonged in the shelf." My chest warms at the memory of her climbing into my lap, insisting we christen the couch. "I knew she was bipolar. She told me right away. I could tell when she was hypomanic or depressed. I rode those highs with her. I was there. At least, I thought I was. I thought she could tell me anything. I didn't always take it well, but… I guess she couldn't."

Ariel's shoulders tense.

Her fingers grip the counter for dear life.

It's not like before. Something is different. Wrong.

"She promised she'd tell me if she was ever thinking about hurting herself." I swallow hard. "I worried sometimes, but I thought she meant it. I thought we were okay. She'd been pulling away for a while. She did that sometimes. I tried to bring her back, but it only made her pull harder. Then..." My chest gets heavy. "I got home from work one day and she was there, in our bed, not moving, barely breathing. There was a note. An apology about being an inconvenience."

It's all over Ariel's face.

She needs to flee.

She needs to save herself.

"It was like time had stopped, but it was moving fast too. I called nine-one-one. They brought her into the ICU. Pumped her stomach. Put her on a seventy-two-hour hold. Her parents found a better program for her." My eyes go to the image of her tattoo. "I visited her every weekend. I thought we were moving on together. But when she got out, she ended things."

"She broke up with you?" Ariel asks.

"Yeah. She said we weren't good for each other. That being with me wasn't good for her."

"Maybe it wasn't."

"It wasn't." I turn to Ariel. Try to face the dread in her eyes. "She bloomed after she left."

"Maybe it wasn't about you."

What?

"Chase, do you really think... do you really think you were responsible for your ex-girlfriend's mental health?"

"She's better without me."

"So?"

"Hunter's sober. My mom's finally trying. Everyone does better when I leave."

Her brow furrows. "You really believe that?"

"What else can I believe?"

"You really think you're that important?"

Huh?

"I… I have to go."

What?

"I'm sorry." She moves to the couch. Grabs her backpack. "I, um…"

"Ariel."

"I think, um… I need to think. I'll text you."

"We're supposed to do this every day this week."

"Yeah. Um… I… I'll call you."

What?

She looks at me like she wants to come closer.

But she doesn't.

She turns and walks out the door.

Chapter Thirty-Two

ARIEL

Dear Chase,

I really like having sex with you. It's fantastic. And, despite your clear signs of depression and your genetic predisposition toward alcoholism, I still want you to father my child.

Maybe I should be more concerned about those two risk factors. But something tells me they aren't coincidental. They're probably related.

Would it be wrong if I talked to your mom and your brothers? Got the 411 on their conditions?

How about if I asked someone in the psych department for a referral?

I know you're in love with your misery, but you don't have to marinate in it.

That's kind of over the line. Even I know that. But, hey, I can't really handle talking to you anymore.

I can't say "Chase, don't be ridiculous. You can't save people. They have to save themselves. They have to want to get better. You're being ridiculous and self-involved."

I want to say that, because it's true, but I can't.

Because I'm just as bad.

Even now, composing this note in my head as I drive back to my house (which is taking forever, of course. There's traffic on Lincoln. Ocean might have been better. Honestly, I should walk next time. It's not even a mile. I'm sure I can get here faster on foot. But now I'm the one getting distracted).

Even now, composing this note in my head, my heart is screaming "Ariel, you can save him."

I want to turn the car around, drive back to your apartment, drag you into bed.

I want to promise that you'll finally get over Grace.

I can see it's more than that. That you're sure you have the weight of the world on your shoulders. That you're just as martyr complex as Matt Murdock—the picture of Catholic guilt. And you're not even religious.

So you're either fucked up or depressed.

Or both.

Though "fucked up" is about as accurate a diagnosis as "plagued by mommy issues."

Even though I know it's hopeless, I want to save you. Or at least break through your walls, teach you how to love again, prove that your love is the best thing in the world.

Even as I try to come up with tactful ways to say "hey, Chase, get over your need to save people," I keep thinking of ways to save you.

I'm officially bonker balls.

That's not in the DSM V, but maybe it should be.

You see, I'm not ending this. Just clarifying it. I still want your, ahem, donations.

But that's all.

No, I want more. I want everything.

I can't have everything.

So it's going to have to be donations or nothing.

I just have to find a way to phrase that. Tact isn't my strong suit. I know you appreciate my honesty, but something tells me you won't appreciate "Chase, I'm falling in love with you. You're obviously a mess, so please stop being all sweet and caring and protective so I can stop falling in love with you."

Yeah, that's not going to fly.

I'm going to think of something.

I'm going to redefine our boundaries.

I'm going to figure this out.

Somehow.

Chapter Thirty-Three

ARIEL

"**H**ey." Skye nods *hello* from her spot on the couch. She's watching a gritty TV drama and she's the picture of comfort. Like this is her house. Like she could die here.

"Where's Forest?"

She nods to the stairs. "Shower."

The water is running. That makes sense. Sorta. "What are you—"

"If I'm in your way—" She hits pause on the remote and motions to the door *I can leave.*

I shake my head. I don't want her to leave. She's always been like a big sister to me. And if she leaves, it's just Forest and his suspicion that I'm fucking Chase.

I'm a terrible liar most of the time.

When every part of me is aching?

Uh… pass.

"How long do you think he'll be in there?" I ask.

She chuckles. "You need to call your secret boyfriend?"

I clear my throat.

She pulls her legs onto the couch and crosses them. "You really like him, huh?"

Next topic. "You want something to drink?"

"I'm good."

I cross the room. Grab a glass from the kitchen. Fill it with water. It soothes my throat but fails to offer clarity.

"Loverboy screw something up?" she asks.

Is it really that obvious? "Not exactly." I turn to Skye. Study her expression.

Her light eyes are fixed on me. They're sincere. Like she wants to save me from the heartbreak she knows so well.

"You, uh, you've have bad relationships," I say.

"Understatement of the year, yeah."

"But you and Forest…" I bite my lip. "You're close."

Her brow furrows. "Of course."

"Since you moved here."

She nods *yeah, and*?

"But, um… you're just friends…"

She bites her lip. "You know Forest. Ever since the ex…"

"But you're…" I move closer. Drop my voice to a whisper. "You're… the way you look at him." I'm just going to say it. Even if it's not at all tactful. "You like him."

Her cheeks flush. Her teeth sink into her lip. "No."

"You do."

Her eyes fill with concern. "Are you going to say something?"

I shake my head. "Girls have to stick together."

"Oh." Her brow softens. "I guess it's obvious."

Very, yeah.

Her voice gets low. "He doesn't see me that way."

"Doesn't that hurt?"

"Sometimes."

I nod to the couch.

She pats the spot next to her.

I sit. "But you're still here. He's upstairs, showering, naked—" I fight my cringe. "And you're here. Not…"

"Touching myself to the mental image?"

"No"

She laughs.

"I just mean… isn't it worse, being that close?"

"Worse than what?" Her gaze shifts to the stairs.

"Being far."

She shakes her head. "He's my best friend."

"But…"

"What am I going to do? Ghost him?"

"No, but you could get some space. Leave. Fly to the other side of the country for grad school. Spend the summer in Europe and find some French dude."

"Don't speak French."

"You can speak with your body."

"Like a gender reversed *Before Sunrise*."

An older independent film from the golden age of indie. I know that much. And only that.

Skye is really into movies.

Whereas I stick to animation and comic books.

Her laugh is equal parts happy and sad. "You have no idea what I'm talking about."

"None."

The shower turns off. Her shoulders tense. Her gaze shifts to the stairs. "You loved Phillip?"

"Of course."

"You know that feeling, when you're around someone? Like you're dizzy because you're floating so high above the ground?"

"But when they don't want you back… doesn't that hurt?" I bite my lip.

"Mystery Guy or Phillip?"

"Both," I say. "You know Forest so well. That must be harder?"

She nods *yeah.* "Like a stone in my stomach, yeah."

"So why do you…"

"Wouldn't you rather have something than nothing?"

Maybe.

The door upstairs opens. Footsteps move into the hallway.

Skye's eyes turn down. She looks at me like she's terrified I'm going to spill.

But I'm not. I'd never. Even if I did, my brother wouldn't believe me.

I motion *my lips are sealed*. "Don't mention—"

She nods *of course*.

"That you, Ariel?" Forest calls from upstairs.

"Yeah," I call back. "Could you go back to the bathroom? I'm trying to convince Skye you're the worst."

His chuckle echoes through the house.

She bites her lip. "We can go to my parents' place. Talk more."

I want to tell someone. I want to understand this. I want to understand myself. "I know he'll never love me but I still want him so badly."

Her eyes turn down.

"I'm guessing you don't have any advice on that front."

"If only." She offers me a hug.

I take it.

Then I head to my room before Forest can get any ideas about asking me questions.

———

DESPITE MY BEST EFFORTS, WORK FAILS TO CLEAR MY

head. My thoughts stay tuned to Chase. I can't concentrate enough to crunch numbers, much less tackle complex problems.

For a while, I grade undergrad assignments. It's easy, mindless work. But it only fills my brain for so long.

Thoughts of Chase creep in.

Student 11, Problem One. Wrong.

Am I falling in love with Chase?

Good show of work. Halfway to the answer. Calculation went wrong here. Circle in red.

Is he really hopeless?

Problem Two. Right.

There must be some way I can figure this out.

Problem Three. No answer. Problem four. No answer. See me after class.

I'm not giving up our mission. That's out of the question. Even if it means the agony of heartbreak.

I'm making this baby.

That's the baseline. The place where we start. From the premise that I'm continuing our meetings.

Student 12, right, right, right, right. Great work.

I breeze through the rest of the assignments. Pick up my cell. Tap a text to Chase.

I have to explain my sudden departure.

And I have to underline our new terms.

No more falling in love. No more ideas of saving him. No more cooking dinner and watching TV on the couch and melting into his chest.

No more of those strong, safe embraces. The embraces that make me feel like the entire world is okay.

I... Uh...

Shit.

I have to give that up. I have to draw these lines. I have to protect myself.

But I also need to fuck him tomorrow.

Ariel: Sorry I left so quickly. I had some thinking to do.

Chase: Are you okay?

Ariel: I am. Thanks for asking.

Chase: You didn't offend me.

Ariel: Good.

Chase: I know I'm a mess. You don't have to pretend you don't notice.

No, that's not true at all. Chase is a great guy. He makes me all warm and squishy. Like I'm basking in the glow of the sun on a beautiful day.

Ariel: It's not you, Chase. It's me. I'm getting confused about our arrangement. I need to remind myself of our terms.

Chase: Right.

Ariel: I need a breath.

Chase: It's easy to mix sex up with other things.

Ariel: Are you too?

Chase: Does that matter?

Of course. If he feels the same, if he wants me too…

God, I want that. I want it too much. I can't say it. I can't even think it.

He's so not there.

Ariel: You're right. It doesn't.

Chase: I still want to do this.

Ariel: Good. Me too.

Chase: What do you need from me?

He's so clear and direct. How did he have such a problem communicating with his ex?

He's just…

Ugh, I'm getting all fluttery again.

Nope. Uh-uh. Not what we're doing here.

Ariel: We'll still meet this week. But only for sex.

Chase: I'm making you come.

Ariel: Okay.

Chase: And calling you princess.

Ariel: Only during sex.

My heart thuds against my chest. My stomach flutters. My sex pangs.

This makes sense.

Everything else is a confusing mess.

But sex with Chase makes perfect sense.

Ariel: Is that okay with you?

Chase: It's what you want, isn't it?

Ariel: Yes.

My phone is quiet for a moment. I stare back waiting for an objection. A plea for more, a confession he's falling in love with me, a total rejection of the idea of drawing stronger lines.

I don't get one.

Chase: My place still work?

Ariel: I'm low on time tomorrow.

Chase: Oh?

Ariel: Maybe you can meet me at school.

Chase: I thought you didn't have an office.

Ariel: I'll figure it out.

Chase: Tell me the time and place and I'm there.

Chapter Thirty-Four

ARIEL

After my first class, I find an empty office. Text Chase the suite number. Request he meet me on his lunch break.

Then I dive into work.

It's impossible to concentrate.

My heart keeps screaming for his smile.

My head keeps screaming *run away*.

My body—

It's in overdrive.

The clock strikes one.

Every thought in my brain tunes to him. And the demand on my cell. The same as last time.

Wear those tight jeans. Nothing under them.

He's so hot. He's too hot. It's wrong.

That thin layer of denim does things to me. Winds me tighter and tighter.

When he finally knocks on the door, I'm halfway there.

I pull it open. Press my lips into a smile.

Remember, Ariel, no feelings. Just sex.

Wham, bam, thank you, sir.

Can I call him sir?

Fuck, that would be so hot.

Is he all demanding because it's hot?

Or because he's Chase? Because he has this obsessive need to take care of people.

Ahem.

Thinking of calling Chase sir—yes.

Thinking of Chase's out of the bedroom needs—no.

Boundaries. In my brain. They're happening.

He pushes the door closed. Clicks the lock.

There's no smile on his face.

There's nothing on his face.

Sure, he's usually a stone wall, but I know him now. I know how to find the feeling in his eyes.

Right now—

"You follow orders, princess?" His voice drops to that demanding tone.

My limbs shake. "Yes, sir."

His eyes fill with something I recognize—desire.

Maybe he wants this too.

Maybe he only wants my body.

Maybe this really is best for both of us.

Chase presses his back against the door. Pushes his palms into his jeans.

He's already hard.

That's what I'm thinking about.

His cock, not his feelings.

I need to turn my thoughts off.

Now.

I stand. Slip my laptop into my bag. Sit on the desk.

He moves closer. "Always wanted to fuck a hot teacher." His fingers skim my temple. He pulls my glasses off my face. Sets them on the bookshelf.

Chase doesn't waste any time. He places his body against mine. Brings his hands to my thighs.

Undoes my jeans.

Rolls them off my hips.

His lips go to my neck.

His hands go to my clit.

He works me to an orgasm. He turns me over. He fucks me hard.

I come three times.

Then he helps me dress and he leaves.

No kiss. No embrace. No offer of lunch or coffee.

It's just sex.

Exactly what I want.

Exactly what I asked.

———

THE NEXT DAY, IT'S THE SAME.

I meet him at work—it's Forest's day off and Skye assures me they have plans that take him away from the Westside all day.

(Holden is much too oblivious to notice and not over protective enough to care. He's also not working. And he posts his location on Instagram constantly, so I'm pretty sure that's safe).

Sure enough, Inked Hearts is quiet.

Chase's coworkers stare at me like I'm an alien from another planet. One of them whispers something to another. I only catch *is Chase actually with a girl*.

We go to his office.

He keeps his hand over my mouth the entire time.

He whispers dirty demands in my ear.

Fucks me from behind.

Rubs me through two orgasms.

I want to nip at his fingers. I want to crawl onto the desk and beg for his cock. I want to get on my knees and suck him off.

I really, really want to kiss him.

But I can't.

I have to keep these lines.

I have to follow his lead.

He's drawing the lines for me.

He's doing what I asked.

He's protecting me, again.

It doesn't matter that I leave feeling more empty than full.

WE MEET AT HIS PLACE AT TEN. WELL AFTER DINNER. Late enough either one of us can say *I better get to sleep* after.

I go straight to his bedroom.

He strips me out of my clothes. Orders me onto my stomach. Rubs me until I come.

Fucks me hard.

When he's done, he presses his lips to my shoulder. "I'm going to shower."

It's all he has to say.

I stay put for fifteen minutes—sure, there's no scientific evidence it will help, but at least gravity is on my side—then I dress and move into the living room.

Chase steps out of the bathroom. His eyes meet mine. They're so blue and deep and full of hurt.

Then he blinks and he's a stone wall again.

I want to stay. To ask what's wrong. To collapse in his arms.

And I want to slap him and tell him to stop treating me like a plaything.

But he's not.

He's doing what I asked.

It's not his fault it makes me empty.

It's not his fault my heart is aching.

It's not his fault I hate this.

"I should go." I grab my purse. Sling it over my shoulder. "I'll see you…" This is the last fertile day this cycle. So I guess… "I'll let you know what happens."

He nods *sure*. "You can call me."

"Oh?" Because he's in love with me. Because he needs me. Because he wants me.

"If you need anything." He doesn't explain what anything is.

I don't ask. I just nod. "I'll see you around."

"You going to Holden's Halloween party?"

"Of course." My brother throws a Halloween party every year. He's obsessed with the holiday. "Are you dressing up?"

He nods. "Won't hear the end of it if I don't."

"Right. Me too. Uh… I guess I…" Need to find a costume. And leave right now. God, there's all this hurt in his voice. He's talking about Halloween costumes and I want to jump into his arms.

This isn't normal.

I need him following these rules.

No matter how much it hurts.

"I'll see you there," I say.

He nods *sure*.

I make it all the way to my car before I start crying.

It doesn't make sense.

Protecting my heart should protect me from this. It should feel good. It shouldn't make every part of me ache.

I shouldn't fall asleep craving Chase.

But I do.

Chapter Thirty-Five

CHASE

The Ballard Halloween party is a yearly tradition. It started in high school, the first year Mr. Ballard was away on business the last week of October.

Holden took advantage of the parent-free house. Invited the entire school to his place. A dozen kids shared cheap Trader Joe's vodka then played spin the bottle with the empty container.

The next day, rumors spread. The party took on a life of its own. It wasn't lemon vodka and Sprite. It was Absinthe and Champagne

It wasn't spin the bottle. It was an orgy.

It wasn't a dozen students. It was every hot chick from UCLA and drug dealers passing out free ecstasy.

The next year, attendance was booming.

When Holden graduated, tattoo artists and clients replaced high schoolers.

Holden must know every woman on the west side.

The packed room screams of holiday debauchery.

Black lights cast the living room in a deep purple glow.

White-green spider cut outs line the walls. (They're glow in the dark, of course). Webbing covers the archways.

Fake spiders cluster around the punch bowl (a cauldron, of course). And next to it: every liquor or mixer imaginable.

I cut through the crowd. Pour a drink. Rum and coke.

It's good. Sweet and rich with enough bite to relax the tension in my shoulders.

Ariel is here somewhere.

I have no fucking idea where. Or what she's wearing. Or how she's feeling.

We've texted here and there over the last few weeks, but it stayed all business.

She didn't complain about her undergrads. Or gush about her current read. Or bait me with claims of her innocence.

She didn't say shit about our new terms.

Not that I need an explanation. She wears everything in her big, brown eyes.

My stomach churns at the thought of her empty groan.

It shouldn't surprise me that something could feel so good and so bad at the same time.

That's what shit was like for me, before Grace.

I didn't get it. I thought all guys liked all sex. Maybe not with all people—my cousin Daryl came out when he was twelve. But with anyone they found attractive.

Fucking hot chicks is supposed to be a thrill. An accomplishment. A rush.

And it is. For a few minutes.

But after… It was like someone ripped out my soul. I'm left empty, lonely, confused.

The one time I mentioned it to a friend, he looked at me like I had two heads, and complained that I didn't appreciate how good I had it.

Eventually, I stopped trying to get something out of casual fucks.

It wasn't until Grace that I understood why people loved sex. That sense of connection. The thrill of a partner's pleasure. The sound of their groan.

It's music. It's poetry. It's art.

Those quick and dirty fucks with Ariel—

I read a few books about conception. A lot of people get to that point. Where sex is mechanical. Where it's just about making a deposit.

But that wasn't it.

That was something else.

Like every part of my body was desperate to connect with hers and something was stopping it.

Her rules are fair. Smart. Necessary.

Sure, it hurts, but it's worth it if it keeps her safe.

I finish my rum and coke. Pour another. It takes three sips for my head to go to Hunter. He's probably here. He's probably sober.

I'm not worried about him.

For once, I believe he's okay. I actually believe it's possible he'll stay okay.

I don't know where I found this revelation. Only that I need to hold on to it.

I need us to be okay too.

I really need to find Ariel.

The room is packed with people I don't recognize, friends of friends, coworkers.

Forest. He shakes his head as he emerges from the crowd. "You look ridiculous." He laughs as he mixes a Moscow Mule. "Fuck, I thought he looked like an idiot on the show, but there's something about how tall you are that makes that outfit look even dumber."

"That for you?" It's Ariel's drink. But she's not drinking. Unless—

I don't have her updates anymore. Has it been long enough? Is she upstairs taking a test? Does she already know it didn't happen?

Is she celebrating two pink lines?

My chest gets heavy.

My shoulders tense.

My jaw cricks.

I need to find her. Hold her. Share her news. Whisper *congratulations* or *I'm sorry*.

But I also need to stay away. She asked for space. She asked for coldness. Sure, it kills me, but that doesn't matter.

I'm protecting her.

"Skye," he says.

My shoulders relax.

His eyes narrow. "You okay?"

"Getting in character."

He chuckles *of course*. "Gotta say, that suits you."

"You've never looked more at home." I nod to the handcuffs hanging off his belt. Point to the badge on his chest.

Forest makes a perfect cop.

"Damn, finally found your alter ego." Wes bounces to the bar. He looks me up and down and bursts into laughter. "You should have fought Hunter for the right to dress as Daredevil."

"Finally, someone more moody than Chase." Forest laughs.

I shrug. It's not like I can argue. My attitude is… fuck, I don't know what it is. Only that I've been miserable the last two weeks.

I miss Ariel's warmth.

"What are you supposed to be?" I take another sip.

Wes points to his fedora and his trench coat. "Rick."

"Rick…" Is that a person I should know?

Wes motions to Quinn, who's sitting on the couch, chatting with Griffin's wife, Juliette. Quinn's linen suit is adorned with a shiny broach. Her outfit seems vaguely related to Wes's, but I've still got no clue what it is.

Now, Juliette and her Dodgers uniform. That's an easy guess.

The woman loves the boys in blue.

"We're Rick and Ilsa. *Casablanca*." When we don't respond, Wes rolls his eyes. "Philistines."

"And you've been a fan of this classic for how long?" Forest asks.

"As long as your girlfriend introduced you to it?" I ask.

Wes shrugs *whatever*. "You look like an idiot, you know." He gives my all black outfit another once-over. "I guess it suits you."

"It's supposed to look ridiculous," I say.

"Haven't you seen the show?" Forest asks.

Wes raises a brow. "No, I have this thing called a life. I don't sit around watching TV."

"You sit around watching classic movies with your girl-friend," Forest says.

Wes nods *yeah*. "What do you think happens after we watch the movies?"

"Wow, you have sex? First I've heard of that." Forest chuckles. "Not like you mention it at every opportunity."

"If you don't like hearing about it, don't listen," Wes says.

"There's no way to avoid it," I say. "You're loud enough the entire shop can hear it."

Wes smiles *of course*. "Hunter's around here somewhere. You two could share your revelations. Gush about your love of mopey bastards. And your love of acting like mopey bastards."

"Tempting offer." This is getting serious. Yeah, he's right. I need to reconcile with my brother eventually. But not now. Not until it feels right.

Hunter gets that.

I hope he still gets that.

Forest's gaze moves to the stairs. Goes right to Skye.

She descends slowly. Dramatically. Like she's channeling her alter ego.

She's dressed as Elvira, mistress of the dark, complete with a 70s black wig and a tight dress cut to her bellybutton.

"Fuck." Wes clears his throat. "You must be hard as a diamond right now."

Forest shakes his head. "You're an idiot."

"Oh yeah, stick with that story that you're not into her." Wes shakes his head *yeah, right.* "But you should think about something—"

"You know about thinking?" Forest teases.

"Yeah, I do it every so often." Wes watches Skye move to the main floor.

Half the room turns her way.

Halloween is always an excuse for women to show off without judgment. (Not like I'm complaining). But Skye is taking it to the next level.

She looks like she's about to claw the nearest guy and demand he serve at the mistress of dark's commands.

Forest's eyes stay glued to her. "Don't strain yourself."

"She's gonna give up on you one day," Wes says. "If you don't figure shit out."

"We're just friends." Forest's voice trails off.

"Just friends who want to fuck each other." Wes rolls his eyes. "Who are totally in love with each other."

Forest stares at Skye like he's lost in thoughts of stripping her naked.

Maybe he is.

He mumbles some comeback to Wes, but it's more vowel than word. His eyes stay on Skye until a familiar voice interrupts.

"Hi." Ariel pushes through a happy couple—Princess Leia and Han Solo. Shit, that's Iris and Walker.

I nod *hey*, but they don't notice. They're too busy dancing to *Monster Mash*.

"Damn, Ariel. Didn't know you were packing that kind of heat." Wes winks.

Ariel blushes. "I, um… it was the only thing I had lying around." She gathers her arms behind her back, pushing her chest forward.

Fuck, she looks good in that purple bikini top.

She's not wearing a red wig, but between the shiny shell bikini top and the scale-print green skirt, she's every part the little mermaid.

Her pale skin glows under the blacklight.

Her dark eyes stay on Wes.

She's still in her glasses.

Still the Ariel who gushes over comic books and mint leaves and chai lattes.

"You gonna let your sister walk around like that?" Wes nudges Forest.

Finally, he pries his eyes from Skye. Turns to Ariel. Frowns. "You're wearing that?"

She rolls her eyes. "I'm twenty-four."

"Still…" His voice drops to a protective older-brother tone.

"She probably needs to get laid." Wes offers Ariel his hand. "I'm a great wingman. Give me your top three traits, and we'll go."

Her gaze flits to me for a split second. "No, I'm okay."

Wes raises a brow. "Ariel, babe, you have the look."

"That is my sister," Forest says.

"You think your sister is a virgin?" Wes scoffs *okay, sure.* "Maybe you can't see it, with your hang-ups. But Ariel obviously—"

"I'm actually good, Wes. Thanks though." She pushes her glasses up her nose. "I know your pushiness is your way of helping."

Forest chuckles.

Wes lets it roll off his back. "You change your mind; you know where to find me." He nods to his girlfriend, wishes us goodbye, leaves.

Music and conversation fill the silence. There's all this space between me and Ariel. It feels obvious. Like anyone can see the severed tie between us.

"I should mingle." I motion to the couch, hoping it's a clear enough *meet me later.*

Ariel nods.

"You can't mingle until we mock you more." Forest motions for his sister to come closer. "Doesn't he look ridiculous?"

"I don't know. Miserable yet charming martyr with a lust for violence suits Chase." Ariel's lips curl into a half smile.

"Shit, I forgot you're a fangirl." Forest shakes his head *where is your taste?*

"I enjoy the show. That doesn't make me a fangirl," she says.

"And the comics—"

"Mom's comics?"

"Uh-huh." He shakes his head. "Wait until you get her talking about *Jessica Jones.* She'll never stop."

Ariel holds up her hand *shut up, Forest*. She turns to me. "Maybe he'll show off some moves later."

"You have moves now, Keating?" He chuckles. "You want to join me at aikido?"

"If you're ready to lose." I scan the room for a distraction. Brendon and Kaylee are dressed as Prince Charming and Cinderella.

Griffin is joining his wife on the couch. He's in an Angel's uniform. She's teasing him about something—probably his team's losing record.

He pulls her into his lap. Kisses her like he's going to fuck her right here, right now.

Maybe he is. The guy isn't shy.

And there's Leighton and Ryan, hanging out in the corner of the room, with Dean and Chloe.

Leighton and Ryan are dressed as Jack and Sally, from *The Nightmare Before Christmas*. She's in a full face of makeup, wig, sewn together dress. He's wearing a skeleton outfit, with nothing on his head.

Not that she seems to mind. She runs her fingers through his wavy hair like they're the only two people on the couch.

Dean mutters something to them, probably about how they should fuck so everyone can watch. Chloe rolls her eyes. I think. It's hard to tell from here.

They're dressed as each other. She's in board shorts, checkered Vans, and a bright blue tank top. He's in tight black jeans, a tight black tank top, clip on earrings, combat boots, thick black eyeliner.

It's ridiculous.

And completely them.

They really nailed each other.

"I'll leave you to your violence and misery, Devil of

Hell's kitchen." Forest pats me on the shoulder. He goes straight to Skye.

Scares off the guy who's flirting with her.

The rest of the room disappears. It's just me and Ariel. And all the confusion in her big, brown eyes.

Does she hate this as much as I do?

Or is she right? Maybe I've overestimated my importance. Maybe this has nothing to do with me.

Maybe it's—

Fuck.

I lean in to whisper. "Can we talk?"

"Forest is watching."

We need a plan. We need to tell him. But I'm not having that argument again.

"My room. Ten minutes. I'll go first." She takes a step backward. Motions to the stairs.

I nod *sure*.

She disappears into the crowd.

My attention turns to the music. A cloying remix of *Thriller*.

It fills my ears.

But it doesn't fill my head.

I finish my drink. Make conversation with a friend from high school. Say hello to couples from Inked Hearts.

Finally, I slip away from the conversation. Move up the stairs. Down the hallway.

To Ariel's room.

She's sitting on her bed, arms folded over her chest, gaze on the window.

It's a dark, cold night. With the curtains drawn, the blue-black sky blankets the room. The sky never gets black here. Even blocks from the beach, there's too much light pollution.

I press the door closed.

She stands. Drops her arms. Stares into my eyes. "Chase."

"Are you okay?"

Her teeth sink into her lip. "No, I... I don't know if we should talk like this."

Maybe. But I can't bring myself to leave. "What happened?"

"Nothing."

No, something.

There aren't any clues in her room. Same teal and turquoise walls. Same purple bedspread. Same stack of text books.

She takes a step toward me. "You do look ridiculous."

"So does Matt."

Her fingers curl into my chest. "It suits you."

"The ridiculous part?"

She nods. "And the violence."

"Mommy issues."

She laughs. "Martyr complex."

"I didn't forget."

She brings her hand to my head. Pushes my mask off.

Her fingers skim my temples.

My heart thuds against my chest.

It's not like our quick fucks. I feel her everywhere. I'm warm everything.

I didn't know how badly I needed that. But I do. I really do. "What happened, princess?"

"Chase..." Her eyes meet mine. She stares back at me like she's about to hand over her heart.

Chapter Thirty-Six

CHASE

I know the answer, but the words still cut.

She shakes her head. "I'm not…" She presses her forehead to my chest. "I took a test. And I'm not… I'm not pregnant."

I wrap my arms around her. Pull her closer.

She digs her fingers into my shirt. Sucks in a shallow breath. "I knew the odds weren't good. But it still… Fuck."

"Ariel." I bring my hand to her cheek. Catch a tear with my thumb.

She blinks and tears curtain her lashes. "What if it doesn't happen?"

"It will."

"You don't know that." She wraps her arm around my waist. "What if I never…"

"You'll become a mother, Ariel."

"But…"

"Whether you adopt or marry a single dad or kill one of your brother's baby mommas so you can take over—"

She stifles a laugh. "Oh my God."

"You want it badly enough; you'll make it happen."

"Aren't you supposed to be against killing?" She tugs at my black shirt. "You really look ridiculous."

"You're right. Don't kill her. Hit her until she's in a coma," I say. "That doesn't count."

A laugh spills from her lips. "Don't make fun of Matt. He's got his priorities more figured out than you do."

"Probably, yeah."

"And he gets laid more."

This time, I laugh. "Not that he cares."

"Yeah, I mean, have you ever thought about how he could use his powers in other ways?" She wipes a tear. "He could be the world's greatest chef. Or composer."

"Or lover." The guy does have the ability to tune into his senses to hear, feel, smell, taste anything. He can feel cracked ribs, smell the exact brand of whiskey on someone's breath, hear a cry four city blocks away.

But he never uses those skills for sex.

The guy may be fictional, but he's still wasting his life.

"God, could you imagine? If you were that good at reading someone else's body? Their feelings." Her eyes fix on me. "I… I wish I could do that with you."

"You can."

She shakes her head.

"Just ask."

"Chase…" She presses her palm into my lower back. "You… you're such a smart guy, but you miss so much."

"Then tell me."

"I…"

Fuck, I just have to say it. "I miss you." I brush her hair behind her ear. "I miss the smell of your shampoo. I miss the digs you take at Matt. I miss the way you gasp over action scenes. I miss the groans you make over your chai lattes."

"I don't—"

"You do. And I miss that. I miss those first few times, when I felt all of you."

"Me too."

"I really fucking miss your laugh."

Her lips curl into a half-smile. "I miss your laugh."

"I have one?"

Her smile widens. "Yeah. It makes your eyes so bright. I love that." She brings her hand to my hip. "I thought… I don't know. I know I asked you to act less… caring. But I hate it."

"I do too."

"Really?" Her eyes fix on me.

"Yeah." I cup her cheek with my palm. "Do you want to talk about it?"

Her brow furrows with confusion.

"The test," I explain.

"No… I just… I want it to work. Talking won't make it work faster."

"It can still help."

She shakes her head. "I want… I want to not talk. But not like last time. I felt so empty after—" She motions to the bed. "I can't do that again."

The thought of handling Ariel like an anonymous hookup makes my stomach turn.

But the alternative—

"Fuck, princess. I want to taste you so badly." My body begs me to forget my concerns. But this is too important. "I want to bury myself in you. Tease you until you're begging me to come."

"Chase—"

"I want to watch every ounce of pleasure spill over your expression."

She swallows hard.

"I can't do that halfway."

She nods with understanding.

"I can fuck you with everything I have. Or I can fuck you with nothing." I don't have a better way to say it. "I'm committed to this. But if you want more… It's more of everything."

"That's… okay… I get that."

"I don't." Maybe I should understand, but I don't. I shouldn't want everything with Ariel. I need to protect her. To keep her from my toxic influence. To help her then leave.

"You… you still blame yourself for Grace?"

"Not exactly."

"But you think you're responsible for everyone's happiness?"

"It sounds ridiculous when you say it like that."

"It is ridiculous." Her voice softens. "But I understand… Mostly."

"I don't know. I… I'm working on it."

"Yeah?"

"No." My chuckle breaks up the tension in my jaw. "But I want to."

"I'm not a shrink. I can't… I'm not going to help you sort out your messed up head."

"Good."

"Good." She repeats the word like she doesn't believe it. "I… that's the thing, Chase. I want to. I wanted to tell you 'get over yourself. You can't save someone.' But I want to save you." Her eyes meet mine. "I really like you."

"I like you too." The words feel good on my tongue. It's true. I care about Ariel in ways I don't care about anyone else. I want the world for her. I want the best for her.

"You… do you want something serious?"

"I don't know."

"Oh." Her breath is shaky. "Okay."

"Do you?" I ask. "Want something serious?"

"I guess I don't know either." Her hand goes to her stomach. "I... I can handle my heart breaking, Chase. But if this works... if we... You need to be all in for him. Or not at all."

"Okay."

"Okay?" The furrow in her brow deepens. "Is that a yes or a no?"

Everything inside me screams *yes*. Maybe this isn't how I expected fatherhood to go. But it's still everything I want.

A little boy in a baseball uniform.

A girl in a tutu.

Hell, a boy in a tutu. Whatever he wants. Whatever he feels.

Ariel is going to be such a great mom.

I want to be a part of that.

But not if it means fucking up someone else. I can't do that anymore. I can't hurt anyone else.

Her fingers skim my temple. "You don't have to say now."

Good. I have to be sure. I have to know I'll be what's best for this kid. "What if you meet another guy?"

"Because no divorced parents have ever had relationships?" Her fingers skim my chin. "You're... I... I don't want to talk anymore." She slips her hand under my shirt. "Can we?"

"I can't do that halfway."

"I know."

"I don't want to hurt you. That's the last thing I want." I shudder from her touch. "But, Ariel, this—"

"It's supposed to be intimate." She presses her lips to my neck. "I like it that way."

"Fuck." I need to stay something. To stay in control. "Your brothers are downstairs."

"The music is loud enough."

"I don't want you to stay quiet."

"Me either." She drags her lips over my skin. Watches as my eyes close and my chest shudders. "I like when you're under my thumb."

"Princess, you have no idea."

She arches her hips, so her stomach hits my crotch. "Fuck." Her sigh is needy. "Already?"

"Yeah."

She rocks against me again. "I love the way you feel." Her slick skirt slides off my cotton pants. "I'm not trying… so we… We can do whatever we want." Her eyes light up. "I can suck you off."

Fuck. Where did she learn to talk like this? "No."

"No?" She pouts. "But I—"

"I need to feel you." I bring my hands to her lower back. "I miss you so fucking badly."

"Chase—"

"Top off." I release her. To give her room. "Now."

Her pupils dilate. She stares back at me, equal parts defiant and eager.

I need both. "Don't make me ask twice."

Chapter Thirty-Seven

CHASE

Ariel reaches behind her back and undoes the clasp of her bikini top.

The shiny purple fabric falls to the ground.

She's only wearing that tight green skirt.

Fuck, she looks like an actual mermaid. A mermaid who spends all her time in the ocean library, torturing every merman who looks her way.

She steps forward. So our bodies connect.

Her hands find my lower back.

Her lips find my lips.

She kisses me hard. Like she needs everything I've got.

Maybe she does. I sure as hell need to give it to her.

I scrape my teeth against her bottom lip. Softly. Then harder. Then hard enough she groans into my mouth.

Her fingers dig into my arms, press the cotton into my skin.

My tongue slips into her mouth.

My head spins.

My heart pounds.

My body buzzes.

This is right. Maybe it's wrong and risky and confusing as hell.

But it's so, so right.

I cup her ass with my palms. Pull her body into mine.

She groans as my hard-on brushes her stomach. Breaks our kiss to pull my t-shirt over my head.

Her eyes go wide at the sight of my bare-chest. "God, I missed this." She traces the Latin quote on my chest. *Semper ad meliora.* The shaded roses wrapped around my shoulder. The skulls that surround them.

She traces my sleeve all the way to the tip of my index finger. Then back up, from my wrist to the crook of my neck.

Her fingers curl around my ear. "You know all my buttons."

"Yeah?" I cup her breast with my palm. Draw circles around her nipple with my thumb.

She groans. "Fuck."

"What do you want, princess?"

Her groan gets louder, lower. Her palm slips from my hips.

She cups me. Rubs me through my pants.

Fuck, this fabric is thin. I can feel all her heat. All that pressure.

"I want to make you come." She rubs her palm against me. "I want to drive you out of your mind."

"You do."

"I want to see it."

I motion to the mirrored closet.

Her eyes go wide. She turns. Watches our reflection. Her palm against my crotch. The black cotton stretched over my cock. Her tits bouncing with her movements.

Her gaze sticks on my crotch.

Her tongue slides over her lips.

I want those red lips around me. I do. Fuck, the thought of coming in her pretty mouth—

Next time.

Right now, I need to feel her.

I need her skin against mine.

"How do you want it, princess?" I bring my hands to her hips. Roll her skirt lower. Lower. "You want it like this?" I pull her body into mine, so my chest is pressed to hers. "Or like this?" I turn her around. Press her back to my chest. Turn her to the mirror.

I take her hands. Place them on the mirror.

She groans as she rubs her ass against my cock.

Her skirt is binding her. She can't move her legs.

Fuck, having her at my mercy—

My balls tighten. I need to be inside her. I need to make her come.

Now.

"Or maybe like this?" I bring her to the bed. Place her hands on the mattress.

She bends at the waist. Turns her head to the mirror. Watches as I slide her skirt lower.

Lower.

There.

I peel it off her ass, over her hips, down her thighs.

All the way to her ankles.

She steps out of it. "The second one."

"This first." I flip her over. Pull her to the edge of the bed. Hook my fingers around the straps of her panties.

"Chase…" She lifts her hips.

I peel her panties to her ankles.

She kicks them aside. Spreads her legs. Digs her fingers into the bedspread.

She's ready.

She's eager.

She's aching.

But I need to tease her more. I need to be the only thought in her head. I need to be the center of her universe.

I can't have it anywhere else.

I need it here.

"You wear that outfit to torture me, princess?" I place my body between her legs.

She nods. "It's called strategy."

"Strategy?"

"Yeah." She groans as I nudge her legs apart. "You like boobs."

I can't help but chuckle. "I like boobs?"

She nods *of course*. "Not that I'm complaining. You're very talented in that way. I just…"

God dammit, she's adorable.

I'm not sure what I want more—her rambling or her groan.

"I wanted you to see what you were missing," she says.

"It worked."

"Not yet." She looks up at me. "Chase, I…"

She's scared.

But then I am too.

This is different than before. There's no pretense. No reason. No excuse.

I'm fucking her because I want her.

She's fucking me because she wants me.

The walls are down.

I don't know how to get them up.

I don't want to.

"You want to come on my face?" I drop to my knees.

She nods *hell yes*.

I motion to the mirror. "Watch."

"But—"

"Watch, princess." I push her thighs apart.

She groans as I bring my lips to the inside of her knee. Then as I drag them higher, higher, higher.

She tastes so fucking good. Like tangerines and soap and Ariel.

I bring my lips to the apex of her thighs.

My cock whines. It wants to be inside her sweet cunt. It wants to taste every inch of her.

I missed this.

I pin her legs to the bed. Then I nip at her tender skin.

"Chase." She tugs at the bedspread.

"Watch." I bring my mouth to her other thigh. Bite her softly. Then harder.

Harder.

There—

"Fuck." She groans. Turns her head toward the mirror.

Her eyes widen as she takes in her reflection.

She's a goddess. She must see it. She must see how perfect she is.

I kiss my way to her inner knee.

Then back up.

Down her other leg.

Then it's soft bites.

Harder ones.

Higher and higher and—

There.

She digs her fingers into my shoulder. "Chase." Her hips shift. "Please." Her voice dips to a whine. "Make me come."

I nip at her skin.

She groans in agony.

I do it again.

Again.

Again.

I do it until she's shaking. Until her groan is a plea. Until her nails sink into my skin.

She sighs as I bring my mouth to her.

"Fuck." Her legs dig into the bed. Her eyes close.

"Watch, princess." I remind her one last time. Then I lick her up and down.

I take my time tasting her. Like it's the first time. Like it's the only chance I'll get.

Slowly, I toy with her. Nip at her lips. Suck on her clit. Plunge my tongue inside her.

I slide my hand up her torso. Tease her nipple with my thumb and index finger.

She groans as I toy with her.

As I explore her.

Then I bring my tongue to her clit and her groan gets lower, deeper.

The agony fades to pure ecstasy.

I pin her to the bed, lick her exactly how she needs me.

Higher. Softer. Faster.

A little to the left.

There—

"Chase…" She claws at my skin. "Fuck."

I scrape my nails against her thighs. So she knows she's mine.

Here, she's mine.

I may not know what happens when we dress.

But right now—

Fuck, I need her to be mine.

I keep that same steady pace and pressure. I bring her all the way to the edge.

She claws at my skin. "Chase, fuck."

With the next flick of my tongue, she comes.

She shakes and shudders, groaning my name as she claws at my skin.

She gets sweeter. Wetter.

I don't release her. I keep her pinned. Work her with that same pressure.

Agony melts into her groan.

Then it melts away.

Until it's pure bliss.

I bring her to the edge again. She comes fast and hard. She claws at me, groans my name like it's a curse.

She tugs at my hair.

I help her up. Stand. Bring her to the mirror.

She brings her palms to the slick surface.

I strip out of my pants and boxers. Then I wrap my arm around her waist. Hold her body against mine.

Through the mirror, her eyes find mine.

She nods *yes, please, now*. It's more than *fuck me*. She's asking for everything.

I want to give her everything.

I just don't know how.

Through the mirror, I stare back at her.

Her brown eyes fill with need. Her cheeks flush. Her chest heaves.

I shift my hips, bringing our bodies together.

Her eyes close. A groan falls off her hips. Her fingers dig into the mirror.

She feels so fucking good, but it's nothing compared to watching bliss spread over her expression.

Slowly, I fill her.

I savor every second. Every inch of her sweet embrace. Every furrow of her brow. Every twinge of her lip.

"Watch, princess." I hold her in place with one hand. Bring the other to the back of her head.

She turns her neck.

My lips find hers. I kiss her hard.

I claim her with my tongue.

When she breaks our kiss, she turns back to the mirror. Nods *yes*.

It's a plea for more.

This time, I know exactly what she needs.

I fill her with a steady thrust.

She watches our reflection for as long as she can. Then her eyes close and her teeth sink into her lip.

I rock my hips, driving deep inside her.

Again and again.

I pull her closer. So I can feel her back against my chest, her thighs against my hands.

I need her skin against mine.

I need her groan.

I need her.

"Touch yourself, princess." I press my lips to her neck. "I want to watch you come."

Ariel groans and brings her hand to her clit.

I drag my teeth over her neck. Watch as she works herself.

Fuck, it's the best thing I've ever seen.

She comes hard and fast, groaning and shaking and struggling to stay upright.

I hold her close. Flip her over. Bring her to the bed.

She looks up at me for a second. Then she wraps her arms around me. Pulls our bodies together.

A few thrusts and I'm there.

My orgasm is quick. Intense. Pleasure spills through my body. Takes over every inch.

But I feel so much more than that.

I feel all of her.

It's so fucking obvious now.

I have no idea how to be what she needs. But I'm going to figure it out. I have to.

Chapter Thirty-Eight

ARIEL

Venice switches from boardwalk debauchery to suburban chillness as soon as you cross Main Street.

But tonight, Holden's party is spilling onto the street. I scan the crowd for my brothers, but I don't see any cops or Spider-Men. Spider-Mans?

Of course, Holden could put on a mask and I'd have no idea it's him. But, uh…

Maybe I should have picked a costume with a mask. Or a wig. Anything less obvious than my namesake.

Goose bumps spread over my skin. It's a cold night. Or maybe that's my outfit. Most of my skin is exposed, including my toes.

We should move Halloween to the middle of summer. Or I should move to Hawaii. There's no other place in the US where Halloween is actually warm. Even here, in Southern California, the perfect weather capital of the world, late October nights are chilly.

Chase nods to a friend. He moves to me. Takes my hand.

The warmth of his touch fills me with butterflies. I'm not being smart. I'm not pulling back. But I don't care.

The last two weeks were torture. Taking that test, staring at the single pink line, holding my phone, wishing I could tell him, that I could tell anyone—

The simple act of holding his hand fills that emptiness. It fills me in spots that have been empty for far too long.

I loved Phillip. But it was different. More steady and easy. Safer somehow.

With Phillip, it was like we both looked at a pool and decided to take the stairs into it.

With Chase, it's like I'm at the top of the high dive, staring down at the deep reservoir of turquoise.

It's the same water, but it's a hell of a lot more thrilling.

He brings his lips to my ear. "I passed Forest and Holden."

"Inside?"

He nods *yeah*. "Holden's teasing Forest about Skye's outfit."

"Right?" I doubt any of the guys know, but Skye is insecure about her curvy figure. She's beautiful and sexy as hell, but she's also larger than the average Southern California woman. "Do you think it's going to work?"

"Worked for you."

"Now I have to think about whether or not Forest is a boob guy." My nose scrunches in distaste. Gross.

"I'm gonna break something to you, princess."

My chest warms at the pet name. How can it be so sexy and sweet at the same time? It defies reason. "Yeah?"

"All guys are boob guys."

"What about guys who like guys?"

"All guys who like women—all people who like women, like boobs."

I nod. It's probably true. I mean—"It's hard not to like them. They're so soft and comfy."

Chase raises a brow. He's not wearing his mask. It turns his costume into *random all black outfit*, but it means I can look in his eyes.

God, he has such pretty eyes. So blue and deep and full of love.

Does he realize that? There's this well of love in his heart. He's been holding it back for so long. He's afraid it's a tsunami.

Maybe it is.

Maybe this is dangerous.

Or maybe I'm learning how to surf.

If… uh… if it were possible to surf a tsunami. I mean, uh… God, I need work on my metaphors.

"Something I should know?" His voice drops to a low, dirty tone.

"Don't tell me you're into the idea of two girls hooking up." I roll my eyes. "Why are guys into it?"

"Guys? Or me?"

"Guys."

"They think the girls are secretly desperate for dick. That when they show up, the girls will fall all over each other trying to suck them off."

I guess that makes sense. It's stupid, but it makes sense. "Some girls do that. Make out for guys' entertainment value."

"You?" He slides his arm around my waist.

I should pull away. This is Holden's party. His friends are everywhere. They might recognize us.

But I don't.

I can't.

It's physically impossible. "You know me. I do whatever

it takes for a man's attention. There's nothing I love more than pretending I'm interested in… anything, really."

"You've never faked interest in something for a guy?" he asks.

"Am I supposed to?"

His chuckle is low, hearty. "I love that about you."

"You love—" The word feels so good in my ears. On my lips. "You love what about me?"

"You barely know about the usual bullshit people do."

"I know about it…" Sorta. "I mean, when Forest was dating his ex, he pretended he loved coffee. But he really thinks it tastes like dirt."

"No," he says.

"Yes." I nod. "He's never told you?"

Chase chuckles. "Only every time we go to a coffee shop."

"Oh." My cheeks flush. "Sometimes I forget you're best friends." I want to forget. I want this to be easier.

He nods. "Me too."

"Why do um… why do you like the idea of two girls together?"

"What's not to like?"

I have no idea how to answer that.

He chuckles. "I guess I just like to watch." His fingers skim the waist of my skirt. "I'd watch you with anyone."

"But then I'd be with someone else."

"Yeah. But if my choice is watching you or not watching you—"

"Wouldn't that hurt?" My teeth sink into my lips. "And where's the consent here? Am I giving you permission to watch or are you spying?"

His laugh gets louder. "It's a fantasy, princess. It's not supposed to make sense."

"So you fantasize about watching me with another—"

"About watching you fuck yourself, yeah." He brings his lips to my neck. "Why? You want to make my dreams come true?"

My sex clenches. God, that's a hot idea. For a second, I forget I'm freezing cold. I nod *yeah.*

His lips curl into a smile.

"You're like dreamy Matt right now."

His chuckle lights up his eyes. "He has pretty eyes."

"Not as pretty as yours."

"He's more charming than I am."

"Only sometimes." My heart thuds against my chest. I love the way he looks at me. No one has ever looked at me like that. "Should we, um…"

"Yeah." He presses his palm into my lower back.

"Are you okay to drive?"

"I walked."

"It's freezing."

"I can go inside. Get your coat." He pulls me closer. "Or you can take my shirt."

"You'll be cold."

"And you'll get a view."

It's a tempting offer, but I shake my head.

His smile spreads over his cheeks.

Then it disappears.

"Ariel, is that you?" A familiar voice cuts through the crowd. It's feminine. Supportive. All *girl power, let's stick together.*

Whereas I want to stab its owner in the eye.

That's not a healthy response. By all accounts, by Chase's account, she never did him wrong. She broke up with him because it was best for both of them.

Even if it was only best for her, how is that different than what I've asked of Chase?

At the end of the day, a girl's got to look out for herself.

I turn to the sound.

Grace waves hello. She moves closer. She's, well, graceful in her floor length orange dress.

Princess Buttercup.

And there's her boyfriend, next to her, dressed as the Dread Pirate Roberts.

My heart climbs into my stomach.

Say nice things. Say hello, it's nice to see you, but I have to run. Normal social skills. Easy.

"Grace." I take a step toward her.

She takes one toward me. "You look so grown-up." She laughs. "Your boobs look great."

"Thank you." I bite my lip. How the hell am I supposed to take that? I mean, I can't say *wait until you see how good they look when I chop them off and replace them with saline. I'm thinking I'll trade up. Might as well, right?*

"They were so much... uh... doesn't she look cute, John?" She motions to her boyfriend.

He just laughs.

Finally, Grace pulls her eyes from me. Surprise spreads over her expression as she takes in Chase.

It's all over her face.

"Oh. Chase." Her cheeks flush. A blush of embarrassment, not desire. "I didn't... I'm sorry. I thought—" She turns back to John. "I thought this was Steve's party."

"That's what he said." The Pirate—I can't call him John—wraps his arm around his girlfriend.

God, they're cute together. And not just because they're dressed as an iconic couple. Or because she looks so pretty and regal with her long blond hair.

Is that her real hair? It's not a wig, but it could be extensions. Skye would be able to tell. She's great with this stuff, whereas I look like a raccoon every time I apply eyeliner.

There's a comfort to their gesture. Like they've been together forever. Like they're madly in love.

"Oh, uh, I guess you don't know John." Grace clears her throat. "Chase, this is John. John, this is Chase."

John extends his hand.

Chase shakes.

"Guess Grace has a type." John taps his black mask. Nods to Chase's all black outfit.

God, they are dressed the same.

There are small differences—The Pirate has black gloves and pull on boots. Chase is in combat boots and he's out of his mask.

But it's basically the same outfit.

We saw her Instagram.

We saw the Buttercup costume. Maybe that's why he… maybe he's not channeling Matt Murdock and all our conversations about the Devil of Hell's Kitchen.

Maybe he's dressing as Grace's other half.

With a smidge of plausible deniability.

My stomach churns. My veins buzz. It's the same ugly feeling as when Phillip talked about his boss.

I shouldn't be jealous.

But I am.

"You look good, Chase." Grace's voice is honest. Earnest. "Are you good?"

Chase stares at her, dumbstruck. Finally, he picks his jaw up off the floor. Nods a casual *yeah*.

Her smile is sweet. Loving. "I didn't realize… We should go."

"We're leaving," Chase says. "It's all yours."

"No." She looks to her boyfriend. "Your friends hate me."

He shakes his head. "They're on your side."

She bites her lip. "So you're still..." She takes a step backward. "I... uh... I'm sorry."

"There aren't sides." The words spill from my lips without passing through my brain. "Chase doesn't really talk about you. I just... I don't think anyone knows the details of what happened. Except, well... I checked out your social media. You're very open about it. That must be hard. But good. Uh..." Shit, I'm still talking. "It's brave."

Her laugh is wry. "It's not brave."

"Yeah, it is." I bite my lip. This is so not the time for this conversation. At all. "You, um... I should go."

"Isn't this your house?" Grace asks.

Yeah, that's true. But—"Chase and I were leaving."

"So you're..." Her eyes light up with realization. "Oh, that's great." Her exhale is heavy with relief. "I'm so glad, Chase. You deserve to be happy."

His eyes fill with confusion.

"We're—" Grace mimes *my lips are sealed*. "Our secret."

They have a secret.

No, it's our secret. All four of us.

But it's theirs too.

They're so...

Ugh.

My gaze goes to her wrist. Her sleeves are too long. I can't see the tattoo.

I'm not sure why I need to see it, but I do. I need the evidence she's the same girl I've stalked on social media. That she's okay with everything that happened.

That she moved on and survived.

I don't know why I need it—it's really none of my business—but I do. Not just for Chase. For me too.

Even though I hate her, I want her to be okay and happy.

324

I mean, I don't even hate her. It's just this ugly, jealous part of me. It hates her for having Chase's heart.

But that look on her face—

It's not her. She didn't take his heart. Maybe she hurt him, but she did everything she could to make it okay.

He's the one holding on.

Or maybe he's not.

Maybe I'm caught up in nothing.

It's just…

Why isn't he saying anything? Why isn't he saying *sorry, Grace, but Ariel is twice the woman you are, we have to go. I love fucking her and I need to do that now?*

Okay, no one would ever say that.

And, well…

Uh…

"We should really go." I wrap my arm around Chase's waist. It's a possessive gesture. It's not like me. But I don't care.

Grace nods *of course.* "You must be freezing in that."

I nod *kinda.* "I'll be okay, thanks."

"You sure? We're gonna leave, so we could give you a ride." She looks back to her boyfriend *is that okay?*

He shoots her a *really?* look, but he says nothing.

"No, it's not far." I nod goodbye. "I'm glad you're doing well."

"Yeah." She looks at me a little dumbstruck. "It was good to see you, Chase. Take care, okay?"

He just barely nods.

I pull him closer. Force myself to move forward.

He follows me.

I try to think of something to say, but my head is blank. I focus on moving forward—it's impossible to walk in this skirt. On turning the corner. On taking the next block.

It's a ten minute walk to Chase's place.

He fishes the keys from his pocket. Opens the door. Motions *after you*.

I step inside.

He closes the door behind him.

His apartment is quiet and warm and small.

It's like we're the only two people in the universe.

I turn to him. "Are you okay?"

He stares back at me, slowly formulating a response.

Chapter Thirty-Nine

ARIEL

*D*id *you wear that costume for my sake or hers?*

Are you thinking about her right now?

Do you think about her when you fuck me? Was that your go-to that time in my office? Is that why you needed me on my stomach?

Are you ever going to get over her?

Are you ever going to love me?

I swallow the jealousy that rises up in my throat.

He's not... we're not... I need to wait for him to respond.

"Yeah." He sucks in a shallow breath. "I can barely breathe, but it's not the same way it was."

I swallow hard. "Do you need something?"

He shakes his head. "You're shivering."

I pull my arms over my chest. "I'm okay."

He grabs the blanket from his couch. Drapes it over my shoulders.

Fuck, that is better. "How... how is it different?"

"She's happy."

Yeah, she is.

His expression stays dumbstruck. "I knew she was, but seeing it—"

"Are you jealous?"

His brow furrows with confusion.

"Of her boyfriend?"

"No." His voice is honest. "I'm happy for them."

"Yeah?"

He nods *yeah*.

I pull my blanket around my shoulders. I want to wrap it around him and hold him and kiss him.

But I need to hear this first.

I need to know he isn't still in love with her.

I can deal with his Daredevil-esque martyr complex. But not a Daredevil-esque inability to get over his ex.

God, the super powered lawyer offers insight into so many things.

"Do you miss her?" I shift my weight to my foot. God, these shoes are ridiculous. I move to the couch. Tug at my skirt.

Chase drops to his knees. He peels my skirt to my ankles and undoes the buckle of my left shoe. "Parts of me do." His fingers skim my calf, ankle, heel. "It's the same way I miss varsity basketball." He sets my left foot down. Moves to the right. "I miss the smell of the ball, the squeak of sneakers, the thrill of a win. But I don't want to go back to that."

"You play basketball with Forest once a week."

"Yeah. One-on-one. And he kicks my ass every week." He undoes the buckle on my right foot. Slips my shoe off. "It's fun. And it scratches that itch. Mostly." His eyes meet mine. "It's not about basketball. It's about being sixteen and not—"

"Feeling like you were responsible for the entire world?"

"Yeah." His brow softens. "I didn't realize how bad shit

was with Mom. Hunter was… he wasn't even partying yet. Wes… well, Wes is Wes, but he's always been okay."

"He and his girlfriend are cute."

Chase nods *yeah*. "She's good for him."

"Was Grace good for you?"

"Sometimes. I miss those times. But it's not about her, not really. I miss that feeling of walking on the beach, talking about our futures like we really believed they could go anywhere."

"They still could."

"Maybe. But it doesn't feel the same."

I nod. I know what he means. I remember that feeling of being seventeen and having the world at my fingertips. "Like when you finally get your driver's license."

He nods *exactly*.

"The rush of your first kiss with someone new. The first time you say *I love you*. The first time—"

"Your friend asks you to get her pregnant."

My laugh is nervous. "Are you expecting a second time?"

He shakes his head. "Not sure I could go through this again."

"Because, um… so…" I can't ask about our future. Not yet. I'm not ready for an answer. "She's pretty."

He stands. Shakes his head *so not going there*. "You're gorgeous, Ariel. I'm not gonna let anyone say otherwise. Including you."

"But she's prettier—"

"I don't compare you to Grace."

"Ever?"

"Ever."

"But you must think about how she has blond hair or how she gets art—"

"Your mom was an artist. You surround yourself with

everything she loved. You know more about pop art than I do."

Oh. That might be true. "So you think about how I'm smarter."

"Princess…" His voice is sincere. "This has been haunting you."

"No."

"Yeah."

"A little."

He sits next to me. Turns to face me. "I don't love her anymore."

"Okay."

"I'm not saying I'm over the damage she did. Not that she did it—"

"I know what you mean."

"But I am over her."

"Yeah?" My voice is needy. "Are you sure? You don't think about her ditching Pirate Boy for you?"

"No."

"But…" I tug at his black shirt. "It's basically the same outfit."

"I didn't have time to spring for the red suit."

"God, it looks so much more stupid."

He nods *yeah*. "I had to narrow it down by all black outfits."

My lips curl into a smile.

"Didn't leave a lot of options."

"You swear you didn't?"

"You had your strategy?" His fingers outline my bikini top. "I had mine."

"You think reminding me about your mommy issues and your martyr complex works?"

"Didn't it?"

A laugh spills from my lips. "Did you really?"

"No." He brings his hands to my waist. Pulls me into his lap. "Wanted something you'd notice."

"I'd notice you in anything."

"Wanted something that mattered to you." He cups my cheek with his palm. "Plus, it shows off my ass."

My smile widens. "It does."

"You telling me that doesn't help?"

"I love it when you're like this."

His eyes flare with hurt.

"Not that... I like all the versions of you. Well... No, I still like the Chase that blames himself for everything. But I don't want you to feel like that." I stare into his eyes. "You're such a great guy. I wish you could see it the way I do."

"Me too."

"I wish I could do more—"

"You are." He digs his fingers through my hair. Pulls me into a slow, deep kiss.

Mmm, he tastes so good.

"You need to talk more?"

I shake my head.

"Good." He kisses me again. It's faster, more demanding.

It erases my thoughts.

Convinces me we make sense.

God, there's so much to think about. It didn't happen this time, but it will.

We're going to make a baby.

We're going to make a baby and I'm atwitter over whether or not he loves me.

But then it's not like the two are unrelated.

If we could have everything, if I could really believe he's all mine, that he won't leave—

I'm scared to want it.

But I do.

I want the dream. A doting husband, a healthy kid, a booming job, a house with a picket fence.

Chase would be such a good dad.

He will be such a good dad.

He breaks our kiss. Tugs at my hair as he stares into my eyes. "I mean it."

"Huh?" I'm lost in those baby blues.

"I want to watch you fuck yourself."

Oh.

"You made a demand earlier." He catches my lip with his thumb. "You sticking with that?"

"Yes."

"Yes?" He raises a brow *you can do better than that*.

"Fuck yes."

His lips curl into a smile. "Mine first."

I shake my head. "Mine first. Take it or leave it."

He smiles. "Princess, you're gonna be the death of me."

———

I wake up in Chase's arms.

November first. What a beautiful day. Big yellow sun. Bright blue sky. Brisk breeze.

Chase's strong tattooed arms.

His ink is so sexy. I was never into that before. Having older brothers with tattoos kinda ruins the appeal of the so-called bad boy.

But Chase wearing his heart on his sleeves—

Mmm.

I pry myself out of bed, brush my teeth, wash my face, fix tea.

He joins me in the kitchen. Wraps his arms around my

waist. Brings his lips to my neck. "You think you're going somewhere?"

"Work." I melt into his touch. "I have a class at eleven."

"It's eight thirty."

"I have to get dressed." I exaggerate my voice, so it's obvious my protests are empty. "And, well, I do need my chai…"

"I need you groaning over that chai."

"I might be able to arrange that."

He nips at my neck. "I might fuck you right here."

"I might be okay with that."

"You might?"

My lips curl into a smile. "I'd prefer the bed."

He hooks his thumbs in my pajama bottoms. "After the chai."

"And the coffee. You're even more miserable without it."

"Of course. I'm intolerable with coffee most times. Without it—"

"I don't want to imagine."

———

A PERFECT MORNING SPILLS INTO A PERFECT DAY INTO A perfect night.

Chase and I fall into a routine.

After work, we meet at his place. I teach him how to cook a Vietnamese dish or he teaches me how to cook a… well, any non-Vietnamese dish.

We eat dinner, watch TV on the couch, break for, ahem, other activities, fall asleep in his bed.

Then it's chai and coffee and bacon and eggs and another day of texts about everything and nothing.

We go to the Huntington Gardens on his day off.

We hike in the Malibu Hills.

When I complain about his pace, he teases me that exercise is good for the baby. And neither of us has to say it. There isn't one yet, but there will be.

I keep thinking about that.

About this being our life. About us being parents. About us having it all.

Okay, so I don't think about it when we're actually trying to make a baby. It's impossible to think, at all, when Chase is ordering me around and growling into my skin and nipping at my neck—

But after—

Before—

All day, every day—

It's there, running through my mind, until it's time. Five days before my period.

Four.

Three.

Two.

The morning of day one.

The test is 99.7 percent accurate three days before. It's 99.9 percent one day before.

I could wait until tomorrow. To see if I actually…

But I can't handle that level of disappointment.

I need to know now.

I meet at his place, but I don't bring dinner. I bring a stack of pregnancy tests. "What if I'm not?"

"What if you are?"

I'm not sure which is scarier.

Chapter Forty

ARIEL

I wrap my fingers around the plastic stick. This is the fourth time.

I checked every day with my last cycle. I thought, maybe I had the timing off, that I got it wrong.

Today…

There's only one more chance. One more month. If I'm not—

I can push my doctor's orders, but…

Fuck. I suck in a deep breath. Push out a heavy exhale. I need to think about something else. Anything else.

Chase runs his fingers through my hair.

The gesture is calming. He's way too calming. It's wrong.

"I… uh… will you come?" I ask.

"After this? Sure. However you want me, princess."

"No, uh. I mean, yes, but to Thanksgiving?"

"That's in two days."

"Yeah." I bite my lip. "I know it's last minute. But Dad is home and Forest and Holden will be there. And Skye will stop by. And, uh… I'd like it if you were there."

"Won't Forest—"

"He hasn't invited you?"

"He has, but—" He plants his hand under my chin. Tilts me so we're eye to eye. "I can stop by."

"Oh."

"Keating Thanksgiving is a big thing now."

"No, you should… I don't want to—"

"I'd rather be at your place. But—"

"Can I come? Instead." The words spill from my lips before I can stop them. "I mean, before ours. Early. Or maybe after. Uh, when do you do dinner?"

"Late." His eyes bore into mine. "Are you sure?"

I nod.

"You using this delicate moment to manipulate me?"

"Maybe. I don't mean to."

"Are you gonna tell your brothers?"

"Not yet."

"They'll be happy for you."

"No. It's more…" My lips press together. "If I don't make it through the first trimester, I don't know if I can handle their disappointment on top of mine."

He nods with understanding. "Princess, you look so nervous."

"Too nervous?"

"No." He runs his fingers over my jaw. "I get it. But it's not exactly—"

"It's obvious something is up?"

He nods *yeah*.

"And your family… if I come to Thanksgiving, they'll know—"

"They're good at keeping secrets."

That's true. "I had no idea your mom was an alcoholic."

He chuckles.

Oh, shit. "Sorry, that was—"

"Perfect." He leans down and presses his lips to mine. "You're invited. I'll make sure we do dinner at seven. And I can stop by your place first. But they will ask questions."

"Okay."

"We should decide how we want to answer them."

That's true. "Maybe I'll just go to your place."

He nods *sure*.

"And well... I should probably." I hug the test tighter. "I should probably find this out first."

He nods *yeah*.

"So, uh... I guess there's no sense in waiting. And I, uh... God I really have to pee." I break our embrace. Move to the bathroom before he can reply.

I can't answer any questions.

I can't think.

I just have to do it.

I take my position. Uncap the stick. Hold it in place.

Five. Four. Three. Two. One.

There. I recap it. Finish up. Wash my hands. Stare back at the mirror. Set a timer on my smart watch.

Three minutes.

Three minutes and I know whether or not I'm going to be a mother.

Fuck.

I pace around the bathroom. It's too small for pacing, but I do it anyway.

Chase moves toward me. He presses his hand to the door. "You freaking out, princess?"

"No... A little."

"Come here."

I shake my head. Not that it conveys anything. There's a door between us. "I just have to..." I run the water until it's cold. Splash my face. It should help. Why isn't it helping?

Deep breath.

Steady exhale.

My future.

No big deal.

"Ariel…" Chase taps on the door. "Tell me you're okay."

"I'm okay."

"Convince me."

"I am." Deep breath. Steady exhale. "Really." I just… "I can't look at you yet."

"Why not?"

"If I'm not… I just can't."

"Okay." His voice is clear. Understanding.

God, he's really understanding. But also good with boundaries. And authoritative.

He'll be a good dad.

A tactful other half.

Not that we're… I mean, we might… God, I hope we are.

Buzz, buzz.

That's it.

The three minutes are up.

It's time to face my fate.

To see if this is really happening.

I close my eyes and pray for two pink lines.

Chapter Forty-One

CHASE

Ariel shrieks. "Oh my God."

I reach for the handle, but it's still locked.

"Chase… Oh my God." Her fingers hit the door. The handle. The lock.

Click.

I turn the handle, press the door open.

She stares back at me, her eyes wide, her smile wider. "It's…" She turns the test over.

Right there, in that tiny display, my life changes forever.

She's pregnant.

This is happening.

Fuck, this is really happening.

It hits me all at once—

I want that. I want this with her. I want everything with her.

How the hell do I do that?

She throws her arms around me. "Thank you." She squeezes me tighter. "I'm so… I don't know how to say it enough."

I don't know what to say, so I stick with something simple. "You're welcome."

She laughs as she digs her fingers into my skin. "I… God… what do I do now?"

"How about breakfast?"

She nods into my chest. "Breakfast is good. But I need more. I need big."

"You're not feeling any symptoms?"

She releases me. Looks up at me with a hazy smile. "Just a little… the ginger tea helps with the nausea. I thought it was nerves, but—" She jumps into my arms again. "I… I asked my adviser how she felt about her first pregnancy."

"She knows?"

"No, I told her my brother and his wife are trying."

"Your brother got married?" I tease.

She laughs. "She said she knew she wanted a baby, but when she saw the pregnancy test… all of a sudden, it was real. Terrifying and exhilarating and everything."

"You're terrified?"

"Yeah." She presses her lips to my collarbone. "But mostly… I don't think my heart has ever been this full." Her eyes meet mine. "Do you feel that too?"

I don't know what to say. It's still her kid. I'm still the sperm donor. Uncle Chase, at best. But I can't say those words. I can't accept that. "It's everything."

Her smile spreads ear to ear. "Thank you." She rises to her tiptoes and presses her lips to mine. "I know we haven't figured out everything, but you… I… this is good."

"It's great, princess."

She steps backward. Looks up at me like I'm the answer to her prayers.

Fuck, she's beautiful like this. Glowing. Is this why everyone says pregnant women glow?

She's bursting with light.

It warms me everywhere.

Ariel is pregnant.

We're having a baby.

But then—

It's not us. Not yet. I can't fall in love until I know this is ours.

"Chai oatmeal?" I take her hand. Motion to the kitchen. "Sit. I'll make it."

"I can't sit." She bounces into the kitchen. Fills the kettle with hot water. Sets it to boil. "This is…" Her voice is dreamy, far off. "Is it possible to say amazing too many times?"

"No."

She looks at me with the world's biggest smile. "We have to celebrate."

"Chai oatmeal isn't enough?" I tease.

Her laugh is light. Easy. "Chai oatmeal sounds amazing." Her tongue slides over her lip. "But we need more. And, uh, well, you must have practice celebrating without alcohol."

I can't help but laugh.

She bites her lip, but she doesn't jump to her usual *oh my God, that was rude, I'm sorry*. "Right. I mean—"

"Call in sick," I say.

"No…" Her eyes go wide. "I can't."

"I'm off today."

Her fingers tap the counter. "I did have a class canceled." Her gaze shifts to the kettle. "The other… no one really tries the week of Thanksgiving."

I motion *come here*.

She releases the counter. Moves toward me. "What are we doing with our day off?"

"Besides fucking like rabbits?"

"Will we have time for anything else?" She wraps her arms around my waist.

I pull her body into mine. "Barely."

Her laugh is pure joy. "We can do that all night."

"Are you rejecting me, princess?"

"No." She slips her palm under my t-shirt. Presses it against my bare skin. "I'm making you wait."

"Cruel."

She nods *yeah*. "While we… you'll do anything I want?"

"Anything."

"What if I want to get a tattoo?"

"Not sure you're supposed to. But I insist on doing it."

"Right here." She points to her lower back. "MILF."

I burst into laughter. "Yeah?"

"Yeah." She holds her poker face. "You don't think?"

"Let's go to Inked Hearts right now." I slip my hand under her tank top. Trace the letters over her lower back. "I'll make a stencil. It'll take twenty minutes, tops."

Fear streaks her expression. "No, I, uh… I should follow the guidelines."

"You need an extra prenatal vitamin?" I motion to the cabinet. She's been taking them for weeks. I guess that's standard operating procedure.

She shakes her head *no*. "Too many is just as bad as too few."

"You're informed."

"Of course." She slips her hand between us. Places it over her bellybutton. "Charlotte needs the best."

"Charlotte?"

"Or Charlie." Vulnerability drips into her voice. "Unless you object."

"Not a bit."

She's naming her kid after her mom. That's pure Ariel. My heart melts.

It's too much.

I'm falling head over heels.

I need to hit the brakes. If that's not what she wants—

"But what about Matt? Karen? Foggy?" I pitch names of *Daredevil* characters until I run out.

Her nose scrunches with distaste. "At least Matt and Karen are normal names people wouldn't notice. But, really… UGH."

"Should I move to another series?"

She shakes her head *no way*. "You're lucky you're a tattoo artist."

"Is that right?"

"You never have to name anything." Her expression gets warmer. Brighter. It shouldn't be possible, but it is. "You're not good at it."

"Not good at many things."

"Well… you're a good cook, a good tattoo artist, a good friend."

"A good fuck?"

She laughs. "Great."

"That's the one that gets great?"

"Show less skill if you want less recognition." Her voice gets floaty.

My chest warms. Fuck, I love seeing her like this. I want it so badly. Want this so badly.

If it's what's best for her. And Charlotte.

It's so perfect it's wrong.

It really is.

"You don't want to experience my skills today," I say.

"I do." She tugs at my t-shirt. "But later."

"After…"

"You'll really do anything?"

I nod. "Anything."

"This will be perfect."

Chapter Forty-Two

ARIEL

I take Chase to the Museum of Contemporary Art.

He laughs. "Princess, you really think you had to convince me to go to a museum?" He motions to his tattooed arm.

My thoughts evaporate. Logic… There was some logic to this decision. To the surprise. This was Mom's favorite museum. That's why I'm here.

But everything else is so fuzzy.

Chase's inked arms are just—

It's not even that they're yummy, though they are so, so yummy.

I look at him and I see him cradling a baby. I see him holding a little girl, cooing over her, letting her tiny little fingers wrap around his tattooed forearm.

Why is that so sexy?

I don't care to find the logic at the moment.

Life is too good for thinking.

I'm spending a beautiful, blue day with Chase.

With the smoking hot father of my child.

It's perfect.

———

After wandering around MoCA all morning, Chase and I head to Chinatown, share sweet and sour chicken, beef and broccoli, and copious piles of white rice.

Then we head to Silverlake, window shop hip boutiques, drink expensive coffee (decaf for me. It's good, but I don't get the fuss), stop at a baby store.

I know it's early. Too early to get this excited. But I can't help myself.

I buy a tiny onesie printed with *cutie pi*.

I hold it close through ice cream, dinner, a walk in the hills, the drive back to the Westside.

To a shop with lingerie wearing mannequins in the window.

Chase motions to a sex toy—a giant glass dildo—on display. "Come on." He turns the car off. "I still owe you a vibrator."

Chapter Forty-Three

ARIEL

Wide windows let in the soft blue evening light. The curtains are drawn. The merchandise shines in the twilight.

Everything is on display.

I'm on display. To anyone in the strip mall.

Anyone who drives along the busy street.

Okay, maybe it's not all that busy this far into Santa Monica. It's past rush hour. There's nothing nearby except a bunch of car dealerships. And the hospital.

God, what if Phillip was driving home and he saw me here?

I mean, he doesn't live in this direction. And, really, what if he saw me here? It's not like I was some sort of virginal prude. We had sex. We had good sex. It wasn't Earth-shattering, but—

"Princess, you there?" Chase wraps his arm around my waist.

I lean into the gesture. I need the steadiness. I need the weight of his limb. The pressure of his touch. It's right. It shouldn't be right. But it is. He is. We are.

This is just…

My hand goes to my stomach reflexively. Not my stomach exactly. The space below my belly button. I know enough about anatomy to know where this is happening.

There's a tiny being the size of a seed inside me. She's so small. How can she make my life feel so full? It defies reason.

But then, reason is still incredibly unappealing.

"Ariel?" Chase brushes my long hair behind my ear. His eyes meet mine. They fill with all the happiness in the world.

He wants this as badly as I do.

He must.

I get lost in his blue eyes. They're so pretty. So deep. So blue.

Will Charlotte have blue eyes?

God, a tiny baby with big eyes the color of a lake—

"Where are you going?" he asks.

"Aren't we…" I clear my throat. Motion to the sex toys against the far wall. There are so many. Dozens. How can there be so many?

There are only a few basic functions.

"Yeah." He motions *after you*, but he keeps his arm around my waist.

I nod *of course*. Take a small step forward. Then another. My stomach flutters. Nausea or nerves or both. I have an excuse now. A get out of jail free card. But I don't want to use it. I want this. I do. Just—"Do we still need this?"

He arches a brow.

"I mean, before, it was because you thought I would—" My eyes dart around the room. There's an older woman perusing glass dildos. She studies them like they're works of art.

They *are* works of art. They're beautiful, like the stained glass windows in a Catholic Church.

I step behind a wall of products. DVDs this time. There are even more possibilities. Gay. Straight. Lesbian. MILF. Interracial. Barely legal.

God, that's so…

Why?

Why do guys find the idea of a woman on her eighteenth birthday so attractive?

Chase presses his palm into my lower back. "You want one?"

"No." My chest flames. "We don't need a vibrator anymore. Because we don't have to, uh, finish, in any specific way." My fingers brush the skin below my bellybutton. "I'm already—"

"I know."

"Oh."

"Still want one."

"But—"

"Still want to feel you coming on my cock."

Oh my God. This is a tiny shop. There's no music. Only the hum of the air-conditioning. In Los Angeles, everything hums with air-conditioning, all the time. The sun heats the glass, makes shops warm every afternoon, even if the temperature stays in the sixties.

His low chuckle fills my ears.

I look around the shop for signs someone heard. That they're shaking their head *so uncouth*. But no one is watching. And even if they were. So what?

We're all in this shop for the same reason.

There's nothing to be ashamed of.

Sex toys are healthy. Sex is healthy. Masturbation is healthy.

This is a totally normal activity.

So why am I dizzy?

Maybe it's not nerves. Maybe it's the baby. Maybe it's lust.

Maybe it's love.

Not that I can think it at the moment.

This trip isn't about love. This is about sex. No, it's about coming, pure and simple. "What if I want something else?"

"Do you?"

"No."

He rests his hand on my cheek. "You've never used one?"

"Never."

"Never wanted to?"

"My hand is effective. Why mess with nature?"

He chuckles. "How do you know it's the best unless you've tried something else?"

That's very logical. I really can't argue the logic. "But, uh, it's just… not as tactile."

His chuckle deepens. "True. But hands get tired. Machines don't."

"So you…" My gaze shifts to his hand. The one that's reaching for the shelf. For a toy in a bright pink box. "You admit that?"

"Of course."

"But, uh, aren't guys all obsessed with their dicks being good enough to get women off?"

"Which guys are these?"

"I hear things."

He rubs my temple with his thumb. "From who?"

"Holden's friends."

"When they were in high school?"

Probably, yeah. I don't really talk to guys about their sex lives. Not at the moment.

Phillip didn't have hang-ups. (The rumors about Asian guys aren't true. He had plenty of, ahem, equipment). He didn't get upset if I didn't come from penetration. He made it happen another way.

"You don't want to know the shit Holden says now." Chase takes my hand. Places the bright pink box in my palm. "But, trust me, he's using toys."

"Oh."

"Did your ex have a complex?"

"No. This guy I dated in college did. He was kind of a dick." I can't help but laugh. "Maybe that was the problem. He was obsessed with it."

"Yeah?"

I nod. "He wanted to know how he measured up to other guys. He'd always ask about my high school boyfriend. If he was bigger. If he was better. And he thought... well, I mean, it was never about that. It felt like plenty, but uh—"

"Was it not?"

"No. I mean, he was smaller than my high school boyfriend, but it didn't really matter. It was more... he was so into his dick that he neglected other things."

"He didn't eat you out?"

My cheeks flush. "Never."

"Asshole."

"Maybe he didn't like it."

"Then he's not just an asshole. He's an idiot." Chase drags his fingertips to my chin. He tilts my head so I'm staring at the sex toy. "You like this one?"

"I don't know how to pick."

"You want something inside you?"

I fight my blush. "I thought I was coming on your cock." My voice wavers. It's not strong enough. I need to channel Chase's sex god confidence. "I want to come on your cock."

His pupils dilate. "Fuck, princess." He drags his eyes away from me. Turns to the shelf of toys.

There are so many. Long rods. Short ones. Tiny ovals. Strange curves.

He motions to the left side of the wall. "I want to buy one of these later. And fuck you with it." He taps a vibrator with rabbit ears on the box. Oh, it's got the long rod for vaginal stimulation. And the ears for clitoral stimulation. But that's too clinical. I need to say it in a sexy way. I try to find something. Come up with, "oh."

"Oh?"

"I, uh… okay."

"Okay?"

"Yeah. Sticking with okay."

He chuckles. "It might be too much." He points to the box in my hand. Curved handle. Six inch cylinder. Hot pink and white, with a heart shaped logo. "It's more—"

"For either?"

"Yeah." He reaches for something on the top shelf. A display unit. "You want to try it?"

"Here?" But, we're… Uh…

He chuckles. "Like this." He places the box on the shelf. Takes my hand. Brings it to the, uh, rod.

He turns the toy on. Presses the silicone against the pad of my thumb.

His eyes go to mine. He studies my reaction as he turns the vibration higher. Higher. Fuck, that's a lot.

He turns it down. Switches from a steady buzz to a rhythmic buzz-buzz-buzz. Then one with longer gaps. With longer holds. With an erratic pattern.

"You like it," he says.

I... don't know. But, God, the anticipation in his eyes. "I think so."

"Good." His lips curl into a half-smile. "I'm gonna take you home and make you come until you beg me to stop."

Holy shit.

Chapter Forty-Four

CHASE

Ariel shifts back and forth on her heels. She eyes the bedroom nervously. Like she's never been there before.

Fuck, it does something to me, seeing her so wide-eyed and innocent.

"You're still nervous." I set the plain white bag on the dining table. It's not the black plastic of an old school sex shop. It's white, paper, proudly bearing the shop's name in a girly shade of pink.

Her eyes go to said name. "Maybe. But not just because of that." Her lips press together. "This is… we're… It's different."

It is.

She's pregnant with my child.

Fuck, it still makes me dizzy.

It shouldn't change things. Not here. But it does.

Her feet steady. She kicks off her shoes. Leans down to do away with her socks. "So, uh, I guess we should unwrap it?"

"You want to do the honors?"

"Okay." She bites her lip. Shakes off her nerves. Moves to the table. "Have you used one before?"

"Yeah."

"On Grace?"

"Don't do that."

She swallows hard. "Right. That doesn't matter. It would be silly to be jealous. I mean, you're not with her. And you don't want to be with her."

"Princess—"

"I'm not jealous." She plucks the box from the table. Runs her nail along the plastic wrapping until it snags. "I mean, it's not like she's the one having your baby."

"My baby?"

She skips right over the clarification. Lands in a big, dopey smile. "I can't get over it."

"Me either."

"I just…" She peels off the plastic. Sets the box on the table. Pulls off the top. "All the books I read, they say it's good to have sex."

"Do they?"

"Yeah, I mean, it's never putting the baby in danger." Her eyes meet mine. "Can I keep saying it?"

"Yeah."

"Don't you want to—" She motions to the bedroom. "Get to it."

"It's not a rush." The opposite, actually.

"Some of us get tired easily."

"Some of us?"

She nods *yeah*. "Maybe that's another symptom. Charlotte is taking all my energy." Her smile widens. "I'm going to keep saying it."

"Good."

She stares back at me with every bit of happiness in the world. "What if I fall asleep?"

S, Windsor Gdns

5. 12. 2023

Dear Valerie & Roland

I have just re-read last years

letter enclyed for your grandchildren

1689-00

9.50
4.00

51.00 57-00—Tesco — 10/12 *
18.99 — Amazon 4/12 ✓

"Damn, you think that little of my abilities?"

Her cheeks flush. She trips over her words. "No, I just mean… orgasms help you sleep."

"Trust me, princess. You'll be plenty awake."

"I just, uh…" She runs her fingers over the toy. "It's the first time. Since we know. That's…"

"I know."

"So you—"

"Yeah." I move to the table. Wrap my arms around her. "Ariel, I want to fuck you. I want to feel your cunt pulsing around me. I want to watch you writhe until you can't take it anymore."

Her breath catches in her throat.

"But I want to hold you just as much."

"Oh."

"This is… it's everything."

"It is."

"And, fuck, this sounds cheesy. But I don't have the words to explain it." I place my hand over hers. "I need to show you."

"Oh." She arches her back, rubbing her ass against my crotch. "That is cheesy." She wraps her fingers around the toy. "But, I like it." She steps forward, breaking our touch, and leads me into the bedroom.

I press the door closed.

She turns the main lights off. Turns the string lights on. The room fills with the soft glow of stars.

It casts faint highlights off her dark hair, her sharp nose, her strong shoulders.

Fuck, she's beautiful like this. She's beaming.

I need to have her.

I need to hold her.

I need to fuck her senseless.

What is it about knowing she's pregnant? It's doing shit

357

to me. Shit these jeans are—

God damn, I need both of us naked. Now.

She tosses the toy on the bed. Pulls her top over her head. Undoes the clasp of her bra.

The fabric falls on the floor.

Her eyes meet mine. She motions *come here*.

I do.

My hands go to her hips.

She melts into my touch. Looks up at me, those big, brown eyes full of trust and need.

I run my hand through her hair and bring my lips to hers.

She kisses back with everything she's got.

I pull her closer.

She arches her hips, rocking her crotch against mine, gasping as her cunt brushes my hard-on.

I hold her body against mine.

She groans against my mouth.

My body hums. Every part of me is awake and alive and every part wants her.

It's torture staying this close without touching her properly. But I do it. I hold her close until I can't take it anymore. Then I break our kiss. Do away with my t-shirt.

Her eyes go wide.

Her hands go to my jeans. She unzips them. Pushes them off my hips. Wraps her hand around me.

Ariel rubs me over my boxers. She stares up at me with this perfect mix of defiance and obedience.

My balls tighten. She's too fucking good at this. I'm too fucking eager.

I need her brimming with bliss.

Now.

"Take off your jeans." I pull back, breaking our touch.

She nods. Sets her glasses on the side table. Stares into my eyes as she unzips her jeans and kicks them off her feet.

She doesn't wait for instruction. She pushes her panties —black cotton with cream lace trim—to her feet.

Fuck, she's gorgeous.

I soak in the sight of her for a moment. Then I wrap my arms around her. Help her onto the bed.

She looks up at me with hazy eyes.

I push her up the bed. Nudge her knees apart.

Ariel knots her hand into my hair. She pulls me into a slow, deep kiss.

I sink into her.

She wraps her legs around my waist.

Fuck, she's exactly where she needs to be. Only I'm still wearing these fucking boxers.

God dammit, if she keeps touching me like this, I'm going to come in these.

I break our kiss.

She lets out a whine. "Chase. Please."

I kick off my boxers.

Her eyes go wide. She takes in the sight of me. Like it's the first time. Like I'm a piece of art she's studying.

Her teeth sink into her lip.

Her fingers dig into the sheets.

Her toes curl.

She looks so fucking good on my black sheets. Like she belongs there.

She does.

She belongs in my life. In my world. With me.

I just—

Fuck, that's still confusing. I can't want that yet. I can't have that yet. Not until I'm sure it's what's best for her.

She climbs up the bed. Wraps her fingers around my cock. Brings her lips to mine.

She pumps me with steady strokes.

I kiss her hard for a moment, then I flip her onto her stomach.

Ariel arches her back. "Fuck me."

I push her legs apart. Run my fingers over her cunt. She's wet, but not enough.

I reach for the toy.

She gasps as I turn it on.

I press it against her inner thigh. Softly. So she can get used to the pressure. Then harder.

Hard enough she groans.

"Chase." She rocks her hips. "Please."

I move the toy a little higher.

"Please." Her voice is a whine. "Fuck me. Please."

"Not yet."

"Please." Her voice lifts. "Chase—" She gasps as I bring the toy to her clit. "Fuck."

I keep the pressure soft.

She digs her fingers into the sheets.

I bring it a little higher.

"Oh my God." Her toes curl. "Chase... I... fuck." Her head falls to one side. Her hair goes with it.

Fuck, seeing her like this—

It's everything.

I hold the toy against her until she's panting. Until she's groaning and writhing and clutching the sheets like she can't take it anymore.

Then I bring my hand to her hip and I pull her body onto mine.

She groans as I slide inside her.

Fuck, she feels good. And this, knowing she's mine, knowing we're one—

My head fills with every cheesy metaphor in the universe.

Then Ariel groans and my thoughts dissipate.

She arches her hips.

I press the toy against her clit.

"Fuck. Chase…" Her groans run together. They get louder. Higher.

She reaches back for me. Rakes her nails against my ass as she comes.

Her cunt pulses around me.

My name falls off her lips.

It's the best thing I've ever heard, but it's not enough. I need more. I need everything.

I place my free hand outside her shoulder. Then I lower my body onto hers. Fill her with steady thrusts.

"Chase… Fuck." She turns her head to the side. Presses her eyelids together.

I wrap my arm around her shoulders. Bring my hand to her neck.

She lets out a heady gasp.

I press a little harder. Not enough to hurt. Enough she knows she's mine.

Ariel responds with a low, deep groan. "Chase…" She rolls her body into mine. Making room for the toy.

I hold it against her clit. Hold her close as I fuck her.

It's pure beauty, watching bliss spill over her expression. Watching her eyes close, her lips part, her brows furrow and relax.

She pulses around me as she comes.

Fuck.

It's too much. She feels too fucking good.

A few more thrusts, and I'm there. I hold her close, groaning her name as I spill inside her.

She knocks the toy away.

When I'm finished, she collapses beneath me.

I untangle our bodies. Roll her over. "You think I'm done with you, princess?"

She nods. Then shakes her head. "Later."

"Later?"

"After we shower."

"In the shower."

Her teeth sink into her lip. "In the shower."

Chapter Forty-Five

ARIEL

By the time I step out of the shower, my legs are jelly. My body is still buzzing. And my—

Fuck, I didn't know it was possible to be this sore.

I reach for a purple towel. It's new. I think. I mean, the last time I was here, all of Chase's towels were white cotton.

Now, they're purple.

He grabs the regal fabric. Wraps it around his waist.

My lip corners turn down reflexively. As much I can't take more—I really can't—I still want to see *all* of him.

Don't get me wrong. He looks plenty good in his towel, water dripping off his short hair, down his broad shoulders, along his hard torso.

Mmm.

Ow. My body whines. It wants him. And it can't take any more stimulation.

"I have something for you." Chase motions to the bedroom. Holds up his hand *one minute*.

I nod *sure*. Watch as he moves to the closet.

He pulls the door open. Grabs something. Turns back to me.

Oh, it's a robe. A purple robe.

He holds the shoulders open like it's a coat he's putting on a king. Or a princess, I guess.

I join him in the bedroom. Drop my towel on the floor. Let him help me into the robe.

I tie the sash. "Thank you."

"Comfortable?"

"Yeah." It really is. And it's important. He's buying things for me to keep at his place. He's inviting me into his life.

Does he want the same thing I do?

Does he want us to be a family? A real family?

God, I want it so badly it steals my oxygen. It sucks up every thought in my brain.

Then he brings his lips to mine and my thoughts disappear.

Mmm. Chase.

That's a flashing sign in my brain.

Chase, Chase, Chase.

I want him, yes, but it's so much more than that.

He holds me close. Kisses back with every bit of affection in the world.

Does that mean something? It must. But I don't want to ask at the moment. I just want to bask in the glow.

I'm pregnant.

It's fucking amazing.

I pull back with a sigh.

He runs his fingers along my chin, down my neck, over my collarbones. All the way to the loose neckline of the robe. "I could get used to this."

"Me too." My flush is light. I'm too exhausted for

nerves. But then… no, I need to keep that in the back of my head. For a while.

Today is good. It's pure perfection.

Nothing is ruining that.

He cups my cheek with his palm. "You want something to drink? Decaf chai?"

My nose scrunches in distaste. Even if I wasn't pregnant, I wouldn't be drinking caffeine this late, but the decaf chai is so inferior to the original thing. "Maybe the rooibos. No milk."

"You think I don't know that?"

"You drink coffee. What do you know?"

He chuckles. "I'm a philistine?"

"Well… yeah, kinda."

"Harsh." He steps back. Unwraps his towel. Pulls on a pair of boxers.

"Coffee is so strong. It kills your taste buds. You can't appreciate the nuances in flavor."

"Maybe you don't appreciate the nuances in coffee."

People say all these things about how a certain blend has notes of maple or grapefruit or honey, but it all tastes the same. Thick and overpowering. "I'll take your word for it."

"Harsh."

"The truth is."

His smile lights up his eyes. It's such a pretty smile. I want more of it. I want it all the time.

He steps backward. Winks. Turns and moves into the kitchen.

Okay, yes, I do stare at his ass the whole time. I'm only human.

When Chase disappears from view, I move to the dresser. I could go home, but it feels like it's a million miles away. I need pajamas. His t-shirts are too big for me, but only makes them extra comfy.

I find an old Inked Hearts t-shirt. It's adorable. Black with the logo screen printed in hot pink.

I toss it, and a pair of boxers, on the bed.

My eyes go to the mirror. To the robe hanging off my chest.

They're already bigger. My boobs.

I thought it was all the noodles I was eating, but it's not.

They're going to get huge for a while.

Then they'll be gone.

Everything will be different.

It's not just that I'll have a tiny human being to feed, clothe, protect.

It's not even that I'll gain weight and stretch marks and, uh, looseness in certain regions.

I'm not looking forward to that, exactly, but I'm not afraid of a less than tight stomach (it's not like I'm rocking abs now).

Losing my breasts?

That's… I don't even know.

Sure, I can have the kind of double mastectomy where I keep my skin and nipples. I can trade my natural breasts for saline. Hell, I can trade up if I want.

But no matter how good they look, it's different. There are foreign parts in my body. Parts that aren't me.

Will I still feel like me? Will Chase still want me the same way? Will anyone want me the same way?

There's no shortage of fake boobs in Southern California. Certainly no shortage of guys who want to date women with fake boobs. But those women—

They're so different than me. They wear heels and short dresses and curl their hair in beach waves. They just scream sex appeal.

Maybe I'm stereotyping. There are plenty of girls who trade up in a less noticeable way.

But still…

I'm a fertile woman with breasts now.

In a year, I'm going to be a hormonal mess (a hysterectomy does that) with fake tits.

Footsteps move closer. A cup clinks on the dresser. Chase taps the wall like he's knocking. "What are you doing?"

"Thinking."

"About?"

I motion to my chest. "They'll be gone soon."

He nods. "How soon?"

Does it turn him off? Does he not want a woman who's all saline? Chase doesn't seem like that type. Fuck him if he's that type. But… "I still have to talk to my oncologist. To work out the timeline. But… I can't imagine they'll still be here next year."

He nods with understanding.

"Do you think…" My gaze shifts to my reflection. I pull the robe tighter, so I can see the reflection of my figure. "They're bigger now."

His eyes go to the mirror. "Yeah."

"They'll get bigger as I get further along."

"They always do."

"I might be able to nurse for a few months. I… I don't know."

"Plenty of kids do fine on formula."

That's true. There's all this pressure to breastfeed now. Breast is best and all that bullshit.

"I know it's a loss. Fuck, Ariel, I can't imagine." He moves closer. "But it's not gonna hurt Charlotte."

My lips press together. "Maybe."

He wraps his arms around me. Holds my body against his.

For a moment, comfort overwhelms me. This is right. This is where I belong. This is everything.

"I just…" My eyes go to the mirror. We look good locked together. He's so tall and broad. I'm more… I guess I'm tall for a girl, but I'm more than half a foot shorter. Next to Chase, I look small. Dainty even.

His skin is darker. His eyes are lighter. His sandy hair makes my dark locks look black.

"I'm not going to have boobs," I say.

"You're not doing reconstruction?"

"Would it bother you?"

"Not my body."

"But would it?" I turn around so I can look into his eyes. "Would you want me less?"

"Princess…"

"Would you?"

He cups my neck with his palm. "I love your tits, Ariel. They're fucking gorgeous."

My stomach twists. He's a boob guy. All guys are boob guys. I'm not going to have them anymore. I'm going to be marked. Different.

"But you know what I love more than that?"

"No." I swallow hard.

"The sound you make when I do this." He pushes my robe aside. Brushes my nipple with his thumb.

Fuck, that's intense. My eyes close. My heart races. My fingers dig into the cotton. "Chase…"

"Yeah, I'm gonna hate that I can't make you groan like this. But I'll find another way."

"You don't… You'll still want me?"

"You think I want you because of your tits?"

I force myself to look into his eyes. "Don't you?"

His brow knits with concentration. "I love your body exactly as it is now. I love your soft hips and your curvy waist, and, yeah, I love your lush tits. But that isn't why I want you."

"It's not?" That doesn't make any sense.

"It's your smile. The way your dark eyes get big. The way they fill with need. The way you touch me like you adore every inch of my skin."

"I do."

"I do too, princess. I love your body. It's beautiful, yeah. But I don't love it because it's beautiful. I love it because it's yours."

He loves my body. Because it's mine.

Does he love me?

God, I want him to love me so badly.

I want him to want me so badly. I'm used to his lust. I crave it. I run on it.

"So you don't…" My brow furrows. "They'll be all hard and weird."

"So?"

"So…"

"So what?" He brings his hand to my chin. Tilts me so we're face-to-face. "You're gonna look beautiful no matter what."

"Even if I stay flat as a board?"

"Even then."

"What if I go huge? Porn star huge?"

He chuckles. "It doesn't sound like you."

"Maybe it's the new me."

"Then it's the new you." He leans down to press his lips to mine. "I get why you're scared. It's fucking terrifying. But you don't have to worry about whether or not I'll want you. I'm always going to want you."

"Always?"

He nods. "Always."

Always as in forever? As in he wants this relationship forever? As in I really can have the dream of the nuclear family and the white picket fence?

I should ask.

But I'm not ready for the answer.

Chapter Forty-Six

ARIEL

A blood test confirms it.

Everything else fades away.

The world is a beautiful, bright place full of love and happiness and bliss.

Students, coworkers, actual tenured professors ask questions. I answer with a shrug and a smile *it's just a beautiful day*.

Thanksgiving morning, we go for our usual family walk. Dad, Holden, and Forest spend the entire trek debating my good mood.

When Dad heads to the store to pick up forgotten green beans, my brothers launch into questions. *What's up? You look different? Are you getting laid? No way that's it. No one's that good.*

Maybe Phillip was that bad.

Wait? Are you and Phillip back together?

Are you fucking his best friend, getting the best kind of revenge?

That's stupid. The best revenge is living well.

How is that revenge? It doesn't hurt the other person.

That's not the point.

Uh, yeah it is.

How does hurting your ex make you feel better?

How are you asking that question?

The shrug and smile does nothing to convince them. "None of your business" only encourages questions. "It's just a new vibrator" buys me a moment of *ew, my sister has a vibrator*, but it rebounds into a billion inquiries about my sex life.

I want to tell them.

It's bursting out of me. The words climb up my throat, claw at my lips, beg me to spill.

I'm pregnant. That's why I'm so happy. Because I'm having a baby.

But I keep my mouth shut. Not until the second trimester. Not until I'm sure it's happening.

At the very least, I need to figure out what to say about me and Chase.

He's still just Uncle Chase.

Usually, that would weigh on me. Usually, I'd spin in circles asking myself if he'll ever love me, if he'll ever be mine, if I'll be able to offer Charlotte a real family.

But I'm too fucking happy for that.

I beam as I help with dinner, as I shrug off wine (more questions), as I dine on marshmallow covered sweet potatoes.

On the drive to Chase's and the walk to his door and the knock—

I beam.

Then his Mom answers the door and all that confusion crawls back into my throat.

"ARIEL, RIGHT." HER SMILE IS SOFT. WEAK. "IT'S NICE to meet you." She extends her hand.

I shake. Mrs. Keating is exactly as Chase described her. A thin woman with subtle makeup, designer garments, and very expensive highlights.

She's wearing those shoes, the expensive ones with the red soles. They're fancy. One of my professors gushes over them.

I don't get it. The red soles look ridiculous. Why would anyone want to walk around with fire-engine red on their shoes?

Maybe it's my distaste for the color red and all the stupid questions about my hair.

I mean, red isn't so bad when it's a dress Chase is stripping off my shoulders.

Ahem. I'm meeting my baby's grandma. I mean… if he's just Uncle Chase, I guess she's just great aunt… whatever her first name is.

"You too, Mrs. Keating." I release her hand.

She smiles and motions *come in*. "Please, it's Melody."

"Right. Melody." That's a nice name. So sweet and innocent and not at all what I see in my head—a witch holding Chase's heart. She's the first person who broke him.

My anger usually fixes on Grace. But Melody—

How can someone who hurt him so badly smile so kindly?

I follow her through the huge, clean foyer, into the equally pristine dining room.

Chase is sitting at the sleek wood table, one leg folded over the other, his hands wrapped around a mug of coffee. A mug on a coaster. An actual coaster.

His gaze flits from his brothers—he's actually talking to Hunter—to me. "Hey, princess."

My cheeks flush. I love that nickname. But there are too many dirty associations. It sends me straight back to his low growl *come for me, princess*.

Mrs. Keating smiles. "Princess? That's a new one."

Chase's smile fades. "Her name is Ariel."

Mrs. Keating nods *of course*. "If you'll excuse me. I've got to check on the pie." She motions to the kitchen.

"Oh, Chase told me you ordered in." I bite my lip. That was the wrong thing to say.

She nods. "Yes, Mr. Keating is grabbing dinner. But I wanted to try my hand at dessert." She smiles at the table. "Westley helped."

"Westley." I laugh. "No one ever calls you that."

Wes shrugs, not at all moved. "You look nice, Ariel."

"Thank you." I smooth my black dress. It's a simple fit and flare style. Fashionable and parent pleasing (at least, according to Skye). My fingers go to the pearls around my neck reflexively (also Skye's suggestion).

"Nice?" Hunter chuckles. He waits until his mom moves into the kitchen, then he shifts into a teasing tone. "That's the first time you've ever paid a woman a compliment that tame."

Chase laughs at his brother's joke.

He's actually laughing at Hunter's joke? Maybe they've made up. Maybe they're best friends. Maybe Chase is finally learning how to forgive people. And himself. And the world.

Maybe he finally realizes he's amazing and worthy of love and—

Uh…

Wow, can I blame my recent news on my brain's zero to sixty?

I want him to be mine, yes. But I want him to be Charlotte's so much more. After Phillip dumped me, I thought I wanted to do this alone.

No, I did want to do this alone.

But it's different now that I've tasted a supportive partner. A possible co-parent. Someone who wants a family as badly as I do.

Fuck, that might not be zero to sixty but it's fast.

I'm here, meeting his parents.

That's a step.

It doesn't mean he's prepping for a Christmas proposal, but it's something.

It might be for Charlotte, not me. But that's okay. Yeah, it will break my heart if he says *I want to be this kid's dad, but that's it. We're co-parents. Period.*

I'll push through it. For her.

I guess I shouldn't assume she's a girl. I hope she is, but I'll love a little boy just as much. I'll love her no matter what.

"Would you prefer, *damn, Ariel, you look good enough to eat?*" Wes offers.

Hunter chuckles. "Sounds more like you."

"Not gonna say that shit in front of my girl," Wes says.

"So you'll say it behind her back?" Hunter asks.

Chase nods *he's got you there.*

"Where is Quinn?" I ask.

He motions to the backyard. "On the phone with her brother."

"Asking for pictures of the baby," Hunter says.

"Oh." My stomach flutters. That's all it takes. The word baby. God, I want to tell them. I want to tell everyone.

Wes nods. "Her brother and his husband are adopting a little girl."

"A little girl." My heart sings. My eyes go to Chase.

He smiles. "Her name is Ilsa."

"Like the Disney princess?" My nose scrunches. "That's cruel. Don't do that."

"Oh yeah? You looked like you were gonna cream your panties when Chase called you princess." Wes raises a brow *get real*.

Hunter laughs. "You never change." He reaches out to muss Wes's hair.

Wes slaps his hand away. "Who the fuck started that?"

"It suits you." Chase takes his turn messing with Wes's hair.

Wes slaps Chase's hand, then combs his hair with his fingers. Not that it does much. He has these messy California boy waves. Like Chase's, but longer and lighter.

Maybe Charlotte will have those too. Maybe she'll have golden hair and blue eyes and look just like her daddy.

Ahem.

What is happening to me? I'm not myself when it comes to Chase, but I'm not all fluttery and lovesick either.

It's not just the life growing inside me.

It's being here. There are photos on the walls. I need a tour of those photos. I need to see a tiny Chase.

Maybe Charlotte will look exactly like him.

Oh God…

Must. Stop. Daydreaming.

"You all right, Ariel?" Wes asks. "You look like you're thinking about Chase naked."

"You flirt with every woman you meet?" Hunter asks. "Or just the cute ones?"

"And you don't?" he asks.

Hunter shakes his head *hell no*.

"Yeah, I guess you don't have any game." Wes laughs. "What do you think, Ariel? If you were gonna date one of us—me or Hunter?"

"Hunter," I say.

Hunter laughs.

Wes jumps to his feet. Mimes pulling a knife out of his back. "That's cold, Ariel. Cold as ice."

The sliding door opens. Quinn steps inside. "Hey, Ariel." She looks at her boyfriend and laughs. "Who betrayed him now?"

"Ariel would rather date me than Wes," Hunter says. "Not sure why he cares. What with you being the light of his life."

Wes mimes tossing the knife aside then he turns to his girlfriend. "Everything good, angel?"

She nods *yeah*. "You flirting with poor Ariel?"

"No…" He motions *a little*. "Can't help myself when I see glasses."

"That's our entire relationship? Your lust for librarians." She pushes her glasses up her nose.

"Pretty much." He wraps his arms around her. "Is that okay?"

"Well…"

He kisses her neck. "Because I have this idea about sneaking back to one of the stacks."

Chase clears his throat. "You realize Mom is in the kitchen?"

"Oh, yeah, I forgot, you never hooked up with a girl in this house." Wes rolls his eyes. He slips right back into his seductive tone. "I think I learned something new in the last book I read. I want to show you."

Quinn stifles a groan.

"Take it upstairs." Hunter rolls his eyes. "Nobody wants to watch."

"Griffin would," Wes says.

"Then go to his place." Hunter shakes his head. "Is he always this annoying?"

"I'd know?" I ask.

"He is." Chase's voice is different. Harder. "He's worse at the shop."

"Always flirting with Em." Hunter nods.

Quinn just laughs. "Down boy." She takes a step backward. Smooths her fifties style dress. A velvet shift dress in a deep shade of plum.

God, she looks like she walked off a magazine cover. How does anyone get their hair and makeup that right?

How am I going to teach Charlotte about these fashion rules?

Maybe Quinn can help. Or Skye. If she and Forest are set on staying friends forever…

God, my head is spinning.

"You need a drink, princess?" Chase stands. He cuts between Quinn and Wes. Moves around the table to me.

I hug him hello.

He pulls me closer. "You're glowing."

"Thank you."

"Fuck, I want to take you upstairs." He pulls back enough to kiss me. It's hard, hungry, aggressive.

It's about more than how much he wants me.

It's about something going on behind those impenetrable blue eyes.

But I don't ask what it is.

It feels too good being the center of his attention. It feels too good believing his love is for me.

Chapter Forty-Seven

ARIEL

Dinner is surprisingly easy. Sure, Chase eyes his mom carefully. And his laugh gets stilted when his brother makes jokes. But it's easy for everyone to focus on Quinn and Wes.

They're happy and in love and adorable. She and Mr. Keating gush over classic movies. *Casablanca* is just so romantic. But what about *Roman Holiday*? Or *His Girl Friday*? Or *The Philadelphia Story*?

Mr. Keating can't pick a favorite.

She's adamant about *Casablanca* being the greatest film ever made. An unsurpassed and unsurpassable work of cinema. Not just the greatest movie, but the greatest story of all time.

I don't have it in me to tell her I don't like it.

Yes, it's beautifully shot and well-acted and the music is fantastic.

But Ilsa leaving with Victor? Because duty is more important than love? Because Rick knows what she wants more than she does?

I guess it makes sense, what with them fighting Nazis, but it's not romantic.

It's just sad.

———

HUNTER SETS A MUG OF MILKY COFFEE ON THE TABLE. Then a black one. "Decaf."

I hug Chase's blanket around my shoulders. The one from his old room. (All black, of course).

Mmm. It still smells like him.

Hunter sits across from me. Takes a long sip of his black coffee. "From Chase."

"Oh." The mug is warm against my skin. It feels like love. It's just a cup of coffee, but it still feels like love. "Thank you."

"Thank him. He insisted," he says.

"But you made it?"

Hunter's laugh is easy. Like there's no frost between him and his brother. "Chase can't make coffee for shit."

"He drinks it every morning."

"Drip." Hunter's nose scrunches in distaste. "That isn't coffee."

"Oh?" I take a sip. It's rich, warm, creamy, sweet. But it's still coffee. It tastes like any other cup of coffee.

Hunter nods *yeah*. "Drip is basically swill."

"I didn't realize." The warmth is exactly what I need, but it's just… so much less good than tea. "I'm more of a chai girl."

"You have a favorite?"

"I make my own."

"Impressive." His gaze shifts to the dining room.

The warm, yellow light surrounds Quinn and Wes in

an angelic glow. They're sharing a piece of pie. Feeding each other.

It's sickeningly sweet.

Or it would be. If I didn't want that so badly.

"Where's Chase?" I hug my blanket tighter. It's a cold night, but I need the fresh air. My stomach is… ugh. I'm not sure if it's the hormones or the marshmallows.

"With Mom," he says. "She snuck out for a cigarette."

"She smokes?"

He nods *yeah*. "Since rehab. You know the cliché? You trade one addiction for another."

"But you don't smoke."

His lips curl into a half-smile. "I used to smoke when I drank. They were too mixed up."

"So now…" When he doesn't respond, I clear my throat. "Sorry, I'm overstepping."

"It's fine."

"I do that sometimes. I, um… do you have a new coping mechanism?"

He laughs.

"That was also out of line." Ahem. "I…"

He laugh gets louder. "Fuck. I can see why Chase likes you. You're the opposite of Grace."

My lips curl into a frown. That name again. Even his brothers think about her. Why does everyone still think about her?

"Not that he—" his voice softens. "He's not still into her."

"Would you know if he was?"

"Probably not."

Damn, that was another overstep. But he doesn't seem to mind. "Where, um, where's your girlfriend?"

"In New Jersey with Kaylee and Brendon."

Right. Emma and Kaylee are best friends. God, that

must be weird, what with Kaylee dating Emma's brother Brendon.

But I guess Emma is dating Hunter. Who's Brendon's friend.

And, uh...

Shit, I need a diagram for all these Inked Hearts couples.

"You share her with her best friend?" I ask.

He nods.

"Is that weird?"

"I'm glad she has someone else she can count on."

"And her brother."

"Yeah." He takes a sip. "Brendon would do anything for her."

"Would you?"

"Of course." His eyes meet mine. They're just as blue as Chase's, but they're a little lighter. A little easier to read. "You and Chase?"

"I don't know yet." Under the blanket, I cross my legs. "What was that like? Falling for Emma when you were friends with her brother?"

His laugh is knowing. "Harder than it needed to be."

"I, uh..."

"Forest and Chase are good friends."

"You should tell him."

"It's none of your business."

"You should still tell him," Hunter says.

It's true. It's none of his business, but it is true. I clear my throat. As much as I appreciate Hunter's personal experience in this topic, I need his personal experience in another topic more. "Were you invited to New Jersey?"

"Yeah. But I wanted to be here."

"For your mom?"

His eyes meet mine. He doesn't clarify *and for Chase*. He just nods *of course*.

I guess it's obvious.

"Chase told you everything?"

"Most things. Chase is—"

"Yeah." He chuckles. "He is." He crosses one leg over the other. "You two are serious."

It's not really a question. I nod anyway.

"Good."

"Why?" I don't doubt him. But I need his insight. Why does he think Chase needs me? Why is he here, when Chase is so completely unable to make up?

"He needs someone who doesn't sugarcoat things."

"Chase doesn't sugarcoat things."

"He wants people to believe he doesn't." Hunter's gaze shifts to the living room. It's still just Wes and Quinn. Chase and Mr. and Mrs. Keating are off… somewhere. "Part of me is here for Mom."

"It's her first Thanksgiving sober."

"Yeah." His smile is sad. "And Chase… Fuck, Em is right." He lets out a heavy sigh.

"Right how?"

"She thinks I have a martyr complex."

"No."

"Yeah."

"I say the same thing to Chase." Is it genetic or how they grew up? "He's like Daredevil."

His laugh is loud. Hearty.

"Is um… Chase said Daredevil is your favorite. That you used to read it together?"

"I don't know about favorite, but—"

"You really identify with his need to protect everyone with violence?"

"Hey, I'm not the one listening to music about how my ex should die in a fire."

"Do you have an ex?" I ask.

"I have a brother who won't forgive me." His smile is bittersweet. "Sorry, it's not your problem."

I bite my lip. "He forgives you."

Hunter looks at me like I'm crazy.

"He wants things to be easier. He wants to make up."

"Maybe."

"You could push him."

Hunter shakes his head. "He asked for space. I gave it to him."

"Offered to disappear from his life?"

His laugh is sad. "Am I really that obvious?"

Yeah, he is. But only because I know his brother so well. "You're like Chase."

"Really?"

So much. I can tell already.

"It's got to be hard, loving someone who can't move on." He takes a long sip. "I guess neither one of us is great with comfort."

"You've known your brother for longer."

"You know him better."

Do I really?

"You probably know him better than anyone," Hunter says.

I guess I do. I'm Chase's only confidant. His closest friend.

He's mine.

Doing this together—

It changes things.

"Can I offer you more advice you don't want?" Hunter asks.

"Can I stop you?"

"Yeah. I'm big on boundaries."

"You sound like a shrink."

He chuckles. "I've been to enough."

"Oh, you're—"

He leans back in his seat. "Since rehab, yeah. And I go to meetings every week."

"Do you worry about relapsing?"

He just laughs.

"Am I not supposed to ask that?"

"I don't know. More people should." His expression gets serious. "It terrifies me."

"But you…"

"I try to make something of the fear. But—" His gaze shifts to the black sky. The stars are dull and small. There's too much light here. "I get why Chase has all these walls up. It's hard for me, loving someone, when there's a big part of me that believes I'm going to let them down."

"But you're trying."

"Trying isn't always good enough."

I bite my lip. He's so aware of his flaws and limitations. But that's only done so much to help him piece his life back together.

Hunter is happy. He has friends and family that love him. A girlfriend who adores (and torments) him. A great job.

But all the sobriety and therapy and love can't do anything to change how Chase feels.

Nothing can change how Chase feels.

"Do you think you'll make up?" I ask.

"I don't know." His gaze shifts to the moon. "The sale went through. After the remodel, Inked Love is opening."

"Inked Love?" I ask.

"The new shop." His eyes meet mine. "A little obvious."

"But cute."

He nods *true*. "Brendon offered Chase a gig managing it."

"He'd change shops?"

"Yeah."

"Leave Inked Hearts?"

Hunter's voice softens. "He specifically requests shifts where I'm not working."

"Oh."

"I quit. For him, Wes, and Griffin. I didn't want to be the reason why they couldn't find work."

"You blamed yourself?" I ask.

"It was my fault. I'm the one who lied to Chase. Who picked up a bottle and refused to put it down. I'm—"

"Still plagued with self-loathing." Like Chase, but so different.

"It's a process."

"Does it help?"

"My brother staring at me like I punched him in the stomach? No." He takes another sip. "We used to be best friends. I want that. But if he doesn't… Maybe it's better for him to take the gig."

Maybe it's a way for Chase to move on. But it feels like a step backward. "Does that make it harder? To stay sober?"

"It's hard no matter what."

Under the blanket, I bring my hand to my stomach. Chase was upfront about his family history of addiction. And I knew… everyone knows about Hunter's struggles.

Chase doesn't have that problem.

But Charlotte still could. The fear in Hunter's eyes—

It's terrifying.

And it's just one of a million things that could go wrong for her.

There's so much I can't do for her.

"Isn't that giving up?" I ask.

"There are battles you can't win." His gaze shifts to the sky. "I can't erase the past. He can't control how he feels. I don't blame him." His voice gets soft. Contemplative. "The heart wants what it wants. Nobody can change that."

.

Chapter Forty-Eight

ARIEL

Skye drags me into her Black Friday shopping. My gaze is magnetically drawn to the maternity store. Its windows are adorned with images of smiling women with round bellies and small children by their sides.

A sunny day at the park.

A picnic under the blue sky.

A doting husband off in the distance.

The total package.

I don't need that.

I don't even want it. Not with anyone else. Only with Chase.

His brother is right. The heart wants what it wants. I can't talk myself out of my feelings for him.

Or talk him into loving me.

Not that I love him. I mean, I might, but, uh, there are more pressing concerns at the moment.

———

Week five is easy. Nausea nips at my throat. Ginger

tea chases it down.

Week six, my body screams for mint and lime. I appease it by cooking Phillip's favorites.

The details escape me. None of the online recipes are right. I need the secret.

I call Phillip.

He answers on the second ring. "Ariel?" His voice drips with concern. "Are you okay?"

Oh. People don't call their exes for recipe tips. Maybe I should ask to talk to his sister. No, that would be worse. I think. "It's not that kind of call."

"Oh." His exhale is heavy.

"I was wondering…" Actually, it is that kind of call. "Well, um, I was wondering how much mint you put in your spring rolls."

His voice is incredulous. "Mom or Becks would know better."

"I couldn't call."

"Becks asks about you all the time." He calls his sister by her English name. She stopped going by her Vietnamese name last year. It took forever to get used to calling Van Rebecca, but I have the hang of it. "She'd love to hear from you."

"Yeah?" Rebecca is a sweet kid. And the opposite of Phillip. Loud, bubbly, excited. "I thought she—"

"Calls me an idiot every day for ending things."

"Oh." My heart warms. I miss her too. "That sounds exactly like her."

His laugh is easy. The way it was when we were together.

I miss that. The easiness. The familiarity. That feeling of his family being mine and mine being his (even if Forest and Holden never really believed he was good enough for me).

The line goes quiet for a moment. Finally, he asks, "Is that it?"

"Well…" Yes. No. Maybe. I want to talk to him. More than I should. But then he was the most important person in my life for a long time. "How are you?"

"Honestly, Ariel, I miss you. It's hard. But I know—are you still pursuing that?"

"Yeah."

"Is it… happening?"

My teeth sink into my lip. I want to tell him. I want to tell someone. And I want to tell Phillip. It might upset him, but it's worse if he hears it from someone else. "You sure you want to hear—"

"Yeah."

"And you can keep a secret?"

"Who am I going to tell?"

My laugh is soft. I miss him. I miss knowing he loved me. I miss having a best friend. "I'm pregnant."

"Fuck."

"Only five weeks. So it's still… but I… It's good. I… uh, are you sure you want to hear this?"

He's quiet for a minute. "I wish things had been different. But… I'm happy for you, Ariel. You're gonna be a great mom."

"Thank you." A tear wells in my eyes. Stupid hormones. My emotions are in overdrive. "I…" I can't say he'd be a great dad. He would. But that's a different life. One that isn't mine.

"A white guy?" he asks.

"Oh my God, Phil."

"Everyone knows mixed kids are cuter."

My laugh is big. Hearty. "You're not supposed to say that."

"Why? It's true."

I laugh a little louder. "Yeah, he's Caucasian."

"Anyone I know?"

"We're um…" God, how do I explain our arrangement? What we said? Or what I want it to be?

"Whoever he is, if he doesn't treat you right, send him to me."

"And you'll what, punch his lights out?"

"Please. I'm a doctor. I'm going to use a scalpel to inflict as much pain as possible."

"I'll consider that." It's a sweet offer. "I… um… I should go. I'm glad you're okay."

"Congratulations."

"Thanks."

"I love—fuck, it's hard not saying that." His exhale flows through the speaker. "Take care."

"You too." I hang up. Drop my cell in my lap.

A million things flit through my head. All these visions of the life I was supposed to have.

Of the life I could have.

I hover over Chase's contact. Try to think of exactly what I'll say.

My stomach flutters.

Then it twists.

Then—

Oh God.

———

WHY DO THEY CALL IT MORNING SICKNESS?

It's dinnertime.

Only dinner no longer holds any appeal. The thought of fish sauce makes me cringe. And not in the usual *that feels too much like a home I don't have anymore* kind of way.

Not even in a *oh my God, that smell is strong, did I just gut eight thousand fish* kind of way.

In a whole—

Ugh…

A wave of nausea hits me. Is that seven or eight? Am I ever getting out of here?

I press my palm into the white wall. Suck a breath through my nose. Sitting next to the toilet isn't helping. It's too close to everything.

I try to stand, but another wave hits me.

Shit, Dad is out of town until Sunday. No, that's a good thing.

I'm not telling them until the second trimester. But I have to say something.

Maybe I can pass this off as the flu.

Or mono.

A food sensitivity?

There must be something.

It's just morning sickness. (Sure, I know, from the books that it isn't always morning, but can't someone come up with a different name? It's just inaccurate).

I can excuse it.

I can handle it. The ginger tea is downstairs. I just need to stand.

I press my hands to the toilet lid. Push myself up.

My head spins. My knees knock.

Nope.

Back to the ground.

I reach for my cell. Call Chase.

"Ariel." His voice is the picture of concern. "What's wrong?"

"I'm just a little—" Ugh. I swallow another wave. "I'll be okay."

"I'll be there in ten." He hangs up before I can object.

Chapter Forty-Nine

CHASE

Ariel answers the door with a giant white bowl pressed to her chest. Her eyes narrow. "How could you do this to me?"

I arch a brow.

She presses the bowl to her chest. "You've put me in this condition."

"I'm responsible?"

"Yeah, you shouldn't have listened to me. Pregnancy isn't beautiful. It's horrible, hideous torture."

"I brought club soda."

Her gaze softens. "You're still evil."

"I know." I wrap my arm around her waist. "Come on, princess."

"I'm trying to hate you."

"I know."

"If you're sweet, it's harder to hate you."

"Should I be cruel?"

She nods. Stops. Squints like she's about to throw up. "At least—" She coughs. "Be stupid or something."

"Something about how statistics are lies."

"Well, yeah, but it's really more complicated than that. They're objectively true, but the way you look at and present data is subjective."

"Not stupid enough?"

She shakes her head. "That was practically perceptive."

"Damn. I didn't realize."

That earns a glare. "Of course, you realized."

"Come on." I help her onto the couch.

She looks up at me with a tiny smile. When I smile back, she turns her lip corners down. "You're being too cute."

"Too cute?"

"Yeah, just look at you." She draws a circle around me with her finger. "All tall and smiley and happy."

"You're letting me take care of you."

"Oh."

"You needed help, so you called."

"It's not too much?"

"For the mother of my child?"

Her frown disappears instantly. She beams. Catches herself. "No, I'm… this is a terrible condition."

"The first trimester is supposed to be rough."

She bites her lip. "You're still being understanding."

"How about this? *Daredevil* is an amazing show except for the fight scenes. They're trying too hard."

She stares back at me. "That's the best you can do?"

"I can't lie to you."

"You don't think that." She sets her bowl to the side. Pulls her legs into my lap. "Did you see that hallway sequence? That was amazing."

"Amazingly showy."

Her eyes fill with disbelief. "And I suppose your tattooed arms are incredibly subtle?"

"You tell me."

"Ugh." Her gaze shifts to my arms. "I want to say something bad about them."

"Do your worst."

"They're just so—"

"Say anything. About my arms, my hair, my eyes, my personality."

"They're so strong and safe and beautiful."

"My personality?" I ask.

She shakes her head. "Your arms. And your hair... it's this perfect shade of brown. Halfway between the inside of a chestnut and a mushroom." Her nose scrunches. "Ugh, mushrooms."

"You eat dinner?"

She groans in agony. "No. No food."

"Charlotte needs nutrition."

"That's so manipulative."

I can't help but laugh. "You're supposed to be worried about her."

She sets both hands on her lower stomach. "Are you kidding? All I do is worry about her. But she only needs an extra few hundred calories a day."

"How about plain pasta with butter?"

"Plain pasta?"

"Tell me what you want on it and I'll make it happen."

"No... plain sounds perfect. But I... I hate plain pasta."

"Don't over think it, princess," I say.

"It's just—"

"Plain stuff always sounds good when you're sick."

She tries to stand. Falters.

I move to the couch. Hold her down as gently I can.

Ariel looks up at me with that same *I'm totally going to hate you* stare. "Okay. But add something. As long as it's not spicy or chewy or rich or—"

397

"I'll make it work."

"You're supposed to complain that I'm difficult."

"Aren't you always?"

"Hey!" She folds her arms over her chest. "Oh. You're teasing."

"Am I?" I move to the kitchen. Fill a pot with water. Set the stove top to boil. Honestly, Ariel is easy. She's a little stubborn, sure, but she tells me what she wants. She asks for help when she needs it. She shares her feelings.

She laughs at my bad jokes.

She melts into my embraces.

She beams like the fucking sun.

I'd watch any shitty superhero show on the couch if it meant I got to sit with her.

She watches as I scan the fridge. It's packed with fresh food.

It must all be hers. "How often is your dad here?"

"About half the time." She pushes through a wave of nausea. "He's a great cook. He took over after Mom died. Mostly… well, I guess he mostly makes pasta. The same three dishes too."

"You never noticed because you love pasta?"

"No, it's more… I could feel the love he put into it, you know?"

I nod. I do.

"I hope I can do that."

"You will."

"But what if she doesn't feel it?"

"She will. Trust me. You're brimming with love, Ariel."

"What if… I've been thinking, um, well… I just worry. What if it's not enough, having a mom and her uncles? What if she needs a dad?"

My chest gets light. I want that. But I can't push her. Not now.

"I guess... uh..." Her eyes go wide. "That's not it. I just... uh, can you give me a minute?"

"Sure." I turn my back to her. Focus on dicing chicken, warming butter in a pan, starting a sauté.

The water boils.

I crack pasta. Set the timer. Add spinach to the sauté.

Ariel sits on the couch, fingers wrapped around the bowl, eyes on the floor.

She stays like that as I finish dinner and bring it to the kitchen table.

I pour her club soda and water then I help her to the table.

She looks up at me like I'm her savior.

I love that feeling.

I love the way she looks at me.

I love all of this.

"You're still glowing." I place her silverware next to her plate.

"Is it the nausea face that's doing it?"

"No, it's you."

"I still can't... ugh." She turns to the bowl. Hugs it to her chest. "Sorry, you don't have to stay."

"I'm staying."

"But you don't have to—"

"I know."

"Okay, I just... you didn't agree to take care of a needy pregnant woman."

"Try and stop me."

———

ARIEL STRUGGLES THROUGH DINNER. SHE HEADS TO the couch, munches on saltines as she starts a new series.

I hang out next to her until she falls asleep, then I carry her to her room, lay her down, help her into her pajamas.

She pats the spot next to her. Mumbles, "Come to bed, Chase." Rolls onto her side.

Her bed is small, a full, but I still slide under the purple covers.

I still fall asleep next to her.

It's the best sleep I've ever had.

———

THE NEXT DAY IS THE SAME.

Ariel texts curses, against me or the demon leeching her life force *how could I call her Charlotte? She's clearly something pure evil. Rosemary's baby. Or Lilith. Or some other being from another plane of existence.*

I text back, teasing and comforting in equal measure.

I go to her place, cook her dinner, walk along the moonlit beach, watch bad TV.

Even after her dad gets home, I stay with her.

Even after her brothers notice I'm hanging out way too often.

I want to tell them. But I let her lead. I keep my lips zipped.

Even though I'm desperate to spend Christmas with her, watching her family open a tiny box with a little onesie.

I spend Christmas with my family.

Sure, she comes over for hot chocolate and marshmallows (she can't get enough of marshmallows), and we talk about when she's going to tell the rest of the world (twelve weeks, and that's not up for negotiation).

And, yeah, I take her back to my apartment and spend the night with her.

But it's not enough.

I want more of her.

I want the world to know.

Well, most of me does.

There's that other part, the one that still believes I'm an anchor around her neck.

I try to stop that voice. I pour myself into work. I focus on the Inked Love remodel. I'm in charge and it's taking forever.

It's fucking amazing, being in charge, making it happen, watching the place go from a shack to a palace.

But it only underlines the question.

Can I forgive my brother? Can I help my family heal? Can I be the person Ariel needs?

But with every passing week, the voice gets louder.

This isn't a relationship that might go wrong.

It's her entire life.

It's Charlotte's life.

I have to be sure.

Chapter Fifty

CHASE

For the first time, Inked Love is booming. The remodeled shop is exactly as I pictured it.

Big open lobby. Bright pink desk. Flash art in fuchsia frames.

A softer, bigger, even more feminine version of Inked Hearts.

It shouldn't work, but it does. It's perfect. None of that typical shop snobbery. This space invites everyone.

And it's mine.

Until the end of the month, it's mine.

I'm handling the transition. Making sure Inked Love offers customers the full Inked Hearts experience.

But this task only has a few weeks left.

After that—

Fuck, I don't know.

Brendon pats me on the shoulder. He hands me a champagne flute. Holds his to toast. "You did it."

"We did it." I fight a blush. Clink my glass with his. This place is amazing. Perfect. New.

There's no baggage.

No memories of my brother's hurt stare.

Or my other brother's *get over yourself* eye rolls.

Or that ache in my gut when everyone slips into easy conversation.

Not that it's going to last.

Sure, this is a chance at a fresh start. At drawing that line between me and Hunter. Accepting my inability to forgive my family.

But—

Can I do that?

I want to look at this as a business move. A promotion. A chance for more responsibility.

But there's no denying it: I'm running away. Giving up. Throwing in the white towel.

I can't exist in limbo forever. I need to make up with Hunter or move on.

This is a good thing. A step forward.

So why does it feel like I'm about to step off a cliff?

I down a sip of champagne. Fruity bubbles burst on my tongue. Warm my throat. Take my head to other celebrations. All those times I didn't see the truth even though it was right in front of my face.

"You ready for the opening?" Brendon takes a sip of champagne. He looks around the empty room. Watches as Wes and Forest enter through the front door.

Wes holds up a bottle of wine.

Forest laughs. "You've been bragging about that bottle all day."

"My girl picked it out," Wes says.

Forest rolls his eyes. "Really? I haven't heard that."

"I know you're jealous because no one wants you." Wes crosses to the counter. Sets his bottle down. Grabs a flute. "Damn, is this Trader Joe's champagne? That's some good shit." He winks at Brendon.

Brendon chuckles. "I go all out for my employees."

"You too, Chase?" Wes pours two glasses of champagne. Offers one to Forest. "You gonna treat Forest and Holden like kings?"

"Kings?" I ask.

Wes nods.

Forest chuckles as he takes his glass. "Won't Chase be the king?"

"Damn, a monarch. No democracy." Wes shakes his head. "Sounds like my entire life." He holds up his glass to toast. "Better you than me."

Forest clinks glasses. "Chase isn't a complete tyrant."

Wes nods *okay, sure*. "Glad you're happy."

"It's only three months," Forest says. "I can scare him off."

"Or you'll turn him on with that bratty shit." Wes downs his glass. "I've seen your search history."

"And?" I can't help but laugh. Wes is Wes. When he isn't giving me shit about Hunter and I'm not giving him shit about Mom—

This is easy. Why can't it always be this easy?

"And you like to order around chicks who disobey." Wes stares at me, waiting for a response.

I just shrug. "And?"

Forest chuckles.

Wes turns to Brendon *help me out*.

Brendon raises a brow. "Really?"

"Fuck, surrounded by pervs who love ropes." Wes shakes his head. "Nobody is gonna back me up." He nudges Brendon. "You into that too?"

"Didn't we just cover this?" Brendon's eyes fill with amusement.

"Yeah, but not in enough detail." Wes holds his hand

over his mouth. Stage whispers, "Tell me that cute blonde loves to disobey."

Brendon doesn't punch Wes. He doesn't even threaten Wes. He just shakes his head *you're ridiculous*. "You think you can ask me anything Dean hasn't?"

Wes pouts. "Fucking Dean. At least your brother is going to be here."

"You can stay the most annoying person at Inked Hearts," I say.

"With you gone, maybe." Wes laughs. "Dean is stiff competition."

Brendon cringes. "I don't need to hear about Dean being stiff."

"What's that?" The door swings open. Dean enters, with Chloe on his arm. He shoots us a shit-eating grin. "You were talking about me, weren't you?"

"How the fuck did you hear that?" Wes asks.

"Don't ask questions. It only encourages him." Chloe releases her boyfriend. She shakes her head *he's ridiculous*. Makes a beeline for the champagne. "More drinks, less discussion of—"

"You want to hear about the Prince Albert, don't you?" Dean asks the room.

Chloe rolls her eyes. "Every day."

"You don't like it, sunshine?" He looks her dead in the eyes. "'Cause if you don't like it, I can always see about getting it removed—"

Her cheeks flush, but she holds strong. "Would you really be capable? I mean, how would your dick know it's special without jewelry?"

"You'll make it feel plenty special." He crosses the room. Wraps his arms around her. "That look you get when you—"

She puts her hand over his mouth.

"You think that's going to stop me?" he mumbles.

She nods *right*, rises to her tiptoes, kisses him hard. She's a full foot shorter than him. He has to bend over.

At first.

Then he wraps his arms around her. Sets her on the counter.

She hooks her legs around his waist.

And they're off.

"You think they'll stop?" I ask.

Brendon shakes his head *no*.

"She will. She's shy." Wes laughs. "Chloe, baby, you know we're dying to see what you're packing under those tank tops."

Forest rolls his eyes. "How did you ever charm that sweet girlfriend of yours?"

"Same way Dean did." Wes motions to his crotch.

Forest's poker face breaks. He laughs so hard he doubles over.

"You don't believe I'm skilled?" Wes shakes his head. "That's cold."

Forest's laugh gets louder.

"The lady doth protest too much," I say.

"Oh, you want to see?" Wes reaches for his zipper.

Brendon shakes his head in horror.

I do the same.

Forest laughs harder.

Chloe and Dean continue making out.

"Well, that's too bad. You're gonna have to wait for my girl to get here." Wes shrugs *you wish you could see*.

"Yeah, Quinn is going to fuck you in front of us," I say. "That's plausible."

"You don't know." Wes's smile gets wicked. "And you don't get to know."

"So, why are you offering us a show?" Brendon asks.

"'Cause he's trying to win *most annoying person in the room*." Forest breathes through his laughter. Slowly, he straightens himself. He looks at Wes like he's ridiculous. "Competition is tight with Chase as a boss."

"I've been difficult so far?" I've been Forest's boss for the last month or so. But only technically. Inked Love is up and running starting tomorrow. Which means I'm stepping into an actual boss roll tomorrow.

Tonight…

I guess it's my last night as one of the guys. Shit changes when you're the boss. It has to.

"We'll see." Forest refills his empty glass. Holds it up.

I clink glasses.

The door swings open.

Hunter steps inside.

The whole room goes silent.

Everyone knows I'm a miserable fucker.

I'm the only one who can change it. I want to change it. I want to be a better guy.

A guy worthy of Ariel.

A guy worthy of a family.

But when I open my mouth, nothing comes out. I nod *hey*.

Hunter holds up a bottle of sparkling cider. Wes pulls him aside to gossip about something.

Slowly, the mood shifts back to teasing fun. But it never gets quite there.

———

BIT BY BIT, THE PARTY FILLS. RYAN AND LEIGHTON HANG out with Walker and Iris.

Holden brings a cute girl.

Emma and Kaylee come together. And stay together, away from their respective boyfriends.

Hunter stays away from me.

Skye and Ariel arrive last.

Ariel's in one of her tight black dresses and she's glowing.

Under the soft string lights, she looks like an angel.

Her red lips curl into a smile. She's wearing makeup today —all courtesy of Skye. But surprisingly restrained. Ariel has something highlighting her eyes, whereas Skye looks like—

Well, she looks like a Goth princess.

Forest's eyes go to her. They flit over her body quickly, like he can't help himself. He clears his throat. Nods *hello*.

Her eyes stay glued to him.

Fuck, it's so obvious they're into each other. How are they the only people who can't see it?

I wish I could get on my high horse, but I've missed so many things, so many times.

Those thoughts dissolve as Ariel moves closer. Her dark eyes light up as her fingers hit the counter. "Hey."

"You want a drink?" Forest asks.

She shakes her head *no thanks*.

"You've been skipping them lately." He looks her in the eyes.

They exchange something, some Ballard family thing I don't understand.

"I have a lot of work to do tomorrow." She shrugs off her brother's stare. "School. You remember that?"

He nods, accepting her answer. "You're working Sunday?"

Or maybe not.

She nods *of course*. "Yes, I work most weekends. Do you know how many hours it takes to finish a thesis?"

He studies her expression.

She folds her arms over her chest.

Skye breaks up the tension with a smile. "Who wants to pour my Moscow Mule?" She holds up a bottle of ginger liqueur. "Which Ballard makes it best?"

His attention turns to her.

Ariel mouths *thank you*.

Forest fixes her drink. Skye pulls him aside, to another conversation, but my shoulders stay at my ear.

"We need to tell him, princess." I press my palms into my thighs. It's the only way to keep them off her.

She glances at her brother—still deep in conversation with Skye—then Holden—practically making out with the cute blonde in his lap. "I'm officially in the second trimester tomorrow."

"Yeah?"

Her smile spreads over her face. "Only a few weeks until we'll know the sex." Her hand goes to her stomach. "I…"

Fuck, I want to touch her.

She looks up at me, her smile goofy. "We will. I promise."

"We should—"

"Can we… um, so I know you want to talk. And talking is really important. But here's the thing." She rises to her tiptoes. Brings her hips to mine. "I need to fuck you." Her fingers skim the waistband of my jeans. "Like right now."

My balls tighten.

"Are you gonna make me beg?" Her voice drops to something low and breathy.

I step backward. Hit the counter. "Princess—"

"I will." She presses her lips together. "If that's what you want."

I do. I really fucking do. Right now, I don't care that it's a bad idea. I don't care that the entire shop is here. Only that I need her body against mine. "Not here."

She nods *okay*. "How long do we have to stay?"

"I'm running the shop. I have to stay."

She pouts. "It's only five minutes to my place. Or—" She stares at my crotch. "I can be fast." Her teeth sink into her lip. "I want to suck you off."

Fuck. "Later."

She clears her throat. "If you change your mind..." She motions to the girls gathering in the corner. Iris and Leighton are hanging out, gossiping about something. "If I stay here, I'm going to rip your clothes off." She grabs a red cup. Fills it with club soda. "I don't have your self-control."

I nod *okay*, watch her walk away, watch her join the conversation.

I try to mingle. I talk technique with Brendon. Discuss music with Juliette. Listen to Quinn gush about classic movies.

The whole time, my attention stays on Ariel. On her red smile, her dark eyes, her lush curves.

She's only gained a few pounds, but there's something about the way she carries herself. Like she's screaming *I'm a woman*.

I need to tear that dress off.

I need to make her come.

I need to feel her skin against mine.

After an hour of chatting, I break away from the conversation.

I text Ariel.

Chase: Meet me in the office in five minutes.

Ariel: Are you sure?

Chase: Come before I change my mind.

Chapter Fifty-One

CHASE

I want to take my time, to savor every inch of her, but that's going to have to wait.

I push her dress to her waist, tug her panties to her knees, warm her up with my fingers.

Ariel melts into me. She groans into my hand as I fill her.

We're too loud, even with the music muffling us, but I can't bring myself to quiet.

When we're like this, connected, her body responding to mine, her voice all low and breathy—

I come too fast. Finish her with my fingers.

We rush into her clothes. Kiss as we dress.

I know I need to leave. I know we need to separate. I know I need to figure out my shit.

But it feels too fucking good holding her.

It's perfect.

And then it's not.

Voices flow into the room. Something about showing someone an office.

Then the door pulls open.

Ariel jumps backward.

I smooth my t-shirt.

Forest stares at me like I'm the scum of the Earth. "What the fuck?"

"Forest—" Ariel steps forward, protecting me.

I can't let her do that. I can't fuck up any more families.

I hold out my arm. Stand in front of her. "This was all—"

"You got my sister pregnant?" His eyes fill with pure hate. "What the fuck, Chase?"

Ariel's face flushes. With embarrassment. And anger. "What… But… How…"

"Maybe we should go." Skye tugs at Forest's shirt. "This isn't our—"

"What? You love her too much for a condom? What bullshit did you feed her?" Forest glares at me.

"No…" Ariel steps sideways. I try to reach for her, but she ignores me. Her gaze goes to her brother. "I don't have to justify anything to you. This is my life. And my business. And Chase didn't… I asked him to do this."

Forest's face streaks with disbelief. "What?"

Skye clears her throat.

Forest ignores her. "You—"

"No, I don't." Ariel steps forward. She stares daggers at your brother. "If you'll excuse me, I'm going home."

"No you're not." He holds his arms. Adopts a protective older brother stance.

This is their battle.

But I have to do my part to ease the tension. "This was my fault." My chest gets heavy. This is what I have to do. I hate it, but I don't have a choice. "I asked Ariel to keep it a secret. I asked her to lie."

"Chase—" Ariel squeaks. "That's not—"

"Of course, it's your fault, asshole. She's in love with

414

you. Everyone knows she's in love with you, and you're, what, using her to get over Grace?" Forest's eyes narrow. "Fuck you." He glares. "Leave before I do something I regret."

Skye pulls at his shirt. Pleads words that run together.

Everything runs together.

He's right.

I'm fucking this up.

I'm the problem again.

And the solution—

It's obvious, the same way it always is.

I nod in agreement. Then I leave.

Chapter Fifty-Two

ARIEL

I don't give Forest a chance to reply.

I go straight home. Lock myself in my room. Blast The Eurythmics.

Send Chase frantic texts.

Ariel: Where are you?

Ariel: Are you okay?

Ariel: Are you leaving? What did that mean? Can we talk about what Forest said? I don't know if it's true or not. But I should be the one to say it. He doesn't get to say it for me.

But that isn't true.

I do know.

It's there in my heart. I love him. I love him so fucking much. And I want this so fucking bad.

But I can't take another person abandoning me.

I can't open myself up to that heartbreak again.

If he wants to leave—

What good is it, stopping him? It will only delay the inevitable.

Ariel: Call me, please. We need to talk.

The albums repeats twice.

Finally, Chase texts back.

Chase: Give me a few days. Your brother needs to cool off.

Ariel: I need to see you.

Chase: You need to make things right with Forest.

Ariel: I can do both.

Chase: He's your family. You need him.

I need Chase.

But I can't say that. I can't even verbalize it.

It's one thing if he leaves.

If I beg him to stay and he still leaves—

I'm not sure I can take that.

I turn my phone off, bury myself under the covers, and cry until I fall asleep.

Chapter Fifty-Three

CHASE

I reschedule my appointments for next week. Manage Inked Love from afar. Stay busy at the gym.

Nothing clears my head.

My thoughts stay on Ariel and the hurt in her dark eyes.

I want to call her. To go to her house. To hold her and promise her it will be okay.

But I can't lie to her.

Wednesday, I head to Inked Hearts for an appointment I can't move.

Forest is at the other shop. He isn't here, staring at me like I'm the scum of the Earth, but I still feel his disdain.

The entire shop hums with tense air.

Everyone knows I fucked shit up. Again.

Everyone knows I'm an anchor around the neck of the people I love.

Everyone knows I'm miserable.

Maybe that's the case. Maybe it's my fate. But I have to know.

After I finish the back piece, check my client out, accept congratulations, I leave.

I go to the only person with insight.

Chapter Fifty-Four

CHASE

"I guess I should offer you something to drink." Grace motions to the tiny dining table. "You still drinking coffee as black as your soul?"

"I like a splash of milk now."

"Your soul is lighter?" Her voice is soft. Teasing. A tone I haven't heard in ages.

I try to find a laugh, but it's not there. This is a snapshot of the life I could have had. Of the life I wanted more than anything.

Grace's lips curl into a smile. She's wearing the same red lipstick as always. Brighter than Ariel's shade. As bright as the sun.

It suits her.

"John's into coffee too." She moves to the counter. Pulls a carafe from the coffee maker. "He can't stand when I make drip."

"Hunter's the same."

Her laugh is easy. "How is he?"

"Sober."

"Really?" Relief spreads over her face. "That's great, Chase."

"It is."

She nods, pours two cups of coffee, sets them on the counter.

Fuck, it's weird being here. I need to do something. Anything. "Let me help." I go to the fridge. Grab the milk.

She brings sugar to the table. Sits.

I take the seat across from her. Cross one leg over the other. It's not comfortable. Not right. But then neither is this.

"You look good." She stirs milk and sugar into her coffee. Brings her spoon to her lips. "Like you've spent the last two years at the gym."

"Was I lacking before?"

"I don't remember complaining." She raises a brow *did I?*

I shake my head. I was always fit. Three hour practices do that. But working out only became an obsession after she left. I needed routine more.

Grace takes a long sip. Stares at me, waiting for me to go on. When I don't, she clears her throat. "If this is one of those *I miss you* things, you should probably go now."

"It's not."

Her eyes turn down. "What is it?"

Fuck, that's a hard question.

I fix my coffee. Take a long sip. It's mediocre, at best, but it's still warm and familiar.

"I want to know you're okay," I say.

Surprise streaks her expression. "I am. I'm good."

"You're selling art?"

"Here and there." She sets her spoon on the table. Wraps her fingers around her mug. "It's competitive." Her gaze travels down my body. Slowly. Like she's assessing me as a human being, not a potential fuck. "You have a lot of new work. It suits you."

"And you." I motion to the tattoo on her left wrist.

Her brow furrows. "Chase I… I cut you a lot of slack, because I know how hard that was for you, but I'm not having that conversation again."

"Which one?" I rack my brain, but I can't put my finger on anything. We've had so many fucking conversations that one of us swore off forever.

She releases her cup. Warps her arms around her chest. "I know it hurt. I know it was scary. I hate that I did that to you. I do. But, Chase, get over yourself."

What?

"You don't get that." She presses her hands into her chair. "It's mine. It's messy and ugly, but it's mine."

"I'm not—"

"Yes, you are." Her eyes narrow. "I'm sure you have a lot of feelings about it—"

"I found you."

"I'm sorry that I scared you. Really. I hated myself for a long time. For hurting you. For scaring my mom. For making that choice. But it wasn't about you or her or school or work." She rubs her wrist with her right thumb. Traces the outline of her tattoo. "I didn't attempt suicide because you weren't a good enough boyfriend."

"Why…" I swallow hard. This isn't why I'm here. Not exactly.

"You know why." Her eyes meet mine. "You sat there and held me when I cried so many times. You were my light. My rock. The only thing that got me through so many depressive phases."

"I wanted to help."

"I know." Her voice is soft. "But that's not how it works.

423

I have bipolar two. I have a messed up brain. There's no fixing that."

"It wasn't like that."

Her gaze goes to the table. "I know you believe that, Chase. I know you think you wanted to stay by my side, no matter what. But when I'd share my ugly thoughts… you looked so scared. So hurt. Like I'd told you I slept with your best friend." She stares at her tattoo. "I was asking too much of you, and that's on me. I wanted to believe it too. I wanted to believe you were my knight in shining armor."

"I loved you the way you were."

She nods *I know.* "But you still thought… you thought I was the princess at the top of the tower. And that's on me too. I believed it too. I let you believe it. We were… we were kids. We didn't know better." She forces herself to look me in the eyes. "Do you remember the day you graduated?"

"I promised I'd do anything to hold you together."

She nods *yeah.* "It inspired so many bad poems." She laughs, lost in a memory. "I loved that you loved me like that. I loved that you wanted to kill the demon in my brain."

"You wanted that too."

"More than anything." Her lips purse. "I thought if you loved me, I had to be okay. I had to be worthy. But—"

"It wasn't like that, Grace. Yeah, I wanted to save you. But that wasn't why I loved you."

Her lips curl into a soft smile. "I know."

"We were good sometimes."

She nods *true.* "I still remember that bonfire on Forest's birthday. We snuck away with that blanket. And I dared you to strip and swim."

"We practically caught hypothermia, because we were both too stubborn to admit we were cold."

424

She laughs. "You told me there was shrinkage and you needed the chance to prove it."

I can't help but laugh. Fuck, I was such a dumb kid. But in the way all kids are dumb.

I thought I could save the world.

"We christened the backseat of my car," I say.

"The first time I… I wasn't very good at it."

"You got the hang of it."

Her smile is soft. "It wasn't just that you wanted to save me. I loved the way you lit up about tattoos. And the way you looked at me when I pushed you. And your total inability to admit how often you read comic books."

"That again?"

She nods *that again*. "But that became bigger and bigger. You wanting to save me. Me wanting to be saved. It held me together sometimes. It did. But when I was having an episode… I felt like I was letting you down."

"You weren't."

"I was. You were disappointed. You were hurt. Maybe you didn't realize it, but you were. You made my mental health your responsibility. I'm not blaming you, Chase. I let you. I wanted you to. For a while… but after… After I tried to kill myself, I had to face a lot of shit." Her eyes meet mine. "I couldn't look you in the eyes anymore. All I saw was fear and disappointment."

I want to deny it, but I can't. She's right. I was terrified. I tried to hide it, but it was everywhere.

"It's sweet that you want to help the people you love. But you can't. People have to save themselves."

"I only wanted to help."

She looks at me like she doesn't believe me. "It was messy, but it worked out. You backed off. We both moved on."

"You're doing better."

She stares at me, assessing me. "It doesn't have anything to do with you."

"Doesn't it?"

Her lips press together. "I had to change a lot of things. I had to switch my meds and start seeing a therapist and exercise every day. And, yes, I needed to end things. I needed to get away from that pattern."

It makes sense. I want to believe it. To believe that I wasn't the thing holding her back.

She's right. Who the fuck do I think I am, giving myself that much power and importance?

Is it that simple? That we were misguided kids who couldn't break our pattern?

She pulls her arm over her chest. Wraps her fingers around her elbow. "I should have gotten in touch. But I... I still couldn't look you in the eyes. I hadn't forgiven myself yet."

"I forgave you."

She blinks and a tear catches on her lashes. "Yeah?"

I nod.

"But you... you were so mad and hurt. And you're not... you really..."

"I do."

She wipes a tear. "You swear?"

I do. There's still a part of me that hurts, that can't believe how much I missed, but I get it.

She was hurting and she didn't see another way.

It was about her. Not me.

And she got better when I gave her what she asked. What she needed.

Maybe...

Maybe if I take Mom and Hunter and Ariel at their words—

Maybe that will be enough.

Chapter Fifty-Five

ARIEL

My brain shifts into work mode. The way it did after Mom died.

I turn off my phone. Check only my work email. Ignore my brothers and my dad. Eat dinner in my room.

It's a comfortable routine.

Wake up. Breakfast. Work. School. Work. Lunch. Work. Dinner. Work. Walk. Work. Sleep.

The walk is the hard part. The place where thoughts threaten to ruin my sense of calm.

I shut them out with podcasts. Music is no good. It leaves too many gaps. Brings my mind to Mom and how much it hurt when she was gone.

To how well she did this. How scared I am I'll mess it up. How hard it will be doing it alone.

But that's better.

No one to leave.

No one to abandon me.

No men to disappoint me.

Why do they always disappoint me so thoroughly?

Sunday evening, I spend an hour on the beach. The cold seeps through my black hoodie, but I don't mind. Between the shining stars, the crashing waves, and the soft moonlight, it's a beautiful night.

The kind of night you spend with a lover.

Where you drop to your knees and beg for forgiveness.

Or, well… for other things.

I give up on blocking out thoughts. Pause my podcast. Listen to the roar of the waves.

They're so steady. Crash, recede, crash, recede. The same pattern, over and over again, until the end of time.

What's it like to feel that steady? That stable? That sure?

Of course, the ocean isn't a person. It doesn't feel anything. It's a force of nature, controlled by gravity the way I am.

But, still, to have that power, that fury…

The roar fades to white noise as I leave the sand, walk the blocks to our place.

Forest is sitting at the dining table, hands around a mug of coffee, eyes on me.

It's not the first time he's sat here, waiting for me, and it's not going to be the last.

This conversation is not happening.

"I need to shower." I pull my hoodie over my head. Toss it on the couch. Cross the room.

He stands. Gets in front of me. "We need to talk."

"Talk? You mean that thing where two people get equal say in a conversation? I didn't realize you understood that concept."

"Ariel."

"I fuck who I want."

"Did I say—"

"Yes." I push my brother.

Stupid strong basketball player. He doesn't budge.

God, I really need to start lifting. So I can hold my own against assholes who think they can dictate my life.

"Please move." I blink and see red. Forest is there, in one of his usual *look at me, I'm an aloof tattoo artist* outfits. Jeans and a t-shirt. Sneakers. But God knows what color they are. Everything is red. It's fury. It's righteous indignation.

I am the Samuel L. Jackson character in a movie.

And I'm going to bitch slap the idiot trying to put me in my place.

Verbally at least.

"We need to talk." His voice is steady, even, calm.

"You need to go."

"Ariel."

"Saying my name in that tone isn't helping your case."

"Chase is miserable."

My cheeks get hot. "And, what, that's my fault? Fuck you, Forest. You're the one who told him this can't happen. You're the one who looked at him like he betrayed you. You're the one who made him miserable." I push him again, a little harder. "Get out of my way. Now."

"What the fuck, Ariel?"

"Excuse you?"

"My best friend got you pregnant and you didn't think to tell me."

"It's none of your business."

His eyes turn down. "You're my sister."

Fuck this. I can move around him. I don't need to convince him to move. He's unconvinceable.

"Ariel."

"Stop it." I take a step backward.

He follows. "What happened?"

429

"I'm going upstairs." I move faster. Turn at the table. Break into a jog.

My hand hits the railing.

My feet find the stairs.

I make it halfway up, then his voice stops me.

"I'm sorry." Forest moves toward the stairs. "You're right."

What?

"It wasn't my place to say that. You're an adult. You can make your own decisions."

"You realize that?"

"But, Ariel—"

"Nope." I should run to my room. I should lock the door, blast the stereo, refuse to speak to him. But I need to say this. "My life. My body. My decisions. You don't get a say."

"You're twenty four. Why—"

Frustration surges through my veins. I just have to say it. That's the only way he'll understand. "I'm a carrier."

"What?" His hands fall to his sides. His dark eyes fill with fear. "You're… you're sick?"

"No, but if I don't—"

"How soon?"

"My oncologist wanted me to do it right away, but—"

"You have an oncologist?"

I nod.

"Fuck." His face goes white. "Isn't this dangerous? You should do it now. Before you—"

"Don't."

"I'm just…" He moves onto the first stair. "Ariel… I can't lose you. We can't lose you."

I swallow hard.

"You—"

"I know." I'm not doing the safest thing. But I don't

care. "It's a risk, I know. But I want this. I… I'm scared, yeah, but that's not… isn't everyone scared of becoming a parent?"

"How far along?"

"Thirteen weeks."

His eyes go wide. "Already?"

I nod.

"And Chase is the father?"

"I asked him to help me."

He stares at me like I'm crazy.

"At first, he was helping me find someone. But then… that didn't feel right. And he's a good guy. And—"

"Tall."

A laugh breaks up the tension in my shoulders. "He is tall."

"Blue eyes."

I nod.

"But he… his family—"

"I know."

"This kid is going to inherit a lot of shit."

"At least he'll have the world's most annoying uncle."

Forest's smile brings color to his face. "You're really doing this?"

I nod.

"How did it happen? How the hell did you and Chase happen?"

"It's a long story."

He motions to the table. "I'll make tea."

"Decaf."

Realization hits his face. "Shit, you switched to decaf four months ago."

"I still have my morning chai."

"Is that okay?"

I shoot him a *mind your own business look.*

He shakes his head *no way*. "Uncle Forest has to protect —do you have a name?"

"Charlotte."

"She's a girl?"

"No. It's too early. But I hope." My lips press together. "Or Charlie."

"Fuck, Ariel, that's not fair." His voice wavers. "How am I supposed to stay mad when you're doing that?"

"You're not supposed to stay mad." I move down the stairs.

My brother pulls me into a hug. "I'm sorry."

"You should be. You're an idiot."

He chuckles. "I know."

"You fucked things up for me."

"Yeah, but… don't take this the wrong way, Ariel. But if Chase can't handle my scorn—"

"Then how can he handle a tiny, helpless human being?" I ask.

"I was gonna say your relationship, but yeah."

"I know." I pull back. Move to the table. "He… I want to believe he'll get over it. But he's just…" God, what do I say about Chase?

Forest motions *sit down*.

The chair is a relief. This is so much. It's so fucking exhausting.

"I'm sorry, Ariel. Really. Even if Chase had knocked you up by accident… I'd punch him in the face, but—"

"That's not a great apology."

He chuckles. "I'm always gonna protect you. But you're right. I need to step back. Let you make your own choices. Even if I think they're mistakes."

"Did Skye coach you on that?"

He holds up his fingers *a little*. Then he chuckles, pulls his fingers apart *a lot*. "Earl Grey or chai?"

"Are you really asking that question?"

"You bought the decaf Earl Grey."

I stick my tongue out. Earl Grey is fine. It fits a certain mood. But chai is life.

He puts the kettle on. "Tell me what happened." His voice softens. "If you want."

"You'll lay off the judgment?"

He nods *yeah*.

"And you'll… you are Chase's best friend."

"I am."

"So if you have any insights…"

"They're yours."

I wait until he fixes two massive decaf chai lattes. With extra cinnamon. And cardamom.

Then I tell him every detail.

Well, most details. I'm not about to share… *ahem*.

When I'm finished, Forest nods with understanding. His expression stays kind. Concerned. Loving.

Free of unique insights.

"He left. And he asked for a few days. And I… He doesn't want something complicated." Or maybe he does. My cell is still off. I'm still refusing contact. I just can't handle an *I'm sorry, but you were right. I should stay Uncle Chase. Not even that. I should disappear from your life forever. Enjoy the genetic material!*

"Chase lives and breathes complicated."

"Maybe. He… he's pretty much cut everyone out of his life."

Forest's gaze goes to the table. He stares at his half-empty mug for a long moment. Then his gaze shifts to me. "He's very—"

"Stupid?"

"Yeah." My brother chuckles. "He always took responsibility, but something changed when Grace left him. It was like he stopped interacting with the world."

"With you?"

"We still play every week—"

"This week?"

He shakes his head. "First one we've missed in a long time."

"Oh."

"Which is my fault."

"That's true."

Forest's laugh gets louder. "He's a miserable fucker, right now. He's not doing well without you."

"But does he realize that?" I try to take another sip, but my mug is empty. "He can't get over this idea he has that he's toxic. It's ridiculous. He's done so much for me. But he can't see it. And I can't make him see it." I set my mug down. "I told him you can't save someone. I meant it. But I still want to save him."

Forest's eyes flash with epiphany.

"You think I need a therapist?"

"I have an idea."

"What idea?"

"Do you trust me?"

My nose scrunches.

"Give me a week. If he wants to stay away, he will. But if he doesn't…"

"You really think it will work?"

"I don't know. But it'll do something."

Chapter Fifty-Six

CHASE

I wake to a voicemail from Forest and a flurry of texts. I only catch the latest.

Forest: You fucked up bad, but you can fix it.

That could end a threat to kill me or a request for an apology or a demand for a shotgun wedding.

Usually, I know how Forest is going to react to something.

Right now, I don't have a clue.

I will talk to him. After this.

I skip breakfast. Dress in a hurry. Pick up coffee on the way to Hunter's place.

He opens after two knocks.

Surprise streaks his expression. He rubs his eyes. Blinks three times. "Chase…"

I hold up his drink. "From the place down the street."

His fingers brush mine as he takes it. "Drip or pour over?" He tries to make his voice light, but he doesn't quite get there.

"What do you think?" My attempt at teasing is even

worse. Fuck, this is bizarre. I'm on my brother's doorstep. Asking *him* to let *me* into his life.

For the past two years, I've kept him out of my life. I'm still not sure I can handle him in my life.

But I can't wait anymore. I need to make this right.

We might never be best friends again. We might never be close again. But we can be okay.

He takes a sip. Lets out a low sigh. "Fuck, that's good."

"Save it for your girlfriend."

He pulls the door open. Motions *come in*.

I take a deep breath and step inside. "Is she here?"

"Class." He motions to the dining table in the living room. *Have a seat.*

It's an invitation, not an order, but I still feel like I'm being called to the principal's office.

He sets the takeout cup on the sleek wood table. Slides into a matching chair.

I sit across from him. Wrap my hands around my cup. It's warm but I can barely feel it.

"How's the new shop?" He takes a long sip. Swallows hard.

"Good." My phone is flush with updates on Inked Love, but I haven't seen enough of it. Not in person.

"It's nice. Beautiful." He tries to make his voice even. Gets most of the way there. "Suits you."

"The hot pink suits me?"

"The black."

I can't help but chuckle. "I look good in misery."

He laughs too. "You do."

"Maybe not as good as you."

He holds up his cup to toast. "You're the king."

"Then you're the prince."

"Maybe it's just a Keating thing." He takes another sip. Lets out another moan. "Fuck, that really is good."

I nod.

"I'm going to have to look past those uncomfortable chairs." He lays his palms on the table.

I try to think of some response. Chairs. Coffee. Black. None of that shit matters. I have to say the shit that matters. "I'm sorry."

His eyes go wide. He repeats my words like he's translating a foreign language. "You're sorry."

"Yeah. Not for the last year. I was pissed. I needed time."

He nods with understanding.

"Before that…" I suck a breath through my teeth. This is hard. But I can do it. "I made it too personal. Made your drinking about me. Yeah, it hurt that you lied. It hurt that I missed it. But I get that you weren't an alcoholic at me."

He stares at me, dumbstruck.

"Mom… Fuck, you think it's gonna stick?"

"I don't know." His voice is honest. "I hope so, but… I know better than anyone—"

"It doesn't always."

He nods *yeah*.

"Do you think you will?" I stare into my brother's eyes.

"Do you?"

"Yeah." The tension in my shoulders eases. "I do. I really fucking do."

"Chase—"

"You don't have to say anything. I get it now. It's your fight. Not mine. I'll always be there, cheering you on, but I'm not gonna get involved."

"Okay."

"You're my brother. I love you, Hunter. I always will."

"Uh…" He picks his jaw up from the floor. "Have you been seeing a shrink?"

"I probably should."

"Yeah." His laugh is awkward. "It helps."

"You still?"

He nods. "I'm still on meds."

"They help?"

"Yeah. Fuck with my sleep. And my appetite. But they help." His eyes go to the take out cups. He studies them like they're works of art. "That's genetic too."

"I know."

"You… no offense, Chase, but what the fuck?"

My chuckle is a little easier. "I, uh… I can't spontaneously forgive my brother?"

"No." He picks up his coffee cup. Goes to sip. Stops himself. "This poison? Are you granting my final wish before you kill me?"

"You think I'm that clever?"

He shakes his head *hell no* and takes a sip. "This about Ariel?"

"No."

He raises a brow *yeah right*.

"Kind of." I press my hands together. Bring my gaze to his eyes. Fuck, they're just like mine. Like Wes's. Like Mom's. It's terrifying how much he resembles Mom. "She's pregnant."

"What?"

"Yeah. We… we're having a baby. I mean… fuck, I don't know if she still wants me."

"That's a pretty big—" He trips over his words. "Since when?"

"It's a long story."

"What's the short version?"

"She asked for my help."

"Coming? You could buy her a toy."

I can't help but laugh. "Getting pregnant. But now… I really fucking like her."

The Baby Bargain

"You love her?"

"Fuck, I haven't said that word in so long."

"You just said you loved me."

"You know what I mean."

He leans back in his chair. His shoulders fall from his ears. His jaw softens. "No offense, Chase, but what's that have to do with me?"

"I want to be better. For her."

"Ariel or the kid?"

"Both."

"She's a girl?"

"Too early to say."

"Fuck." He shakes his head in disbelief. "Chase Keating is gonna be a father." His eyes meet mine. His lips curl into a smile. "It suits you."

"Yeah?"

"A lot."

"You don't…" Fuck, I don't know how to say this. I channel Ariel. Go for bluntness. "You don't hate me?"

"Never hated you."

"The other shop—"

"Not like you were hanging out with me at Inked Hearts."

"But if I—"

His eyes fill with understanding. "You like managing Inked Love?"

"I do." I really fucking do.

"It's a promotion."

"But—"

"It doesn't have to mean you're giving up on me."

"I'm not." I run my hand through my hair. "Fuck, this is hard."

"Why do I think I'm in therapy?"

I can't help but chuckle.

"Not gonna get easier when you have a kid."

"I know."

"But you'll be good at it."

"I hope so."

He nods *you will*. "You need the extra money now."

"It's only a little more."

"Still. Gotta save up for private school." His lips curl into a half smile. He's relaxed. Easy.

How is that possible?

How am I the one tangled in knots?

For the last two years, Hunter has been staring at me like I punched him in the jaw.

Now that I'm trying to make nice, I'm the one who's nervous about winning his respect.

I try to shift into the teasing conversation. Shake my head *hell no*. "We're in the Venice Santa Monica school district. That's the good one."

"She's moving into your tiny apartment?"

"Fuck, I don't know."

"You really love her, huh?"

"A lot." She's bright. Like the stars. "I want to do this right."

"You don't need my blessing."

"I know, but… I want her to have a family. I want us to be a family."

"So, if your girlfriend wasn't pregnant, you wouldn't bother with me?" he teases.

"Pretty much," I tease back. For once, it's easy. Well, easy ish.

"Take the job, Chase. It's good for you."

"But we—"

"It's not like I'm far."

That's true. "Her family does Sunday dinners."

"Aren't you joining?"

Hopefully. "We could do another day. If you're not too busy for me." I raise a brow *you think you're that important?*

His laugh is easy. "I'll have to check my schedule."

I nod *sure.*

He looks at me differently. Like he's the older brother. Like he's the one who's proud of me.

Maybe he is.

This is fucking hard.

This is a lot.

Fuck, maybe Hunter has it worse than me. Proud of me for forgiving him.

Keatings are a fucking mess.

But we can get there.

I want to get there. For me. For Hunter. For Ariel.

For both of our families. And the one that's just ours.

Fuck, I hope it's just ours.

"She looked pretty pissed when she walked out of the party," Hunter says.

I nod *yeah.*

"Forest too."

"You know how that goes."

He chuckles *don't I.* "I've talked to him."

"Do I want to know?"

He nods *yeah.* "It's not as bad as it looks."

"You promise?"

"Yeah, but then again, I could be fucking with you."

"I'd deserve it."

He nods *yeah, you do.* "Good thing I'm a bigger person."

"Too bad Wes isn't here to comment on that."

His laugh is easy. "Fuck, how did he ever win over Quinn?"

"Maybe he's as good as he says."

Hunter's nose scrunches. *Gross.* "I think she likes his personality too."

"No accounting for taste," I say.

Hunter stands. Offers me his hand. "Let me help. With Ariel."

"I should be the one helping you."

"Yeah, but let's be real, Chase. You need a lot more fucking help."

I stand. Hold out my hand.

He pulls me into a close hug.

He's right. I do need help.

For once, I'm accepting it. "Tell me you have a plan."

"Yeah, but you're not going to like it."

Chapter Fifty-Seven

ARIEL

s promised, I give my brother a week.

For seven days, I ignore my cell, I focus on work, I stay off social media.

Day eight, I wake up to a letter on the dining table. There's a Post-it note on the envelope.

Dropped this off. Give him a chance.

-Forest

P.S. Skye says I'm still an idiot.

P.P.S. Skye wrote that.

My lips curl into a smile. The P.S. is in Skye's handwriting. And she...

Whatever happens with Chase, I have the support of my brother and his friend. My friend. Holden and Dad—

We need to have a bigger conversation. But they'll support me too. Whatever happens, this baby is going to have a lot of love in her life.

I take a deep breath. Push an exhale though my nose.

It doesn't calm my racing heart.

This needs to be good. It needs to be *I love you forever. I'm sorry I was stupid. I figured out all my shit. Please forgive me.*

And maybe a little of *and come without panties because I'm going to fuck you senseless*.

Okay, so it's not the moment for sex. But, God, sex is so much easier than everything else.

If only Chase and I could stay there forever.

This has to be good.

What kind of person would leave a note on the dining table for a break up?

That's cowardly.

Chase is a lot of things, but he's not a coward.

My stomach flip-flops. I can't blame hormones. I'm well past morning sickness.

This is all nerves.

I don't know how I get the letter open, but I do.

Paper flutters to the ground.

I flip open a handwritten note.

Ariel,

Come to my place as soon as you can. I'll be here all day. I know you want to make me wait, but I do have chai.

- Chase

Sure enough, my custom chai blend is missing from the cabinet.

Dastardly.

Devious.

Genius.

I dress. Chug a glass of water. Brew a decaf chai. Even with three tea bags, the flavor is weak. More milk than tea or spice.

This is it.

I need to go there.

For him.

For my chai.

For everything.

I grab my purse and head out.

It's a short walk, fifteen minutes at most. And it's a beautiful morning. None of the typical beach grey.

The sun is bright, the sky is blue, the clouds are fluffy.

The soft breeze raises goose bumps on my arms. It must be sixty-five degrees, but I'm freezing and warm at once.

Every step feels like a million miles.

Every familiar sight—the coffee shop where Chase and I planned, the street that Inked Hearts calls home, the one the new shop claimed, the turn that leads to his apartment —makes my limbs light.

I'm not sure how I make it all the way to his apartment, but I do.

I walk up the steps.

Knock on his door.

"It's open," he calls.

His voice makes my legs weak. It's been too long. I miss him.

I miss him in ways I've never missed anyone.

I want this to be okay.

For me.

And Charlotte.

And Chase too.

He's a good guy. He deserves to be happy. Does he finally see it?

God, I hope he finally sees it.

My fingers graze the door handle.

Deep breath. Slow exhale.

I push the door open.

Step inside.

He's leaning against the counter, eyes on the door, mug of tea sitting on the table.

"Is that my chai?" I don't know what else to ask.

He nods *yeah*.

"How long has it been sitting there?"

"I've been making a new one every fifteen minutes."

"That's such a waste."

"Drank everything so far."

"That must be—"

"I think I'm at nine." He pushes off the counter. Takes the mug from the table. Brings it to me.

My hands brush his as I take it. "Thank you." Fuck, it smells good. Ginger, cardamom, cinnamon, tea. "You must be bouncing off the walls." Oh, the walls.

They aren't black anymore.

They're a soft shade of purple.

Why are they purple?

He follows my gaze. "Seemed appropriate."

"But…"

"Are you gonna try that, princess?"

"I…"

"I'm still a novice chai maker, but I'm getting the hang of it."

I take a long sip. Mmm. It's spicy, sweet, rich, creamy.

"Good?" His eyes fix on me. They fill with honest vulnerability.

"Perfect." I get lost in his blue eyes. They're so pretty and deep. I want to swim in them. I want to stare until I understand him.

Will I ever understand him?

Do two people ever really understand each other? Or is it the kind of journey that takes a lifetime?

My stomach flutters at the thought of waking up next to Chase every day. Rolling over, brushing brown strands from his cheeks, watching his chest rise and fall. Teasing him about his attempts to make chai oatmeal (he never gets the spices quite right). Watching his hands move over his sketch book. Tracing the ink on his arms.

Diving deeper every day.

Understanding more every day.

Loving him more every day.

His fingers brush my forearm. "It's your blend."

"Forest stole it?"

"His idea."

A laugh escapes my lips. "Was that his entire plan?"

Chase shakes his head. "Most of it was slapping sense into me."

"Did he?"

"Hunter helped too. But… You should probably be the judge of that." His fingers curl around my forearm. He nods *follow me*.

But I'm too transfixed by his eyes. And the room. "It's purple."

He chuckles. "Yeah."

"Why?"

"You love purple."

"I do?"

He nods *yeah*. "Your bed and all your towels are purple."

"Oh. That's just… Mom… uh…"

"You don't like it?"

No, it's gorgeous. Soft and feminine, but still regal and powerful. "It's not you."

"It's not supposed to be." He drags his fingertips down my forearm. Over the back of my hand. "I want to show you something."

I just barely nod.

"In here." He takes a step backward. Pulls me with him.

I follow Chase down the hallway.

Into his bedroom.

Only it's…

Oh my God.

The black walls and bedspread are gone.

The walls are painted teal—the same teal in my room. And the bedspread—

It's the same purple as the one in my room.

And right there, next to his bed, there's a crib.

A soft white, perfectly put together crib.

I…

He…

I nearly drop my mug.

He takes it. Sets it on the dresser. Takes my hand.

"I… You…" My eyes go to his. "You… I…"

"You okay, princess?"

"That's a crib."

He nods *it is*.

"For…" I nod to my stomach.

"For Charlotte."

Oh my God. "You want to?"

"You were right, Ariel. I need to get over myself."

My laugh is awkward.

"I can't say that I have. Or that I've stopped blaming myself for Mom or Hunter or Grace. I can't say I'm over it. But I'm trying." He runs his thumb over my palm. "I want to get there. I've never wanted that before."

"Where?"

"I want to believe I make your life better."

"You do." I squeeze his hand. "Chase, I—"

"Let me finish, princess. I have a whole thing." His cheeks flush. "I've been practicing."

"Yeah?"

He nods *yeah*.

I reach out. Brush a hair from his eyes. Rest my palm on his cheek.

He feels so good against my skin.

Like he's mine.

Is he finally mine?

Finally ours?

Chase squeezes my hand. "Ariel, I freaked out when your brother caught us. Not because he was pissed. Because his words were my words. They were what I've believed about myself for a long time."

I bite my tongue so I won't interrupt.

"I'm not sure when I started believing I could save everyone I loved. Or when I started blaming myself for their failures. But it's been weighing on me for a long time. I thought I was helping by removing myself from the equation. And I was. But not because I'm an anchor around everyone's neck."

I nod.

"Because I was making their problems about me. I was making my brother's addiction about me. Staring at him with betrayal, asking him to prove he loved me by giving up his coping mechanism—it wasn't fair. It was asking too much. Putting too much pressure on him."

"He's okay now."

"Yeah. Because I stepped away. Because I stopped asking that of him. People got better when I left, yeah, but not because I'm toxic. Because I was pushing them further than they could go. I talked to Grace—"

My stomach flip-flops. "You talked to your ex?"

"Yeah. But not like that." He moves a half-step closer. "I didn't go to win her over. I don't want to win her over. She's happy. And I'm finally happy about that. I finally get it. It wasn't her and it wasn't me. It was us. This pattern we'd made."

"Yeah?"

"Yeah. We were kids. We were naïve. We thought we

could save each other. And we couldn't let that go without letting each other go."

"But now… if you're healed now, couldn't you… couldn't you be together?"

"Maybe. But I don't want her. I don't love her." His eyes bore into mine. "I love you, Ariel."

"What?" There's no way he said that. I must be dreaming. That's the only reasonable possibility.

He nods. "Ariel Ballard, I'm madly in love with you. And I want a life with you." He motions to the crib. "Maybe we did this out of order, but I don't care. I want to be the father of your child. I want us to be a family."

"You do?"

"More than anything."

I blink and a tear catches on my lashes.

Chase brings his hand to my cheek. He catches a tear on his thumb. "Those happy or sad?"

"I love you too." I wrap my arm around him. "And you… you don't think you're going to ruin this?"

"I'm scared. But I'm getting there." He stares back at me.

"How fast?"

"I don't know, princess. But I promise I'll go to you with those fears. If you promise you'll tell me what I need."

I nod. "I will."

"Yeah?"

"Yeah." I move closer. "And right now—" I slip my hand under his t-shirt. "I really need you to take off your clothes."

"I'm trying to have a romantic moment."

"All of your clothes." I reach for his waistband. "As quickly as possible."

He chuckles. "Are you ordering me to strip?"

"It's a request." I look up at him. "I'd rather stick with you issuing the orders."

"But naked?"

I nod. "Is that a problem?"

"No, princess." He breaks our touch to pull his t-shirt over his head. "Your wish is my command."

Epilogue

CHASE

"**Y**ou sure it's not too late to switch to all black?" Wes holds out my purple tie. Shakes his head *oh, the horror*. "This isn't you."

"It's not?" I try to find a teasing tone, but it's impossible. Every part of me is buzzing.

I can't tell if it's nerves, excitement, too much coffee.

Lack of champagne.

Hunter insisted there was no reason to keep the groom's suite dry, but... well, I guess I'm still over-protective.

He tells me it's ridiculous every other day. I actually talk to my brother enough he can tease me every other day.

It took a while to get there. Months of weekly dinners. Mc officially joining Inked Love full time. (I'm still managing the shop. I'm good at it and I fucking love it). Hell, that was the turning point. Once I stopped seeing Hunter because I had to and started seeing him because I wanted to, something changed. Shit was easier for both of us.

Don't get me wrong. It was tense for a while. Dinners were quiet. Then they were nonstop debates on comics (with Wes providing plenty of eye-rolls about our terrible taste). Everyone gushing over Charlotte. Everyone teasing about the new shop.

Then, one day, it was easy. We talked about everything and nothing. We teased like we used to. Mentioned Hunter's sobriety like it was the weather or a new pair of jeans. We didn't have wine at dinner. No big deal.

"You spent three months trying to convince Ariel." Griffin taps his fingers against the arm of his leather chair. He raises a brow *you're ridiculous*. "You ran that joke into the ground day two."

Wes flips him off.

Griffin just shrugs. He's the picture of confidence. And comfort. When he steps into his suit, he's a different person. This guy who's incredibly proud of his status as a husband.

No, he's always that person. But it's extra obnoxious when he dons a suit.

"You need any last minute tips on married life?" Griffin asks.

Wes rolls his eyes. "Chug half a bottle of tequila before the ceremony and the rest after?"

Griffin copies Wes's eye-roll. "It's sad how jealous you are."

"Jealous of what?" Wes holds up his left hand. Wiggles his adorned ring finger.

"Such insecurity." Griffin shakes his head. "Poor Ingrid. Growing up with a daddy who doesn't think she's enough."

At the mention of his daughter's name, Wes completely forgets his irritation. He *does* turn into a different person.

It's bizarre. Beyond bizarre. My little brother is a dad.

Hell, Charlotte is completely enamored with her cousin. She lights up about everything. But she especially lights up when she gets to play with Ingrid.

"You have to admit. Chase could use a drink," Wes says.

The door swings shut as Hunter steps into the suite. He surveys the room, nods hello to everyone. "He really could."

Wes chuckles. "Even he thinks so."

"I'm good." Nerves aren't always a bad thing.

My whole body is buzzing, sure, but it's anticipation as much as anything else. Like before my first tattoo.

I'm marrying Ariel Ballard.

I'm marrying the mother of my child.

I'm marrying the woman who brings joy to my life.

Fuck, I thought I knew what it meant to love before. But after the last few years—

My world is open in a whole new way. A way I never imagined.

The first time I saw Charlotte—a tiny ultrasound that's still taped to the fridge—my heart nearly burst. But actually meeting her? Holding her in my hands? Feeling her tiny hand wrapped around my finger?

I've never felt so much love.

I'd die for her.

I'd die for Ariel too.

And even more importantly, I'd live for them. I stay on top of my shit—I journal, I go to therapy, I set boundaries with my mom—for them.

The big gestures are easy.

It's the little shit every day that's hard.

But I wouldn't have it any other way.

"You gonna put that thing on or stare at it?" Wes holds up my tie.

I suck a breath through my teeth. It shouldn't feel this monumental. Ariel and I already have a kid together. We live together, share finances, plan our lives around each other. Getting married is a formality.

Only it's not.

In an hour, I'll be able to call her my wife.

She'll call me her husband.

Fuck, it's—

"You're gonna run out of time." Wes clears his throat. "Keep your hands at your sides." He moves closer. Loops the tie through my collar.

"When did you learn to do that?" Griffin raises a brow.

"You want to mention your wedding again?" Wes cinches the knot and slides it into place. "It never gets old."

Griffin just chuckles.

Hunter too. "Poor kid, huh?"

Wes pouts. Even though he's a married father—with another on the way—he's still Wes. (Soon, he'll be able to compete with Dean for most obnoxious father, not just most obnoxious guy at Inked Hearts. Chloe is a million months pregnant. Poor five-foot-one girl looks like she's about to pop).

"Good thing she takes after her mother," Griffin says.

Wes's frown turns upside down. He steps backward. Lets out a dreamy sigh. "She has new freckles."

Griffin and Hunter share a look. *Not this again.*

Wes was a lovesick puppy when he fell for Quinn. Now that he can gush over his daughter?

I'd find him annoying if I didn't feel exactly the same way about the women in my life.

Not that Hunter loves Emma less than I love Ariel. He adores his fiancée (she's making him wait). But he's like me.

He wants to hold it close to his chest. So it doesn't disappear.

Once a fucked-up Keating, always a fucked up Keating.

Mom is... Mom. I wish I could say she stayed on the straight and narrow forever. But she didn't.

About a year ago, she started drinking a little. Then a lot. Fuck, it was probably earlier. I probably missed it.

But it's not like before. I can handle it.

Yeah, I'm not happy my mother refuses further treatment. I certainly don't like thinking about her drinking herself to death.

But it's not my battle anymore.

It's hers.

You can't help someone who won't help themselves. Not with tough love. Not with a lot of slack. Not with anything.

I get that now.

The door swings open and Forest steps inside. He shoots me a shit-eating grin. One that screams *I know something you don't.*

He's in a royal purple suit. One that matches my tie. And the bow around Ariel's bouquet. And every flower here. (Our colors are royal purple and crimson. Her pick. Completely perfect).

He's in the bridal party.

And, well, he really is wearing that suit.

Forest holds up a bottle of champagne. "We have extra." He nods to Hunter *you mind?*

Hunter shakes his head *no worries.* He's laid-back about recovery now. Or maybe he's used to being around temptation.

It's been years.

He's okay.

I really believe he's going to stay there.

"He's wearing the purple better than you are." Griffin nods *hey* to Forest. "He's gonna upstage you."

"Gonna upstage Ariel with that smile." Wes chuckles. "You know you're supposed to let the bride shine."

"How could anyone shine brighter than you, Wes?" he teases.

Wes just laughs. "Is Ariel as terrified as Chase?"

Forest mimes zipping his lips. "Just dropping this off."

"And getting intel for the bride?" Griffin raises a brow.

Forest shrugs *maybe*.

Griffin shakes his head. "You dirty dog."

"Yeah. But only for my girl." Forest winks at Griffin.

Griffin winks back.

They exchange some look. Something about how they love dirty sex.

Fuck, I don't need those details.

Forest sets the bottle on the white side table—everything in the room is stark white—then he steps backward. "Gotta say, bridal suite is a lot nicer." He nods goodbye and steps out the door.

Griffin chuckles. "What a dick."

"Your favorite dick," Wes says.

"I think Griffin's favorite dick is his," Hunter says.

"You have some questions?" Griffin raises a brow. "If you need tips on pleasing your girl, I can help."

A laugh spills from my lips. Then another. Another.

I double over, clutching my stomach.

These guys…

The more they change, the more they stay the same.

We're here, minutes before I walk down the fucking aisle, married men, fathers, business owners.

But we're gossiping the way we did in high school.

"He's laughing at your skills," Wes says.

Griffin shrugs *I know what I've got*. He shares a look with Wes. Even though their lives have gone in different directions—Wes is father of the year, whereas Griffin and Juliette are incredibly uninterested in children—they're still best friends.

We're all close. Yeah, we're dysfunctional, and ridiculous, and sometimes immature, but we're family.

Griffin stands. Grabs the champagne. "I'm popping this fucking thing."

"'Cause it reminds you of coming?" Wes raises a brow.

Griffin's smile gets wicked. "'Cause it reminds me of licking champagne off my wife's tits." He grabs a corkscrew, holds the bottle against his hip, pushes the sharp edge into the cork.

Bam—

The cork hits the ceiling.

Foam spills over the bottle.

"Should I go on?" Griffin looks to Wes for an answer.

"You know you want him to," Hunter says.

Wes grabs the champagne flutes from the side table. Brings them to Griff. "It's up to the groom."

"You need a dirty story to rev you up enough to fuck your wife later?" Griffin asks.

His words dissolve the second they hit my ears.

There's only one thing in my head.

Tonight, Ariel is going to be my wife.

Tonight, I'm going to fuck my wife.

What could be better than that?

"Shit, we lost him too." Wes shakes his head.

Griff fills the glasses. "He's not as bad as you."

Wes brings a glass to me. He nudges my shoulder. "Look alive, kid. You've only got ten minutes until show time."

I take the glass. Let the bubbles burst on my tongue.

We shift into our usual teasing. The same shit as always. Only it's not.

Everything changes today.

Everything.

———

ARIEL

FOREST SHOOTS ME A SHIT-EATING GRIN. ONE THAT screams *I know exactly what Chase is thinking and I'm not going to tell you*.

He's pure evil.

He really is.

"You want one more?" He nods to the champagne on the vanity.

I lean back, teeter on my heels, catch myself.

For the last three months, I've been practicing my walk. Well, walking in heels, period.

I'm far from graceful, but I can move. Ish.

Maybe I should take them off. Sure, I want to be eye to eye with Chase (well, closer to eye to eye. He does have seven inches on me). And my dress is hemmed for four inches of lift.

But there's something about walking barefoot in the grass.

It's romantic. Natural. Beautiful.

Forest's chuckle fills the room. "I'm not sure which of you is more nervous."

My cheeks flush, but my reflection doesn't show it. The entire bridal suite is mirrors. Seriously. My reflection bounces off every single wall.

She isn't the usual Ariel. With her carefully coiffed hair,

her perfect makeup, and her elegant sheath dress, she's some kind of goddess.

But I guess that's how all brides feel. Even though most aren't focused on their, uh, upgrades.

At first, the fake boobs were weird. I'd catch a glimpse of my reflection and go *who's that*. But it was like a new hairstyle.

I got used to it.

My entire body was changing. Like all new moms, I didn't bounce back to my pre-pregnancy body. I carried extra padding, stretch marks, loose skin.

And, well—I lost a lot of parts.

Gained these.

Once I got used to them (and let Chase drag me on enough hikes I felt fit... ish), I started to like them. I can skip a bra, run without bounce, wear dresses that scream *knock-out*.

Sure, the hormone changes were a bitch for a while (I'm still super temperature sensitive), but I got through it. Found my new normal.

Even with the big boobs (they look natural ish), and the less defined waist (not that it was ever slim), I love my body.

I love all the things it does for me.

All the things Chase makes it feel.

I was scared the first time he toyed with my new breasts. It wasn't quite what it used to be. The sensation wasn't there.

But after a while, it came back. Or maybe he got that much better.

He stared at my boobs even more post-surgery.

He still loves my body as much he did that first time. Not just because I'm, ahem, well-endowed.

Because it's mine.

"Ms. Ballard, you're up." The wedding coordinator

peeks her head through the door. She presses her bright pink lips into a smile. Holds her clipboard against her black suit. "Your father is ready for you." She looks to Forest. "You first." Her composure breaks as she takes in his purple suit.

Sure, my brother isn't the most conventional choice for Maid of Honor, but I don't care.

After I told him about my pregnancy, he stepped up. He's been there for me and Chase and Charlotte… well, always.

He answers my three a.m. calls (there were so many the first year. Babies. Never. Sleep). He drags me to aikido (I'm still terrible). He watches trashy superhero movies with me. Dives into memories when I cry over how much mom would have loved it. (That's another thing about having a baby. I cry all the time now. I cry at cereal commercials. I cry when Charlotte tries on a new dress. I cry when I buy a new toy. It's nonstop waterworks).

"Ms. Ballard." The coordinator clears her throat. "Are you ready?"

Forest nudges me *you've got this*. "You look beautiful."

"Yeah?"

"Like you don't know." He pulls me into a tight hug. Leans close enough to whisper. "I'll grab the car if you want to run."

"And Charlotte?"

"She's with Holden." His voice is light, teasing. "He'll bring her out. Unless you want to bail. Head back to Vegas. Hook up with a stripper."

"That's okay."

"You sure?" He releases me. Smiles wide. "This is your last chance to walk. And who knows, you might find a stripper who's six four"

I can't help but laugh. It's the perfect thing to say. "I'm sure."

"Good." He winks. "Just testing you."

"Uh-huh."

"Uh-huh." He nods *really*. Mouths *you've got this*, turns, follows the coordinator into the hallway.

I've got this.

I've got this.

Really. I do have this.

It's not a big deal. Sure, I'm legally joining my life with Chase's. And all of our friends and family are here to watch that union. And I haven't seen him since the bachelorette party—Forest, Skye, Holden, and some friends from work—dragged me to Vegas.

But uh…

Fuck, do I have this?

Why didn't I stick with the *let's elope in Hawaii* idea?

"You ready, sweetie?" My dad's voice fills the room. He peeks his head through the door. Looks at me with a soft expression.

No. Yes. Maybe. I nod and cross the room.

Dad smiles as I take his hand. "You're taller than me in those shoes."

It's weird, towering over my father. "As tall as Forest."

He laughs *true*. "He's right. You look beautiful."

I squeeze his arm for support. "Thanks."

"Just like your mother did." His eyes turn down for a moment. "Well, a little older."

"Hey."

Dad laughs. "We married young."

"You're not supposed to call your daughter old."

"Not old. But… you'll always be my little girl, Ariel. You'll see what it's like with Charlotte."

I already do. It's amazing how fast she grows. I swear,

yesterday she was this tiny helpless thing who did nothing but eat, poop, and cry.

Now… well, she does eat, poop, and cry an awful lot. But she's already an explorer. She's already trying to learn everything she can about the world.

Dad nudges me. Motions to the closed door *shall we?*

God, this is really happening.

I nod *we shall*. Let him lead me out the door, around the corner, all the way to the ceremony site.

The sun shines over the well-dressed guests, the purple bows, the rose covered arch.

It's a beautiful afternoon. Bright blue sky. Big puffy clouds. Ocean for miles.

We're on the Malibu cliffside. We're so high above the ocean we're practically in the clouds.

It's pure California indulgence.

Mom would have loved it.

But then she would have loved anything. Her heart was always so big and full. It was always expanding.

She used to say the more you love, the more capacity you have for love. I didn't believe it. Not after she died.

But the first time I felt Charlotte kick—

I didn't think it was possible to love that much. I still have trouble believing it. But, somehow, my heart gets bigger and fuller every single day.

For a moment, my eyes move over the crowd. There are almost a hundred people here. Chase's family. Mine. Friends from work and school. Every tattoo artist we know.

And Charlotte.

Holden is standing there, at the back of the bridal party, holding my daughter.

She's fussing. Of course. She likes to move on her own. And she hates wearing fancy dresses.

But, God, she looks so cute in that royal purple dress.

She's going to throw it off the second she can. I need to appreciate it now.

I swallow hard. Tune into the music. Focus on moving one foot in front of the other.

Walking in heels is hard.

Walking in heels on the grass—

Those little plastic things that stop shoes from sinking into soil only work so well.

The sun fills my eyes. Casts the world in bright white highlights.

Then I take another step and Chase comes into view.

My groom.

My husband to be.

My other half.

His blue eyes meet mine. He smiles the widest smile in the history of the world.

The rest of the world falls away.

All I can see is Chase's smile.

I move closer to him with every step.

Then close enough to touch him.

Dad kisses me on the cheek. "I love you, sweetie." He crosses the altar. Takes Charlotte from Holden. Sits in the front aisle.

I look at my daughter for a moment. She's so big now and she looks so much like her daddy. Big blue eyes. Long limbs. Bright smile.

My little girl. Our little girl.

We're already a family.

This is where we make it official.

My gaze shifts back to Chase.

I take his hands. Squeeze them tightly. Stare at him as everyone sits.

The officiant moves to the podium. He makes some

joke about how we did everything out of order. And how he's never seen such a tall couple.

Then he's reciting Mom's favorite poem. Talking about love and marriage and forever. Taking the rings from Forest.

He hands the shiny silver wedding band to me.

My fingers close around the metal.

I'm surrounded by people. I'm speaking in public. But the second I stare into Chase's eyes, my fears dissolve.

I recite my vows from heart, then I slide the ring onto his finger. "I do."

He takes the ring. Stares at me with every bit of love and devotion in the world as he slides it on my finger. "I do." His hands go to my hips.

He pulls me into a slow, deep kiss.

The officiant is saying something.

Friends and family are clapping.

The waves beneath us are crashing.

But there's only one thing in my head:

Chase is my husband.

I'm kissing my husband.

He's really mine forever.

Stay In Touch

Thank you for reading *The Baby Bargain*. I hope you loved Griffin and Juliette's story as much as I did, and I hope you look forward to Forest's book *The Best Friend Bargain*, coming fall 2019.

If you enjoyed this novel, please help other readers find it by leaving an honest review on Amazon or Goodreads.

Want news about new releases and sales before anyone else? How about exclusive sneak peeks and bonus scenes? Sign up for the Crystal Kaswell mailing list.

Want to talk books? I love hearing from my readers. You can find me on Facebook or join my Facebook group.

You can find more of my books here.

Author's Note

There's a tendency in romance novels. This assumption that all women love, want, understand, expect kids. There are so many books where the hero and heroine never discuss kids, family, or pregnancy. But, somehow, they make it to the epilogue with a couple of kids. Like it just happens. Like everyone always wants the same things, on the same timeline.

This trend irritated me—it still irritates me. I did what I do whenever something irritates me. I decided to use my skillset—writing romance novels—to comment. To twist expectations. To write my own "baby book," one that didn't ignore the reality of timing and expectations. One where two adults made a decision together.

The concept hung out, in the back of my mind, for a long time. It poked when I wrote particularly paternal heroes, but I never gave it time to play. Until I met Chase. Immediately, I knew he was the one.

For awhile I tried to deny it—I wrote the first few chapters of Chase's book as a second chance romance. But it wasn't right. It wasn't Chase. I needed to push him hard—

the characters who don't want to change need the hardest push—and what would be harder than offering him everything he wants… with one condition.

It's funny. Once I started writing *The Baby Bargain* as a book about a guy helping his friend get pregnant, it flowed. It wasn't easy, exactly (it never is), but it clicked. It made sense to me. I stepped into the characters' heads, understood what they wanted, sympathized with their need for a biological family. It didn't matter that I don't want kids myself. I got it.

It turns out baby making is all about having sex. (Who knew?) But the implications of parenting push the characters to, ahem, deeper places. Chase's possible fatherhood forced him to evaluate his ideas about masculinity. What does it mean to be a man? To protect the people you love? To help? At what point does it become about you? At what point are you hurting more than you're helping? Do good intentions really matter? What if the only way to help someone you love is by walking away?

I'm sure I drove my husband crazy with my references to Daredevil, but, hey, great minds think alike. Okay, I'm not sure the showrunners always understand when Matt's brooding is eye-roll inducing and when it's aww-poor-baby inducing, but the show makes a lot of coherent points about martyr complexes. (Also, Charlie Cox is super dreamy). Some guys want to help, even though it's not their duty or their place. Some guys need to learn to listen before they act. To hear other people's boundaries and respect them, rather than assuming they know best.

Heroes are always a hot topic in romance. One person's alpha is another's eww. I don't want to comment on other authors' books or heroes (you'll have to buy me a drink first), but I will say that it took me a long time to realize I could write my heroes as people. When I started writing romance, so many told me heroes have to be X or Y. For a long time, I thought heroes needed to be indestructible "alphas" who were hot and cold for no reason, who had no interiority, who had no flaws beyond sleeping around or working too much or playing with the heroine's heart.

But heroes don't have to be "alpha male" constructs. They can be wounded, vulnerable, hurting and still be strong. The people who are hurting the most are often the ones who are the strongest.

I never explicitly said that Chase had depression. I never forced him to face that. I have my own ideas about his mental health, but I like to leave something to the reader. Where's the line between brooding and depressed? When does someone need medical attention? And why is it so great hanging out in the heads of miserable men? (Really, tell me! I can't figure out why I love it so much).

I guess this is a long way of saying thank you for reading. I'm so grateful I can write books that I love that readers love too. I'm able to explore things like toxic masculinity, consent, martyr complexes, and the difficulty of wanting the best for someone when you can't stomach that their ideal life doesn't include you.

When I was in high school, I wanted to write books about how beautiful and fragile relationships are. About how fucking complicated feelings are. And now, I do. I won't lie. This job is hard. It's the most demanding job I've ever had, and the most nerve-wracking. But it's also the most fulfilling. Nothing compares to the satisfaction of finishing a book that's *mine*.

Thank you for reading. Inked Hearts has been a ride. I haven't felt so much like a series made my career since I said goodbye to Sinful Serenade. (Pete will forever be my #1 BBF).

It was hard saying goodbye to the Inked Hearts family in this book, but they aren't gone forever. Chase and Ariel will be appearing in the Inked Love series, coming this fall, starting with Forest and Skye's book *The Best Friend Bargain*.

Who knows, you might see some of your other favorites too.

Sincerely,

Crystal

P.S. Forgive me for taking creative liberties with Ariel's health condition. For the most part, her condition is accurate, but I did speed up the usual timeline. There are genes that cause increased risk of certain cancers. Please don't take medical advice from fiction, including this book. If you're worried about your cancer risk, talk to a doctor.

P.P.S. Fuck cancer, seriously.

Acknowledgements

My first thanks goes to my husband, for his support when I'm lost in bookland and for generally being the sun in my sky. Sweetheart, you're better than all the broken bad boys in the world.

The second goes to my father, for insisting I go to the best film school in the country, everything else be damned. I wouldn't love movies, writing, or storytelling half as much if not for all our afternoon trips to the bookstore and weekends at the movies. You've always been supportive of my goals, and that means the world to me.

Thanks so much to my amazing audio narrators, Kai Kennicott and Wen Ross. You always bring my characters to life in a way that blows my mind.

A big shout out to all my beta readers. You helped give me the confidence to put out a book a little more heartbreaking than usual. And also to my ARC readers for helping spread the word to everyone else in the world.

To all my writer friends who talk me down from the ledge, hold my hand, and tell me when my ideas are terrible and when they're brilliant, thank you.

Acknowledgements

Thanks so much to my editor Marla, my designers Okay Creations and Tempting Illustrations, and to Regina Wamba for the amazing cover photo.

As always, my biggest thanks goes to my readers. Thank you for picking up *The Baby Bargain.* I hope you'll be back for Forest's book *The Best Friend Bargain*.

Also by Crystal Kaswell

Sinful Serenade

Dangerous Noise

Inked Hearts

Inked Love

The Best Friend Bargain - Forest — coming in 2019

Standalones

Broken - Trent & Delilah

Come Undone - A Love Triangle

Dirty Rich

Dirty Deal - Blake

Dirty Boss - Nick

Sign up for the Crystal Kaswell mailing list

The Best Friend Bargain

Printed in Great Britain
by Amazon